Rob,

I hope you enjoy
your read and please
review on Amazon.

Max Millard

# BLOOD DILEMMA

*Kith and kin,
where have you been?*

# MARYL
# MILLARD

# ACKNOWLEDGEMENTS

## To courageous pioneers and educators:

Lee Campbell, Ph.D., Arthur Sorosky, M.D., Annette Baran, M.S.W., Reuben Pannor, M.S.W., Florence Fisher, Joyce Maguire Pavao, Ed.D., LCSW, LMFT, Mary Jo Rillera, Carol Schaefer, BA Psy, Sharon Roszia, M.S., Kathleen Silber, MSW, ACSW, Lois Molina, Author, Lorraine Dusky, Author, Sandy Musser, Author, Carol Chandler, Author, Jed Somit, Atty., Martín Brandfon, Atty., Ellen Roseman Curtis, Educator, Anhei Morningsong, M.A., Jim Gritter, Karen Wilson-Buterbaugh, author, Ann Fessler, author,

Corruption/crime history/policy authors: Sarah Chayes, M.A., Ioan Grillo, Tim Weiner, David Skarbek, Ph.D, and Don Winslow.

Special appreciation to Dr. Michael Beckwith and Dr. Ricki Byers Beckwith, and the Agape International Spiritual Center. Agapelive.com.

Last but never least, Pam Smedley's Writer's Gym, and the creative women writers therein.

# APPENDIX

For information about the author, email address for contact, recommended reading, research publications related to Corruption/Crime, Drug, and Adoption Policy, and a description of the author's non-fiction research and professional history, see pages 395-414. The author welcomes readers' comments regarding any personal relationship to themes in this story, or any part of this publication, including English-Spanish translations, cultural observations, or errors.

# DEDICATION

To my four daughters, Kathleen, Amy, Lara, and Kate. I think about each of you every day and celebrate your growth, happiness, and creativity! To your children, and theirs, born or yet to be born, my love abounds. For Betty and Dewey, Jim and Eleanor, Kim and June, Karen and Anhei—we do what we can, when we can, and we learn—loss hurts, love heals.

To my husband, Larry Kasparowitz, who has supported me in countless ways over the last 40 years. Every project I chose received a vote of confidence from him, and, regardless of life's difficulties, he has stayed my faithful friend. My soul found a supportive structure in this relationship, without which it might never have organized itself enough to create what it came to create. Larry knows about structure; he's an architect, even at the level of the soul.

## SPECIAL DEDICATION

To Jody

I'm always going to treasure the memory of the time you raced your tricycle across the backyard lawn right into the swimming pool! You proved you were a speedy driver and a great swimmer, too! The stress of adolescence weighed on you, and heroin brought an end to that pain. You missed the joys and difficulties of adulthood, and we have missed you. No doubt you have found loving support in your sphere, and have found the joyous groove of being you.

PS: About the high chair conversation we had when you were two years old. I'm sorry for wasting your time trying to get you to appreciate string beans.

Theologians may quarrel,
but the mystics of the world
speak the same language.

.

Meister Eckhart

Adoption, at its best, is a
loving, thoughtful relationship.
At its worst, it's a kidnapping.

Maryl Millard

# 1

The night air in the Oaxaca City square assaulted her senses from every direction. The body-slamming pulse of the mariachis' trumpets, guitars, violins, and voices blared from the bandstand. A slight scent of sulphur rested on her skin and clothes from clouds of spent fireworks. The enveloping margarita bouquet of fresh lime, tequila, and agave nectar wafted from dozens of curbside tables. Joy's interest in talk was flagging; her attention was fixed on the swirling pungent liquid she held in her mouth, finally observing its descent with pure pleasure.

Ángel and Rosa, young Oaxacan locals who had been groomed to work in Mexico's bilingual tourist industry, and Joy, a vacationing art major from San Francisco State, were toasting Christmas Eve 2015 with their third round of margaritas. Mateo's restaurant, Oaxaca City's favorite with locals and tourists alike, was packed for the festival. Scrunched around a street-side patio table, they looked out on the zócolo, the city square. Fireworks, in the red, green, and white colors of the Mexican flag, filled the sky. Joy raised her glass and proposed another toast.

"To Rosa, the best art aficionado and travel guide ever, thank you for a wonderful week!" An unexpected breeze blew through the restaurant patio as if to punctuate her salute.

"Joy, you are very generous," Rosa leaned close to entice her. "Most of the artists I introduced you to this past week will be at Casa de Artistas tonight for their Christmas party. You want to go, don't you?" Ángel interrupted Rosa, raising his glass to Joy.

"They want to have a drink with the talented Latina art student from San Francisco. Your beauty is not overlooked by them either!"

Ángel teased Joy with his irresistible smile. Rosa's intricately etched silver earrings danced as her head bobbed in agreement. Joy stalled a moment and adjusted her snug indigo dress; aware of the uncomfortable relationship she had with the very low-cut neckline. She attempted to justify a question she had asked Rosa earlier.

"Rosa, I only asked about criminal activity here because my parents threw a fit about us going out tonight. I had to threaten I'd sneak out later if they said no. After all, I am a legal adult now, not such an issue here, but at home it's a big deal." She heard herself shouting to be heard over the music and fireworks.

Rosa pushed her half-eaten dessert aside and placed a hand on her friend's arm. Joy loved the gentle caress; her inebriated brain focused on the silver pendant that rested just above the cleft of Rosa's breasts. She lifted her eyes to Rosa's, noting her intentional expression.

"Joy, the Mexican cartels can be very violent, yes, but tourist venues are more protected. The cartels know they won't make any money extorting the tourist industry if they scare tourists away, and this city's main industry is tourism."

"Well, that's reasshurring" Joy responded, slurring her last word a bit, tilting her head back, shaking her long black hair behind her. "Look at the crowd," she said, "if this was a big festival in the US., gangbangers would be busy selling drugs to locals and tourists, not attacking them. I guess it's not a lot different here, and Ángel, I love eating your gourmet meals at our hotel; it helped that you offered to go with us tonight, so my parents could chill out a bit."

Ángel, the youthful, gregarious day chef for one of the city's premier hotels, Refugio Tropical, was indeed out of his apron; dressed for clubbing in a dark purple dress shirt, slacks, and fancy black western boots. He sat a head higher than Rosa, about the same height as Joy, and was twice as wide. Reaching for Rosa's dessert plate, he spooned the flan into his mouth and declared his plan.

"Ladies, I am going to get one more drink, then we will go." Rosa and Joy looked at each other and rolled their eyes as he headed to the bar.

Joy smiled at Rosa, admiring her jewelry and her fluorescent red dress; a faux Zapotec design with a modern form-fitting flair she loved. They looked over the crowded city square. The Christmas parade was in full swing, passing Mateo's customers as they waved from their patio tables. Indigenous tribes from surrounding areas, Zapotecs, Mixtecs and others, paraded in their traditional regalia around the zócolo. A few young boys set off small fireworks here and there—fiery fountains that hummed and popped, and spinners that hopped across the street, spitting sparks.

"Joy," Rosa raised her voice over the noise, "I know you are leaving for home in a few days, I want to give you a Christmas gift." She put both hands on the chain that held her silver pendant, and pulled it over her head, then stood, placed it over Joy's head, and leaned back with an expression of total admiration.

"We have years of friendship ahead, Joy, you have become very special to me." She squeezed Joy's hand as she sat down, and smiled.

"Oh my God, Rosa, thank you! I know how much this pendant means to you." The mariachis' music pulsed, smiles multiplied.

The small wrought-iron table that held her third margarita and untouched flan was crowded with other outdoor tables right up to the curb. Joy could have touched the costumed women that danced past them; the music tingled along her skin, pulled her; a passing dancer urged her to join them, but she demurred. She reached for her drink as her other hand stroked the pendant. Ángel appeared at the doorway to the restaurant and bar, waving at them.

The explosion that followed was close, loud, and painful. Joy's ears felt as if they'd been stabbed—she screamed as she and Rosa bolted from their seats. Plates, glasses and desserts flew onto the concrete as everyone ran screaming for cover inside the restaurant. Joy collided with Ángel just inside the doorway. His were the eyes of a soldier on a mission; the jovial chef was nowhere to be seen.

# 2

"Stay inside, don't move!" The command in Ángel's bass voice arrived muffled as it passed through her shocked eardrums, but his actions intimidated Joy such that she moved without question, turning at the last minute to look. He ran onto the patio, then to the street. A local policeman walked toward Ángel; two young boys dangled like doomed chickens from the man's powerful fists. Ángel leaned down to hear the policeman, then he raised his arms, tossed his head back, laughing, and scurried back inside, still laughing when he reached Joy and Rosa.

"It was a cherry bomb! Loudest one I have ever heard; no one hurt but those boys' butts! Time to go, I think." Patrons passed the word along and calmed themselves with nervous chatter, then stood at the bar three deep for a free drink while the patio was cleaned up. Ángel grinned, showing interest in the free drink possibilities.

"Perhaps I'll get just one more before we go," Ángel said with a smirk.

The humor Ángel embraced was lost on Joy. She couldn't shake the terror she'd felt.

Rosa, twisting her hair and securing it into a bun at the back of her neck, winked at Joy, and spoke more like a purring cat than a controlling wife.

"Ángel, I want to go to the club, mi amor, it is time for fun!" Charmed by her seductive invitation, he consented.

"If you insist," Ángel said, kissing her hand. Joy and Rosa looked at each other, affirming Rosa's skill at managing her husband's excesses. As they began to leave, a waiter walked up with a tray filled with straight shots of mezcal.

"Gratis," the waiter offered; Ángel urged the women with a booming cheer.

"Rosa, Joy, one free drink for the road!" Joy, Rosa and Ángel grabbed their shots, choked them down, placed their glasses upside down on the tray, and headed for the door. Joy laughed, surprised that no flames flew from her mouth and nose; every breath burned, incoming and outgoing. Her terror began to melt. Like school kids bursting out of a classroom onto a crowded playground, they rushed to the curb.

Joy welcomed their dash into the blaring energy of the festival, felt the fresh mezcal high swim its way through her, delivering freedom from every confining thought.

"We can buy buñuelos and get a cab by the cathedral," Ángel urged, and led the way through the crowd, his girth clearing ample space for the women. Joy, her high heels catching on the uneven cobbles, struggled to keep up with Ángel's pace. She hated the walk, but her competitive nature spurred her ahead for the short trek until they finally stepped onto the expansive plaza.

Looking up, she felt dwarfed by the cathedral's glowing stone facade, perhaps five stories high; the fully illuminated Cathedral of Our Lady of Assumption—Nuestra Señora de la Asunción—where families strolled on the plaza, swarmed around kiosks, and sniffed the heavenly scent of frying pastries. Ángel slowed, took each woman by the arm, and walked to a nearby kiosk.

Joy's unusual height, plus her high heels, gave her a view over most of the locals. She salivated when the vender doused the steaming pastries with powdered sugar and served them on terra cotta plates; the sweet aroma a balm for the mezcal heat dancing through her nose and throat.

"After you eat it, you break the plate onto that pile there," Rosa pointed. In less than five minutes they ate, broke their plates into the pile with a drunken flourish, and stood licking the soft sugar from their fingers.

"I will get a cab," Ángel said over his shoulder as he headed for the curb. Rosa and Joy, giggling over each other's powdered faces, followed him. A yellow cab approached, Ángel waved it down, and opened the rear curbside door for the women. Joy looked at Rosa, raising her voice over the din.

"Time for girl talk?"

"Sí!" Rosa giggled, slid into the cab, followed by Joy, who relaxed into the seat and kicked her tight high heels off for a few minutes of relief. She wiggled her toes, caressed her bare feet against each other, and eagerly embraced her adventure with a celebratory cheer.

"Oh my God, this is so much fun!"

5

Ángel gave her a smile and a thumbs-up. Puffing on his cigarette, he closed Joy's door, exhaled smoke into the night air, then opened the front passenger door. Joy could see he recognized the driver as he slid into the seat.

"Rico, que tal! Trabajando esta noche?"

"Necesito mas dinero. Cinco niños comen mucho!" Rico grumbled.

"Rico, Jesus never said a word about birth control being a sin. That's just the church's way to guarantee more followers!"

"Ángel!" Rosa scolded, "Rico does not understand English well, you better hope he missed what you said!"

"You are so correct," he smirked. "I should have said no to that last shot of mezcal."

The smoke from Ángel's cigarette changed direction as the cab lurched forward. Joy emitted an uninhibited complaint.

"Hey, open a window if you're going to smoke, okay?"

"Pardon señorita," he effused with an inebriated smile, rolling down the window. Joy sniffed at the fresher air coming in, then discovered the cab's interior had an entrenched army of odors she'd be happy to leave.

"Rosa, how far to the club?"

Rosa pulled her hair loose from its bun and shook her head; a cascade of thick black curls competed for space as they descended.

"Diez minutos, no mas. Relax, Joy, you will love it. Remember Eduardo, that handsome sculptor you met at the museum yesterday? I just got a text from him, he is at the club holding a table for us!"

A visceral tingle of anticipation burst through Joy; her face flushed. She pulled out her compact and checked her makeup. Brushing some powdered sugar off her dress, she congratulated herself for choosing the low-cut indigo knit, even if it tended to hike up her thighs. *I can't believe Eduardo texted Rosa he'd see us at the club!*

A vision of Eduardo's intriguing smile, his thick brown ponytailed hair, his knife shaping that intricate wood carving, appeared in her thoughts. Rico startled her out of her haze, accelerating as they headed through town, swerving around people, cars and venders' carts faster than Joy could comprehend.

Their drive from downtown gave way to a mix of homes and

6

small shops. As if she had read Joy's mind, Rosa presented Joy with a flask and a comment to assuage her worries about his driving.

"We're not too far now...here...you can see the posada." She pointed to a small parade of people in the street; Rico muted the music in the cab, slowed to a crawl, and finished lowering the windows as the wide tones of a wooden flute entered on a breeze and surrounded them.

The group of families, from stooped gray abuelos with canes to bushy-haired niños in strollers, advanced toward them, some of them costumed and carrying battery-operated candles. Young parents chased after scurrying toddlers, scooping them up when they got too close to the cab, the kids' squealing protests flew in the open windows uninvited. Rosa launched into her tour guide mode.

"These are neighborhood posadas, treks on foot to represent Mary and Joseph's search for lodging." Rosa waved a greeting to a young girl about seven. She wore a grown woman's makeup, with a sparkling shawl draped over her hair and shoulders. A boy walked next to the girl, both within an arms' length of the cab.

*He's smaller than that adorable girl...perhaps a little brother,* Joy thought, *what a cute Joseph.* He wore a shiny blue robe, a long beard, and a red yamaka. Joy waved, and felt the boy's eyes lock onto hers when he looked into the cab, a wide grin flashed above his drooping synthetic beard. Joy felt charmed to her bones. *This is such a beautiful night,* she sighed, sinking back against the seat, closing her eyes to savor the feeling.

The cab passed the last few stragglers, then turned onto a smaller street. Joy felt the change in direction, opened her eyes, seeing mostly closed shops, a few holiday lights here and there. Rico cranked up the music, Rosa sang along, Joy moved her body to the beat, scanning ahead to see the club. The evening breeze swept through the open windows, cooling her flushed face.

To the left a small restaurant with a hand-painted closed sign. Ahead of them on the right sat a vacant lot fenced in with caution tape; except for a space that appeared to be a temporary entry. Stacks of building materials, concrete blocks, bags of cement filled the lot along the line of yellow tape.

Joy felt a smile coming and fell into a fixed stare out her open curbside window, eyes entranced by the yellow tape as the cab moved slowly along its length. The tape ended in a knot around a metal fence pole that marked the driveway. A car pulled out of the lot, and Rico swerved to miss it. The loud, heavy-metal thunk from the collision concluded with a crunching sigh as their fenders met. Joy's head almost hit the back of Ángel's headrest; she was pissed and shared it.

"Just what we need, some drunks who stopped to steal a few concrete blocks!" Rosa was upset too, cussing in Spanish; Joy turned to her and burst out laughing. Rosa had been in the middle of looking in her mirrored compact, putting on fresh lipstick; it had smeared on her face from the force of the collision. She gave Rico a slightly hysterical earful.

"Rico, está borracho?" He shook his head back and forth, a supplicating palm of his hand raised; he shrugged his shoulders.

"I think you are drunk!" Rosa yelled, "You are going to make us late!"

Four men got out of the other car, a distressed Chevy sedan, their tall driver in the lead, and walked toward the cab. Joy leaned close to Rosa and whispered so Rico and Ángel wouldn't hear.

"Don't tell me they're going to argue over whose fault it is, we don't have time, Eduardo's waiting for us!"

The absence of street lighting had given the advancing men the benefit of the doubt in her mind until she saw the ski masks and dark long-sleeved shirts; no visible tats, no crew advertising. She watched two of them walk to the open front windows.

A third man stood by Rosa's window with a small pistol, demanded her purse, checked it for weapons and threw it back to her. Joy saw one man put a pistol to Rico's head; his partner stood at the open passenger window, with a pistol aimed at Ángel's head. The tall guy had stationed himself at Joy's window. He shouted so fast and so loud every muscle in her body contracted at once.

"Manos Arriba! Fuera del coche, ahora! Hands up, get out!"

## 3

The men opened the doors. In seconds, everyone was out; their hands quickly immobilized in plastic restraints behind their backs. Joy, her shoes and purse in the cab, was pulled to the graveled edge of the pavement. Small, sharp rocks shot pain through the soles of her bare feet. Her long legs, barely covered by the short dress, vibrated like loose guitar strings, playing out the silent screaming in her brain.

Joy's captor moved in front of her, dark eyes threatening her through the ski mask; he pushed her hair away from her face. His accent made him a home-grown Mexican; his perfect English continued to shatter her stereotype.

"Close your mouth, keep it closed." He jerked, then spun around ready to fight. There was no one there.

"I felt someone hit me in the back. Did you see anyone?"

"No, I saw no one…but it's very dark here." Joy had seen him spin around, as if he'd heard something, then he'd turned back to her. *He must be on drugs, hallucinating someone hitting him. Oh God, what are they going to do to me?* She shut her mouth tight. He cris-crossed two strips of duct tape over her lips, pressing it hard against her skin, triggering a reflexive arc to her bladder.

The liquid heat burned down her legs onto her feet as she watched her companions lined up against one side of the cab. Is this some kind of execution? The horror of the thought knocked her off balance. Her captor grasped her upper arm to steady her, his eyes darting around the unlit street for witnesses.

His men backed Ángel, Rico, and Rosa against the closed doors of the cab, frisked them, checked their wrist restraints, restrained their legs at the ankles, taped their mouths, then shoved them into the back of the cab and fastened their seat belts. The smallest of the men scooted into the driver's seat of the cab and waited, while the other two headed for their car.

"Do not move one inch," Joy's captor ordered. He squatted to put her ankle restraints on, then rose quickly and startled her when he yelled at the man in the cab to hide it in the unlit construction site and lock it.

"Manejar en el lote! Ciérralo!" She lost her balance again, felt

9

his hand grasp her arm as she swayed, holding her upright. He swiveled his head around to scan the area again. Obedient to his command, his man started the cab's engine, backed it away from the other car far enough to drive behind it, then snaked forward into the black cave of the construction site.

Joy watched; her breath heaving, acid squirting into her throat, her stomach in spasms, arms and legs twisted and cramped from the restraints, urine stinging her legs. He pulled a black cloth bag from his back pocket, drawstrings dangling from the bottom. She woke to its purpose; in one motion, he released his hold on her arm, opened the bag with both hands, pulled it over her head, and secured it around her throat. She reacted with a muffled high-pitched scream. It reverberated inside her skull, too weak to escape.

*Can't see anything but black, can't stand this acid in my mouth, burns to swallow. He's going to take me…what can I do?* Her father's cautionary words about sadistic, brutal cartel gangsters burst out unbidden. She thought of her parents, who had brought her to Oaxaca as a birthday gift. They had begged her to pass on the club invitation just two hours ago.

She waited, her ankle restraints seemed to have a sadistic will of their own, tugging, almost daring her to fall over. She knew what was next; her panic burst from the top of her head and flew screaming over the city, though no audible sound was made.

Then it happened. Lifted like a child half her size; swept off her feet, put down in the back seat of the gangsters' car behind the driver's seat, strapped in a seat belt, her door slammed. A second later, the other three doors slammed shut. Her captor's voice, this time in Spanish, offered a succinct order in a tone no one could disregard.

"No le digas ni una palabra a la señorita, ni la toques, ¿entiendes? Llamaré a la policia desde el telefono publico despues de que te deje, para que puedan llegar al taxi."

*What? He's telling them to not talk to me or touch me? Someone's in the back seat with me. I can smell him, sweating; one of the other men…breathing hard. Maybe he said that just in time!* Her own breathing reminded her of her first scuba dive, but in reverse—this required breathing only through her nose— every breath a conscious breath. Snorting in the air, fingers of gripping fear forced down her throat, into every organ, every muscle.

Fear, like clawing hands, sprouted desperate and angry,

weakening her sculpted muscles. She felt her strength retreat, like the tendrils of a sea anemone; taking the rest of her into hiding. She felt almost invisible. *What am I now?*

No one talked. The old Chevy crept forward, away from the construction site that sequestered the taxi and its inhabitants. *I heard him say something about stopping later to call the police, so they could get to the cab soon. I bet he's doing it to taunt the police, probably enjoys laying it in their laps on Christmas Eve…at least they won't be tied up in the cab all night! Poor Rosa!*

The taxi hit a deep pothole and bounced. Joy's entire body vibrated, her screams constricted inside her lungs with violent force, forcing one gagging acidic groan after the other. Foreign sounds and feelings convulsed from uncontrollable reactions inside her body. She heard another command from the leader.

"Deshacer su cinturón," he ordered; then he spoke directly to her.

"Señorita, you must lie down so no one can see you, and for your safety, make no sound."

Joy's backseat guard unlocked her seatbelt, reached around her back and pulled her onto her side, head and neck rigid. His body odor made her gag, penetrating the hood as her head hit the seat next to him He covered her with a blanket. Stiff, Joy lay facing blindly forward toward the front, legs bent at an awkward angle, bare feet dangling down to the floor of the cab.

The right side of her enshrouded head bumped on the seat as they moved forward. Eyes squeezed shut, nose sucking rancid air and blowing it out, lips pulling against the suffocating tape. The vibration from tires rolling over rutted asphalt traveled up through the seat into her skull, and mixed with the terror and booze in her brain.

# 4

They knew it wasn't going to be any good unless it involved no holding back. The white Arabian mare, pounding at full force through the wet California sand and high tide foam, the rider, her butt up off the saddle, knees bent, all her weight on the stirrups, her back almost horizontal to the mare's, her long dark hair flying from the thrust of the mare's passion; their manes spinning into a merged fan of curls in the morning mist. *We are one, baby, we are flying!*

She turned her head, looked out over the breakers, showered by the spray bouncing off the rocks from the biggest wave of the morning. Her hair, falling over her shoulders, soaked more cold sea spray into her tank top.

"Wow! Doesn't that feel great Amira? And look at the dance up there!" Thousands of curlews, celebrating with their life-long mates, dove in acrobatic formations over the churning gray sea. Addie always cheered their winter arrival on the California coast from inland breeding grounds. *Papa and I used to ride under them like this, and shout our welcome as loud as we could, again, and again.*

"If only we could fly like that, Amira! Let's catch 'em!" They galloped until they fell into their seemingly effortless 'flying' rhythm. Above, the flock shape-shifted over the sea with instantaneous changes in direction. Against the light of the morning sky, they emerged from gray to black; the flock folded over and through itself, as if blown by a sentient wind. With the birds' display, her entire being felt airborne, and coursed through the sky, infused with joy. Amira gathered more speed and dashed forward, heightening Addie's sense of flight.

The ringtone she reserved for FBI calls ripped her attention out of the heavens and onto her phone. Exhaling in frustration, she signaled Amira to canter, then slowed to a walk, answered, put it on speakerphone, and re-clipped her phone case to the waist band of her jeans. Amira ambled across the wet sand with slow, rhythmic steps, her breath active, her white hair soaked with sweat and sea spray.

"This better be good, Agent Chung, you just interrupted something really beautiful."

"Addie...so sorry...you and Jake engaged in something I shouldn't have interrupted?"

"No, if I were having some long overdue fun with Jake your call would have gone to voice mail, believe me. It's only the day after Christmas and he's already gone, researching a story for Wired Magazine; something about a human trafficking ring with a heavy internet presence. On the positive side, Amira and I are illegally tearing up the beach in Pescadero, out here in the surf, just running for the pure pleasure of it. What's up?"

A wave washed a long piece of kelp around them and Amira hopped sideways, then scooted forward fast to get it off her legs. Addie kept her seat and focused on hearing what Isabel had to say.

"Oh, well, good luck with Jake when you get around to it," Isabel chided, "but thanks for picking up. We really need you on board today. Urgent case. Kidnapping. Clients are Mike and Ana Doyle. They took their daughter Joy to Oaxaca Mexico for a twenty-first birthday gift. She was kidnapped Christmas Eve in Oaxaca City. Their flight from Mexico got here around 5 a.m., I met with them to work out logistics, introduce them to Emil, and discuss the ransom. The call from her kidnapper came about an hour ago, and…"

"Let me guess, Izzy, he talks like a real smoothie."

"Oh," Isabel teased, "having a psychic news flash? Doesn't matter how often you do this, Addie, it always unnerves me."

"Well, check this out; no visual, completely auditory. I just started to tune in to what you were saying and next thing I knew, I heard a voice; deep, resonant, calm, focused, and he's fluent in English."

"Spot on, you hit the psychic bullseye. Yeah, his voice, like a Latin TV news anchor, his English, perfect. Now that you mention it, he was the opposite of what we expect; not your typical cartel soldier, that's for sure. Calls himself Ramiro."

"Well, it will give Emil a break; he won't have to translate every call for the girl's parents. Izzy, I wonder what it means that I heard his voice; I adjusted to having these psychic visions, like little video clips, like you see in a dream, or when you recall a dream, but I've never actually heard anyone talking before."

"Okay, Addie, it seems logical you would have new skills show up; I think it's a nice addition, but enough on that subject. I don't have time to analyze it with you, and the girl's parents are probably not in any frame of mind to hear about your psychic skills right now. I need you to give them a dose of Dr. Addison Diaz, Forensic Psychologist. We need them emotionally squared away before they lose their ability to help us." Addie listened as her plans for a day off faded.

"They're beating themselves up for letting Joy go with friends to a club, because she was kidnapped from her cab on the way there. Please say you can meet with them today; and while you're considering why you should give up such a stunning day at the beach, I'll tell you why I need you and no one else for this job."

"Go ahead, if you have a compelling reason, I will do it, you know I will."

"I'm worried about them because there's a factor that's complicating their PTSD symptoms, especially their guilt and anxiety. You're the only therapist I know in the Bay Area who is a former FBI agent trained in our kidnap protocol, who also has a specialty in infertility and adoption therapy."

"Oh God, they're adoptive parents?"

"You got it. And the fact that you're an adoptive parent will help them feel less judged; they'll know that you understand them more than someone who's never been through it."

"And they would be right; especially in a situation like this. Of course, I'll see them. Today for sure; not a lot of time to get them grounded enough to cope with this. Got a date set for the exchange yet?"

"We're tentatively looking at Wednesday, but you know how that usually goes. I have to run everything through our International Ops Division in D.C. and the assigned legal attaché in Mexico to work out coordination with Mexican law enforcement. Right now, we're assuming it's a cartel kidnapping." Addie felt a chill that had nothing to do with the sea spray; Isabel's report proceeded apace.

"Could be independent though, the local police report stated that the three people they found restrained in the taxi saw no tattoos, and heard no comments that identified the kidnappers. All three were interviewed separately. They all told the same story, that Ramiro did all the talking, English to the victim, and Spanish to everyone else. Usually the cartels leave their calling card, to claim bragging rights, but not these guys. Two of the victim's companions in the cab are trusted employees of the hotel where the victim was staying with her parents. Both are acquainted with the taxi driver, and he's the only one of the three who's ever been arrested; stole a dirt bike some years back. So far it looks like the Doyles' daughter was sighted and followed from the cathedral by the kidnappers."

"How did they target her, any ideas?" Addie reined Amira around, and headed up the beach toward the parking lot. She could sense her imagination working its way south to Oaxaca. She focused on the location and tried to hone in on the kidnapper and the clients' daughter. Izzy interrupted her reverie.

"They may have seen a news article on the internet. The father of the victim, Mike Doyle, was concluding a US-Mexico prison construction partnership on Mexico's second maximum security prison, this one in Oaxaca; it's more isolated than the Penal del Altiplano which is only fifty-five miles from Mexico City. Perhaps they wanted to locate this one in a state with low population, like our super max facility in Colorado. The article mentioned his wife and daughter would be celebrating Christmas with him in Oaxaca City."

*Obviously, the guy deserved a vacation after all that work; might as well bring the family down,* Addie thought, as Isabel forged ahead with more.

"One silver lining in this, Mike Doyle's business has an international footprint, and I located an FBI specialist in international ops with Mexico who may work with us if all goes well. For now, I need you on the home front here to help these parents."

Addie sighed, reined to a stop, then leaned forward over the saddle horn and hugged her mare's damp, smooth, scented neck; a loving long-time signal that the ride was over, time to head back home. Amira, unlike Addie, showed no signs of reluctance, for the end of most rides came with a shampoo, a hose down, and a delicious tub of alfalfa in the corral.

"Addie? You there?" Isabel's voice broke through.

"Okay Izzy, put one of them on the phone, we'll set it up.

Gonna take me till eleven to get to the office."

"Thanks, they've been waiting in the next room. I'll go give Mike the phone now. And just so you know, the police are doing what they can to avoid news coverage of this, for now; we don't want this kidnapper's competition to hear about it and try to get a piece of the ransom. That would ratchet up the danger for the victim and our team exponentially. I gotta go. Check back with me after you meet with them?"

"Sure, no problem." Despite the loss of her day off, Addie felt deep gratitude for her bond with Isabel, twenty-five years strong, and the lengthening string of cases they had successfully navigated together since Addie's transition from the FBI to her private forensic practice.

"Hello?" Mike Doyle's heartbroken, tortured voice reached out. Addie released her reverie about Isabel's importance in her life.

"Hello Mr. Doyle, this is Dr. Diaz. Let's see, it's eight o'clock now, let's meet at eleven if that works for you. Eat before you come, it will take us a few hours. We're all going to be making sacrifices until your daughter is home where she belongs."

"I understand, Doctor, Agent Chung has provided us with your card. You're on New Montgomery…" His raspy voice started to break up.

"Between Mission and Market, the Sharon Building, across the street from the Palace Hotel. There's a crowded, expensive parking garage in my building. I use the public garage on Fifth and Mission or the independent lots on Mission."

"Very good," he sighed, "we will be there at eleven." His parting response communicated a modicum of relief rising through his angst.

The kidnapper's voice found a niche in Addie's brain from which it refused to budge. Her psychic skills had never included clairaudience, until now. Why now? Why him? *All these years of working cases and I'm feeling like a scared rookie.* Glad to be home, if only briefly, she rushed through her shower, toweled down, even gave herself a pep talk in the slightly steamed mirror of the master bath.

"Pretty fit for forty-six, if I say so myself." A fast makeup effort ensued as she thought of her hours of training with Isabel. She looked closely at her eyes... *just like Papa's; big, dark, Izzy always says 'I love your eyes, there's always so much going on in there'*...She rushed through her makeup routine, eager to get moving, energized from the beach ride. Addie's cell started echoing in the tiled space. She grabbed it, saw it was Grandma Luisa, put it on speaker, then propped it on the table by her closet as she picked out something to wear.

"Buenos días."

"How was your ride this morning?"

"Oh, I can't even begin to tell you, it was magical, beyond my expectations! Except for the FBI call. It's perfect timing that you called me. Izzy called with an emergency referral, a kidnapping case, so now I have an appointment at eleven in the city. Jake's not here, and the girls are still asleep." *If I wake them up ... forget it.*

"Can you wake them up around ten and let them know I won't be home 'til this afternoon? They have chores to get done in the barn, and the Christmas mess all over the living room to clean up, and a plan to help Star get ready for the Sunday service." Addie started picking out her clothes from the closet as Luisa responded.

"Si, I will bribe them out of bed with breakfast. By the way, Addie, was that kidnapping in Mexico? Southern Mexico?" Addie almost zipped her skin into the zipper of her slacks—Luisa's guess was spot on. But then, Addie's talent for visions had come from her.

"You know I can't talk about cases, Grandma, but I'll say you must have had your ear to the ground on this one."

"I was sound asleep until a few minutes ago, dreamed I was wandering in the hills looking for someone down there. Anyway, I'm not trying to pry, but now I don't have to spend the day wondering what that dream meant. I'll see you when you get home…te amo."

Addie heard the dial tone, tossed the phone in her bag, then finished getting dressed. Aubergine slacks, her favorite silk blouse, new faux snakeskin loafers, and a light jacket in case the fog blew in. She brushed the tangles from her damp unruly hair, tucked it neatly into a clip, then rushed through the living room with a quick glance at the Christmas tree, still surrounded by evidence of their family's gift-opening frenzy the day before.

Wishing her brief holiday wasn't over, she went out the carved cherry wood front door, happy to see Nita had taken their Christmas purchase; a Yukon Denali, through the carwash yesterday. Scrounging in her bag, she realized she hadn't gotten the keys back from her. With no time to lose, she gripped her briefcase and purse, walked away from the paved driveway, and headed for the barn. *I'll just take the truck; beats waking up a grouchy teenager and watching her search for keys for ten minutes.*

She glanced at Grandma Luisa's cottage, and not far away, the newly vacated farm manager's home. *The orchards, crops and greenhouse plants will be fine, thanks to our crew, but it didn't help that Jake left hiring the new manager to me.* She could feel that task slipping to the bottom of her to-do list behind whatever this current case demanded. *Oh, well, it won't be the first time Grandma Luisa stepped into the gap. The land and climate here in Pescadero is ideal for farming—makes us look like pros.*

Forcing herself to focus, Addie entered the barn entrance to get the truck. The barn's interior greeted her, with the familiar scent of barn wood, alfalfa, tack, molasses-laced grain, and three stalls in need of mucking out. A loud squawk told her Red, the Rhode Island Red rooster, and Ali, the calico barn cat, were deeply engaged. Addie's ruminations about the case were jolted out of mind as Red startled her with a louder squawk and leaped off a rafter onto Ali's back; a noisy routine of theirs that evolved into a chase as Addie opened the truck, climbed in, and reached into the unused ashtray for the key.

The truck had a few unloaded bales of alfalfa in it, a chore half done, she noticed and dismissed. Amira had seen her enter the barn and neighed from the corral, just her quick hello. By noon, the girls will have let her into the pasture with her pals…what a great life that horse has!

Addie drove out of the barn, her thoughts mulling over the

quick talk with Grandma Luisa. *She has never picked up on a case before I've even met with the clients, and here she's already searching in the hills of southern Mexico! I suppose we can't rule out the possibility the kidnapper is hiding up in the hills to protect his investment from any cartel-affiliated crooks in Oaxaca City. Something strange going on here.* Her thoughts shifted to Jake as she saw their house recede in the rear-view mirror...*well, maybe he'll be home when I get back.*

Off kilter from that moment on, she drove down the hardpan driveway until the wind-bent cypress trees beckoned her onto Highway One. The moist air from the kelp-strewn beach greeted her through the open window, but she held her focus on the road, with both hands in a white-knuckled grip on the wheel; the opposite of her usual one-handed driving style.

She glanced at the dashboard clock—9:15—pushed play on her Audible phone app, determined to listen to Grillo's book. *If he has the guts to risk his life with years of on-site reporting about these Mexican cartels, I should at least have the courage to listen to it!* So, on she went; the mud-spattered truck, with two bales of fresh alfalfa still aboard, obediently powered its way north through Half Moon Bay toward San Francisco.

She had bought Grillo's audiobook version of El Narco in 2013, but every time she listened to it, the bad news had been overwhelming; she could barely stomach the accounts of Mexican cartel violence the acclaimed journalist reported. Both the descriptions and Grillo's erudite analysis made it clear, this book wasn't the typical 'Cartel for Dummies' publication.

*How many other people in the US pretend this isn't happening, and why aren't more people rethinking our US drug policies if that's making the violence worse?* The beautiful California landscape surrounding her was a stark contrast to the images of carnage Grillo described, but with this case in her lap, she was committed to hearing him out.

When she arrived, the Fifth and Mission parking garage wasn't crowded, but she drove to the roof regardless; it felt safer, she could see around the roof easily. She checked the time—10:45—off she went; riding the elevator down to Mission Street, then walking a few blocks to New Montgomery.

*Usually when I'm heading to work I'm feeling confident, even eager to help, but the Doyles' case?* Her intuition, abetted by the grim facts from

19

Grillo's book, sent her images of treading through a quagmire, wondering if her next step would sink so low it wouldn't let go. When it was an urgent FBI kidnapping referral, she was usually calm, upbeat, and ready to lead someone through the tearful, fear-filled maze that would, hopefully, take them to their lost family member. But not this time. Short on facts but long on intuition, she knew this day seemed to portend unusual difficulties.

She walked across Mission at the crosswalk, hurried along the sidewalk on New Montgomery, and approached the entry to number 55, the old beaux-arts style Sharon Building, on her right. An angry man yelled something unintelligible. Chills ran down her legs, she jerked her head toward the sound, grateful to see the men were farther away than she had imagined. The shouter, a large gray-haired man, stepped off the curb in front of the Palace hotel across the street, arguing with a younger man. They were headed straight for her.

Addie, her hand on the pistol she kept in the outside pocket of her bag, watched as the men angled their approach and headed toward Market Street. The young man was getting an earful.

"We should have parked at the fifth and Mission garage and walked. Now we'll have a parking ticket! Hell, for what that costs, I could have paid to park in the Sharon Building garage!"

The comic relief in the man's plight lightened her concerns about imminent danger. But as she walked in, she hoped she wouldn't encounter some druggie who had sneaked in to sleep in the elevator and have him...or her...wake up in a violent mood.

*As edgy as I am, there'd better be no one there*, she grumbled. *Izzy and I honed our martial arts skills to a peak this past year. I might just enjoy getting rid of this wacked out energy if someone gave me a good enough reason.* Her conscience objected. *That's a bit off the deep end, no one's tried to bunk in there for years, just stay focused on the case.*

There was a strange aura developing around this new client relationship. She recalled her prescient auditory clue about the kidnapper, and it played a low minor chord through her entire body. *I'm unnerved by a criminal who's 2,500 miles away? Not my typical response, that's for sure. Something new going on. Would it happen again? Probably.* Addie knew she'd have to wait until it was revealed, which annoyed her. Intuitive visions had unique symbols and characteristics over which she had no control, she knew, including their timing.

*Just stop whining*, she reminded herself, *these people are desperate, and Isabel needs me.* As she recalled Isabel's poignant entreaty, the unnerving auditory intrusion of the kidnapper, and the sound of Mike Doyle's tortured soul coming through her phone, she realized the gravity of this case had her locked in its orbit.

The Sharon's entry door closed behind her, its reverberating sound highlighted the emptiness of the foyer. She thought she heard something, and came to a sudden stop, feeling the morning chill inside the antique building's marble-tiled space. The elevators waited for her at the long end of the rectangular foyer like tight-lipped butlers begrudging Saturday work. She waited. Her intuition, as if it had responded to her pique over having to wait for more answers, opened her to receive the clincher right between her ears, just to make sure she heard it loud and clear. This time, a woman's voice.

*Addie, this is like no other case. Someone you love dearly is going to die…but if you don't stay with this case all the way to the end you will regret it for the rest of your life.* Addie was startled stiff; the voice sounded just the way Mama used to mete out dire threats to her when she was a teenager. Except this didn't sound like a threat. It was a promise.

**6**

Addie's eyes scanned the elevators as she struggled to decide between the stairs and an elevator, headed for each then turned away, then finally pushed the up arrow on the elevator nearest the stairs and stood impatiently, still shaking, gripping her shoulder bag with one arm and holding tight to her briefcase with the other. Trembling from the tension and the chill, her body gripped her until she bolted and chose the stairs. Every quick step echoed in the deserted musty stairwell. *Yet another reason to wear loafers, I'd hate to hoof it up three floors in heels.*

The Sharon Building was a hundred and three years old and she'd been working there ten years, avoiding this notoriously creepy route up to the third floor. *Surely, I'm not the first to ascend these stairs in a panic. Good thing the office isn't on the ninth floor!* Her breath tightened in her chest as she sighted the door to the third floor, made it to the landing, struggled with the ancient doorknob, then burst into the long hallway expecting the worst.

*No one. Well, where the hell are my clients? I'm the one who's getting here at the last minute; they should be standing outside the door.* Addie hated being late; most of her clients arrived already believing the universe was punishing them for some transgression, and she saw it as her job to help them rebuild their trust. Having been on the receiving end of life-saving therapy herself, she knew that having a therapist arrive late just added insult to injury.

The door to her office seemed to recede as she hurried. She wanted to get inside so she could calm down before they arrived. She half hoped for a no-show; her lungs were feeling tight; their generous flexible motion stunted, doling out air in piecemeal fashion. *I run about twenty miles a week no problem, but give me a scary message and I can barely make it up the stairs.*

She stopped at the door, and out of sheer luck the inhaler was the first thing her hand hit when she searched her purse. *Calm down*, she cautioned herself as she administered the medication, *no asthma, no panic, off limits for the day. PTSD is an acronym, I'm the only power it has.*

Fumbling for her keys, cursing her inability to consistently put them in the same place every time, she said a silent blessing for the ADHD that kept her humble, and searched amidst the 'junk drawer' midsection of her bag, containing her phone, wallet, hair brush, nail clippers, pens, a flash drive, loose coins, a crumpled coupon, a pen-sized tire gauge, handy 'updo' hair clip, Swiss army knife, backup inhaler, lipstick, and…keys! Finally, keys in hand, she proceeded to unlock the door, but sensing no resistance from the bolt lock tumblers gave her pause.

She heard her phone ring, but wanted to get inside the office before trying to locate it. *Did the janitor leave the door unlocked or is there someone inside, or both?* At this point her caution was overridden by her anathema for botched appointments; she pulled out the key, and opened the door.

Addie practically crashed into a stocky red-haired guy holding a cell phone to his ear. She gasped loudly and felt as if she'd sucked all the air in the room into every cell of her body. The man jolted backward, eyebrows raised high, his eyes stretched open, exposing blue irises surrounded by so much white they seemed to be retreating into it. His entire body leaned back, apparently unaware he was still holding the cell phone to his ear.

Behind him, rising quickly from her chair, was an attractive woman with beautiful shoulder length blond hair, tied with a small silk scarf. Addie dropped into her therapist mode immediately, ready to roll, regardless of her discomfort or theirs.

"Hello," she began, "I …"

"Wait!" The man waved her off, then burst out defensively.

"Doctor, you weren't here, we tried the door, thought it was into a waiting area since it was open, then figured you might be in the restroom or something so we just came in." The subtle structure of an Irish accent with a chip on its shoulder called for a subdued response.

"It's fine," Addie said with her most disarming hypnotic demeanor; using body language, facial expression, and tone of voice honed through years of experience.

"You may call me Dr. Diaz or Addie, whichever is most comfortable for you. This is the first time I've ever known the janitor to leave the door unlocked, but it appears that relieved you of having to stand in the hallway; so sorry I was late."

The man pulled the cell phone from his ear and looked at it, and hung up on the call he'd been making.

"No, actually, it's eleven a.m. right now, you're right on time." He mustered a half smile and backed toward his chair.

Addie heard her phone vibrate its subtle buzz one last time, then stop. The man had heard it too, and gestured self-consciously as he spoke.

"I was calling you, this whole thing was so nerve wracking I thought you might have forgotten our appointment. By the way," he said as he made an obvious effort to relax his face and mellow out his tone of voice, "feel free to call me Mike, and this" he said as he took a step sideways, sweeping his arm out, extending his open hand toward his wife "this lovely woman here, is Analisa."

"Good morning, Doctor, we so appreciate your willingness to help on such short notice." She smiled, "call me Ana, and just to get it out of the way, my name's pronounced like the opposite of off…just think off-on, on-a."

"I love it when people help me avoid mispronouncing their names," Addie said.

"Oh yeah," Mike said, clearly attempting to lighten up a bit, "Ana knows all about short notice appointments, she's been a zoo vet for 15 years. One minute you think you're heading downtown on your way to a birthday dinner, next minute she's on the phone talkin' bout an escaped Siberian tiger shot by police, and up Sloat Boulevard you go instead."

Addie recalled the tragic 2007 incident at the zoo and acknowledged it to Ana. She didn't want to dampen Mike's attempt at humor, but knew the pain of the event had to be acknowledged.

"Tatiana's loss must have been horrible for you, Ana…my sympathies."

Mike looked a little sheepish; perhaps regretting he chose the least humorous example of Ana's job-related emergencies.

"Thank you," Ana replied, "the enclosure's improved now, fortunately."

Ana bestowed a smile upon Addie that expressed a desire to please, to connect, and strangely, to comfort. There had been a depth to her voice that penetrated Addie's heart with such peace; it reminded her of something wonderful she had experienced, then forgotten.

"I'm pleased to meet both of you. Just have a seat," she said gesturing to a roomy upholstered loveseat flanked by rattan tables, each with a small box of tissues.

"I could use a glass of water," Addie said. As Mike and Ana settled in, Addie walked over to the desk by the large window, stashed her bag and briefcase there, and from years of habit, walked to the water cooler, filled her glass and poured it into the drying soil of the five-foot-tall bamboo plant by the window.

It gave her pleasure to care for the healthy plant. She had rescued it from Izzy's windowsill when it was about five inches high, cramped in a tiny pot, and almost dead from dehydration. Addie refilled her glass as well as preparing two for Mike and Ana. She placed theirs on the end tables, and sat down across from them in a matching chair, sipping her drink.

"Ok." said Mike as he squirmed, shifting his weight impatiently in his seat, glancing at his phone before stashing it in his pocket. "We ate before we drove over; you said it could take a few hours..." Addie felt his attempt to forge on with little more than raw energy.

"Yes, Mike. Sometimes an emergency requires a more intensive investment of time and resources, all of which we can evaluate to our mutual satisfaction as we move forward. Are you prepared to continue up to two hours this morning if we agree it makes sense to do so?"

"Ah, well, I guess that's okay," said Mike, "money's not the issue, it's just that I'm not one hundred percent clear why we are here or what our objectives are, and in the movies people seem to see a therapist an hour a week and that's it, so I'm a bit muddled, but go ahead. I told Ana I would help and that's why I'm here."

"You don't see yourself as needing help?" It may have been gently spoken, but it was the first confrontation, right off the bat. His eyes locked onto hers. She continued cautiously, then, as if her words were gently blowing a small feather off the upraised palm of her hand, she added just enough force to carry the words to him.

"Mike...do you see yourself as *deserving* help?" The feather rocked its way over to his space and settled on his heart.

"Oh, uhh, ah..." Mike frowned, squinted his eyes, pressed his lips together tight, his jaw sawed back and forth, as though his mouth struggled to contain something. Then, quickly, his lips parted, he sucked in a fast breath, and almost simultaneously emitted a choking sound.

The usual strong volume of his voice cracked, then trailed into a groaning whisper as he slumped forward, elbows braced on his thighs. His muscular hands rose, covering his face, but not before the tears came and his body jerked with each unbidden sob.

"Ah…" he struggled to speak through his hands. "Oh please." Tears fell down his wrists and onto his spotless slacks. "I just want our girl back," he growled, "and Doctor, I dunno how this is gonna help!"

Despite her desire to stay asleep, Joy was beginning to wake up. As she moved her head, she felt the pillow enough to know she wasn't home in her own room. *Maybe it's a hotel pillow or something.* The silence she encountered invited her to sleep again, so she did. She heard her mother's soothing voice. *What's she saying? Is this a dream?*

"Joy?" She felt bathed in love, and relaxed into it, she moved her mouth but couldn't make any sound.

"Joy?" *Mama, I love you, you are the best; I can feel your love all through me. Mama, I'm scared, really scared!* She tried to open her eyes, but the lids stayed closed.

She felt people looking at her but couldn't open her eyes to see them. She felt Mike and Ana, and someone else. A few other people nearby as well. Maybe she had fainted. She heard herself talking.

"What's going on?" She thought she saw her family, and reached out to them, tried to grab her father's hand; she felt desperate, terrified, like she was falling off that old Titanic ship, and he was her only chance to live.

"Joy…you're going to be okay, my darlin' just hold on, this might take a few days," her father said. His response really pissed her off; roused her just enough to recall the terror of her abduction.

"A few days? How can you say that? I got yanked out of my life the way a child yanks a praying mantis off a leaf, throws it in a jar, throws in some leaves, puts the lid on and pokes holes in it!"

She heard no response, thought her parents didn't understand what she meant, so she strained to explain, without losing a beat of her frustrated tirade.

"You know, the kid says 'Oh, let me keep him, the bug's got food, he's got air, see? I'll keep him by my bed on the table' see?"

"Oh, yeah," said Mike, still too slow on the uptake.

"But *I'm* not fine!" Joy felt the relief. "He didn't hurt my body when he took me, but I was brought inside this cage, not *my* world. I'm in *his* world now," she growled. "Help me, dammit! Help me! Get me outa here!"

Joy waited for their response. Her mother's voice called to her but she couldn't make out the words, then her dad's voice, lower and louder, but still incomprehensible. Then a stranger's voice, whispering.

"We're coming for you."

Joy struggled to sit up, still asleep, could not open her eyes, felt nauseous, then dizzy. Eyes open at last, she began to recall the dream. She sat up, and saw she was in a narrow bed, set against one wall of a small, dark rectangular room. No windows. Smelled like a neglected attic. Pillows and warm blankets. Kitchen cabinets and a sink along the center of the opposite wall. Her mind raced. As her vision cleared, she remembered the kidnapper giving her a Valium to help her rest. *How long ago was that?* She had no idea.

*We're coming for you? What the...?* She looked around the dim room in terror. *Some kind of basement?* A faint glow came from a lamp at the far end of the room, next to a recliner chair. *Is there someone sitting there?*

Addie watched as Mike remained hunched over, his face in his hands, shoulders jerking with each staccato breath. He had large hands which matched his muscular build, but weren't that consistent with his height, which at first meeting, had failed to exceed Addie's five-eight.

"It's okay, Mike, take your time," Addie said softly. Facing Mike's quivering form directly, Addie didn't move from the leaning-in position she had acquired.

"You're a bit of a master, aren't you doctor?" he said as he looked up at Addie, the whites around his blue eyes reddened.

"Only my dear mum could get to my heart in that fashion. And yes indeed," he sighed, and sat up straight again, "I am lost until I know our Joy is safe."

Ana got up, walked to the water cooler and refilled her glass. Instead of sitting down, she walked behind the loveseat, placed a hand on Mike's shoulder, and spoke directly to Addie...cautiously, *as if,* Addie thought, *she's lifting the lid on Pandora's box, and she knows it.*

"Isabel said she chose you for us not only because you were formerly with the FBI but because you're also a specialist in the psychological issues related to infertility and adoption." Addie met her eyes and nodded.

"Yes, I am personally and professionally involved with adoption; my husband and I experienced infertility, and our two teenage daughters were adopted at birth through open adoptions with their birthparents. Both girls have some Mexican ancestry."

"So does our daughter. Do you visit with their families?"

"Well, Ana, more with Lizbeth's birth family than Nita's. Our contact varies, the way it often is with extended family members; we would have visited more but we live a long way from each other. I always feel like reunions with any family members or friends, can be picked back up quick and enjoyed—as long as no one's holding a grudge. Once the girls became teenagers they wanted me to back off and let them be in charge, so I have. Frankly, I miss the talks I used to have with their birthmoms, but the girls don't want any triangulated discussions going on, and I understand."

Ana returned to sit by Mike; he took her hand and patted it

gently, then spoke.

"We had two private adoption situations where we met the birthparents."

"Ana, don't go into the details, please." Mike's face was getting red, he looked ready to walk out the door.

"Okay, well, both of them took a lot of time, travel, money, and heartbreak. Neither of them worked out. We switched to a licensed adoption agency. We were about to age out of the eligibility requirements when we got the call from the agency about Joy, her birthmother agreed to Joy contacting the agency for a meeting once she turned eighteen, but Joy hasn't done it." Mike had heard enough, and changed the subject quick.

"Doctor, I wanted to tell you that Joy was watching the TV documentary where you and two other criminal justice specialists were interviewed about using your psychic skills in investigations; she pulled us into the TV room for the second half of the show."

"Yes," said Ana, "So we feel we've already met you in a way. We were glad agent Chung referred us to you; I didn't discuss it with her at the time, but when she gave us your name I kind of thought your psychic connection with Joy might be helped by the fact that she connected with you watching that TV show, though when I say it out loud I wonder if I'm grasping at straws." Addie responded before she could second-guess herself further.

"To the contrary Ana, your hunch makes sense. If Joy has a mental video of me in her mind, it could make it easier for us to connect." Mike leaned forward with an idea.

"I can show you a short video of her that I took at her twenty-first birthday party, the Sunday before we left for Mexico. It's on my phone, then you'd have more connection with her. Maybe you could try to connect with her." Addie looked at him, then got a strong image showing the connection he suggested had already happened.

"I just got a déjà vu vision, Mike; kind of like watching a rerun on TV; looks like Joy and I have made that connection. I see that she is safe and unhurt, she's telling us to hurry up and get her." *No point in me describing just how pissed off Joy was in my vision, but I see she has some really serious spunk.*

Ana and Mike both gasped; Addie watched their tears and

smiles emerge.

"Wow," Mike exclaimed, "It's one thing to know about these perceptions in the abstract; it's quite another to experience it first-hand." Ana wiped her eyes, nodding in agreement. Addie gave them some more details.

"Looks like she's wearing a dark indigo knit dress with a low-cut neckline, elbow length sleeves, she tugs the dress down because it's shorter than she likes. Beautiful long black hair, no shoes. She's ok; someone's coming to feed her." Ana looked up at Addie with a smile, wiping away more tears and the last of her mascara with a damp crumpled tissue.

"Now I know for sure you saw her, that's the dress she had on night before last. You're right about the shoes, too, the police found her high heels in the cab, along with her purse."

# 9

The door to the underground bunker, rusty from its proximity to the dirt, made a screeching sound as Ramiro opened it. He propped it open against a large rock and began to climb down the steps. Then he turned, looked up at the white blur of fur as his dog bounced in a circle. He responded in a low affectionate tone.

"You want to stay by my side and explore the bunker? Bella, que preciosa, si, si, if you are to come, be muy tranquillo."

Bella sat like a statue at the bunker opening. Her eyes focused on Ramiro, her ears and one side of her neck sported black fur, the rest glowed white.

"Okay, you come, help her feel better. With one tip of his head, the 'yes' signal to her 'please,' Bella descended the steps, stopped midway at the riser where he stood, and sat like a statue, her eyes on his again, her head tilted in loving expectation, and awaited his lead.

"Tonio!" He barked up to his son. In a moment, Tonio appeared at the opening.

"Si Papa?"

"Cierre la puerta, regresa en trienta minutos!" He knew the boy was both repulsed and reluctantly curious about the girl; the knowledge shamed Ramiro in the worst way.

Ramiro nodded to Bella, and continued down the stairs with a bag of food and some sodas, pausing every few steps to accommodate his sciatica. The door closed, cutting off the light above him. Tonio had let the door down slowly to avoid the heavy clang; Ramiro hated the sound.

He held the bannister, and proceeded at his cautious pace. Reaching the bottom of the dark stairwell, he waited. He knew Bella was curious about the scent Joy's bare feet had left on the stairs; Bella, her companion knew, 'saw' the location of each footstep clearly.

Ramiro, taking her cue, sniffed the air; it had been many years since they'd used the bunker, but the musty smell wasn't as bad as it had been before. He'd taken a risk and left the door open for a few days before Christmas Eve, and had turned the battery-operated fan on; some fresh air was managing to circulate through the vents. They entered the room together.

He saw the girl curled in the recliner chair at the far end, reading by the camp light on the table by the chair.

"We could use more light in here," he paused and turned on the light over the kitchen counter, hoping the batteries would last. Bella sat at Ramiro's side, eyes fixed on Joy. As soon as Joy looked up from her book, Bella tilted her head, disarming any fears that moved in her direction. Joy's head tilted in reaction, and a quiet, inviting "hello" gave Bella the green light. She looked up to Ramiro for final confirmation, he nodded, and Bella set off gently toward Joy.

Ramiro watched, appreciating that his wife Adela's adoration of Bella had been expressed for years through daily grooming and weekly shampoos, providing Bella with the softest, most irresistible coat of long fluffy fur attainable. Bella started a slow tail-wagging climb onto Joy, who made her more than welcome.

Ramiro watched their embrace with much pleasure, then interrupted.

"Señorita?" Ramiro kept his voice calm and quiet as he stood by the kitchenette which abutted the stairwell wall.

"Tengo mangos, cantaloupe, y un burrito, y sodas. ¿Tienes hambre? You hungry?"

When he got no response, he put the bag in the sink, reached in, then placed the contents on the countertop. From his pocket, he pulled a jackknife, opened it, sliced the cantaloupe, scraped the seeds into the plastic bag, rolled it up, and set it aside. He turned to face her, unaware the knife was pointed in her direction.

"Señorita Doyle? I will speak more English." He self-consciously pulled at his bushy gray mustache to separate it somewhat from his untrimmed beard; a habit just before he ate anything, to keep his mustache away from his mouth. He had no plan to eat any of her food. It was just one of many habitual gestures that came with age. He looked at her, doing his best to come across as a kind grandpa. He wanted to be as non-threatening as possible, wanted her calm, cooperative and healthy.

"I have brought you some fruit, a burrito, and some sodas. Please eat, your mother has made it clear to me that you need to eat every day, and I agree."

"I'd like to say I'm not hungry," she said, her voice quivering.

Ramiro strained to hear her as the fearful words came out of the girl's mouth. Her eyes were fixed on the knife. He wiped the blade on a paper towel, closed his knife, and buried it deep in his pocket.

"I will bring you something, please eat it, think of your mother's worry." The sliced cantaloupe, a burrito and a plastic bottle of soda now sat on a tray with some more paper towels, and he carried it to the small round dining table next to the recliner. It was strewn with English novels and magazines he'd left for her; she shoved them out of the way to make room for the tray. Bella jumped off and watched as Joy sat up straighter in the chair and leaned toward the food.

"I need to use the bathroom before I eat. Please wait here for me, I have some questions for you."

"Está bien." He backed up and sat tentatively on the front half of the small upholstered armchair opposite the recliner. As Joy walked by on her way to the bathroom, he put his nervous energy into tickling Bella behind both ears and along her back, pretending he hadn't noticed Joy wearing the green cotton dress he'd left the day before. The sash from the dress had been repurposed, and pulled her thick hair into a black waterfall down her back, over the flowers Adela had embroidered around the scooped neckline.

Joy barely fit in the dress, giving Ramiro yet one more reason to be pleased that Adela had put on some weight over the years. The hem just touched Joy's knees, while on Adela, it reached mid-calf. Joy's youthful form reminded him of his wife Adela's first visit into the bunker after their escape from the cartel fifteen years before. Their Zapotec crew had laboriously completed the modifications on the railroad shipping container and slid it down the ramp into the excavated earth. The mountain hideout was a testament to their fear. Even though they were hidden in an isolated Oaxacan forest, 2600 kilometers from their cartel's Nuevo Laredo headquarters, they had feared pursuit, capture, torture, and execution.

As Joy entered the closet-sized bathroom, she slammed the door, startling him out of his dazed reflections. But what could he do; he knew the bunker was too confining. He drifted into the past again, another habit of his advancing age, memories disappearing and reappearing in random fashion. His memories of their split with his brother Miguel made him shudder. Their escape from decades of cartel

34

slavery would never have been safe with him around; he had insisted that Miguel leave them before their hideout's location was chosen. The drunk accepted the exclusion, took his cut of the money, then became just another ubiquitous old man in Oaxaca City.

Ramiro dove deeper, wistful inside the scenes the bunker stirred...Tonio had been only five...Adela's oldest brother had led them to the uninhabited mountain site; close to a mountain spring, and only three miles from the highway that led to Oaxaca City. The Zapotecs from Adela's village, especially the shaman, had seen them through very dark days, and nights of terror-stricken paranoia.

Terrible images of their cartel years caused him to fidget in the chair. He moved forward on the seat again, considering the comfort of food, when Bella turned her head away. The bathroom door opened. Joy emerged, Bella joined her, they went to the sink while Joy washed her hands, then walked over to the tray of food. Ramiro could see Joy had been crying, and tried to cheer her up.

"I had a feeling you were hiding in there because you were upset. We will keep you safe until you go to your parents on Wednesday, no one here is going to hurt you." His shame pained him; doing a bad thing for a good cause felt so indefensible at the moment he was forced to change the subject.

"Good that I brought down the rug before Christmas Eve since you are barefoot...I will bring some socks when I come back with your dinner. You said you have questions, Señorita?"

"What day is it? What time? I thought I'd know, but I forgot."

"Saturday, almost 10 a.m.

She tossed her head and shoulders back in a defensive posture, a sneer on her mouth.

"Saturday? Are you kidding me? That can't be right, you're playing tricks with my mind, there's no way I've been here that long. It's the twenty-sixth, then, isn't it?"

"Yes, it is. Do you remember arriving?"

"Well, no." She quieted, closed her eyes, let the tears flow. "It's...my twenty-first birthday." She looked up, pouting.

"Can I just call my parents' office landline at home, so I can at least hear their voices on the message?"

Ramiro's bottom lip curled out slightly from within his silver beard, his wiry eyebrows raised. Now he felt slightly guilty about the valium. Palms up, shoulders shrugged, he felt like a child admitting guilt with veiled mirth but no real regret.

"First, your lost time was from medication. One or two valiums here and there. You slept a lot. Good for your fears, just to stay relaxed until you go home. As for your phone call, you can leave a quick message, because it is your birthday."

"I thought your voice was familiar...you're the one who put the tape on my mouth." Her hands clenched. She stood like a stone.

"When am I going home? Am I really going home or are you just tricking me? Who are you?"

Joy studied the old man and came to a decision. *I'd better stop pushing him; don't know what kind of crazy he might be, not going to give him any excuse to hurt me.*

"If you eat, I will talk with you."

Joy stared at him. She shook her head in frustration. Willing herself to move, she walked to the table by the recliner, picked up a slice of cantaloupe and a paper towel and started chewing the melon off the rind, wiping the juice as it slid down her hand. With a quick move, she dropped the rind on the tray, grabbed a second piece, and glanced at Ramiro.

"I guess I was hungry." At this point, she moved around the table, sat in the recliner, curled her bare legs underneath her, covered her lap with a small hand-woven throw, and ate while she waited for his answer.

Ramiro got up, walked to the kitchenette, picked up a bottle of soda and returned to his chair.

He sat, but this time slid back on the cushioned seat and made himself as comfortable as possible. He uncapped the soda, dropped the cap into a small trashcan near his chair, and prepared to talk.

"You call me Ramiro, señorita. And no, you will not be hurt. This is business. Not a business to be proud of, but I need to move my family very soon, and that requires a lot of money. To move, have a good life in a safe place, and your parents are very rich, no?"

"I understand," said Joy, "you are going to sell me to my rich parents, so you can get your family somewhere safe, like out of Mexico."

36

"Exactamente."

"What's this place I'm in?"

"A railroad storage car, completamente enterrada. Your location is a secret. Cannot be seen from above, no worry about someone bothering you."

"Where does the air come from?"

"Muy inteligente, señorita, you are thinking about escaping from ventilation ducts, like in the movies?" He pointed to a small air vent in the ceiling. "Nothing bigger than your arm venting that air. Only Alice in Wonderland may get small enough to escape through there."

Joy, distracted by his comment as she reached for the soda, moved fast to pull it to her lap, turned her head at an angle, and looked up, straight in his eyes, surprised enough to demand an explanation.

"People here read Alice in Wonderland?"

Ramiro chuckled, unable to resist her childlike query. He leaned fully back in the chair, one arm on the armrest, head leaning on his hand, stroking over his face to regain his composure.

"I married young, a baby on the way, then another. I taught them both Spanish and English with that crazy story. Speaking English is a common practice for Mexican families who work with Americans. Even good drug dealers speak English; the US is our biggest customer."

"Hard to imagine a gangster having a family."

"That familia es no más, señorita."

"Are they dead?"

"No. Just gone."

"Your choice or theirs?"

"God's, yo creo. I made bad choices, I did not deserve them." Embarrassed and saddened over his transparent remark, he looked at the floor. When he heard no response from her, he looked up.

The girl was more moved by his statement than he had anticipated. Her tears refracted the scant light; she began with quiet measured phrases that evolved into a crescendo of recrimination and rage.

"My mom's always on and on about choices, about how they can take you to the top or run your life right off the road. Like the choice I made to push my folks until they let me go in that cab to the club on Christmas eve. I wanted it bad. I pushed against their warnings

37

until I won…only I didn't win, did I? I wasn't thinking about anything but fun; they just sounded like they were being overprotective. I didn't believe there was any threat to my future or my parent's future at all!"

Her chin trembled, she jerked it down to her chest; she moaned, her anger strangled it into a loud growl. Ramiro felt it reverberate against the steel walls, and deeply regretted his role in her subterranean nightmare. The fact that his regret wasn't sufficient to stop his desperate extortion of the Doyles shamed him even more.

## 10

Addie could not shake the image she'd seen of Joy, and she guessed the Doyles felt the same. She still had no image of Ramiro, but at times thought she heard him talking to the girl. She had to wrap up her meeting with the Doyles, and wanted to conclude their session on a positive note.

On impulse, she leaned forward, took their adjacent hands and folded one within the other, giving them a comforting pat. For a brief moment, as she held their hands in hers, it triggered an image of Ben and Star, so she decided to follow the impulse.

"Have you to ever heard Ben and Star Robinson present a program?" Ana nodded.

"Yes, we have, a friend of ours streamed one for us at her house last month; very impressive, to see how their message spoke to people from so many religious traditions."

"Yeah," Mike agreed, "who'd think that quantum physics and prayer would ever be spoken in the same sentence?"

"Well," Addie said "It's an emerging line of inquiry. We know anecdotal evidence, no matter how frequently it's cited over the course of history, is not scientific proof. So, it isn't clear yet how we can properly study paranormal phenomena like ESP, or how states of consciousness influence illness or healing."

"If you weren't psychic yourself you might be more skeptical," Ana said, "but I love science, for how much it's taught me to keep an open mind. Just because we can't see something or prove its existence doesn't mean it's not there." She made another trip to the water cooler, her passion about the subject energizing the conversation.

"I mean, how many of our inventions have extended our perception beyond what our eyes can see on their own? We thought we understood atoms, then discovered the behavior of subatomic particles like quarks contradicts prior scientific beliefs about matter." Mike was grinning at Ana as she spoke, then laughed openly.

"Oh, darlin' I can see we need to have more of this discussion when we have time." He looked at Addie to explain his comment.

"When I left the Catholic Church, I lost track of God. Ana referred to me as a reductive materialist. But when I learned that our consciousness can function separately from a healthy or disabled brain, as part of an underlying universal consciousness, I could see it is a spiritual mystery worth exploring.

"Enough, Mike," Ana said, "We all need to go." Addie nodded in agreement and focused forward with a suggestion.

"Since we're going to be leaving for Mexico so soon, why don't we meet tomorrow at the Robinsons' eleven o'clock session? My family will be there at the same time; of course, but I won't say you are clients; that's only for you to share if you ever want to. Just Google the Omni Center on Skyline Boulevard."

"Sounds like a good plan," Ana said, "So how did we do today, Doctor?"

"Ana, Mike, I think we've accomplished a lot in the last two hours. You did a good job on the open-versus-closed adoption dynamics, so if Joy decides to connect with her birth family later, you won't feel as threatened as you would have. Save the reading list I gave you for later, there are excellent books on the dynamics of adoption reunions. They're often a real emotional roller coaster. If you read them before her reunion, you'll be more prepared."

"And Joy won't have to avoid that connection just to keep us from feeling threatened, either," said Ana, "I got your point, though, that it's the reality of whatever relationship she finds that is important; so she can adjust to reality instead of fantasies, and so can we." Ana looked at Mike, then back to Addie. "I'm not eager to see her or us disappointed, however. Adjusting to a disappointment would be tough on top of the crisis we are in."

"Doctor…uh…Addie…thanks for everything," Mike said, with what appeared to Addie as a self-conscious grin. "Of course, we will come tomorrow to see the Robinsons, but will we see you at our house Monday for the FBI meeting?"

"Definitely. We're in a time crunch while you secure the ransom, then we need to get to Oaxaca to recover Joy by Wednesday. I rarely do field work these days, but Agent Chung wants me to be available if they need help to find the hideout. I'll tell you right now I have a strong hunch we need to get to Oaxaca as early as possible on Tuesday." Addie saw Mike's eyebrows arch up. Ana spoke before he had a chance to start a new conversation.

"Agent Chung, Isabel, told us she is consulting with other agencies, and with someone new at the San Diego FBI who is a cartel specialist. He'll be at the meeting Monday morning at our house. Isabel, Emil Torres, and this new guy will bring us up to speed, and," she concluded impatiently, "that's all we know right now…"

"I'd like to toast today's meeting," Mike said, "it went way beyond my expectations. You wouldna' happen to have a pint of Irish whiskey in that filing cabinet, now would you?"

"I truly wish I did; it would be all yours, Mike, just so I could hear your Irish brogue get thicker. Have you ever been to the House of Shields Bar?"

"No, but I heard it's one of those big luxurious bars they built in the 1800's, high ceilings, beautiful dark wood everywhere," said Mike.

"If you want a high-quality drink experience, I recommend it. They occupy the first floor of this building. When we go out the front door downstairs, turn right, you'll see the Shields sign." Addie gathered up her things and they left, heading for the elevator.

"Thanks for the tip on the bar, sounds perfect, right Ana?"

"Yes, and when we get home, a real nap; we haven't slept much for days."

Once they were inside the elevator, Mike put both arms around Ana, looked in her eyes, and gave her a quick hug.

"We're gonna make it through this darlin'…just hang on."

Their intimacy jarred her. Addie felt a strong sensation in her chest, as if some part of her was stirring into wakefulness from a profound sleep. She welcomed the elevator's arrival at the first floor, and stepped out first; she had her eyes dry before Mike and Ana caught up with her. Ana spoke first.

"I forgot to tell you, we both took family leave; obviously, we want to be in Oaxaca when Joy is released to the FBI, so we can bring her home ourselves. May I call you if something comes up?"

"Sure, anytime. I need to be up to speed with whatever news you have." Addie noted Mike's appreciative and vulnerable smile. The good vibes moved in her heart again.

## 11

"It's like stepping out of a time machine into the 1800's" Ana said, "this bar is amazing!" A row of booths lined the street side of the room, with the bar opposite. "Let's get a booth," she said, choosing for them and sliding onto the seat.

"Yeah, but you're lucky it's 2015," Mike said as he sat across from her, checking out the street view through the large window. "Because I heard this place operated only as a men's club until the 1970's, no women allowed except prostitutes."

"Then our first toast will be to progress, and after that it's your call." Three drinks later, they were toasted.

"We should have known not to order this third one," Mike said, "with me tippin' whiskey and you into the brandy, I'd say it's a good thing we have a brisk walk to the parking garage…hey…you look like you're getting upset, was it somthin' I said?"

"Kind of, I was thinking what you said to Dr. Diaz about letting go of the fear of Joy's birthmother. You're not as far along as you let on. Felt like you were kissing up to her because you want her helping us, now that you know she has this psychic link to Joy." Mike's left eyebrow went up, indicating he did not agree.

"Don't give me that look!" Ana scowled, "I know she's honest and skilled, but it's just her opinion that we should open our hearts and our home to welcome this woman. Is that really the best idea? Joy could meet with her birthmother at the adoption agency when she finally gets around to asking for it, and if they decide to meet again, they can work it out between them." Ana got more annoyed as she waited for Mike to lower his eyebrow and get on with the argument she saw coming.

"Your tidy alternative pushes Joy to feel her birth mother isn't good enough for us, Ana, that she's someone we don't trust. It also tells Joy we'd rather not be involved with her birthmother, so we are bailing out of supporting them through the ups and downs of the relationship."

"Are you kidding me? That's bullshit!" Ana heard her voice carry farther than she wished, and leaned forward. Her inebriated whisper was only slightly distorted.

"Mr. Flynn," she waved her glass in a small arc, "I think you are missing my point. It would be a boundary that allowed them privacy. A vote of confidence that we trust them. We don't have to embarrass the woman and have her pass muster with us!" Mike tipped his head to sip his drink, then peered up at her.

"Sneaky, Ana, sneaky, but I'm onto you. Your empathy battery must be runnin' outta juice. Ever think about her needin' anything from you and me? I mean Joy can't tell her much about the first two or three years, you know, the years that were the worst for her birthmother. I've heard you tell stories to people you hardly knew, stories about Joy's antics as a baby, the way she begged us to 'go airpot, see panes fy up.'

"Ana, you would light up like a Christmas tree when you told people about taking her to the airport. Yeah, it might be sad for Joy's birthmother, hearin' it for the first time from us. But think of the benefits, she has not one iota of information about what Joy did growing up, things that would reassure her, memories she could cherish. She paid a high price to give Joy up, and until now what could she comfort herself with, what could she share with her closest friends about what Joy was able to do during those early years?" Mike looked straight at Ana, then answered his own question.

"She could not tell herself or her friends one single thing, because we hoarded all of it, even after Joy turned 18. She would have found her before now if we had been open to the good that could come from it, but we never mentioned it. The agency told us they would meet with Joy once she was 18 if she wanted to meet her birth mother, but when Joy turned 18, instead of offering to host a reunion at our home, you just left the agency name and address on her desk on her 18th birthday."

Ana pushed back, hard.

"I didn't see you offering any help either, Mike!" She shoved her glass aside, grabbed her purse, and slid from the booth, her mouth clamped tight, eyes daring him to say one more word.

"I'm walking by myself, see you at the garage!" The booths and the bar looked misshapen and irrelevant through her tears as she headed out the door.

He caught up with her faster than she expected. Her eyes closed to a slit, shutting him out, daring him to speak again.

"You make me out to be the withholding bitch while you demonstrate all your empathy. I thought of her birthmom a lot as I saw

Joy doing special things, but never considered I'd tell her about them later; just seemed like it would break her heart to hear it."

"Ana, we shouldn't be fightin' over what to share with her and what not to share, we should bring her into our home and let her decide what she's interested in; stories about Joy, photo albums, videos we took of everything she did for years. If I were Joy's birthfather and it was me you said that to, why, I'd be sayin' bring it on, I'd want to see it all; maybe not all at once, but over time."

"Stop! I've heard enough!" Ana's tears were flying off her face as she hurried ahead of him.

"All right!" His voice boomed over the sidewalk; people turned to stare as he caught up with her.

"But hear this first, Ana, the doctor's opinion is an educated opinion. Who would you pay to give medical opinions for your animals at the zoo? The clerk at the gift shop, or you?"

"What if her birth mother turns out to be a total bitch?" Ana pressed her case. "Someone who does sneaky manipulative crap to weaken our relationship with Joy? Once we let her in our lives, how would we get her out? And what about the birth father? Plus, all their relatives who might want to meet us. Scared? Hell yes I'm scared!"

Ana stomped forward, aware their argument was spinning in a circle, and could only muster one word.

"Ugh!"

# 12

Addie steered the truck into the Devil's Slide bypass southbound tunnel. Devil's Slide had been aptly named. Persistent mudslides had buried the same section of the highway with tons of life-threatening mud and boulders from the saturated coastal hills every rainy season.

That section of narrow, cliff-hugging highway had, for decades, provided sightseers with a thrilling, if risky, seagull's view of the sea hundreds of feet below the road. It was now closed. Nature had won. Addie missed the old view but not the travel delays between her home in Pescadero and her office in San Francisco.

So, here she was, a few months shy of two years since the Lantos tunnel was completed in March of 2013, and it had become a familiar landmark on her commute. Addie slowed the truck down through the well-lit 4,100-foot tunnel, then emerged, only to enter another tunnel—constructed solely by mother nature—this one made of dense fog.

She was thankful for the increased safety of the new divided highway, but it wasn't long enough. Soon, it devolved into two lanes approaching the landmark Devil's Slide concrete bunker. The fog had lifted just enough; she saw the bunker perched on the cliff edge, its mission during World War II had been to protect the soldiers looking out for Japanese subs and planes. *Another era filled with threats to democracy,* she thought.

With her progress slow, she was glad she had stopped at Tam's in Pacifica for won ton soup. She'd also written her notes of the Doyles' session on her laptop and emailed them to Isabel. The Doyles had given Addie and Isabel a waiver of confidentiality, so the team could communicate as needed when time was of the essence. Being on the same page was top priority.

*I need to stop thinking about the unknowns in this case, let them incubate. When the time's right, I'll get a strong hunch. Until then, I'll chill, have a nice slow cruise to Pescadero, and I may get home before sunset.* The fog had a way of isolating her thoughts, pulling her back into herself. After leaving Tams, she had avoided listening to Grillo's book of drug cartel terror, thinking the view would cheer her up…but now, unable to indulge in the allure of her comfort zone, she lapsed into her own uncensored thoughts about her mama's death a year earlier.

*So, let's think about Mama. And about her cancer, aided and abetted by forty years of chronic grief, alcoholism, and decades of smoking. Grieving her death is so different from when I lost Martín and Papa. I was a kid when they died; and when I look back on those years, there are periods I cannot recall, big blocks of time, months that vanished from memory. With Mama, it's the opposite, I'm remembering everything. I'm older, I can process more, yet it creates such an emotional overload! I just want it to stop!*

Addie pulled a bottle of Starbuck's coffee out of the console. Time to be alert; she knew this fog was dangerous.

*Too bad Mama didn't have a spiritual connection, felt no love, no guidance. At least I understand now; that addictions freeze love in its tracks. Some people grieve the loss of their parents because they miss the love they shared; but there are lots of people like me who grieve only the loss of hope; because of love that never developed.*

*With Mama I grieved the loss of hope, when Martín and Papa died, I grieved the loss of them loving me every day. So, the universe sent me Grandma Diaz; I became the daughter she never had, and she became the mother I never had. What a blessing!*

A portal opened in the fog ahead, the afternoon sun glared, yanking Addie out of her thoughts. A shiny red Yamaha motorcycle, driven by a thrill-seeker dressed in matching biker regalia, came flying into Addie's lane, passing a truck stacked high with wooden pallets. Startled as she was, Addie couldn't help looking for him in the mirror after he sped past, taking his assumptions of invincibility with him.

The phone rang, piquing her already jangled nerves. She was shocked to see the time on her phone, next to Ana's caller ID. Twenty-five minutes had passed since she exited the Lantos tunnel.

"Okay, okay," Addie groaned, "so much for driving undistracted." Rationalizing her actions, she answered with the speaker on.

"Addie Diaz," she said automatically, having returned to enjoying the sun, and the pleasure of watching the now visible sea.

"Addie, it's Ana! I know you didn't expect to hear from me this soon, but I knew you'd want to hear this!"

# 13

*I should pull into the turnout, but Ana sounds happy, how distracting can a quick report be?* Comfortable with her rationalization, Addie drove past the turnout. The sea displayed a soft gray shimmer; a formation of pelicans flew a few feet above the water. She had to roll down the passenger window to catch the humid scent. It poured in, teasing her to relive her morning ride with Amira.

"Go ahead, Ana, I'm listening." Distracted, she sniffed the sea air, and imagined flying over the water. Ana's words burst forth with such excitement, she fully captured Addie's attention.

"Addie, we got a message from Joy on our land line in the study! We had drinks at the Shields, came home, and took a nap. The call must have come in while agent Torres was out. I doubt he checked the land line, we rarely use it. It was kind of hard to hear her voice, but it was her, all right, said she just wanted to hear our voices on the recording and leave a message for us on her birthday. Said she's looking forward to seeing us on Wednesday, then she hung up."

"Her birthday?" Addie, confused, snapped out of her reverie. She squirmed in her seat, pulled her seat belt out to loosen it, and focused on hearing Ana's explanation.

"Yes. The twenty-first birthday party Mike videoed on his phone was done in advance of our trip to Mexico, so her friends could join in. Her real birthday is today."

"Today?" Addie began to look for a place to pull off the road, but tight weekend traffic and no turnoffs in sight forced her to keep driving. Ana's voice was quivering with equal intensity in every word.

"Yes, Addie," Ana continued the familiar use of Addie's first name as if she'd known it forever. "December 26th, 1994, at Stanford Hospital, she arrived at 8:20 p.m. Oh, Addie, we waited for the call from the agency all day, and finally, it came. Baby Girl Doyle, nine pounds, three ounces. You know what I'm talking about, you've been through adoption…"

There was a double click, a brief silence, then Ana's voice. "Addie, wait," said Ana, "agent Chung is calling me, we can talk about this tomorrow at the Robinsons' service, I'll see you there." Ana hung up swiftly without another word.

Addie, who was barely a mile from home, couldn't stand to be contained a minute longer. She pulled into the Pescadero State Beach entry, turned right, and drove to the end of the parking area. She felt for the key, killed the engine, and sat staring out the windshield, her heart pounding.

The sun-sparked breakers smashed against the rocks; her vision fixed on the next wave ahead, as if the turbulence of the ocean could roll back the events of the day, place her back on Amira, back into her bliss.

Addie felt she was blowing apart; she shoved the door open, jumped out, and scuttered down the dirt path to the beach, arms flailing, right hand still locked on the silent phone. Her exploding dread forced her to abandon what little attempt she had made to watch her footing; the worn wooden steps down the five-foot drop to the beach required more control than she had.

She jerked her head back as she descended. Instantly and unexpectedly, she slipped, spun her arms wildly, and sensing the entire incident playing out in slow motion, she observed herself scrambling to regain her balance. Somehow, her feet landed squarely on the sand, her upper body folded into a squat, rebounded to vertical, and switched into fast-forward.

Dr. Diaz, her professional garb the antithesis of beach attire, ran down the deserted shore in absolute panic and disbelief. It was late afternoon, off-season for tourists, but usually there were people here. The earlier fog had likely discouraged visitors, but Addie wasn't noticing, regardless.

A huge and possibly well-meaning wave had rolled in a small injured seal pup during the mid-morning high tide. If she'd seen it she would have realized it had recovered enough to return home, though its progress toward the advancing tide was slow. The assist nature had given to the small creature had, it turned out, one more propitious result. Addie had lost all ability to slow down and calm herself, and the pup's tail, safely away from its bruised flipper, caught the doctor's shoe right at the toe; enough to tweak her fickle balance.

The momentum of the tall muscular woman's stride was significant. No one was there to measure the arc of her forward motion, but the sheer force of it lent an unintentionally artistic air to what became a swimmer's racing dive, as arms instinctively thrust forward to break her fall. A tangled mass of greenish brown bull kelp, covered with the almost imperceptible presence of tiny flies, seemed ready to receive her, to meet her desperate need for a bed of any kind.

It took only a millisecond for her fainting, discarded body to descend fully to earth. Addie's fractured soul had chosen to fly skyward, seeking answers, and to her surprise, she arrived with no questions. She resided in comfort and impenetrable safety. She rested, silently present and slowly moving within this welcome embrace, yet when she searched for and sensed a boundary she found herself already occupying the space beyond it.

Her panic had vanished. She had known overwhelming terror only once before—during the brutal rape that destroyed her hopes for an FBI career—but this time, her fears had all been left behind on the beach. Peace welcomed her, and she rested in its buoyant, warm embrace. She faded into this mothering home, this fertile void, teeming with dark matter and the active sensorium of her memories.

Gently, it presented her with a vision from her past. A long-lost flood of sensations; the hospital's ubiquitous fragrance of antiseptic, the clanging metal trays serving the bland lunch, the round neckline of her thin hospital gown too close to her throat, her view from the window onto the parking lot. Addie heard the voice of pain beckoning her to fall through the window, to escape the hospital room.

*Escape the distended painful breasts leaking wasted milk. Escape the bleeding, empty womb. Escape the walk to the nursery, to hold your baby girl in your arms for the last time.* The memories had been carefully surrounded and eventually obscured by years of repeated analysis and rationalization. The vivid details of heart and soul, of flesh and blood, had respectfully waited in the mausoleum of her psyche, such that she could remain aware of that sequestered event and not feel the longing it held.

Ana's one sentence, 'twenty-one years ago today, at Stanford hospital,' expressed the yin of Addie's empty womb, and the yang of Ana's heartfelt memory of Joy's arrival. In its issue, it had released everything at once. *How could so many sharp, piercing feelings and images occur in an instant?* Her answer?

*I know how it works—physical pain originates and demands all attention in the present moment—but emotional pain can resonate with every relevant loss*

49

*across an entire lifetime and deliver it simultaneously.*

She descended under the weight of it. The smell of antiseptic merged with an encompassing sense of ocean mist. The hospital parking lot morphed into cool, soft sand. Saltwater tears fell into grains of earth as soft as baby powder, scented with pungent sunbaked seaweed.

Addison Marisol Diaz, disembodied yet more present than ever before, floated through time, back to a high elevation midsummer trip she'd taken in August with her papa on her sixth birthday. He had promised her a perfectly cloudless night to experience the cosmos in all its glory. The Perseid meteor shower. Lying close, tucked into their sleeping bags, hands clasped and warm, father and daughter watched the meteor shower in the most star-studded sky she'd ever seen.

From her soul's vantage point, Addie looked down, scanned the mountain meadow and saw her small form, cuddled close to her papa, eyes looking skyward. Addie hovered closer to them. A quiet voice began to speak as Addie listened.

"Papa, I think someone's here with us," whispered her young voice.

"Oh?" He queried with a huge grin, "I should have known your antennae would be working overtime in a place like this, mija. Just relax, it could be my grandmother in heaven, just checking in on us. She used to take me out on nights like this."

"I'm watching meteors, Papa. Even if someone did want to talk to me, I'm too busy!"

The good doctor smiled as she heard this. The familiar rules of time and location, of being and knowing, didn't even occur to her. She descended, entered her little body, curled herself up in her papa's arms, and as the stars blurred, fell gratefully into sleep.

## 14

This second altered state of Addie's day, unlike the distracted drive down the coast, didn't have the shrill ring of a phone to draw her back to her homebound surround; she remained where she was. Was it by chance or by design that she had gone to a new realm?

If watchers of her ilk had observed her body, damp from the heavy incoming fog and the mist of the rising tide; had they seen her snuggled next to that twisting mass of brackish bull kelp, phone still in hand, fingers serving as launching sites for kelp flies, they might have guessed she washed up dead onto the beach from some vessel wrecked at sea. Of greater interest perhaps, would be the enigma that overshadowed all else; how might a person so cruelly discarded by the sea move her lips in such a satisfied smile?

Addie, aware of the scene from her soul's perspective, saw everything moving exactly according to plan; so she stayed connected but knew all was well. No human life but hers was evident, so no alarm was being raised. Instead, she saw that her eyes flickered busily under closed lids, her chest rose and fell gently, and the avian witnesses to her visage saw it as neither distressed nor lifeless. Possibly she was seen as an opportunity for foraging, as suggested by a few gulls landing nearby, alternately walking, and, when disturbed by another gull, hopping forward in search of edibles that might be spilled and currently undefended.

Eventually, the gulls waddled seaward, squawking, launching themselves gracefully over the surf. Their squawks fell, silenced by the pounding, crackling sea; their wings skirted past the bobbing young seals that darted within its buoyant support. The playful seals slowly disappeared; perhaps they went in search of their parents, or the fish they sought had moved to deeper waters.

The tires from an approaching sedan crunched slowly through the gravel entry to the beachside parking lot. Addie's truck, with the door slightly ajar, encouraged some investigation. Once the sedan was parked alongside, a tall well-dressed man emerged. His slacks, pullover sweater, brown skin and short cropped black hair received a swath of the sunset's golden tones. He stepped out to take a closer look, then turned back to grab his jacket.

His companion watched out her opened window as he circled the sedan where she sat looking at the truck. The wind was picking up, blowing through her dark curls, its chill closing the pores in her skin, which, unlike the man's, was as black as obsidian in the waning sunlight.

"Nobody's in there, Ben. It's like the truck Addie's girls run errands in, but they came to help with Saturday chores at the center this afternoon and decided to stay for the yoga class. Addie called me this morning to beg off today's class. Izzy called her, asked her to take an urgent FBI referral that couldn't wait 'till tomorrow—a kidnapping case."

"Those clients are in for a special experience if Addie's working with them." He looked up and down the beach, "If the girls or Addie left the truck here, where are they? I don't see anyone out there." He tilted his head, closed his eyes, then slowly opened them a moment later. "Star, I have a strong feeling that Addie, Isabel, and her clients are headed into an extremely serious confrontation. We need to check in with her as soon as we're done here, and see what we can do."

"You and Addie are both such visionaries," Star said, "whenever I'm with either of you, there are always these moments when you look like you just recalled something important, your eyes dart up and to the side, it comes to you, and it turns out to be a psychic vision of some kind…instead of…oh yeah, I forgot to call and order that book so-and-so told me to get."

"Well, my love, we all have our peculiarities."

He bent over, stared in the open door of the truck, and stood back up looking puzzled.

"Keys are still in the ignition. Let's just leave it as is. If we don't see Addie or the girls I'll walk up and get the ranger to check the truck registration, and we can ask him if he saw who drove the truck in. He's a new guy; if he saw us rummaging in the truck he might have a problem with it."

"Makes sense to me," Star answered. "Too bad Caroline isn't on duty, she knows us. I mean, you don't look like a thief, but you are black, and it ain't your truck, just sayin'." She exited their car and zipped up her fleece jacket to ward off the breeze.

"What did we used to tell our son," he mused.

"I know, racists don't see people, only their own insecurities, and it makes their blood boil."

He turned from the truck, walked over and hugged her. They molded to each other. They kissed, slowly separated, still holding hands, and walked to the bluff.

Addie, watching from her comfortable disembodied vantage point, was thrilled her friends had arrived; she celebrated what she considered a celestial example of perfect timing. Ben, Star, Jake and Addie had been coming here together to watch sunsets for almost twenty years; dubbing themselves 'the sunset view crew.'

"Look Ben," Star pointed and exclaimed in a loud whisper, "in the twilight, the sea's comin' up like a blanket to tuck in the beach…that foam looks like cotton, so soft."

"You're getting downright poetic, Star, next thing you know you'll write a song about it, you'll teach it to the choir, and everyone will clamor for a CD." Ben chuckled at his own joke. "But I see what you mean, especially over that way where it's comin' close to that big pile of kelp, tide's definitely in."

Another wave crashed. A beam of pale ochre from the sinking sun glistened in the foam as the icy wave slapped down on the kelp. Suddenly, like a sea creature from another world, a strange shape leaped out of the tangled vines; sunlit water flew, like sparks from a campfire. The creature grasped at the air for balance, rising a good five or six feet.

"Godhelpus!" Ben prayed.

"Ben!!" Star screamed so fast, so loud, her voice cracked apart; like an animal that just stepped into the biting teeth of a metal trap. The sound surrendered to a shudder as she grabbed his arm, terrified. In that same instant, the form, now human, turned in their direction and staggered forward.

"Ben! It's a woman, she can hardly walk!"

"Come on girl!" Star screamed into the wind, "Hurry on up here! Oh, my Lord, I'll get you." She ran from the parking lot, down the narrow-worn path to the bluff, and scrambled down the stairs. Ben had followed her, but stayed on the low bluff as the women embraced each other hard and strong. The dripping, disheveled woman couldn't yet stand fully erect, nor emerge from the soaked mop of her long hair enough to be seen. He stayed with his feet planted on the hardpan and waited for his cue.

The fog had gathered thick and distinct, more like a low well-formed cloud. The wedge of open sky below the cloud received a buttery swath of sunlight from the horizon, illuminating the women's march across the beach. Star tripped on a rock and the rescued woman instinctively found the strength to steady her in their forward motion.

"Like angels too wet to fly," Ben said quietly. The women marched staunchly forward, holding onto each other as they found footing through rocks, kelp and sand.

"Ben!" Star yelled through the wind, "It's Addie, it's Addie!"

Ben descended the stairs, took off his jacket, and ran toward the women. As the sun extinguished itself in the sea, he met them, and without slowing their forward motion, wrapped his jacket over Addie's shoulders. She pulled her dripping hair away from her sand-speckled face and looked straight into his eyes.

"Ben," she croaked in desperation, "Thank God you're here! Thank you!"

"We got you now, Addie, don't you worry." He stepped between them, wrapped the power of his long arms around Star and Addie and helped both women up the stairs. Ben knew Addie was crying big. He could feel her body convulsing under the jacket he had fitted around her, even though the dusk and the damp allowed no sign of tears.

## 15

Yesterday's bizarre reveal seemed like a terrifying dream. *Now there's a handy defense mechanism,* Addie observed, *if it's not real, I don't have to deal with it.* Her chest was tight. Her stomach hurt. Some part of her mind insisted the event at the beach could not be real.

The experience insisted on its veracity until the lie in her mind drifted away like a mist. Ana's phone call, the beach, and her disembodied return to 1994. Undeniable. Back to square one, where she faced the truth. The time-trapped memory of her beautiful baby had morphed into an urgently updated contest for her grown daughter's life.

The closet in Star's guest room offered Addie a choice of outfits she had left behind through years of overnight visits. A teal pullover, jeans and boots would do for now. *Thank God for that shower last night. I'm still freakin' out...at least I'm clean! But now what?*

*God works in mysterious ways, Addie.* Grandma Luisa's cliché bounced around in her brain, but not to provide a comforting catch-all context for her dilemma. Luisa navigated those mysterious ways more than most. For Luisa, the platitude wasn't something you said to get off the hook; it was an invitation to plumb the mystery.

Addie felt like a scared ten-year-old at a theme park, dared to get on the rides she had always avoided. Her thoughts surrendered to interruption—crystalline chimes called to her from an eave outside Star's guest room window, drawing her closer, just in time to see two humming birds, like neon streamers, orbiting erratically around their feeding station.

Star's lilting piano phrases from the next room pulled her attention back into the house. Addie looked down at the cell phone on the table by the window. Star had activated a spare and loaned it to her. Addie had texted the number to Ana and Mike. Now it was time to face Isabel.

She called, then parked it on the table by the window with the speaker on. Her heart began a steady thump in her chest as she worried about Izzy's response ... *should I tell her about yesterday? No. This isn't the time.*

"Hello, Star?" Izzy was responding to the caller ID.

"Izzy, it's Addie, gotta minute? Okay. I'm using Star's spare cell, you're on speaker, no one's here, you can talk freely. I got my phone soaked, don't think any bag of rice is going to save it this time, so I'm buying a new phone soon. In the meantime, just call me on this number until I tell you otherwise." Isabel, who had patiently listened to Addie's report, came back at her with her own; Addie sensed the anxiety in her voice.

"Addie, get this, the Doyles are having cash flow problems trying to raise the ransom. While they're working on it, I got ahold of that international ops agent I told you about; he's with the San Diego Bureau now; a cartel specialist. He'll join us tomorrow morning at the meeting to help with negotiations, maybe he can get the price down."

"Ok, then, but if there's a cash flow problem coming up with the ransom, that's serious, I'm sure Ana and Mike are freaking out." *Maybe I should sell that ten acres my neighbor's been begging me for. Not an appropriate step for a therapist, but if I step out of that role, then it would be okay. What am I thinking, the cash has to be in hand by Tuesday!* Isabel reminded her of her primary duty in no uncertain terms;

"Right now, you need to work on Ana and Mike and get them focused on this thing working out; their confidence is wavering big time since this cash problem arose. We can't afford to have them getting hot-headed and sabotaging the phone negotiations. Anyway, that's your end of the job, just calm them the hell down, you are so good at that, I have to say."

"Izzy, these are strong people who don't shrink from a crisis, even one with a steep learning curve like this one."

"You may be right. After all, Ana told me they discovered a lot about their infertility and adoption issues in their meeting with you yesterday. That's good; and I love your idea inviting them to hear Ben and Star. Their confidence is irresistible, and their logic is like a stairway to your heart's desire, isn't it?"

Izzy rarely talked this much on the phone. *Something in this case has touched her, too. Everything I haven't told her about yesterday is probably buzzing around her, but she just feels it, doesn't know what it is.* Before Addie could get a word in, Izzy went on.

"Once they listen to Ben and Star, the Doyles will know their cash problem is fixable, and Joy's rescue is under higher supervision than they imagined. Actually, I know it too, I just have times when I doubt everything, then Dana reminds me in her blunt fashion, 'you can't get to found from lost' and I have to agree with her. They don't see it now, but they will. Anyway, gotta go."

Addie heard the dial tone and knew Isabel was off the phone and onto her next task. She smelled the coffee before she saw the steaming red cup behind a stubby vase of flowers and a bowl of fruit.

Balancing the tray with one arm, Star carried it to the table and put it next to the phone. Addie felt the peace Star brought as well.

"Thanks for the over-the-top room service, first a free cell phone, now this."

"We aim to please. Everything go okay with Isabel?"

"We have a meeting with the new clients tomorrow morning at their house in the city. Not trying to be funny, but thank God this is Sunday; I need your eleven o'clock service like I need air. I have to get myself together before tomorrow's meeting, it's going to be like walking through a minefield."

"I've never heard you describe a meeting like that before, what's different about this?" Star walked up to Addie. "You seem actually frightened. Does it have anything to do with your episode at the beach? Are you ready to talk about it now that you've had some rest?" Addie grabbed both of Star's hands and squeezed them hard; unconsciously pumping them up and down, shaking them, and unloaded her bottled up pain.

"Star, what you saw was the tip of the iceberg! Tomorrow's meeting is the first time I'm gonna have to show up and publicly recuse myself from my therapist role in a case." Addie had started off with a bit of bluster, but the truth flooded through her; she backed up to the bed, sat down, then looked up at Star's loving expression and found the words.

"Izzy asked me to be their therapist because the clients are adoptive parents in a closed adoption; she knew it would add another layer of panic to sort out." Star sat next to Addie on the bed and took her hand, gently, just as she'd offered her support sustaining Addie through the agony of Joy's breech birth. Star nodded to Addie, encouraged her to trust the next emotional contraction. Tears balanced on the lower lid of Addie's eyes as she looked at Star.

"Yesterday, my client Ana called me while I was driving home from our first session, to tell me the kidnapper had let her daughter leave a brief voicemail message on the land line in their study. But here's the catch..." Addie lowered her chin to her chest, clenched her quivering lips, stared at the cell phone in her hand, gasped in a desperate breath, then let the tears fall, looking straight at Star.

"When Ana called me right after hearing Joy's message, I was driving, coming up on Pescadero beach. She blurted out how thrilled she was to hear from Joy, because it was Joy's birthday! She reminisced about the birth twenty-one years ago...she mused over what a blessed memory it was...recounted the details the adoption agency relayed to them that day." Addie looked up, tears flooding her face, and dropped the phrase that had torn her apart.

"Stanford hospital...December 26, 1994...at 8:20 p.m. Weighed in at 9 pounds, 3 ounces, a beautiful baby girl. Oh, Star, it was such a happy memory for her! But for me? I felt torn in half."

Star's eyes and mouth flew open with shock; she jumped up off the bed, looked down at Addie with her arms waving in the air like a bird's wings fighting a downdraft.

"Oh my God! Addie! The kidnapped girl is your daughter! I'll never forget that day and night I spent with you at Stanford for as long as I live, and neither will Isabel or Grandma Luisa, or your Uncle Jerry. None of us were surprised she weighed over 9 pounds because you were as big as a house, waddling into that hospital!"

Star didn't hesitate, reached for Addie, pulled her up from the bed and wrapped her arms around her, rocking her while they cried, until Addie's sobs abated. Star took a step back, placed her hands on either side of Addie's face, and spoke to her dear friend in quiet, certain tones.

"Good thing Izzy didn't catch the connection, and who knows if she even recalls the exact date. The way she keeps work and personal life in such separate compartments, it doesn't surprise me."

"Yeah," Addie said in a heavy exhale, "The clients had just arrived from Mexico yesterday morning, Izzy had a rush meeting with them right after they arrived, you know Izzy, she hands them the forms to fill out for the case, then leaves it for her secretary to put in the computer. If any info had tweaked Izzy's recollection she would have asked the clients for more details, just to rule out a possible conflict of interest."

Addie was following Star's lead, and had blurted out her own view to support it. She walked to the window to grab tissues from a decorative dispenser, and continued her attempts to recover her confidence. A thought emerged as she wiped her eyes and blew her nose. She stepped toward Star.

"Ha!" she released unexpectedly, "Izzy's going to be amazed she missed it at their meeting, and when Izzy interrupted Ana's call to me, it was about their panic over the ransom; so, I doubt Ana waxed poetic about Stanford Hospital and Joy's birth during their conversation."

"Addie, you know how fast Izzy moves through her phone calls; there's rarely time for conversation, and half the time she just says 'I gotta run' and hangs up." Star's face brightened, she took Addie's hand and said, "Izzy's oversight created your opportunity."

"Still," Addie's breath hitched a few times, "I'm trying hard to not see it as the worst possible way I could have connected with them."

"Addie, you know when we're anxious we analyze, we get bogged down in details, we don't have the big picture. You became a psychologist and private investigator to help crime victims. Honey…it's all about decisions you made when you were young and passionate about honoring your brother's and dad's memory."

"I thought I'd forgiven myself, for taking a risk with that gangster, setting myself up for a world of hurt from the rape and the adoption."

"You have, and you will again," said Star.

Addie kept shaking her head; new tears poured down her face from Star's summary of Addie's young aspirations and traumatic mistakes. She picked up the tray Star had brought, and made every effort to pull out of her downward spiral, beginning with a smile and an invitation to get some fresh air.

"I'm ready to have coffee in the garden, want to get the doors?" Star smiled, opened the French doors, made way for Addie and the tray, and followed her into the garden.

## 16

The cool air did just what Addie hoped. Gave her a quick swipe in the face as she moved through the French doors into the winter morning, and jolted her into focus. They sat at the table. Addie finished her fruit and coffee in a rush, determined to get her story across to Star before they had to leave.

Scooting her chair back from the glass-topped table, she took sustenance from the lush garden and her beloved friend's patient, loving presence. Star was already dressed for the nine-a.m. service, with a warm shawl over her Ankara print dress, and a smile that promised Addie a brand-new view of her crisis. Star nodded, Addie told her what happened after Ana's jolting phone call, and concluded with her anxiety-ridden hopes for the Monday FBI meeting at the Doyles.

"I can't see myself quitting the case, but I have to explain there's a conflict of interest. Star, I'm fine with recusing myself as their therapist, but how will I get everyone's support to let me stay involved in a different role once they know the truth?" She cried, covering her face with her hands. "They'll say I knew all along that Joy was my daughter!" Star had listened intently, her face close to Addie's, and found the words to comfort her friend.

"Addie, listen to me, you've got your guts in a wad for a valid reason. But at the same time, you know you're in this situation by no accident whatsoever. God's in this, Addie, offerin' you a chance to heal. Now I don't care what you call it, Spirit, Source, God; you are in the midst of a healing opportunity. Not just for you alone, either, but for every single person involved. Just remember—dilemmas are dualities in search of unseen information—there are infinite solutions in universal mind. You need to talk with Ben after today's service, girl, he can help you too." Addie listened, and began to regain her strength.

"Yeah, I need to focus on the solution, not the problem. Wow, this thing really knocked me off track, but I'm coming back."

"Ben brought your truck home last night. Go home, get the family into your first-ever brand-new car, and come to the eleven o'clock service. If you don't mind indulging me, I'd like to park your butt in the front row and let you have undistracted access to the music, to Ben's message, and just see if that doesn't realign your consciousness.

Come on, girl, I've seen you teach classes on this! Let's go to the quantum physicists' realm of infinite possibilities, and get the high sign for your bon voyage to Mexico."

"Amen, sister," Addie said half joking, half crying, rising to join hands with Star. "I'm with you!"

Star held Addie close for a minute, then looked into her tearful eyes.

"Addie baby, we've been through so much together, since we were toddlers for God's sake. I'm always going to be right here for you, no matter what. I love you, girl, and I got your back no matter what's happening, you know that down deep, right?"

"Yes, I do. And I love you too, no limits." As they embraced, Addie remembered how many overnights their parents allowed them during preschool and kindergarten, because they hated to be separated when it was time to go home from school. Addie's heart filled with gratitude for her friend's wisdom and understanding. She put her hands on Star's shoulders, smiling wide.

"Think about it, Star, we even managed to live within a few miles of each other as adults...except for my FBI stint in D.C." Addie felt her resistance melt. *Star's love is woven through every part of me, and her wisdom is unassailable. I know she's right about this.*

"Oh, Addie, I forgot to tell you. A few minutes before we found you down on the beach, Ben had a vision, said he needed to talk to you because you, Isabel, and your clients were going to be up against some serious challenges at your next meeting."

"What a show-off!" Addie laughed, out of control, through her tears, then straightened up, started through the French doors, and turned back to Star for a second to make her intentions clear.

"Well, I may have invited my clients to join us at the service today, but there's no way I'm mentioning anything about my relationship to Joy until tomorrow's meeting." Star nodded in emphatic agreement.

"That's for sure, you need to get your emotions and your visions lined up in the right direction before you walk into that challenge, or it won't have the outcome you want. You know that, Addie, and don't forget, I'm not going to let on that I know your guests are also your clients."

Addie smiled, turned back to the doorway, moving with determination in her step. She wiped her tears, and found her truth. This experience held a bigger promise than the one she'd heard in the office foyer Saturday morning. Her mama's voice had said Addie would regret it the rest of her life if she didn't go to Mexico. *Apparently, Mama is determined to help me locate Joy.* Humbled to the core, she accepted it. Her mama, after decades of emotional paralysis, was now healed enough to be of real service. *Guess it goes to show that it's not in our best interest to hold a grudge when an important relationship seemed to be an apparent failure. No telling how mightily things can change after someone passes!*

## 17

The auditorium of the Omni Center was almost filled. Addie, in a stylish dark green jumpsuit, sat in the front row with Luisa, who had Nita and Lizbeth seated on her left. Two empty seats were saved for the Doyles on Addie's right. Luisa took her hand and squeezed it when Ana and Mike walked up to them.

Star was talking to someone setting up the stage, excused herself and approached; the warmth from her broad smile reached them long before she did. Addie introduced them, and Ana spoke to Star.

"Mike and I saw you and your husband present a TED Talk on You Tube. We had already decided to come here at some point, so when she invited us yesterday, we took it as a sign that we needed to be here."

Star and Addie exchanged knowing but sufficiently coded looks about what had not yet been revealed to Mike and Ana, then Star provided a judicious segue with a down-home greeting.

"Follow those signs, you'll do fine. I'm in charge of the music here, glad you could join us. Did Addie tell you I met her at Montessori School? We've kinda been joined at the hip since we were two years old; shared an obsession with puzzles and collecting roly poly bugs in the schoolyard."

"What better gift than a friendship that lasts a lifetime." Mike's tone infused the cliché with unquestionable authenticity. Ana took Star's hand and spoke in a quiet, confidential tone.

"We are actually clients of Addie's. Our daughter was kidnapped in Mexico on Christmas Eve. We have one goal for coming to hear you and Ben today. We need to focus our off-the-chart emotions into a clear vision of having our daughter home safe."

"Wow," Star exclaimed, "I can see your focus is about eighty percent there already. Excellent…and once you hear our choir, you'll be high enough to fly there without a plane." Star moved from jest to quiet confidence.

"So…I look forward to all of you coming in to celebrate when you return from Mexico." A choir member came up to ask Star for some help, so Star said her goodbyes to Addie and the Doyles.

"Time for me to make music, enjoy the service, all of you."

Addie felt a sense of peace settle within her as she sat down with Mike and Ana. The doors to the foyer closed, and a lilting piano solo cued up the start of the service. The Omni Center was housed in a large building originally used as a conference center. The main room was packed; unobtrusive TV cameras were providing live streaming of the service to thousands of viewers around the globe, and two large TV screens, flanked the stage, high enough for everyone in the auditorium to see the action close up.

The Center had been established by Ben and his like-minded colleagues twenty-five years ago. Their weekly services had a mix of familiarity and creativity Addie loved. The choir was on the tiered portion of the stage, getting seated, and Addie was soaking it up from the front row, as Star had prescribed. She felt supported, even though Jake was working and couldn't join them.

Addie quickly introduced Mike and Ana to Luisa and the girls. The service started with songs, announcements, a meditation, and a beautiful choral rendition of 'I Believe I Can Fly.' *I have a hunch Star and Ben made sure this classic was on the playlist for us today!*

Ben came out at the song's conclusion, dressed in a casual suit with a soft Nehru collar shirt, encouraging enthusiastic applause for the choir. He turned at center stage with the choir seated behind him. His eyes focused on Addie.

Addie was thrilled to be present for Ben's talk; she focused straight up to the stage, into Ben's eyes, and said a silent prayer. Ana's hand rested on hers.

"Are we going to be sitting here with Joy next Sunday?" Ana whispered.

"Tomorrow at the meeting we'll put together a plan that works," Addie whispered back.

Ben walked to the edge of the stage and looked straight at Addie and her crew.

## 18

"Consciousness," Ben said with his upraised palms held out to the congregation, "the part of us that observes every thought, every feeling, every reaction. We get upset over something someone did, and off we go, with that brain chatter in our heads! But what's that part of us that notices our chatter? It's our consciousness; the door to higher intelligence, universal intelligence." He picked up his pace.

"Those of you who are here, or are streaming us internationally, represent the religions of the world, or sometimes no religion whatsoever. When we clear our minds and connect with universal intelligence, and it helps or heals us, depending on our culture, we have a name for it. We give thanks, each in our own way." He began to move as he talked, focusing on each person he saw.

"Mystical experiences have common attributes; an experience of merging with a loving intelligence that is omniscient, omnipotent, and omnipresent. An experience of being one with the One." He began to smile, stepped down the stairs one step, then launched into his lecture. Addie relaxed into his familiar tones and gestures.

"When Buddha or Jesus or Muhammed had their mystical experiences, their cultures were limited in the tools they used to study invisible energy forces and alternate dimensions. Mystics reported what they saw in heightened experiences of awareness." Addie saw his face take on a look of awe and wonder as he spoke.

"They reported out-of-body travel in which their consciousness moved through non-physical dimensions without their physical bodies. In describing heaven, Jesus is reported to have said 'in my father's house there are many mansions,' meaning he saw places and phenomena far beyond the experience of most humans." He walked along the step near Addie, and looked at her as he spoke.

"Mystics see intelligent, non-physical beings living in these dimensions. They use telepathic communication that bypasses language differences. Scenarios from the past, present and future are available to consider. They describe energy that is harnessed by one's consciousness. Energy that carries information can create whatever is desired; visual art, technology, music—plus auditory and light frequencies that guide, inspire, and heal the body." He smiled, headed closer to the center, looked out to the crowd, and pretended to don a hat.

"I'm putting on my scientist hat." He played with adjusting it, including running his hand up to its tall, thin peak; like a wizard's hat. When he got enough people laughing, he launched into his spiel.

"In this day and age, we have scientific proof that the behavior of matter at subatomic levels is influenced by observation. In the simplest terms, when not observed, a subatomic particle behaves like a wave. When observed, it behaves like a particle. Our conscious observation has an influence. We straddle the threshold between consciousness and matter." He walked a few steps to the right and pointed to a woman holding a toddler on her lap.

"The wave-particle example makes me think of my youngest grandson; when you are watching him, his behavior is in line with our expectations; but when you're back is turned, only God knows the nature of his random activity!" Audible chuckles confirmed the comic relief. He stepped up on the stage, keeping the connection going.

"There is growing interest in using quantum theory to describe how a universal intelligent force may have created our universe. On a local level, how might this higher force express through human intelligence?" *You would know, Ben,* Addie mused.

"We know," Ben asserted, "that cases of complete remission of disease have been reported and studied, in which a diseased person or a healer was observed to consciously direct or allow healing energy. Check out the video of Dr. Eben Alexander talking with Oprah." Their large TV screens displayed a quick clip for the audience.

"Eben Alexander is one of the most concise witnesses we have ever seen. He is a prolific research scientist and esteemed neurosurgeon, and a former spiritual agnostic. He contracted a rare bacterial meningitis while at a medical conference in Israel, came home sick and landed in the ER of the hospital where he worked!" Ben's arms rose. "He was on a ventilator and in a coma for seven days. His brain scans confirmed the tissues in his brain's neocortex had been completely destroyed by bacteria, stripping him of the ability to function, or ever recover! Even his brain stem was badly damaged. His family was advised to accept their loss, however, Eben's wife had consulted a psychic friend, who had told her he would recover, so they kept him on life support."

"His book, Proof of Heaven, describes what happened during the coma. His consciousness ascended into non-physical dimensions and operated fully independently of his earthbound disabled brain. He was guided to a formless, healing presence he described as infinitely powerful, pure loving intelligence, and he was healed. All the destroyed parts of his brain grew back. The cells, tissues, organs and functions of his body were fully restored!"

"He regained consciousness, and when his brain was scanned, his post-coma brain stem and neocortex showed up with the cells fully regrown and functional. His You Tube lectures describe it all."

Ben put his hands on his hips and looked over the congregation, who shared in his amazement. He took off the 'hat' and walked over and 'handed' it to a choir member. His voice took on an expectant tone as he began to pace back and forth.

"Now, there might be a few people in here who think I'm talking about their mind, their brain, when I speak of consciousness. I am not. Dr. Alexander originally believed that our awareness was just a brain function. His experience proved to him that his consciousness was part of a higher intelligence that could function elegantly without a working brain or a functional body."

"Now this, my friends, is the absolute kicker! Not only could he function in higher dimensions, his consciousness could channel that healing energy back into his body with the sole intention of returning to this dimension to prove this extreme level of healing could be done. He, and others, want to lead us in that direction, to help us build specialized skills to access the creative and healing power from these dimensions. But first, we have to let go of our limiting beliefs." Addie sensed a wake-up call was coming.

"Let's see some intelligent energy from those livewires in the back row, wave to me if you can hear me…good! Listen up!" He paced the stage, eyes searching. The TV screens displayed the audience.

"Okay, you must be awake for this, because insight from your higher power can re-file your limiting beliefs in a folder that says BS in capital letters on the tab. If you're offended by my BS comment, think of it as a euphemism for belief system." Laughter brought out his trademark grin, then he extrapolated a bit.

"That doesn't mean you'll never accidently open that folder

again, but unless you're intentionally using that data for a project as an artist or an educator, you will know immediately it's BS; like the belief that the world is flat, or that we can accurately judge someone's character based on the color of their skin." He patted his brown face, then gave himself a pat on the back.

"I declare to you. The belief that we only function in one dimension is definitely BS. We have plenty of people right in this room who have developed a multi-dimensional skill set." Addie turned to look at the audience, impressed at the number of people who raised their hands, including Addie and Luisa, and on stage, Ben and Star.

"So where is our access point, to connect us with this unlimited infinite creative dimension? What technology do we use to get there? Meditation is the spiritual technology par excellence. Different styles, same goal; identifying with the part of yourself that is observing your mind and its thoughts. Using a guided meditation with music, or Monroe's hemi-sync, binaural beats, Sacred Acoustics, with three goals: One, you focus brain frequencies from your everyday beta, to alpha, to theta, delta, even to gamma. Two, you create coherence of brain and heart activity. You will notice a feeling of expansiveness, beyond the physical." *Even on a horse*, Addie recalled.

"If you're new to meditation, try some guided meditations on You Tube. Check out Gregg Braden. See the Heart Math Institute, learn to sync your heart's intelligence with your brain. We know from everyday experience that music can calm the heart and brain, agitate it or exalt it." Star's piano refrains begin to fill the room. Ben moved slowly, paused, took a standing meditative pose, then spoke quietly.

"There are specialized sounds that can help your heart and brain activities cohere, with frequencies that help you through the doorway to the observing consciousness. These spiritual technologies have a high level of efficiency; no need to meditate in a cave for ten years."

Ben moved to center stage, closed his eyes, slowly extended his hands in front, raised them above his head, then in a slow sweeping arc to his sides. With eyes closed he spoke softly.

"Now it's time to put this into practice. To create; in the place of the calmest peace and the most heightened awareness." Ben opened his eyes, moved down the stairs from the stage, walked to the front of the congregation, tilted his head back, and said "THERE!" Addie almost jumped off her chair, he was right in front of her.

"Right THERE in that heightened state; that is where you want to plant your vision. If it's health, see the image of your healthy body there, if it's a relationship issue, see the image of forgiveness and resolution, whatever ya got, drag it in there. If you can't create a believable version, trust Source to provide one." *Yes, Ben, I think of times past when I prayed this way and got way better results than I imagined!*

"Sometimes we create a prototype of our solution and, if we're wise, give total artistic control to our higher consciousness, who knows each individual better than we know ourselves, and will deliver us a much-improved version of our limited idea. In fact, that is the rationale behind the statement 'thy will be done,' so trust your higher power." He walked over to the other side of the congregation, grinning wide, and finished his thought.

"As our trust and experience grow, dear ones...our heartfelt gratitude for our need fulfilled can allow divine intelligence to show us the vision and provide fulfillment; vision and fulfillment, two sides of the same coin." Ben walked fast up the wide carpeted stairs that rose to the stage, turned around and held his arms out as wide as they would go, then brought his outstretched hands into a loud clap.

"Now here's the part most people miss when it comes to prayer, but if ya leave it out, it's like leavin' the chips out of the chocolate chip cookies, or the baking powder out of the biscuits, ya get my drift?" He began to pace the stage, reaching out to his congregation, his teeth flashing in a broad smile.

"Don't leave it out...this part is the sauce that rocks the barbeque...it's your emotions...your feelings, you are planting a symbol of your solution in there, and you have to infuse it with life, celebrate over its reality, give thanks; feel that solution, feel that gratitude. You keep your feelings celebrating, and your intended good shall manifest. You start doubting, and it slows to a crawl." Addie thought, *I have to see my desired vision like a completed puzzle; when I doubt, it's as if I'm removing pieces I had in place.* Ben served up another apt metaphor.

"Doubt is to a prayer like a huge anchor is to a small sailboat; it's not moving, except to bob up and down in one spot. Esther Hicks has hundreds of highly effective anti-doubt techniques on You Tube. She channels her higher intelligence and powerfully demonstrates how to stay focused until your results manifest in your daily life. Visualize and feel a scene; that's your magnet." He gestured to the TV screens. A video of Dr. Joe Dispenza working with a large audience appeared.

"Dr. Joe Dispenza, a chiropractor and hypnotherapist, was hit by a speeding car during a bicycle race, dragged under the car then thrown some distance. Among other injuries, his spine was broken across six vertebrae, the disks fully compressed. He was in his twenties, and had learned the principles I've been discussing. He chose to refuse the only surgery approved for that extensive an injury; one that would fuse his spinal column, but leave him partially crippled. Instead, he visualized his higher power building him a perfect spine…this went on for months. Because he believed his life force would heal it, his spine healed completely, with no handicaps. He's now an international teacher to thousands of students, using sound frequencies, heart-brainwave elevation, and neuroscience to guide healing injuries, and diseases like lupus, heart disease, and cancer. But don't take my word for it, search You Tube for Dr. Joe Dispenza testimonials and listen to people from all over the world describe healings they experienced." Ben responded to Star's lilting piano in the background.

"There's the hint that we may need a healing meditation for everyone whose butt has gone to sleep while I drone on. Okay, I'm headin' for the finish line now, boss!" He gave her a mock salute; Star and Ben laughed at each other, then he hunkered down as promised.

"So, for those of you who think this last part about emotions is BS, just think of every important thing you have done, good or bad, and you will recall that it came from a vision planted in lots of emotion. Emotion creates momentum, and once you are at the height of emotion, momentum grows, and carries you further and further in that same direction, while you visualize the end result."

"Your emotions plus a visualized fear, desire, or rage are like gasoline on a fire. Don't put anything into that crucible that you don't want! Everything you focus on with feeling, influences your life experience. Spiritual masters call it the law of attraction, because you attract whatever you passionately or chronically think about and believe; whether it's something you desire or something you hate. Once you confirm the truth of this law for yourself, you can take total power and responsibility for your future."

Addie felt herself tuned into the flow of their intentions for Joy's return, felt it coming to pass, felt her tears of gratitude emerge. Ben looked directly at their group in the front row.

"Let's wrap this up with a beautiful red ribbon so you can take it home with you. Ben's voice softened, like a slow purr. He moved along the stage, connecting with his congregation.

"So, we open to the power that can heal a sick body, we see how a torn relationship resolves in forgiveness, or how we find what we're looking for in life. Go for it," he grinned, "no matter how difficult it is, because all the creative power you're gonna need is as close as your higher consciousness and your deepest beliefs.

"Your brain cells will line up with an entirely new set of marching orders. Conscious creation takes practice and patience. If you are going for a long-term goal, ask for signs that confirm you're on track. It's how the universal mind tells you it's on the job.

"So, this is it! I'm going to leave you with this recipe for a healthy life, and get off the stage. You will get your minds visualizing and feeling your solution, while Star cooks the music for you. Let her help you lock that vision in; then you can go in and rock with it every day until the solution blasts its way into time and space, into matter, into your life." He closed his eyes, placed his palms together in front of his chest, bending forward slightly.

"Bless you. Namaste."

Addie saw it. The vision of flying to Mexico with the Doyles and returning with Joy felt as real as the auditorium surrounding her. The music began, Star and the choir sang Peter Mayer's 'Everything's Holy Now,' her spirits soared even more. She wasn't going to lose sight of this vision. Whatever hardships they found in Mexico would not change this outcome. Her conviction was unassailable.

71

## 19

"How can I help you, Addie?" Ben, looking relaxed after the conclusion of the service, walked with her into the meditation garden of the Omni Center. Addie knew this was his busiest day of the week, so she would bypass the chitchat and get right to the point.

"I only have about ten minutes, Ben, so help me as efficiently as possible." He laughed and gestured to the path ahead.

"No problem, we'll handle it like a quick TV interview. Go ahead."

A gravel trail near them wove out through the flower-filled gardens that surrounded the center. Their ceiling was a blue sky, graced by a few clouds wafting eastward in slow motion. Ben walked slowly along, looking at the garden, and Addie, keeping pace, began to explain.

"Well, I told you earlier how I got assigned an FBI kidnapping case because the victim's parents not only had PTSD from the kidnapping, they had completely untreated PTSD from their infertility and adoption experiences."

"So, they are questioning…again…whether the universe is on their side when it comes to their role as parents?"

"Exactly."

"I can see why Isabel chose you."

"Yes, but now that I've established a good trusting relationship with them I have to show up tomorrow at the FBI meeting and recuse myself as their therapist."

"Because?"

"Star didn't tell you?"

"She just said you were ready to tell me what happened yesterday, that it was urgent." Addie, sighed, reluctant to dive into it again. Still, she described what happened, his eyebrows spiked up with amazement, and his smile broadened.

"Addie, the biggest mystery here isn't how you're going to find Joy. It's the context of everything connected to this adventure, the intricate way the Universe is rolling this out to you." He grinned his Cheshire cat grin.

"I'm not only happy you're about to reunite with your daughter, Addie, I'm excited to see what other blessings have been added."

72

They arrived at a white wrought-iron table off the side of the path, next to a soothing water fountain of variegated stones, and sat on the padded iron chairs. Ben leaned forward and waited for Addie to speak. Addie frowned, and shared what she thought was an exception to Ben's declaration of additional blessings.

"Ben; Saturday morning, walking into the foyer of my office, a voice I believe was Mama's, told me someone I love is going to die while I'm in Mexico. Then she said I'd regret it for the rest of my life if I didn't go to Mexico. Izzy wants me to go, so do the clients, at least for now." A cool breeze brought her a heaven-scent gift from the lilac tree near them, inviting her to relax and trust his wise counsel.

"Addie, from the day I met you, I've felt like you were the sister I never had, especially since I was an oddity in my family; a mystic, like you, but I didn't have a Grandma Luisa to help me. My grandma, bless her soul, was a duality-bound fundamentalist brainwashed to believe psychic visions were evil. Bless her, she didn't realize that fear always puts you on the road to whatever you're fearing. But we know better." He shifted in his chair, looking peaceful amidst the generous display of color that greeted them from every direction.

"So tell me about fear," Addie said. His eyes lit up as he spoke.

"Fear is the puppy dog of mystics, always tagging along in every new adventure, jumping in and out of ordinary daily life when we least expect, tripping us up, chewing holes in our map of cosmic consciousness. Jewish mysticism teaches that fear, or resistance, isn't something we create, it's an inherent feature of growth. We encounter resistance in every new challenge, every inspired dream, and we must learn to not feed it, not grow it into a terrifying mastiff drooling to chew us to shreds. We learn to understand it, and move forward with it; even if you can't calm it down. That's what courage is. Let that mastiff become your scout, your protector, and forge ahead."

Addie leaned back, holding her hand up to shade her eyes, feeling grateful for the fog-free day, the comfort of the sun's warmth, and the words of wisdom from Ben.

"I get your drift, Ben, grappling with anxiety just makes it grow, and your momentum goes in the wrong direction. Once I've made the right decision, I need to just move forward, let the scared puppy do her thing—and keep my momentum in the right direction."

"While you're going through this, take extra meditation breaks, get your heart and brain connected, and ride the waves into coherence." He looked at his watch, "We need to walk back, just keep talking, we'll have time." Addie got up with some reluctance. Ben rose, moved his empty chair closer to the table, and joined her on the path.

"Thanks, Ben. I'm clear it's going to work out, I have no clue how, but that's not my problem. My problem is what to do with my visions. I'm hearing auditory messages in addition to my usual psychic visions. And I'm having more out-of-body experiences; one in which I found myself in the underground bunker where the kidnapper is holding my daughter, and two times while my body was unconscious at the beach. So that's three times in the last two days."

Ben began to respond as if they were discussing gardening craft instead of Addie's more esoteric issues.

"These are skills anyone can learn. We all go out-of-body during sleep, but most people don't remember it. He stopped, ran his fingertips along the petals of a nearby rose, then looked at Addie.

"I'm guessing you have lots of questions about why me, why now, why so much all at once, and so forth. Am I right?"

"Yes! Especially since most of the psychology profession considers out-of-body experiences as depersonalization, a symptom of dissociative disorder; and some people with schizophrenia have auditory hallucinations, which aren't the same as what I'm having either."

"Well," Ben grinned, "don't you think that's the task of transpersonal psychologists? To educate people about the differences? Your weird experiences get good results, while some other people's weird experiences are born and experienced in a state of confusion, to no useful end. I know your skills are ramping up right now—for some people, it comes on like puberty; all these uncomfortable changes barreling into your experience that you can't stop." Addie showed her surprise over his analogy.

"Just seems to be the way it works, Addie, except there's no limit to the growth you experience spiritually. Most of your being extends beyond your physical body," he gestured to her body and his own, "this part we see is just the vehicle we use to interact in the physical dimension, so when we move out of our body we aren't leaving ourselves, we're just moving our attention to our extended being."

"This is making sense...that is what it feels like..." Addie took his outstretched hand, as if he were leading her on a universal tour right in the moment. A breeze caused her to look up; she saw the kids exiting the Sunday School classroom, carrying balloons.

"Look, Ben, look at the colors of their balloons—red, green and white!"

"Cute kids, huh? Yeah, the youth minister picked up those balloons from the Panaderia...the one on the South City main street across from City Hall; when he stopped to get the pastries for the kids."

"Ben, that's the sign I asked for when we were visioning our prayers at the service this morning...the colors of the Mexican flag!"

"See? I told you it would show up as a surprise! Ya gotta love it! Higher consciousness is outside of space and time, so our request and the placement of the sign that confirms it doesn't have to make sense in linear time. So, you can relax about your new skills. We are eternally evolving, Addie, within a universe that is constantly expanding. You can forget about a stopping point. You have absolutely nothing to fear." *It's the unfamiliar that I'm reacting to,* she realized.

"Your higher self probably decided this task in Mexico required more skills, and you started downloading them. It's taking time for your conscious mind to catch up to all this. It's only scary to the ego, and the more primitive parts of the brain that are stuck in habits, in the physical dimension. That's your puppy dog...don't feed it."

Addie's borrowed cell phone began to buzz; she pulled it from her bag and read the text.

"It's the family; they're getting ready to head home. Thanks for the puberty metaphor; a normal, natural part of development that feels completely alien when it's moving you to a new level of maturity." Ben laughed and moved forward with her, launching a new bulletin.

"Yeah, and it's a bit of a roller coaster ride, Addie, but nothing you can't get through. By the way, I got a bit of a psychic flash of my own, about your FBI meeting tomorrow."

"What? What did you see?" Star had already told her, but she wanted Ben's version. Ben stopped walking, took both her hands in his, and conveyed his message, infused with loving tones.

"Looks like it's going to be a hot mess, Addie, which means it's right down your alley. You, sister, are a catalyst for resolution. Mediating conflicts that people have inside themselves and in their relationships; that's what people pay you for, because, you deliver! Speaking of delivering, check your watch...ten minutes! Ha!"

## 20

Sweat soaked Ramiro's shirt. *It is early, and the weather is cool, why am I dripping like this?* He felt it prickling down his spine, into the small of his back. He felt embarrassed to smell it, knowing he was headed down into the bunker to see Joy. *I must be sweating today's phone call with the girl's parents and the FBI. If I let her talk to her parents, she might freak and get them all upset, screw up our plans somehow. I need her calm.* He had thought a lot about his talk with Joy two days before; couldn't get it out of his mind. The discussion they had about choices had cut close to the bone for both of them.

Ramiro had been more moved than he wanted to be by Joy's outburst. Her description of manipulating her parents with her passion to grow up was a hindsight guilt trip. *She wasn't to blame for her abduction. Nor were her parents. I know who the guilty party is.* It hit home hard, and he became annoyed as hell. When he walked in with the food, she looked up from the book she was reading without greeting him. Bella sat next to Ramiro and waited.

She appeared dejected. *She's probably thinking about her family. I am traumatizing her family to rescue mine. Es loco.*

"Señorita, do you want your parents worrying that you're not eating enough?" He put a freshly cooked burrito on the table by her chair. "You need to eat this morning. You have been here four nights, and each day I have to beg you to eat."

He could smell the bouquet of the savory burrito, couldn't see why Joy wasn't interested; *she knows by now how tasty Adela's burritos are.* He perched on the chair opposite hers, doing his best to be patient. Bella sat at his feet, her eyes on Joy, waiting for an invitation. She sat forward, ignoring Bella. He could see she was shaking, upset but acting as composed as possible.

"I feel like I'm rotting here in this chair. I need to get outside, being underground is giving me the creeps! Listen, I'll eat if you let me come outside and give me just one minute on the phone with my mom and dad. Just one minute. I only got to leave a message on Saturday."

She pushed back her neglected, oily dark hair with one hand, put her cola on the table with the other, and leaned forward with that look in her eye he had come to dread. The spirit he saw looking out at him had the same determination. *Maybe there are a lot of women who have this spirit and I just never met them.* The girl interrupted his rumination with statements that were really demands.

"And I need more clean clothes. I don't care if they fit; well, they can't be too tight, but bigger is okay. I need a hairbrush, and a toothbrush. And some flip flops—what happened to my shoes?"

"You must have taken your shoes off in the cab, when you got out you were barefoot. I had no time to deal with that, we had to move fast."

"Oh, don't remind me! I'm begging you, please call my folks today, just quick, they won't be able to trace your call if it's quick, please?"

"Bueno, I will have my son bring what you need; he is waiting outside. You eat at least half the burrito and clean yourself up, and I will call your parents for you." It wasn't escaping Ramiro's notice that he sounded more like a father than a captor.

"Your son? I thought you lost your family." She reached over and picked up the burrito, unwrapped it and started eating.

"Tonio is my youngest child, almost twenty. His father was killed when he was little. His mother and I raised him together, here in the mountains." *Why am I telling her all this, I am loco!* Then, in a clumsy embarrassed effort to conclude the discussion, he paradoxically blurted out even more private information.

"You are my last job, we will be done interfering with other people's lives and will have enough money to start a new life far away from here. You done with that burrito?"

"You only said half," she said. Sounded to Ramiro like a very sweet five-year-old negotiating over vegetables.

"Ok, basta, let me get Tonio." Ramiro got up to stretch his stiff legs and get some distance from her penetrating eyes. It was starting to make his stomach turn over; the fear of what might be in those eyes that could drive this deep into his guts. He walked to the stairwell and called Tonio.

"Tonio! Come here!" The bunker door was open; in a moment, Ramiro saw him peering in. "Have your mother put some clean clothes and a towel in a bag…she needs a hairbrush, a toothbrush and some shampoo. The girl wants to come up to the patio for sun and maybe call her parents for one minute. It will be good to see if her parents are on track with our plan, sí?"

"Don't forget the flip-flops!" Joy yelled.

"Tonio, traer chanclas, ella no tiene zapatos."

"Bueno, Papa, I will be right back." He walked off, leaving the door open.

Ramiro walked back to the middle of the room. Joy was already looking at him when he focused on her. As disheveled as she was, her beauty was undiminished, and once again he responded with an eerie shudder.

"Tonio will bring what you need. After you get cleaned up, one of us will take you up to the patio and make the call. You must understand that trying to get away is dangerous. Even if you did, you could get caught by someone bad or have an accident."

"Maybe, but I'm going to school on a track scholarship." *Oh, why the hell did I say that?*

"Señorita! Do not be naïve. There are pumas and jaguars in these mountains; their tracking ability, day or night, allows them to smell prey up to seven miles. They have binocular 3D vision, and can accurately descend on prey from a tree. So be a smart girl. We want you to go safely to your parents, and for us to get free from this place and live quietly."

"I'm not going to run," Joy faked an apologetic tone. "I don't think I'd run well on Valium, anyway. I will do what you say. By the way, I heard your son answer you. He also speaks English?"

"For him it is very important, so he can go to college in the US. He is a smarter boy than I ever was, he could go far. Señorita, remember that Tonio will be with you every minute you are outside, just in case, and I warn you, none of the young people from the Zapotec village have ever outrun him."

Ramiro shuffled to the kitchen counter and grabbed a soda, then sat in the chair across from the recliner. An uncomfortable silence ensued, during which Joy kept her head down and her eyes on the book. Ramiro whined inside over his feelings about the job. It seemed to be taking forever. Everything seemed to be slowing down more each successive day.

He'd brought her here Thursday night, then Friday dragged. His chagrin and disbelief had given him no peace; after so many years of this quiet life, he had risked another kidnapping. Indeed, Friday had been a bad day. Then Saturday seemed to take forever. Joy had fussed over her birthday, insisting on leaving that message for her parents.

Sunday had moved like a slug; Joy ate almost nothing and barely talked. Today was no better. As he waited, he watched Joy read. Perhaps he nodded off, he wasn't sure. Regardless, he exposed yet another trait of his age, talking to himself. The words startled him before he realized he'd said them out loud.

"Day after tomorrow." Joy heard him, and her head jerked up. Ramiro pretended he'd spoken to her.

"You know, Wednesday, the day you return to your parents." Her eyes fixed on his, he felt a connection, had the eeriest feeling that she was having the same idea; that perhaps some outside force was slowing down time, against their repeated insistence that it speed up.

"Papa!" Tonio's deep voice rumbled down the stairwell. Ramiro rose slowly from the chair, and started up the stairs. His legs were weak, his back was sore. He wanted this whole job to be done. Bella, eager to get back outside, whined a bit at his slow pace. Ramiro, coughing, signaled her to run up to the open door. He looked up at Tonio waiting at the entry to the bunker. Bella ran past him. Tonio then bent over, looking down the stairs.

A stray beam of sun found its way to the bunker stairwell through a break in the trees, exploding into Ramiro's eyes from around his son's silhouette. Tonio moved enough to block the sun; Ramiro felt his vision clear, in time to see the boy's long black curls bouncing around his face—a younger version of Tonio's first father, Diego. *It was a face Adela and I both loved…may he rest in peace.*

Feeling dizzy, he decided to avoid climbing the rest of the way, and reached up for the bag which Tonio dropped into his arms. Ramiro leaned against the wooden dowel they'd installed as a banister, regained his balance, then turned and came back down the stairs, keeping himself steady with his right hand on the banister. Once at floor level, he walked out of the small stairwell into the room. His eyes couldn't adjust to the dim interior.

He wasn't ready for a shock, but was jolted nevertheless. When he stepped out of the stairwell, she was standing there, tall and still.

80

She was right in front of him, backlit from the small lamp at the other end of the room near the recliner chair. In the half light, she was imposing, and her eyes weren't visible at all, just darker shadows on an already shaded face. *What does it mean that twice in two minutes I have stared into a dark face haloed in light?* His superstitions were running amuck, searching for interpretation. Had he pocketed his knife after cutting the fruit this time, or did she have it? Had he even brought fruit today? He couldn't remember.

The girl raised both hands out, and looked like a zombie reaching through the gray light. Ramiro stood motionless.

"What's going on?" The girl obviously had no idea Ramiro was fearing up, from fatigue, from guilt, from all that was unnamed and haunted his intuition with stubborn purpose.

"Here," he said, unsure, pushing the bag in her direction, hoping it was really her.

The girl felt the bag, a symbol of her uprooted status. "I'm sick of this, I want out, I want to be home!"

Ramiro, startled, wanted out of there too, back into the sunlight. He knew Tonio was waiting for him by the doorway. Possibly he spoke faster than he ever had. His servile tone belied the fact that he had nothing to fear from her.

"De nada, señorita. I will send Tonio back to get you later. There is enough water in the tank above the sink to wash your hair. Then we will go up to the patio and call your parents, acordado?"

"Yes, agreed," said Joy, forcing a respectful tone; but it wasn't enough to assuage his demonic fears. Ramiro turned quickly and prayed his way up the stairs to safety.

## 21

Addie drove up to the Doyles' home right on time. They had saved her a space to park in the driveway to the Doyles' garage. *What a relief!* Her eight-seater SUV was a liability when it came to crowded neighborhood parking. On the bright side, Isabel's morning meetings almost always included lox, cream cheese and bagels, so she tucked her fretful, invisible puppy dog under her arm, focused on food, and rushed up the Doyles' stairs.

Addie pressed the doorbell, and quickly saw the door opened by Ana, standing tall and chic in slacks, a burnished gold shirt under a crocheted vest, her hair pulled into a bun, wrapped with a filigree-patterned scarf. Ana's outfit was lovely, but the pinched expression on Ana's face gave Addie pause. She noticed Ana's hand trembling as she beckoned Addie inside.

Entering the warm foyer, Addie saw no one in the large living room off to the right, then heard voices coming from the dining area to her left. The aroma of toasted bagels beckoned. An antique coat rack by the front door seemed overwhelmed with jackets, and Addie began to feel she'd arrived a bit late; it must have shown.

"Don't be concerned, you're right on time, they got here on the early side." Addie was wearing a light pullover sweater and a snug full-length skirt with her most comfortable suede boots. She pulled a stray lock of hair away from her face and tucked it into the clip that for now, was managing to contain her curls.

"Everyone's here. Right now, it's kind of focused on coffee and food, so go help yourself."

Addie walked toward the dining room. The bold aroma of freshly brewed coffee wafted her way, followed by a strangely familiar voice she couldn't quite place. Except for herself and Ana, everyone was seated around a long oval mahogany table in comfortable armchairs. Light bathed the room through the tall windows of the old Victorian; long, sheer linen curtains swirled softly over the open screened windows; she felt the old house was welcoming her.

The men were leaning forward toward Isabel, their backs to Addie. Izzy was passing out some paperwork. Isabel and Ana had claimed the opposite side of the table from the men and saved the end seat near the kitchen for Addie. Smoked salmon, bagels, fruit and coffee had been pushed toward Addie's end of the table to make room for the paperwork. *Good!* Addie thought, *I'm starving!*

"Addie," Isabel said looking up from her task, "Right on time, we got here early."

"You're the second person to reassure me, thanks." Addie grinned at Isabel, sat down, ignoring everyone, and unselfconsciously began to fix a plate of food while Isabel officially got the meeting started.

"I only notified you of the date, time and place of today's meeting, and didn't get the agenda written up until this morning, so I apologize to you all that you didn't have any advanced information about who would be attending and what their roles would be."

Hungry and determined to get some food in her system, Addie ignored Isabel for the siren song coming from the cream cheese and bagels. The bagel, with a slice of lox, kept her full attention until Isabel noticed Addie's preoccupation, and subtly touched her free hand. Addie noticed, and decided to let her next serving wait a few minutes.

The men were staring as she looked up from her food with cream cheese smeared around the corner of her mouth. Addie immediately lost her bearings during the rest of the introductions. Staring at her from the last seat on the left, next to Mike Doyle, was Dean Culhane. No one in the room knew they had been acquainted during her year at the FBI in Washington D.C.

A sudden shock careened down her spine; wasn't the day complicated enough without Dean flying into it, seemingly out of nowhere? She managed to swallow the food she'd been chewing, and welcomed the excuse to look down at the table to get her coffee. While Isabel's voice rattled on, Addie felt her heart pumping, her ears picked up the pulsating pressure, she couldn't look up. She filled her cup from the carafe, willed her hand to stop shaking, put some sugar and cream into the steaming cup, and stirred slowly.

"First," said Isabel, "let me introduce Dr. Addison Diaz, formerly a forensic psychologist for the FBI, now in private practice. She is a licensed private investigator, a therapeutic clinician for crime victims, and also specializes in adoption and infertility cases. You may have seen her on TV recently; an interview show, with criminal investigators who use psychic abilities to help solve crimes."

Addie looked at Isabel during the long, unexpectedly embarrassing introduction. Isabel turned her attention to Emil.

"This is Emil Torres, an IT specialist and hostage negotiator. He's here to support the Doyles, guide communications in Spanish and English with the kidnapper, and investigate Joy's personal effects and relevant data on her computer. Next to Mr. Doyle, is agent Dean Culhane, recently assigned to the San Diego Field Office. He is a Mexican cartel specialist with twenty-five years of consecutive service in the FBI."

Isabel picked up a Mexican news article with a headline and photo of a state-of-the-art prison, and held it up for everyone to see.

"I'll leave this article on the table for anyone to peruse, but just wanted you to eyeball it for now. Mike Doyle is an institutional construction contractor, with both domestic and foreign business. He was recently profiled in the Mexican press for participating in a partnership with the Mexican government to build a tunnel-proof, maximum security prison.

Of course, we all know of Guzman, the cartel boss who paid prison officials to literally walk him out the door to a waiting limousine; demonstrates how powerful the cartels' extortion tactics can be, along with some impressive tunnel escapes. However, not all prisoners have that kind of leverage, so I'm sure the authorities appreciate this well-built facility.

Mike's news profile, which mentioned his family's plans to vacation in Oaxaca City for Christmas, quite possibly made his family a target, resulting in the crisis we now face." Addie noticed Mike was pained by Isabel's last remark.

"Doctor Ana Doyle has been an endangered species specialist and veterinarian for fifteen years at our own San Francisco Zoo." Addie noticed the expression on Dean's face as he acknowledged Ana; she knew from experience it wasn't just surprise, he was genuinely impressed.

"That's it for introductions," Isabel looked at her notes, then put them aside and continued.

"Let me say that this case appears to be moving forward with clear parameters. The profile on the kidnapper thus far suggests he is an older man, probably in his 70's, fully bilingual in Spanish and English, has a lot of experience in negotiations, and has his emotions in check. He refers to himself as Ramiro. Mexican police haven't turned up any info on him that we can use. Emil has spoken to him three times, with the Doyles present. Why don't you tell us your concerns at this point, Emil?"

Emil shuffled through some papers. Addie knew the Doyles and Dean were in for a treat once they got to know him. On the surface, a buff, handsome guy who looked like a jock, and under it all, a brilliant criminal tactician, hacker, and hands-on agent.

"Well, we handled some initial conversation in English, especially the part that included Mike and Ana speaking directly with Joy. Joy stated she was tired, scared, but not being mistreated. Mike and Ana reassured her they were working out the terms of her release and expected to be successful. Fortunately, Joy is old enough to understand that it's to the kidnapper's benefit to keep her healthy, and successfully negotiate payment for her release, so she's likely confident she will be returned." He looked back at Isabel, and spoke faster.

"As for underlying issues, the longer conversation I had with Ramiro in Spanish, revealed some atypical dynamics that can either help or add risk to the case. He states he is no longer cartel affiliated, has been independent for fifteen years. He said the men who helped him carry out the kidnapping were dropped off in Oaxaca City soon after they left the scene, and Joy, in restraints, was taken by him to a well-hidden, completely private compound. By the way, the Oaxaca City police said someone alerted them by phone not long after the kidnapping. He claimed to be a guy who was walking by, spotted the cab in a construction lot. He gave the location, didn't want to identify himself, just trying to help. I think it was Ramiro who called." Addie's head jerked up...*Really?*

"Ramiro said this is his last job," he continued, "states he's leaving Mexico with his family as soon as it's over, and wants it done with no drama or surprises, just a clean exchange. My concerns? Mostly his age, and his health. He has a chronic cough, maybe bronchitis, or congestive heart failure, which involves coughing due to fluid accumulation in the lungs, and cancer is another possibility."

"Finally, we aren't sure about his level of desperation, or how well he handles frustration. In short, I'm concerned about his competency to take on and manage a stressful, complex process he has allegedly been absent from for years." Isabel interrupted.

"That's enough for now, Emil, thank you. A clean exchange is what we want as well, with the added goal of bringing this guy to justice." Isabel stacked her paperwork and looked at her team.

"Dean, your thoughts?" Dean began to speak, his eyes focused across the table at Isabel. Addie took the opportunity to fake her nonchalance, yet was so shocked to be in the same room with him, she could make no sense of his report. Her eyes could not leave his face. It wasn't just his good looks that attracted her.

When she met him in D.C., she'd been amazed how the nuances in his voice and facial expressions communicated such an unusual variety of subtle feelings when he talked. That had not changed, but some things had. His skin showed lines she'd never seen, his dark hair now slightly gray, voice, completely recognizable, but with more of the deep warmth she remembered...and loved. The moment he finished, she looked down to pour herself some completely unwanted coffee.

At Dean's conclusion, Izzy's clipped speech provided their next directive.

"Let's break for fifteen minutes, then join up back here for phase two. At some point we will hear from Ramiro. Until then, we will continue with our agenda. Addie, you get acquainted with Dean a bit while Emil and I go over some details with Mike and Ana in the living room." Addie had an instant excuse to avoid talking with Dean so soon.

"I have to run to my car first and get the charger cord for my phone. Be right back." With that clarified, she left before Dean or anyone else could slow her down. Addie had to adjust to Isabel's invitation that she chat with Dean. She had no emotional space for analyzing all the possible permutations and combinations of Dean's influence on her, and on the success of their case.

She was trembling from head to toe, flooded with memories. The 'hot mess' Ben had predicted wasn't on the meeting's agenda, but she knew they were headed for it. Between Dean and the Doyles, there was so much to sort out. Just how messy was it going to get?

## 22

The Monday breakfast shift at the Refugio Tropical Hotel was over. Ángel had an hour before he had to set up for the lunch crowd, and longed for some open air, especially today; Oaxaca City's weather was postcard perfect. His mind had been churning with questions since Joy had been taken to Ramiro's. *The policia seemed satisfied with the story we gave them, we are in the clear for now.* Still, his conscience berated him for involving Rosa without her knowledge.

With a liter bottle of soda and his cigarettes, he ventured out the open glass doors from the dining room into the large courtyard behind the hotel, his chef's apron smeared with a fractured rainbow of salsa, avocado, beans and egg yolk. The tiled courtyard was accented with a large, flowered, vine-covered pergola in the center. A thick stucco fence, also shrouded in flowering vines, set off the perimeter. The cleanup crew greeted him on their way to the dumpster, assuring him the heavy wooden tables were cleared and ready for lunch patrons.

Eager for a break, he headed for his favorite spot, where brilliant red flame trees accented the wrought-iron gate to the parking lot. Locals preferred this courtyard entrance to the restaurant, and it gave him a chance to visit with people, to arrange catering jobs for private parties, and just relax. Ángel sat at his table, lit a smoke, and took a long drink of the soda to which he'd added a half pint of rum.

*Now Rosa's on my ass for drinking every day; I just need something to calm myself. At least I can count on her uncle Ramiro to keep a clear head. If Rosa finds out I knew about the kidnapping, she will leave me.*

He knew Rosa and Joy had become very close through days of touring shops and museum displays, getting acquainted with artists. Rosa would never have agreed to Ramiro and Miguel's plan, but when Miguel told him he would have enough money to settle in California, get an education, and start his own restaurant business, he had jumped at the chance. *Sometimes women lack the courage for these things. At least the policía saw us as innocent bystanders and thought the kidnappers targeted the Doyles independently. Rosa and I have never been arrested for anything. Rico, I'm not sure, but they let him go, so...*

Ángel glanced over the cars parked outside the courtyard fence, and saw Miguel's car approaching. He parked near the gate. It wasn't unusual for Miguel to join his son-in-law for a drink while Ángel was on his break, but it was very unusual for Miguel to limp across the lot in obvious pain.

Ángel jumped up, ran to Miguel, and stopped in front of him; a trip to the hospital had apparently kept him occupied prior to coming. His nose was bandaged. His left eye was blue-black and swollen shut. Stitches on a long cut from temple to chin looked like someone's foiled attempt to let air out of Miguel's puffy face. *A perfect model for a Halloween mask,* Ángel thought as he grabbed Miguel's arm and stood in front of him.

"What the hell happened to you?"

Miguel hesitated. As he began to speak through a split bottom lip, he winced—Ángel saw two teeth missing.

"Zetas." Miguel said, but it sounded like 'ate-us' to Ángel. Between the split lip and missing teeth, he knew the beating had rendered Miguel almost unable to speak. Ángel sneered and poked him in the chest to make his point.

"Verdad? Last night in the hotel bar, you were all over Lupe. When she left, I saw another Zeta come in to get the big guy. They left through the lobby in a hurry, right on Lupe's trail, then you sneak out the back door. If my boss had not insisted on my help right then, I would have followed you."

Miguel looked around, put a finger to his split lip and whispered.

"Can I trust you?" Again, Ángel deciphered distorted words.

"Miguel…you trusted me to ask my help for the Christmas Eve job," he whispered back, "I have always been straight with you and you know it, what did you tell him?"

Miguel, reeking from the booze he must have bought when he left the hospital, appeared to have taken a pain pill or two with his alcohol—he was stupid drunk. He swiped his mouth with the back of his hand, smeared some of the blood that was still coming out of his nose, and started crying.

"We give them half…or…they kill you and Rosa…and me." Terrified at the mention of his own demise, Miguel began to sob and shake, his battered hands, one with fingernails torn off by the Zetas, held on tight to either side of his head, as if he feared it might fall to the patio tiles.

Ángel cringed, his entire body hardened, he felt his tongue expand dry and useless, his mouth more cardboard than flesh.

"Merde! How did he guess you were involved? Wait—why do I even ask? You were with Lupe, getting drunk, getting horny, you told her you were going to have lots of money to show her a good time, didn't you?"

Ángel had been chugging his soda since Miguel arrived. Rum freed his tongue, and rage overcame his caution. Even with a few customers approaching the gate, he could not contain his fright-fueled frustration.

"Eres un idiota!!! Lupe would sell out her own mother if the price was right. Now we must hide out fast and get Rosa out of here, you have put your own daughter in danger!" Miguel looked down at his feet with intent; perhaps his best answer was hidden there. His response came with tremendous effort.

"The big guy...he...he took pleasure hurting me...could not stop himself...I saw the monster ...El Cuco...riding him...guiding him, policia saved me..."

"Miguel," Ángel said, "you asked for this! You are the reason none of us can know where Ramiro's hideout is! We cannot hide there. No one has lived through more of your drunken mistakes than your brother, and now—with these devils onto us—we are as welcome as Ebola! We might as well have Ebola!" Ángel's fury incited him to spin his corpulent form around, turning his back on his pitiful father-in-law, lest he add to his injuries.

When Ángel paused the confrontation, Agent Ricardo Morales stepped back from the window of his second-floor hotel room. He called Leticia Reyes, who was down in the parking lot recording the action. It rang once, then she answered.

"Yes?" Agent Reyes sat in the front seat of an old Ford with the directional mike on Miguel and Ángel.

"Good thing you spotted Ángel heading for his lunch break. Are you picking up any of this?" Morales said.

"It is bad, Ricardo," Reyes said, "we know from the Christmas Eve police report that Rosa and Ángel are married. Now we know Rosa is Miguel's daughter, Ramiro's niece. It all makes more sense to know

Ramiro and Miguel are brothers. They pulled off the kidnapping together with Ángel's help, my guess is the cab driver Rico was in on it, too, maybe Rosa."

"They are all in it together, then," Morales conjectured.

"Time will tell," Reyes cautioned, "Miguel admitted bragging about his upcoming big payday to Lupe, the woman we saw him with in the bar last night. Ángel said he saw two Zetas follow her out of the bar when she left. She must have told the guys what she knew, including Miguel's relationship to Ángel and Rosa. The Zetas found Miguel after that and tortured the truth out of him."

"Did anyone see them?"

"Not at first, the Zetas told Miguel they would kill Ángel, Rosa and him if he doesn't give them half the ransom. The police stopped the fight and took Miguel to the hospital, probably let the Zetas go. Ángel wants to make a run for it, but Ramiro's isn't an option because he's keeping his location a secret. Ángel's guessing the Zetas haven't pounced because they think Miguel is still in the hospital."

"Ramiro is holding all the good cards," Morales added, "that's for sure. Damn good thing, too, because those two amateurs would get Joy lost to some cartel, then we might never get her back. They're about to blow this thing apart. We need to get Joy fast."

Reyes interrupted him, urgency accenting her voice.

"Ángel just called someone. Hold on."

Finally, Reyes blurted out the change in plans, her words streaming in rapid succession.

"Wait! Ángel called Ramiro. He's telling him that Miguel blew their cover to some Zeta cartel smugglers, maybe down here from Nuevo Laredo.

"Hold on, Miguel is freaking out…wait…Ángel told Ramiro he's calling a friend to pick up Miguel, Rosa, and him. Says if they disappear the Zetas will give up. Ángel's going to have his friend drive them around and then meet up with Rico on the other side of town, so they can make a run for the coast. They're heading back into the hotel to get Rosa and wait for their ride."

"Ok," Morales said with some excitement, "we have enough evidence here to hold them all for questioning on the kidnapping, let's call the local PD for backup, and get them locked up for interrogation."

Leticia Reyes disagreed immediately.

"Their arrest might spook Ramiro and who knows what he'd do with Joy. If Miguel's got some cartel dogs sniffing out the ransom money for this kidnapping, Dean needs to know they are hungry dogs; easy to catch if you have bait. Sit tight, I'll get back to you. When their ride comes for them don't interfere, we'll tail them."

"We may be signing their death warrant if the Zetas find out they made a run for it and track them down."

"That's why Dean makes the big decisions."

## 23

The hem of the white cotton dress brushed Joy's knees. The low-cut gathered neckline was embroidered with Adela's signature designs, and put Rosa's gift—the silver pendant—front and center. The dress, thankfully, allowed more breathing room than the green dress she had tossed on the bed. Next to the bed, a mirror—framed in red enamel overlaid with Adela's design work—a modern rendering of children's figures in indigenous costumes, holding hands, dancing around the edge of Joy's reflection.

Joy stared, finding comfort at the sight of the pendant, feeling it was keeping her connected to Rosa despite their separation. The horrific dream she had about Rosa during the night was still haunting her. *It was the reverse of what happened to us when I was kidnapped...in my dream, it was Rosa who was kidnapped out of Rico's cab, and I saw blood, lots of it. Why would my mind switch it like that? Easier for me to see it happening to someone else? I have to stop thinking about it!*

She stared into her reflection, trying to recall who she had been a week ago, the day of her 'early' twenty-first birthday party. What she had believed came to mind more clearly than whom she had been. *I believed my defining event of 2015 was going to be turning twenty-one!* As if to underscore how off-the-mark that assumption had been, the hinges on the bunker door broadcast their spine-raking screech.

She heard Tonio's voice, and released most of the worry she'd had; an ever-present anxiety that some rival of Ramiro's had killed her captors and was coming for her next. Or conversely, had killed her captors and were never coming for her, because they didn't realize she was locked in an underground bunker downhill from the compound's fence.

"Señorita?"

"Yes, I'm coming," Joy said as she adjusted the dress, checked the scarf holding back her damp hair, and stepped into the stairwell, looking up, initially relieved to see the light of day. As his silhouette cast a shadow on the stairs, she backed up against the paneled wall. She began to picture all the potential threats that loomed above—snakes, scorpions, vicious encroachers. Her breath stuck in her throat, she stared at each empty step, and couldn't take even one.

"Señorita Joy?" Tonio began to descend slowly. Joy stood frozen in place.

"Do you see something? ¿Cuál es tu problema? A spider?"

He arrived at the bottom, looking around the floor and stairs as his eyes adjusted to the light.

Joy hadn't been this close to him before. His eyes were the same color as hers, almost black. Loose dark waves of smooth hair emerged from the hood of his green sweatshirt. The angular hand-painted design on the front of his shirt caught her eye; a luminous scarlet macaw in open flight. He moved closer, pushed the green hood back, and more locks emerged, grazing the top of his shoulders and curving slightly toward his neckline.

He was tall, and had to bend toward her slightly to accommodate the low ceiling of the stairwell. Something about his presence cleared the air of threats. She relaxed with a deep breath. His scent entered her. Her body began to release the frenzied fears that swarmed in her blood and crept through her skin. Tonio's eyes met hers, encouraging her to speak freely, so she confided in him.

"I think it's safer down here, I don't want to go up."

"Por favor, señorita, Papa…he is waiting."

In response to his urging, she continued to stall.

"Shouldn't we introduce ourselves? My name is Joy."

"I am pleased to meet you, Joy, my name is Antonio." She stalled again.

"And your papa calls you Tonio." He caught on, and urged her again.

"Si…yes, and you may as well, if you wish. But now we must go."

"Can't we just try to get reception from here? I don't want to be all the way up there," she lifted her eyes to the light visible through the open doorway. As if Ramiro had heard her plea on the uphill breeze, an impatient, loud whistle demanded her capitulation.

Joy, resigned to Ramiro's order, pushed past Tonio, dragging her fears with her as she stepped up each stair. Once above ground level, she looked down and saw the black cavern of the stairwell as her only route to safety. The rustling woods spoke to her from the windswept pines and the beaks of countless intentional birds.

The forest surrounded her, it looked like a trap; she couldn't move. As Tonio let the door fall shut, Joy jumped. She felt the terror return when she saw her access to the bunker cut off. Tonio held something out to her.

"Put this on before we go through the brush; keeps bugs out of your hair and off your clothes." He handed her a brown pullover sweatshirt with a hood.

She pulled it over her head. It carried the same intriguing scent she'd noticed when he'd gotten close to her at the bottom of the bunker stairs. As her head emerged from the hood, she saw he was watching her, smiling, then he attempted to lift the mood.

"My mama says if we move from here to a city, she will buy me a white sweatshirt; living here in the hills, it's impossible." His full lips broadened, his black eyelashes lowered slowly as he tilted his head and peered at her. His entire face shifted into the kind of smile usually elicited by something uniquely endearing in the object of observation. Joy felt the energy of it enter her heart. He seemed to be ignoring the rest of her body, including her defensive posture.

Surprised, she saw this was a young man who could appreciate important aspects of her being that had nothing to do with sexual energy. Had he been smiling flirtatiously, she would have gotten the message that he desired her sexually, which would have been typical, it was a common enough occurrence, it was stimulating, and it could be a boost to her ego on an insecure day; but the smile Tonio offered spoke more to what he experienced of her that pleased him in the moment rather than triggering something he wanted from her.

Wind unsettled the tops of the tall pines; as if a disembodied spirit had flown in their midst to see what they were up to. The sound forced its way into their secluded exchange. Had Ramiro's anxiety brought it forth? Some of the smallest and driest pieces of the forest floor swirled upward in a circle, lit by streaks of sunlight. Tonio stepped into the space that separated their bodies. Joy felt his every contour even though they hadn't touched. She felt herself leaning forward, and just as quickly realized she hadn't moved at all.

Ramiro whistled again, this time it was louder and closer; Joy felt her muscles constrict, afraid he was upset again. Beyond their sight, dry branches cracked under his boots. Bella's bark called to Tonio, and he gave her a quick whistle back. They began to wend their way through the undergrowth, up the gentle incline, anticipating Ramiro's appearance.

Joy looked toward the source of Ramiro's whistle. Thick green ferns, vines and shrubs filled the space between pines of every size. The cool wind brought tears to her eyes, blurring her vision; the tallest pines became cylindrical hairy skyscrapers. For a moment her eyes fixed on their swaying canopy. Her feet felt as if the ground were shifting under her; a California-borne sensitivity, but in this case purely imaginary.

Bella broke through a cluster of ferns, and in response to Tonio's hand signal, slowed her pace and fell in behind them. Tonio grasped Joy's elbow, made a gesture toward a small break in the foliage ahead, then led her through a maze of scratching pine needles and tropical plants. The ground felt spongy under her feet, the pines and loamy earth exuded a scent so rich, so preferable to the musty bunker, that Joy surrendered her resistance, and found pleasure moving through the woods.

Bella came alongside her, looking up into her eyes for a few steps, then suddenly sniffed the air, flipped around, dove toward a small hole near the base of an old pine, and clawed frantically. The rich earth gave way and opened to her prying nose.

"Bella!" Tonio was stern. "Get your nose out before it gets bitten! Come! Now!" Her head still almost level with the ground, she turned it slightly and peered at him, still looking ready for a kill, annoyed, but unwilling to disobey.

"Bella," Joy called with an enticing tone, "come with us, let's go." Apparently, there was more dignity in following Joy's cajoling call; Bella shook hard, dirt flying around her, and trotted over to Joy, ignoring Tonio completely.

In less than a minute, Joy saw Ramiro. He looked at her as if he'd found a gold mine, smiling from ear to ear. *What's up with him? Oh, well, maybe he's obsessing about my ransom, not worried about Tonio.* Ramiro encouraged her to follow him, turning away from them and stepping over a long branch discarded by an old pine. She followed, aware of Tonio's presence, especially when he reached forward to steady her as they ascended a small crop of boulders and brush. The midday sun had found a route through the clouds and pines. Joy watched Ramiro, as shadows distorted into twisted rivulets across his bent back, then onto the variegated mix of rocks and ferns.

The tall fence, camouflaged by vegetation, emerged just as Ramiro veered left toward the gate only he could see. When he opened the gate, Joy could see the house ahead. Bella ran past all of them, through the gate, to the back door of the house. Adela, looking frantic, pushed the door aside and rushed in their direction. Her jeans and shirt were covered by her painting smock; she had smudges of green and red paint on her face and hands, some cadmium yellow in her waist-length black hair.

"Andele! Ángel is calling! He says a Zeta overheard Miguel last night at the bar and beat the truth out of him when he left. Now the Zetas want half the ransom from you, or they kill Ángel, Rosa and Miguel!" She returned the cell to her ear.

"Ángel? Ángel? Oh no! The call stopped."

Adela stopped too. She stared at the phone. It was silent.

## 24

The Doyles' heavy front door took an extra nudge to open into the warmth of the house. Addie gave it a push with the phone charger in hand, and almost bumped into Emil, who was crossing the foyer toward the living room. He glanced at her, and she took the opportunity to connect.

"Emil, sorry we didn't get a chance to talk yet, I had to grab my phone cord." She realized Emil was on his way to the living room with a file folder. Ana, Mike and Isabel were seated around a big coffee table, apparently waiting for him. They were out of earshot, so Addie continued.

"I'll be interested to hear what you found, if anything. I know Ana told me she hasn't stepped in Joy's room more than once since their return. Just too painful for her."

He looked over his shoulder toward the living room. "I think I'll go in now; I have some information I want to give to Isabel. She will have to decide what to do with it at that point."

"Sure, I get chain of command," she grinned, "I trust I'll be kept in the loop." She knew she wouldn't be hearing anything he had to say to Isabel unless Isabel decided to tell her. Still, Isabel trusted Addie's judgment completely and pretty much told her everything.

As Emil walked into the wide living room, he was greeted by Mike, Ana and Isabel, all of whom bore expressions more serious than Addie expected to see. She headed through the dining room and kitchen, and looked toward the backyard deck where Dean stood, his back against the deck railing, looking at her through the sliding glass door.

She walked out into the crisp air, closed the door behind her, and walked toward him. Dean watched her as she approached, grinning at her, relaxed under a flowering purple bougainvillea that stretched above him along the eaves of the deck's roof. Addie smiled, then pretended to be interested in the back yard. She focused on a beautiful rock garden beyond the deck.

It beckoned, but she was beginning to be pulled by Dean's vibe; a mixed cue, part of it treasured and familiar, part of it new and very intriguing, both of which she welcomed with curious ease. She had expected to feel awkward and anxious, but all she felt in the moment was an uncanny, effortless familiarity.

"Like old home week," Dean quipped, "I expected a roller coaster, but no, it's just us." It wasn't lost on Addie that they were in a relatively parallel process, but with a common destination; like the linear sides of a two-dimensional arrow. She had been afraid of the feelings that might get triggered once their discourse kicked off, possibly say the wrong thing, cry, argue, who knows what, but she had to agree, as soon as she entered his presence, it was as if nothing between them had been lost.

"Dean ..." Addie prepared to speak but he interrupted.

"You don't owe me any explanation. I knew you needed to make a clean break with me and the job. Knew damn well you weren't going to tell me why, so I understood it was private."

Addie noticed Dean's eyes glance over her shoulder, so she turned her head and looked with him through the sliding door. She saw Emil, Isabel and the Doyles were back at the dining table talking, some animated body language was going on, and Isabel was taking notes. Addie turned back to Dean, hoping to get some traction in their attempt to get clear with each other.

"Dean, something happened to me. I couldn't bring myself to tell you at the time. Scared of your reaction." She looked out at the garden, then spoke. "To put it simply, you could be a hothead. I didn't want to put you in control; I needed to handle it my own way."

The half-smile from his lips merged with the loving recognition in his eyes; she surrendered all doubt as he launched a casual entre into their renewed conversation.

"I think I've finally learned how to not be so reactive. Just in time, too, because I have two college-age sons to keep up with." He paused. Addie was relieved he could acknowledge his immature behavior; it was possible he'd outgrown it.

"Go ahead and bring me up to speed, Addie. I'm pretty level-headed after a few decades of responsibility. Believe me; I'll do what I can to help."

"Well," she moved closer, her hand sliding along the smooth polished cedar of the deck's railing, "in late March of '94, when you went to Miami on that Columbian Cali Cartel money-laundering case, I got a call from Luis Vargas. Remember the kid who was the bodyguard for Enrique, that Sinoloa Cartel distributor for Cali? You'd been in Florida a few weeks. He convinced me your life was in the balance, and I got suckered into meeting him without a backup agent. I met him at Alec's Deli, didn't realize he was setting me up. We went into the back room to talk. He locked the door, walked up behind me, and held a knife to my throat. I couldn't fight him; he was so spiked on crack I knew he'd drag me out behind the deli and cut my throat if I fought."

She looked up at Dean. "He raped me. Said he knew you and I were tight. He'd seen us out together somewhere in the city. It gave him a way to retaliate, because you refused to back off the case. By the time you got back from Florida, I had already decided to tell no one. I wanted nothing to do with dragging it through court."

Addie looked at Dean, heaved a sigh and sat in one of the Adirondack chairs. The space between them filled with emotional intensity. Dean walked over to her, bent down close, and looked in her eyes.

"I'm really sorry, Addie...I should have known it had nothing to do with us, but I just took it personally, couldn't think up any other explanation."

Her head dropped down, she focused on her hands clasped in her lap, determined to not revisit emotions about the past when the present held such high stakes. As Dean lowered himself into the chair across from hers, she looked again for the reassurance in his gentle smile, and filled him in on the rest, except for the pregnancy.

"Remember when I took that family leave to see my grandmother? It's true she was having surgery, but she's so strong she could have done that standing on her head. I went because I needed her. She knew about abuse first hand from my grandfather, and she'd taken back everything it ever took from her." She gripped the arms of the chair, feeling as if she'd seated herself in a roller-coaster.

"Visiting her proved to me I had to be on solid ground to get my power back. Not waste time prosecuting that kid, or having to worry that you'd kill him or do something impulsive to get even with his Sinoloa crew for putting him up to it. I didn't want you to get hurt because of a stupid decision I made, and, truth is, I couldn't be close to any man at that time. The wise thing was to go home and get well."

Dean reached up for the coffee cup he'd left on the railing.

"You're right, Addie, I would have lost it back then. I would have insisted on revenge, on prosecution, on justice, regardless of the cost. Everything was black and white to me; I wouldn't have seen the gray." He leaned forward and lowered his voice. "I'm going to tell you something we can't discuss further while we're at this meeting." Addie intuited his news was going to relate to their future as much as the past.

"Luis Vargas got arrested about a month after you left D.C. Got in a gun fight stealing a kilo of crack cocaine from a rival dealer; killed the dealer and one innocent bystander. All the media attention was going to D.C. mayor Marion Barry, getting reelected that year after his crack cocaine bust. So, the Vargas trial got very little press; I'm not surprised you didn't hear anything about it. The judge threw the book at Luis. He had just turned eighteen. He's probably still locked up."

He waited for Addie's response. She was shocked that Vargas had been incarcerated so soon after she left.

"I was so stressed, then. I knew what happened was going to haunt me, and take years to heal. Wish I'd known he was in jail, I would have felt a lot safer." *Would I have chosen adoption for Joy if I'd known he'd be behind bars for decades?* She shook off the thought and continued.

"I never checked on his whereabouts after I left D.C. Just wanted to block him out of my mind. I admit I hoped he'd get killed. I couldn't forgive him for years. Finally, I just said 'God, I know you can heal this, I'm going to trust you to do it, and let me know when it's done.' It took weeks of turning it over, then, finally, I had a dream in which I was with Luis and it was done."

"You created your own healing, Addie, it makes perfect sense. I wonder how it impacted him." Addie wondered *I guess it may have, I never even thought of that being a part of it.* Dean looked up as the sliding door opened and Isabel walked out.

"Ready to reconvene? We have about ten minutes. Emil had to take a phone call."

"Sure," Dean said, rising to greet her, "Addie and I were just recalling our stint at the Bureau in D.C."

Isabel pulled her cardigan around her to ward off the chill.

"I didn't realize you'd been there at the same time. Well, Addie spent too many hours flying us up and down our beloved California to

100

ever settle in D.C., and her horse missed a lot of beach rides. I think we were all thrilled to have her move back here."

"Ok, you two," Addie said as she walked up to both of them, "lend me your ears. Stay calm. Before we go in, I have to tell you both something you won't want to hear."

Dean and Isabel looked at each other, shocked silent.

Addie backed up to the railing; they followed, and sat in the Adirondack chairs, making an obvious attempt to look casual in case Ana or Mike looked their way, Addie began her revelation in a slow, calm voice. A soft, welcome presence seemed to wrap itself around her. She inhaled deeply, exhaled slowly, and launched her reveal.

"Okay, you two, listen up. Fact number one. I decided to keep information from both of you regarding why I left D.C. Please try to understand my point of view at the time, because once you are on the same page with that, I need to tell you something that just happened Saturday which alters my role in this case in a significant way." Addie could see Izzy's eyes jerk open wide; she was obviously nervous about anything that could pull Addie from the case, and nodded at Dean, nudging him to respond first.

"I'm ready to listen, Addie," Dean responded.

"Me too, but it better be good," Izzy said.

Addie pulled another chair close to theirs, glanced through the glass doors to the kitchen to reassure herself they wouldn't be heard, then began her story.

"Here's the whole truth, some of which I shared with Dean a minute ago, but there's more. In 1994, I went without backup to a meeting with a gangster we had tried to recruit as an informant, and…" she looked down at the redwood deck, "he raped me, brutally, hurt me bad…with a knife at my throat. I didn't want to have anything to do with prosecuting him. I needed to get away, to heal, and get my power back." She could see Dean nod in agreement, so she turned to Isabel.

"I never told you when I came back from D.C. that I had an affair with an agent at the bureau." Addie paused, looked at Dean, then back to Isabel, who immediately put two and two together. There was a brief moment when Addie saw Izzy's professional reaction of shocked disapproval, followed by an almost imperceptible 'best-friends-forever" grin of approval telegraphed under the radar.

"I knew you would not be okay with it at the time." Addie sent Izzy a quick BFF grin back; the subtext being their silent observation of Dean's beautifully complex intellect, humor, and well-contained but steaming sex appeal.

"Izzy, I had to let you think that I got pregnant from a random one-night stand for the same reason I kept it from Dean; if I'd told you about the rape you wouldn't have supported my decision to keep the attack a secret."

Now Izzy and Dean were both nodding in agreement; Dean's eyes told it all—he was shocked to hear about the pregnancy.

Izzy put it into words. "Yeah, well, twenty-one years, long enough to learn there isn't just one right way to respond to a trauma." A quick breeze caught Izzy's straight black hair and blew it into her mouth while she talked; they all laughed as she reacted and spat it out in protest.

Addie felt the tension go in one clean exit; every cell in her body felt at peace. For whatever reason, she was convinced that if the first part of her story had fallen into place this well, the rest would find its equilibrium, somehow. She looked straight at both of them.

"You two mean more to me than you will ever know. I would never want to hurt either one of you or make any kind of mockery of FBI proceedings. So, I'm going to tell you about a new challenge with complete faith in both of you. Please have the same faith in me. Let me have the chance to initiate a solution the Doyles can accept."

The specter of a wild card getting introduced at this juncture threw Dean and Isabel out of their Kumbaya reverie. Addie watched Dean's forehead compress into an impressive set of folds, forcing his eyebrows on a collision course with each other.

Isabel stood and walked up to Addie as if a closer look would assuage her fear that the case was imploding. Addie looked at Izzy, and the tension across her friend's face triggered her own fight-or-flight response. She struggled to get the words out, but her voice was strong.

"Fasten your seatbelts, because what I learned Saturday has really tossed the salad; it may be a lot harder to pick out the parts you don't want on your plate, so bear with me."

## 25

The Doyles' deck seemed to vibrate with anticipation; the countdown to Addie's carefully measured disclosure ended with whatever had been left of Dean's patience.

"Okay, Addie," Dean said with a suspicious tone intruding in his voice; "don't soft-pedal it once you start talking. You can see Isabel and I understand this is some bombshell, just drop the damn thing and let's deal with it." Addie could tell he meant it. She delivered, grateful they were on the deck, so no one else would see her cry.

"Saturday, I was driving home from my meeting with the Doyles, had stopped for lunch, wrote and sent my report on the Doyles to Izzy, then headed to Pescadero. So, it wasn't dark yet, maybe half an hour till sunset. I got a call from Ana, telling me they had come home and napped, then Ana noticed a message on their landline in the study. Joy had talked Ramiro into letting her call, and she had left a message saying she just wanted to hear Ana's and Mike's voices on her birthday."

Addie got up from her chair, retrieved her drink, and told them about Ana's swooning description of Joy's birth at Stanford Hospital. Izzy jumped out of her chair, took Addie's hand, and with her other hand touched Addie's cheek, wiped a descending tear with a gentle touch, ignoring her own tears as she spoke to Addie.

"Oh, Addie…when I interrupted Ana's call to you on Saturday afternoon, I told her I had almost no time to talk but needed to tell her what Dean had worked out with Ramiro about the ransom problem. Ana mentioned Joy had left a quick greeting on her voicemail, nothing worrisome, said she could talk to me about it later. "She never told me Saturday was Joy's birthday. They had already told me they gave Joy a twenty-first birthday party before they left for Mexico, so I was going on that info." Izzy stopped, took a breath, and looked at Addie, her eyes filled with tears.

"Addie, if she had said all the details, Stanford, the time of birth, how much Joy weighed, I would have connected the dots right there." Addie nodded at her friend, and looked at Dean, who was slowly shaking his head, unable to hold back his own tears.

"Dean," Addie said, "just some history for you. Izzy, along with our dear friend Star, and my Grandma Luisa, were at Stanford Hospital with me, through the entire labor and delivery. My uncle Jerry even came to see Joy the day I left the hospital." She noticed a telltale look on Dean's face and had to address it.

"Joy couldn't have been your child, Dean, because you'd been gone on that case in Florida for two weeks when Vargas raped me, and you had left for Florida as I was recovering from the worst period I'd ever had. There's no doubt the Vargas family has great DNA, Joy is the proof. Too bad Luis had so few options."

Addie saw Dean's expression change from a focus on his own feelings to concern for Addie's. She knew he was going to reassure her that he understood and supported her decisions, and he did; with unquestioning support for her and complete disregard for his tears.

"It makes perfect sense to me that you made these choices," Dean advised, "I think it will make sense to Mike and Ana as well." Addie sought Isabel's reaction and could see that Isabel was not so sure.

"Ok" Isabel said, "I believe you, Addie, but oh hell, what a mess. In addition to your bombshell, we have another hurdle to jump. Emil found a letter from the adoption agency in a backpack of Joy's that she had left at her friend Terry's house. When Terry brought the backpack here, Emil went through it." Addie faked patience.

"The agency letter was in support of Joy's request to meet her birth mother. The agency had responded without providing the name. They said Joy's birthmother had given written permission and a meeting could be set up. Mike and Ana feel Joy and her birth mom were moving forward behind their backs. They feel betrayed." Izzy shot a frustrated look at Addie.

"Addie, once tiger lady in there knows you are the birth mom who agreed to this, she is going to flip out." Isabel walked up to the deck railing, leaned back against it and looked into the kitchen. Addie followed her eyes, and saw Mike raise both hands in a 'what's up?' gesture. Isabel held up five fingers and mouthed 'five minutes' to him, he gave her a thumbs-up and walked back toward the dining room. Addie spoke up before Izzy could continue.

"Ana and Mike will calm down about any backdoor plans with the agency when they hear that I wasn't contacted by the agency about this, nor was I involved in initiating it. I signed papers at the time of the adoption, giving my permission to be contacted if Joy wanted to meet

104

once she was eighteen."

"Thank God for that! One less hurdle to jump," Izzy said, then continued to voice her concerns.

"I chose to call you in on this case for perfectly logical reasons; I really didn't have another consultant available who had your experience. But Mike and Ana are gonna have that irrational distrust the minute you tell them you are Joy's birthmother." Izzy squinted in the sunlight, with an anxiety-driven frown and continued.

"If you can go in there and work it out with them, I will support you as a proven blood relative of the victim, with some limited rights to stay involved. You have to recuse yourself from your counseling role, and participate as a relative." Those words sounded like music to Addie's ears. Her confidence level soared. Just to hear herself referred to as an acknowledged relative of Joy's for the first time! It infused her final appeal with confidence.

"Izzy…Dean…I think we're going to be okay with this. I've mediated dozens of disagreements between birthparents and adoptive parents in the last fifteen years; half my practice is infertility and adoption work. Just so happens that this time I'm the birthmother. I agree to recuse myself and to participate however I can. Just let me go talk with them now. We don't need to tell them about my relationship with Dean, that's private." Dean interrupted, appealing to Isabel.

"Just for the record, I think I'm gonna have a lasting soft spot in my heart for Joy even if I wasn't lucky enough to be her birthfather, and I support Addie's goal to be involved. I very much want to see Joy safely back here with her parents." Dean looked at Addie. "All her parents."

"OK then," Isabel said with her most authoritative demeanor, "as for your reference to 'all her parents' I would say let's leave Joy's birthfather to another discussion after this case is concluded. He may be rehabilitated, odds are he isn't, but I have a hunch we will be looking into it before too long. Let's get inside." She put her arm around Addie's waist; Addie knew Izzy was doing what she could to shore her up.

"Addie. Dean and I will give you some space to sort this out, but we're going to stay and back you up if you need it." Isabel and Addie looked at Dean for his opinion, so he jumped in.

"Joy would want you to help her. I'd prefer you were on the team even if in an informal capacity. You have skills we don't have, especially your psychic visions, and it makes sense for you to stay on board and go to Oaxaca with the Doyles. But if you can't work it out to their satisfaction, you can go, but you'll be flying solo."

"I'm used to solo when it's necessary," Addie said, "I'd be lying if I said I wasn't shakin' in my boots just to face them. Mike will be upset too; I know he will. This hits their insecurities hard."

"Ok then—time to walk on water." Isabel gestured toward the door. Addie walked past her, opened the door, and Isabel, then Dean, followed her inside.

Addie saw Ana glaring at her as she came into the kitchen. Mike looked afraid to touch Ana, his face was frozen in neutral. Addie walked forward until the three of them stood in the space between the kitchen and dining room. Mike was standing close to both Addie and Ana, and looked poised to jump in at a moment's notice.

Isabel stood just inside the sliding door, Dean had moved to the dining room to join Emil, who was hanging out by the buffet table. Addie could see Dean; perhaps he was telling Emil to watch Addie master the moment. She hoped so. *Resistance, just move through it*, Addie thought, recalling Ben's words, she walked up to Ana.

Ana's anger was radiating in every direction. Arms stiff at her sides, fists clenched, mouth torqued.

"Addie, we just found out Joy and her birthmother got permission from the agency to meet, and Joy never told us anything about it! We are so hurt! Why would she sneak around and do such a thing? What if her birthparents are involved in the kidnapping somehow?"

"Ana, Mike, can we go in the living room and talk privately?" Addie gestured with her arm in the direction of the living room.

"Let's go," Mike said in his most perfunctory tone, like a cop arresting someone.

They walked away from Emil, Izzy, and Dean, into the spacious living room. Afternoon sun streaked through the tall windows; one screened window was open a bit for fresh air, allowing some traffic noise from the street. The room was a welcome change for Addie. A large couch, loveseat, and matching chairs beckoned; she felt the weight of her task and longed for the comfort of the overstuffed chair next to the loveseat. Once they were settled, Addie in the chair, Ana and Mike on the loveseat, Addie spoke.

"I'd like to tell you something before we talk about the agency issue." They nodded, and Addie told them why she limited her self-disclosure at their first meeting.

"I knew time was of the essence in your case. I knew you would trust me less if you knew that in addition to being an adoptive parent, I also placed a baby for adoption, before I met my husband."

The stunned looks she received were no surprise; neither was their attempt to act less shocked and pretend no loss of trust had occurred. Addie had a map to this territory; she forged ahead, knowing in her heart that they all wanted to arrive at the same fearless, shame-free destination.

"You know," Ana said, "I get it. The minute you revealed you were a birthmother before you married your husband, I felt that fear. Addie, how do we get rid of that fear before Joy brings her birthmother to meet us? I don't want to be out in left field freaking out because they started without us, I want to be supportive of Joy in this."

"Now ya' mention it," Mike added, "I feel the same way, I mean, I don' wanna make a fool of myself over this. If Joy is ready to do it, then I'm ready. Only I'm not, if ya know what I mean."

"Mike, Ana, I will tell you what I've told dozens of adoptive parents when they're meeting their child's birthmother for the first time. Think of the most high-stakes successful interview you've ever had. You have to put yourself in the situation first, and just start getting acquainted, the way you would with any stranger you need to deal with." Both Ana and Mike stared politely, looking frozen in place, so Addie coached them.

"The way it happens most of the time, you see she's a human being you can relate to, and you will calm down. Your fear is mostly the fear of exposing your pain and hers. You each bring your experience of loss, shame, and fear to the relationship. Tears are welcome; the wetter the better. A few worries may pop up here or there, but it won't be the truckload of uncertainty you walked in with."

"Would you consider joining us for that meeting? So if anything came up we could talk about it with your help?" Mike was up, grabbing

107

a hard candy out of a dish on the coffee table.

Addie couldn't help but smile. Then she got to the point.

"Please stretch yourselves for one more issue I need to bring up. You may think my timing is terrible, that all of this should have been dealt with earlier, but it just wasn't possible.

"Okay," Mike said, "go ahead." He sat back down with Ana, giving her an extra candy he'd grabbed from the dish. She held it but didn't open it. Addie was relieved, because she didn't want her choking on it when she heard about Saturday.

# 26

Addie had heard about 'speaking truth to power' often enough; but she also knew that speaking truth to people who are feeling powerless was equally confrontational. Mike and Ana sat stiffly, unable to take any comfort from their beautiful sofa, braced for the worst. Addie knew this was the right path to take, but her body had an entirely different opinion—gut twisting, heart pounding, poised to run for the front door. Nevertheless, she held her ground, her courageous vulnerability a match for theirs.

"We need to go back to Saturday, to set the record straight, so to speak. When Ana called to tell me Joy had left a message for the two of you, I heard her reminisce about all the details of Joy's birth." Addie edged forward in her chair, hoping they could feel her truth, not just hear the words. Their eyes fixed on hers as she spoke.

"Mike, Ana, every single detail I heard in that phone call completely upended my life. Everything we had been through together took on a new meaning." They braced for the worst as she continued.

"What you experienced during our first therapy session had laid you bare, I know. My role was to support and guide you; we were focused on your pain, not mine. I had no problem keeping my professional balance…until…Ana's phone call. Why? Because the hospital name, the date, the time, exactly matched those of my baby's birth in 1994. There was no other Hispanic female born at Stanford Hospital the evening of December 26, 1994."

"What?" Ana jolted, but didn't get up. "Let her finish," Mike said.

"Granted, Joy is technically only three-quarters Hispanic, since my mother is a gringa, but I put Hispanic on the birth certificate. Her original birth certificate, which I have a copy of here, has the identical information to Joy's amended birth certificate, except your names are listed as her parents on your copy." She had brought her copy, and handed it to Ana. Mike looked at it next.

Mike was mute. Ana obliged him by freaking out for both of them, rushing to her feet to stand looking down at Addie, she exploded. Addie faced Ana's wrath as if she were bobbing weightless in the eye of a hurricane.

"You lying bitch! You really had me fooled! What you're saying doesn't jive with what we know. Your pretense that you just found out about Joy on Saturday is a lie! Emil just showed us a letter from the adoption agency saying you had given your permission to meet with her. It was written over two weeks ago. They didn't include your name, but said they got Joy's inquiry and Joy just needed to schedule an appointment with them to move forward.

Ana turned to Mike, who hadn't moved. Addie could see he was filled to the breaking point with emotion, his face was flushed, a tic in his eye twitched furiously. Addie knew he couldn't trust himself to speak. Ana, still standing, backed up to create a third point of their triangle. Her mouth moved as if she had to chew her words before speaking. It seemed that some other force was increasing the volume of her distorted sounds. Heartbreak and rage, crying and growling at the same time; finally, her feelings found words.

"I suppose now you're gonna blame us for risking your daughter's life! For neglecting her in a dangerous city! For being the stupid assholes that we are!" Ana broke down, weeping into her hands, her body bending, retreating.

"Ana," Addie searched for an opening; Ana's head raised fast, glared at her, the full force of her rage struck Addie hard, but she knew they were close to a turning point, so she let Ana vent her classic fears.

"Don't try to be nice," Ana warned, backing away, "I know you hate my guts, I spent years wondering about you. Some days I saw you as a loser I could never approve of, someone who could never compete with me.

Mike reached up, took Ana's hand, and got her to sit next to him. He sat, holding her hand as she concluded. Ana's eyes reconnected with Addie's.

"Some days I saw you as a superwoman. I feared you would be better than I ever was at understanding her! What you said in your office was completely true—we worried you would show up at some random time and she'd know instantly she loved you more than us!" Finally, Addie saw her opening.

"Ana, I understand, and I don't hate you, nor did I go behind your back. I signed that permission paper in 1994, agreeing to meet her once she was eighteen. I have had no contact with the agency since then, and no knowledge of Joy whatsoever. For twenty-one years I've had no way to know if she was alive or dead, happy...or heartbroken...loved...or abused." Addie could tell she was connecting, so she didn't stop.

"I had no idea who or where Joy was until you called me after our meeting on Saturday. I had a few photographs from Stanford Hospital to treasure, to remember her. In your call, you were remembering every treasured detail, it was so touching; but then you got Isabel's call and hung up." Addie's stomach twisted, her throat contracted, tears threatened.

"I completely lost it, the shock of finally reconnecting with her only to know she was in such danger!" Addie flashed back to the panic she had felt, began to cry, and with the force of her will, pulled herself back to the confrontation with Ana.

"I just couldn't call you right back and tell you, Ana." Addie sat back on the chair, leaned toward Mike and focused on their prior experience of trust. "Mike, I knew this all had to wait until today to be discussed and resolved with Isabel as well as you, because of the legal issues." He appeared to be calming down, and made it clear he was listening.

"I knew I was going to have to recuse myself as your therapist, something I would never do over the phone. And, I had to pull myself together first. I needed that attitude adjustment from the Sunday service, believe me." Ana looked at Mike and managed a cautious smile.

"I hope you understand, I was doing my best to manage my own shock and panic, so we could move forward as a team. I would never try to alienate Joy's affections in any way. If the three of you didn't love each other fully and completely, I would worry I made the wrong choice to let her go. I was counting on your love for each other."

"Well, ya got no worries there, Addie, our love is huge, we've lived inside it for twenty-one years." Mike had found his voice.

On impulse, Addie put herself in the most non-threatening position she could, to make the most important point of all—she moved from her chair, went to her knees on the soft carpet in front of them, and took their hands in hers. Ana didn't resist. Addie's words poured out.

"Please, open your hearts and take this in. Adoption isn't some

111

zero-sum game. At its very best, it's a thoughtful, loving relationship, with no desire for estrangement and no volatile secrets. At its worst…it's…a kidnapping."

She bent her head down, her tears flowing, then looked up at them, feeling the truth in her bones. Then, her face glistening with tears, she looked at Mike and Ana.

Mike had his head down, moving it back and forth in disbelief. He looked straight at Addie, his tears floating across the blue of his soul-searching eyes, then made his best shot at resolution.

"Addie, I'm relieved you weren't being dishonest. And you were right to postpone telling me at our first appointment that you were a birthmother before you were an adoptive parent. I had no trust that day—for God, for the FBI, for anybody—I would have shut down. Probably would have asked for a different therapist." Ana sat next to him, shoved an escaping strand of hair away from her face, and put her free hand, shaking slightly, around his, as he finished what he had to say.

"I believe now that you don't hold us responsible for Joy's plight. I'm really sorry, Addie, that my project's publicity could have made us a target. It's probably true the kidnappers saw it on the internet and made the connection." Addie's shoulders relaxed, her heart slowed down. She felt as if she had surfed a massive, dangerous wave, moving on experience alone, and the wave had carried her right where she wanted to be.

She released their hands, scooted back a bit, straightened her skirt, and, smiling, leaned back against the base of the big chair that faced their loveseat. She felt Ben's presence with her, his Cheshire cat demeanor in full force, so she spoke freely.

"Please understand, I'm not bitter toward you, or Joy, for this. Joy needs us to be a team right now. The universe has enrolled us in a crash course, to trust this convoluted situation will be resolved. We need to stay focused." She got to her feet, and sat beside them on the couch, leaning against the arm, facing them, her heart filled with hope.

"How is all this sitting with Isabel?" Ana appeared calmer and ready to work it out.

"At the outset of the case, Isabel had no idea I was related to Joy; she chose me to see you for logical therapeutic reasons. In the bigger scheme of things, though, I don't think we were brought together by accident. Every major choice we have made has led us into this together. Who knows what it all means? I'm relieved we're getting beyond our fears. Now we can focus on the mysteries we're capable of solving, like moving forward, and getting Joy back home."

"Okay then, let's go," Mike said. They stood up, and Addie walked up to them. "Hey look, three points on a triangle. A healthy one now, I think."

"Addie," Ana said, touching Addie's arm, "I'm sorry. I lost it."

"Well," Addie smiled, "I've been known to do the same thing. Just because we fall on our faces jumping to conclusions doesn't mean we'll never do it again."

"I'll trade paranoia and estrangement for teamwork any day of the week," Mike declared.

"Well, Mike," Ana quipped, "that's probably why those huge buildings you construct finish on budget and never fall down!"

Addie waved her hand for Mike and Ana to follow her. They looked at each other, grinned through their fatigue, and walked single file through the dining room and out to the deck to fetch everyone.

Once the sliding glass door was opened and they stepped through, the deck felt different to Addie, as if she weighed almost nothing. Everything in the garden had taken on a richer hue. She was buoyant with gratitude.

Ana walked over to Isabel and spoke in a calm, determined voice.

"Isabel, I know you are in charge of this case, and the chaos we've just been through presents one hell of a conundrum." Ana's tears were tears of relief; it appeared that compassion had won over fear. Ana made her point to Isabel.

"I want to say, though, and I think Mike agrees with me, we want Addie involved in this effort, even if it has to be in an adjunct investigative capacity, whatever looks bureaucratically correct, I don't give a damn. Let's pull it together here!"

Mike had managed to grab a whiskey coming through the kitchen; there was an empty whiskey glass in hand. He looked from Emil to Isabel, to Dean, Addie and Ana. His homeland brogue sounded as if an ancestor had risen from the past to spur them on.

"C'mere, I'm openin' a bottle a' Chardonnay; you who canna' drink alcohol kin have orange juice. As for me, I'm havin' another whiskey. I say we move forward…cheers!"

Off he sped to the kitchen, trailing the others in his wake.

Addie's heart felt as if she'd just run a marathon. Her intuition pushed her to assert an earlier schedule for departure. As Mike opened the wine, Addie pressed forward.

"I know we have more plans to clarify today, I'm on board for that, and I know Wednesday is the day for the scheduled exchange, but I have a very strong hunch we need to be down there tomorrow by mid-day. Something big is changing in the case today, I can feel it. Is there any reason we can't fly to Oaxaca really early in the morning? I would fly us, but it would take all day."

"I'll give you another reason why you can't fly us," Mike said, "we've been through a lot of stress, all of us, and it's not lettin' up for a few days. My company has a small jet already chartered for the flight to Oaxaca, for tomorrow mornin', you can join us!" Addie began to laugh; only Isabel knew why, then Addie let him in on the joke.

"Mike. Compared to any jet, going in my Cessna Skyhawk would be like bouncing along in a riding lawnmower. I would love to go with you!" The vision of traveling over twenty-six-hundred miles on a riding lawnmower seemed appropriately ridiculous at that point.

"Addie," Isabel interrupted with her facilitator's agenda, "If you have a hunch, it's probably more than just a hunch, so you should go early tomorrow. Leticia Reyes and Ricardo Morales are already at the Refugio Tropical Hotel undercover, keeping an eye on Ángel, and Rosa. The hotel management may have heard about the kidnapping; but with the police concluding Rosa and Ángel were innocent, they should both be working there today." Isabel looked at Addie.

"Dean and Emil and four other agents have an FBI plane scheduled for tomorrow morning as well. I reserved rooms for all of you at the Posada de Felicidad, a lovely Inn, away from downtown. You will all be there undercover as vacationers; no one has been informed of this mission except the authorities who had to approve it. I have to stay put here in San Francisco; got a new case last night, I'm just getting it set up."

"So where's the call from Oaxaca?" Ana asked.

"Overdue by an hour," Emil said, then quickly added, "but it's not unusual for these calls to be later than planned."

"Let's take five minutes to finish our beverage," chirped Mike, "I'm holdin' on to the high probability that we aren't carryin' the whole burden for the success of this mission. And, speakin' of probabilities, I believe they are definitely in our favor."

Addie exhaled a huge sigh of relief, toasted with everyone else, then felt pulled back out to the deck, an urge she followed, leaving their muffled voices behind her. Tears of gratitude, born in her heart, streamed over her face as she grasped the deck rail, looked out at the Doyles' garden, and closed her eyes. The bond she felt with Joy at that moment was communicating itself in every pulsing cell they had in common. *We're coming for you, baby, we're coming for you!*

## 27

Adela looked up from the phone that had lost Ángel's call. Tonio and Joy ran into the yard toward her as she tried and failed to reconnect. Tonio looked as if he'd just witnessed a terrible accident; eyes wide, mouth agape. Joy stopped. Tonio swung around to urge her on. She had to tell him.

"Tonio, I had a dream last night about Rosa being kidnapped!"

Joy's shaking hand grasped the pendant. Her feet felt as if they were encased in solid concrete. Tonio came alongside, and touched her gently on the back. With a steady gaze, he conveyed enough reassurance to restore her mobility; her feet complied, and Tonio kept her moving toward the house.

The woods outside the compound rustled and cracked as if dozens of men were running through the brush. The wind tore through the trees, and hit them with chilling force. They rushed across the patio as Adela ran toward them, waving the phone. Ramiro's painful gait vanished; he ran to Adela as if chased by a bloodthirsty jaguar. His ancient straw cowboy hat blew off unnoticed, his face flushed, then smeared in a painful grimace. He took the phone from her extended hand, and put it to his ear.

Joy could see that Ramiro's eyes displayed the fright she'd seen earlier in the morning, when he'd entered the dark bunker to bring her the clothes. Tonio's reassurances lost their tentative hold. She involuntarily clenched every muscle and pulled in a massive breath, preparing for a dive into the unknown. Right now, everything depended on Ramiro.

His chest was heaving, his eyebrows were twisting, his mouth repeatedly snapped open and shut, like a fresh-caught fish tossed on a riverbank. Ramiro turned and walked away from them, his ponytailed gray hair and beard tossed by the wind. He futilely tried to reconnect the call, then holding the phone to his ear with one hand, walked up and down the rows of flowers and vegetables, with Bella at his heels, her head tilted up to hear his every word.

Finally, he pulled the phone from his face and shouted to Adela and Tonio. He didn't appear to care that Joy wasn't restrained, nor in the bunker out of earshot. The barrage from Ramiro hit Joy like a train wreck. He seemed only aware of his rage, his disbelief, his failure to control. His revelation only served to throw Joy into agony over Rosa's plight. He stomped across the yard to them but shouted as if he hadn't moved any closer.

"This is what I feared! We wait! He will call us back."

Joy saw more scenes from last night's dream; gruesome scenarios, gunshots, and lots of blood. Nothing she was willing to describe out loud.

"Let us eat while we are waiting, do not worry, eat, eat." She put tortillas on the grill and left to fetch something from the kitchen. Coming back out, arms full, the breeze announced the scorched tortillas from the nearby grill, and triggered Adela's panic.

"The tortillas!" Adela tossed napkins and utensils onto the table, rushed to the grill and took the tortillas off with her fingers, burning a finger and sticking it in her mouth. Joy looked at her, hoping for some sign that things might work out, and noticed Tonio gesturing for the same with his upturned palm held in his mother's direction.

"Tonio!" Adela cautioned him. "Don't pressure me for answers. You and Joy get in the house and wash up. Show her where the bathroom is, Tonio."

Later, when they were all seated, it seemed Adela had put every last morsel from the refrigerator and pantry on the table; chocolates, nuts, salad, fruit, and a main course of chicken mole she had prepared earlier in the day. The event was surrealistic—like stuffing your face at a theater while you watched a terrifying movie—but Joy and Tonio followed Adela's commands. The irony wasn't lost on Ramiro, who vacillated between devouring it as he would a holiday meal, and sitting in a silent panic, refraining from talk and food altogether.

By the time they were finishing dessert, they were calmer. Joy, with last night's horrific dream hovering around her, knew their optimism was wasted, but kept silent. Then the phone rang. The pet birds had been bathing in the garden cistern, but when Ramiro's loud mariachi ringtone went off, everyone was jolted to attention, even the birds, who flew to the safety of their cage.

Ramiro took off, stomping down the garden rows again, phone to his ear, pacing and listening, Bella ran in front of him and stared him

117

down, her head tilted, nose up, insisting on some word, some direction to take. A groan escaped Ramiro's mouth, trailing across the patio. He turned, Bella bolted and ran for Adela, looking back and forth between Adela and Ramiro, her anxiety building. Ramiro brought the bad news up close.

"It was Miguel," he said in a gasp, looking as if he had just dropped a twenty-pound rock on his foot; his eyes and mouth twisted in pain.

"He says they tried to escape Oaxaca City before the Zetas could find them, to prevent their interference. Rico was driving them to Puerto Escondido on 175, and the Zetas caught up to them on the highway. They want half the ransom money or the girl by Wednesday noon at Puerto Escondido. Their leader took the phone and said if we do not come there, he will torture them until they lead him here to our place, he does not believe they have never been here."

"You must stop them!" Adela shouted, "Miguel and Rosa are your own blood! Ángel is so young!"

"Don't sacrifice Señorita Joy! Make the exchange with Joy's parents then pay the Zetas so no one gets hurt." Tonio stood taller than all of them, his increase in height fueled by anger.

"They are torturers!" Tonio's voice exploded like a canon across the yard and into the trees beyond.

"What of Rico?" Joy asked, though she already knew the answer. She had seen the carnage in her dream about Rosa's capture.

"Silencio! Let me think!" Ramiro, his breath labored, his shoulders hunched over, seemed to shrivel with age before Joy's eyes. He looked down, obviously holding back his answer until the effort to do so overcame him; tears descended into the scraggly gray beard.

"The Zetas killed Rico. Their leader said he would do the same to Rosa, Ángel and Miguel if we do not bring the money on time."

Joy's legs quivered, her heartbeat pounded its way upward, into her throat; she inched closer to Adela and Tonio near the big outdoor kitchen. The wind caught the full skirt of the white dress as if she were in a photo shoot instead of a kidnapping plan run amok.

Ramiro walked into the garden again, looked up at the swaying canopy of the trees. He appeared to be fixed on the gathering clouds descending into the treetops. Minutes passed. Joy watched, chewing on her lips enough to draw blood. Ramiro finally took his eyes from the sky, walked a few feet, and bent to retrieve his hat from the dirt. He knocked the dust off and secured the relic snugly on his head, then marched back across the garden, into their questioning silence. He appeared transformed, filled with sheer strength and determination. He stood taller than all of them, his features shifting down the years—back to a time when courage arrived promptly, with a ready plan.

"We are calling Joy's parents, now!"

## 28

Addie was watching Mike top off a second glass of Chardonnay for Ana, and another whiskey for himself. They were standing around the small kitchen table, clarifying plans with Dean to rendezvous in Oaxaca the next day. *I can't blame them for self-medicating; they've been flooded with adrenaline for days,* Addie thought. *Where the hell is Ramiro's call?* A booming voice shouted in her head as if frustrated with her impatience. *We are calling NOW!* The designated phone for Ramiro rang from the dining room.

She felt his presence in the room. They rushed to the dining table and automatically sat in the same seats they'd occupied earlier. Addie took a deep breath as Emil picked up the phone. She heaved a heavy sigh, and closed her eyes to focus on the people at the other end of the connection.

"Señor Ramiro? Inglés, por favor, I have the family here, it's time to finalize our plans for payoff and Señorita Joy's return, si?" Emil was clearly paying close attention to the kidnapper's information. Addie saw Emil's expression change drastically, then he finally responded.

"Señor, this is a complication that could potentially put the girl in grave danger, that is, assuming she has been unharmed thus far by you. We need to talk with her for some reassurance on our end."

Addie's skin contracted, chills floated back and forth across her entire body. Her left leg started trembling, then both legs. She pressed her palms against her thighs hoping no one would notice. A quick look around, and it was obvious all eyes were on Emil. Emil's responses continued to shred what confidence she had. She heard a sob and saw Ana had gone to Mike, clutching him in desperation.

Rage, fear and heartbreak, combined into one discernable expression, radiated from Ana's face. Mike's eyes were startled wide, his brows pulled toward his hairline, his mouth open, in an expression of pure shock. Addie guessed he must have convinced himself the kidnapping was going to proceed as an unusual but straightforward business transaction. This would be his maiden voyage into the turf wars that set the cartels against each other, and put the goods held by independent criminals like Ramiro in their sights. Emil interrupted with a ripping sentence in Spanish, then switched back to English.

"Put the girl on, let her talk with her parents, then when you get back on we need to figure out how you're going to get to us before they get to you and the girl."

Emil listened to Ramiro's reply, then to Joy's first words. Quickly, he said to her, "Joy, this is agent Torres. I'm here with your parents, I'm going to let you talk with them and then I need to make plans with Ramiro to get you home."

Joy's voice burst out of the speakerphone like a multi-pronged electric current; everyone in the room was startled to attention.

"Mom! Dad! Where are you?!"

"We're here at home," Mike blurted out.

Ana leaned quickly toward the speaker and shouted, "We will see you tomorrow or Wednesday, we're leaving early in the morning on a private jet."

Emil urgently signaled the Doyles to stop giving information. Addie passed them a note "Just focus on her and how she is." Obviously, Addie hadn't written the note fast enough to stop the leak about the private plane. Hopefully that wouldn't make them a target upon arrival. Ana continued in the same urgent tone.

"How are you being treated? Has anyone hurt you? Have they been feeding you?"

"Mom," Joy began to lecture in a slightly parental tone, "you need to calm down. I'm not happy, I don't want to be here, but no one has hurt me and I'm eating fine. No one can find us here, don't worry. We're not in the city. But Rosa and Ángel are in real danger, Mom."

Immediately, Ramiro took over the phone. Mike pushed out of his chair and started pacing through the foyer and back again.

"Enough," Ramiro's voice, distressed by a congested cough, echoed, "the girl has said too much." He slowed for a few breaths, his voice in a subdued rough effort. "Take it off speaker." coughing ensued, until Emil turned off the speaker.

Dean's IPhone chirped. He quickly read the incoming message, leaned toward Emil, put the phone in his hand, and told him to discuss it with Ramiro. Emil nodded. Addie felt as if she were rising off her chair; the stakes were being raised, along with her fears; she wanted to fly free of it all.

## 29

"Ramiro, hold on a minute, we just got an email from our agents in Oaxaca City." Emil scrolled through the message, looked around at each anxious face in the room, nodded, and threw his hat in the ring.

"Okay, we have news. You ready? Good. They recorded a conversation outside the hotel between Ángel and your brother Miguel. The recording confirms that Miguel, Ángel and you, Ramiro, were in this together. You'd better tell us what you know about this mess. I'll read it first, then we will talk." Dean gave Emil a nod, as did Isabel.

"Here goes. Miguel arrived at the Hotel while Ángel was on his break in the patio. He'd been beaten, just got out of the hospital. He admitted to Ángel that he got jumped last night by two Zetas who overheard him in the hotel bar. He was bragging to a prostitute about all the money he was going to have on Wednesday. The Zetas followed him outside and beat him until he talked. Police intervened, called an ambulance for Miguel, the Zetas were not detained." Emil scrolled the IPhone message for more.

"Miguel told Ángel the Zetas are threatening to kill them and Rosa unless half Joy's ransom goes to them. Ángel decided they had to make a run for it. They figured if they couldn't be found, the Zetas would have to let it go and focus back on their own business." Emil listened to Ramiro's response, then came back with his own news.

"Okay, we are on the same page with that bad news, have you heard what happened on 175? What? Well, you're right, 175 is a longer route to the coast than 131. Terminates south of Puerto Escondido, right? We just got confirmation from the police that the Zetas must have been tipped off by an informant; they took 175 south and caught up with the taxi. Kidnapped Miguel, Rosa and Ángel, killed Rico, and abandoned his cab at the scene. They smeared their Zeta tag on the windshield with his blood. He was found dead in the trunk."

Ramiro must have interrupted, because Emil fell silent and listened while Addie, Dean, Mike and Ana imagined every word. Then Emil spoke to Ramiro.

"Ramiro, the Zetas must have gotten your cell number from Miguel and called you from highway 175. I know they want cash more than bodies, they sound eager to deal."

Emil waited impatiently for Ramiro to finish his response, then, looking at Dean, he covered the mouthpiece and whispered.

"Shall I see if he might join us in a new plan?" Dean grinned and nodded.

"Ramiro!" Emil interrupted. "Hold on one minute, we have a very high-ranking cartel expert here with us today, Agent Culhane. Are you prepared to negotiate with him?"

Addie understood that Emil and Dean were thinking about a sting operation to capture the Zetas. *Ramiro considers himself a keen kidnap negotiator from his cartel days, so Emil manipulated Ramiro to move forward to prove his capabilities. They're going to let his ego pave the way for his participation in a Zeta sting op!*

Dean got a nod from Isabel, Emil handed Dean the phone, then glanced around the room. Everyone's eyes were on Dean.

"Ramiro. Culhane here. Can you hear me okay? Good. We both know how badly this could go with your three family members in Zeta hands. But the Zetas don't know squat about your skills, especially if they're judging you by Miguel. They could have driven back into Oaxaca City, but the police already knew they were in town and up to no good. They want this to go down at the coast, probably up in the hills, where they can hide and make you bring the ransom to them." Dean paused and listened to Ramiro.

"Good. Listen, Ramiro, the Mexican authorities will coordinate with us. Instead of you having your family's future at risk, you and Miguel could consider a plea bargain. We have an opportunity to sting these Zetas using the ransom as bait. We might be able to negotiate safe passage to the US for your family, claiming that once the sting is over, you will all need refuge from retaliation by Zetas in Mexico."

It was clear to Addie that her prediction of an important new development in the case was happening right before her eyes. Dean pressed his case to Ramiro.

"Once in custody, we can find out which Zeta cells they are working with, and get some very high value intel from them. Is this something you are interested in?" Dean looked around the room and gave a thumbs-up. "Ramiro, I'm putting you on speaker, just want to run one more thing by you. Can you hear me okay?"

"Yes, I can hear you." He was clearly ill, his voice cracking.

"Good. Now, if you move forward to the coast, as if you're negotiating independently, our team can go there undercover and do everything possible to save your family and snare the Zetas. Of course, we could get Joy from you tomorrow in Oaxaca City, then proceed to the coast without the Doyles and rescue your family from the Zetas." The Doyles and Addie quietly cheered the second scenario.

"With respect, señor," Ramiro's voice rose barely audible from the speaker, "if I give you Joy tomorrow, I give up the leverage I have to make you risk a clash with those devils." His words came in a scratching whisper. "You say you want to capture them, but once you have Joy, your superiors may decide to abandon our plan along with our plea bargain, which depends on me helping you with the Zeta sting." He tried for emphasis with a louder whisper, "this deal has to work for all of us." Dean looked at Isabel, she did a mock hand shake with her own hands, telling him to agree with the plan they originally discussed.

"Very well, Ramiro. However, if you are going to the coast with Joy, we need to clarify how your transport and protection of her will be managed with the utmost safety. I am concerned about your health. Can you manage this?" Ramiro's coughing continued, and the entirety of his response was whispered.

"Senor Culhane, please think about this; I will have my beloved wife and son with me as well as Joy; for me to be careless with their safety would be unthinkable. We have air transport to the coast Wednesday morning at sunrise, we leave from a private air strip. My cousin Reuben has a rental cabin about five miles from the area the Zeta leader indicated for the exchange. We will hide out there. We can discuss more details tomorrow." Rasping words became coughs he struggled to stop.

"Fair enough, I will contact you once we are in Oaxaca City. If for any reason we don't connect by two p.m., then you call me. I will send you my contact information tomorrow."

"Bueno." They hung up. Dean appeared a bit humbled by Ramiro's assertive negotiating, but Addie sensed he was also very pleased the Zeta sting was still on for Wednesday. *I bet Izzy told him to try for the earlier exchange for the Doyles' benefit, so Ramiro could either agree and please them, or disagree with a rationale the Doyles' understood was non-negotiable.*

124

Addie gulped, practically choking on her own spit, then felt her own breath coming in short; pulled though by sheer determination. The image of the blood-smeared Z on Rico's taxi lurched into her vision along with the cocaine-dusted moustache on Luis Vargas' face; her D.C. encounter overcame her, like a captor's net pulling her body to the ground.

The memory of the knife scraping at her throat, the weight of the gangster's hard body crushing her face down against the floor, managed to conflate with a vivid vision of Rico on highway 175, confused and reluctant, as his soul rose above the highway, above his frantic friends, away from his lifeless body. She choked again; then came a series of dry coughs that would not stop, and each cough left her less able to get a breath. She grabbed her purse, found the inhaler at the bottom, and gave herself a double dose of Albuteral.

"You okay?" Ana's voice echoed in the room as Addie struggled to get another breath.

Addie replied in a hoarse whisper. "I'm going in the den to calm down. It won't clear unless I do. This is no allergic reaction, it's psychosomatic."

"Do you mind if I come meditate with you?" Ana asked, "If I don't calm down I'm going to freak. I'm worried; Ramiro's very sick."

"Okay," Addie tried to speak clearly, but only a weak guttural response made it into the room. Ana nodded, headed toward the den. Addie rose, took a quick detour past Dean, and glanced at his notes.

He had printed the name *HANNIBAL* next to an undisclosed section of notes he copied from the surveillance team's email. *OAXACA POLICE ID'S ZETA GORDO FROM RICO'S DASH CAM—GORDO IS CAPTAIN OF A ZETA CELL. DOCUMENTED HISTORY OF HORRIFIC CRIMES—EXTENSIVE SADISTIC HISTORY—USES FIRE, ACID, ELECTRICITY FOR TORTURE.* Addie's mind began to ruminate out of control.

*Will Gordo try to locate Ramiro's hideout at the coast on Wednesday? Will he use his interrogation techniques on his captives to assuage his greed? Or, in Gordo's case, perhaps just for entertainment? Dean has decided this man must be stopped. For good.*

She shuddered; the inside of her thighs reacted to an imagined electric shock. When she worked with Dean in D.C., Hannibal was a

125

code name they used for the 'worst of the worst' criminals, the twisted ones. Dean and Emil had held Gordo's information back to spare the Doyles. A quick vision of Gordo passed through her; his fat stomach was extruding thin, writhing snakes. Shivering, repulsed, she focused on Emil to escape the vision.

Emil was back on the phone, talking with Oaxacan police in rapid Spanish; Addie realized Dean had added a new twist to the plan, one which involved a lot more risk, all of it centered, thanks to the Zetas, in the forested hills near Puerto Escondido. When Emil hung up, he exhaled loudly, then looked up at the rest of them. Mike had a question that couldn't wait.

"Emil, did the Oaxaca police set up a pursuit of the Zetas when they found Rico's cab? Looks like help should be on the way now."

"No, Mike, the officers had to handle the crime scene without any backup. The city PD said a Oaxacan politician and his brother were gunned down on the front porch of their house today, in a cartel execution; the police and feds were ordered to make that their highest priority. As for help from the coast, apparently Puerto Escondido authorities had deployed what few police they had to assist with a crime scene south of Escondido and north of Puerto Ángel, so no one from the coastal end of highway 175 wanted to make a Zeta search any kind of priority."

Emil noticed Mike's shock over the phone call, got up, and sauntered over to him. As Addie listened, she realized Emil was trying to normalize the recent twist in the case, without realizing it would escalate Mike's fears instead of assuaging them.

"Mike, just so you know, reeling these fish in with a sting operation was our only hope of resolving this. Ramiro was so upset he was determined to get to the port and make the deal. These things can get messy, criminals get impulsive, paranoid, change plans, it happens."

Mike leaned back, chewed on his lips, ground his teeth, and stared out the window to the street. Dean directed a nod and a subdued smile at Isabel; he seemed to be the only one who had a clear vision of the sting operation working out. Addie ducked into the den with Ana, praying that Dean's cartel appetite was not going to set him up for a contest he couldn't win.

## 30

Addie calmed down in exact proportion to the miles she drove between the Doyles' house and her own home. Her focus was now on the flight to Oaxaca. Hyped from the Albuteral and conversely relaxed by the meditation with Ana, she wanted to stay on task, but had to let Jerry know she wasn't taking her plane to Mexico after all.

Something told her she needed to fly down and see him regardless; *he's been calming my fears for decades, why stop now?* She drove southwest on Portola to Sloat, then opted for the scenic drive down Skyline, past Lake Merritt, onto the 280 freeway toward Pacifica.

Once she exited onto the downhill curve of Highway One which straddled the cliffs north of Pacifica, she sighted the hilly burg. Its topography along the shore, especially at the south end of town, was a flat tsunami zone, filled with homes, businesses and schools, embraced by a semi-circle of fog-kissed green hills year-round.

The hills extended into the sea at the south end of town, creating a cove. The landmark, originally San Pedro Point, had lost its saintly designation, but not its beauty. Addie couldn't get through Pacifica without a rush of fond memories of herself and Izzy the year they graduated from college, celebrating their freedom with a summer of surfing, eating, and flirting at Linda Mar Beach.

*What a lark,* she mused, *sitting on the oceanside deck of that Taco Bell, right on the beach, eating a whole bag of Tacos watching those hot guys surf, then rushing out to the water to out-surf most of them. Admittedly, the waves were rarely a serious challenge.* She opened the passenger window, breathed in the ocean's bouquet, and felt the tension disappear with every exhale.

*Won't even take me twenty minutes to fly to Jerry's, I'll be back home in plenty of time, and getting in the air is going to feel so, so, good.* She called, he picked up in two rings with his usual greeting.

"Goldman Air, this is Jerry." Addie almost cried—just knowing what she was going to tell him when she got there brought it all up again.

"Hi Jerry, it's Addie, just calling to let you know I'm still going to fly down, but I'm not going to take my plane to Mexico after all; I scored a ride on a chartered jet!"

"So, you're coming to brag about your flight upgrade, or am I right in thinking you need to touch base with your old Uncle Jerry?"

"You were sick over Thanksgiving, then Christmas. It's been almost two months since we've seen you. Next year, you're gonna get that flu vaccination for sure. But bottom line? I need to talk about something too important to say over the phone."

"I had a feeling it was important, sorry I haven't come up to see you. Yeah, I've been a bit under the weather. Nothing for you to worry about, just gettin' old."

"Okay then, I'll see you in a while, we can catch up, then I need to get home for dinner; the family hasn't been brought up to speed on this Mexico case, and I'm leaving in the morning."

"You sound like you're worried about their reaction, Addie, is Jake doing okay these days?"

"It's been a bit stressful, but life without challenges is for cowards. Wow, listen to me, I'm getting so supercilious."

"No, darlin' you're just gettin' super silly."

"One of my best defense mechanisms against insecurity," she said, "anyway, I'm going through Pacifica, and soon as I'm home I'll be heading your way. See ya in a bit."

"Roger that," Jerry said.

In less than an hour, she turned off the coast highway into her driveway. As the houses, barn, trees, greenhouses and fenced pastures appeared, she felt herself reconstituted. Amira, who had spent the morning grazing with the girls' horses in the pasture, rushed over to the fence along the driveway, then kept pace with Addie's red Yukon all the way to the pasture gate by the barn. Addie felt Amira's eyes on her as she got out of the car and met her friend by the gate.

A rub on the nose wasn't enough for the mare, so Addie slipped through the long white boards of the gate and threw her arms around Amira's aromatic neck. The dogs came out of the barn. Patch looked like the freshly groomed and fluffy Border Collie from the IAMS dog food commercial, and her brother Zack arrived smeared with fresh, reeking, wet horse dung, in which he'd obviously had a delightful roll. Addie grabbed Amira's mane and gave her a big kiss on the nose, then jumped back in her car before Zack could force her into a shower and wardrobe change.

The Cessna beckoned her. If not for Jerry, she wouldn't have a plane. Jerry started her with simple flying lessons on her eleventh birthday, in a refurbished Cessna 172, and signed it over to her seven years later when she got her pilot's license. The airstrip Papa had used was converted from hardpan to turf. He'd taught her about the turf, the grade, and the drainage. *Safety first, last, and always. He made up his mind I'd be back in the air with him when Papa died, convinced me I was helping him too, so I wouldn't quit.*

With her exterior preflight check completed, she boarded, and completed the interior check, thrilled to be free of the confined space and the stress of the meeting, and excited to get on with the brief flight to Jerry's. Her evening ahead, telling her family about Joy and the urgent flight to Mexico, was going to be a challenge. Until then, she was, in her papa's favorite clichéd flight simile, as free as a bird.

The north-south alignment of the airstrip placed her in a southerly direction. The joy stick vibrated in her hands as she taxied along the grass runway, accelerated, lifted off, stabilized her altitude, and headed gradually toward the shoreline.

Airborne, she felt wholly and completely herself; not far removed from the way she had discovered herself during childhood flights Papa had taken her on. Sailing above the choppy sea, she felt as sure as any hungry pelican that everything you needed to survive was there. A youthful sense of discovery stirred within her again; being lifted completely out of the familiar orientation, sights and requirements of her life, yet safe and headed in the right direction.

The low altitude brought the sea up close and personal; highlighting the shore along her southbound route. The astounding experience that began Saturday still had her in its grip. In contrast, her personal life since marrying Jake had, up to now, run a course of relative predictability. They'd had their ups and downs like any family. Jake's freeway accident had scared all of them. His protracted recovery had been difficult, he still had problems with pain, and pain medication; but her work and their overall family life had felt stable. *We'll get through it okay,* she reassured herself. *But Mexico, I already know it's going to be rough!*

# 31

Jerry insisted on a quick check of her plane, so Addie sat in the massive leather recliner chair in his quiet office. His photo gallery covered the entire wall above his desk, with dozens of small cheap frames filled with snapshots. She loved the 40-year-old photo of Jerry and her papa in tank tops, standing in front of his old Cessna, arms across each other's shoulders, smiling broadly, with their free hands each holding a bottle of beer. Jerry sunburned, with his reddish-blond hair flying in the ocean breeze, her papa's skin browner than his winter shade, his black locks wafting in the same direction.

There were other shots of them; one with little Martín when he was about five, another that someone snapped while Jerry and Papa were walking with Addie when she was about the same age. She still remembered how it felt to sway in between her two heroes, her small hands secured in their huge paws as they walked, swinging her back and forth.

There was another shot of Addie, age ten, with Papa in his plane, getting it checked out before Papa left Addie and her mother for his last trip to Mexico. The import business he shared with his uncle in Mexico had brought a wide variety of indigenous folk art to an ever-increasing US market; their customers were department and import specialty stores, the products destined for people who enjoyed a cosmopolitan decor. Other imports involved high-end jewelry and ancient artifacts for their wealthier customers.

Addie stared at the photo and recalled the day Papa said he had to get back to work; just two months after Martín had finally succumbed to his heart disease. *With Martín gone, I couldn't bear to be left with Mama, I begged Papa to stay home with us, but Mama said she couldn't stand to look at him anymore; she barely tolerated me. Papa said he'd call Grandma Luisa and see if she could come for a visit. Maybe Papa knew Grandma Luisa would need to be there for me, because one week after Jerry took that photo of us, Papa's plane was found crashed in the sea near Baja.*

Only one photo was professionally matted and framed, hung proudly next to the chaotic collection of crooked frames; Addie, seventeen years old, standing tall and beautiful, her long hair flying in the wind. Dressed in jeans and a red 49ers tank top, next to Jerry and his old Cessna, laughing and waving her newly acquired pilot's license over her head. *Looks like the exuberant hiking photo I saw of Joy at the Doyles' house on Monday, Joy with Mike on a peak in the Sierras, waving a bandana over her head.* She felt her past and present merge as she looked at the photo. The vision she had seen in church, a triumphant rescue of Joy, flooded her senses, and filled her with encouragement. *My vision was very vivid, but completely without details of how it's all going to work.* She could almost hear Ben say it wasn't her job to sweat the details. Addie shifted her position in Jerry's ancient recliner, opened her laptop, and checked on the weather. Even if she wasn't the pilot on tomorrow's flight, she wanted to know what to expect.

*Let's see…no major storm fronts approaching. Some small cells in the South Pacific, might bring some heavy rain and wind along the coast in a day or so, no reason to be worried about tomorrow's flight, unless there's unseasonably dense fog.*

She heard Jerry's cigarette cough preceding him into the office, and smiled in greeting when he entered. He was at least six-three, usually weighed about two-hundred-eighty pounds, most of it up front, though today he looked thinner than usual. He reminded Addie of John Madden; one of her favorite TV football announcers—a humble, down-home, silver-haired expert, who never forgot his glory days as a football player and a coach.

The fact that Jerry had bankrolled his flight business with the money he made playing pro football took his likeness to Madden even further. With one exception, Addie recalled; Madden avoided airplanes after the late 1970's after a panic attack. She looked up after closing the laptop, and Jerry bellowed an encouraging message.

"Fog's holdin' off for now, Addie, hope you have a clear morning for takeoff tomorrow, at least enough to see the runway."

"Yeah, me too. There's some precip comin' up the Pacific in a day or two, we may be back before it arrives, just have to see." Addie stuffed the laptop in her case, and extracted herself from the comfort of the chair. Smoke rose from the ashtray on the desk, where Jerry had parked his cig while he shuffled the paperwork for the plane into one stapled batch. Like most ex-smokers, Addie resented cigarette smoke; everywhere but at Jerry's. He and Papa had smoked the same brand, and on this premise only, she treasured it; the aroma was like a nostalgic embrace. When she reached for the paperwork, her eyes met his, ratcheting up her resistance to lay out the truth.

"Jerry, you know protocol, I can't tell you too much about this Mexico trip…but there's an important piece I'm sharing with the whole family tonight; blood relation or no blood relation, you are at the core of our family, this is gonna rock you a bit."

"Well, hell," Jerry blurted out, "thanks for givin' me my recliner back; I wanna be sittin' down for anything earthshaking." She had to laugh, gesturing toward it with her hand. He took her cue, dropped into the cracked leather chair in one move, then looked up with his bushy brows clenching above his nose, a curious squint, and pursed lips, genuinely worried.

Addie watched his face go through more contortions as she told him what happened Saturday, and Sunday, and concluded with her experience at the Doyles' home. Not a tear emerged until she finished.

"Oh, baby," he groaned, then groaned a bit more getting out of the recliner. She walked up to him, crying, saw his tears flood just before they embraced. Holding him was the closest thing to holding Papa. Jerry had been there for every celebration and every crisis in her life, including Joy's birth, and later to welcome Lizbeth, and then Nita as Godfather. He and Luisa had shared responsibility for every nuance of Addie's development after Martín and Papa were gone. Though not technically an uncle, he was dubbed as such from her earliest childhood.

Mama had been convinced that Papa crashed his plane on purpose, and no one could console her; she'd been allowed to nurse her chronic heartbreak and rage with limited outbreaks of frustrated criticism from Addie until she died. As for Jerry, he had told Addie if her papa crashed on purpose he still loved him and would never hold it against him, and Addie had taken his cue.

So, the embrace from Jerry was fully comforting; a shared moment of anxious optimism, fueled from a lifetime of loyalty and love. In their embrace, Addie realized she needed more from Jerry than his support for what she'd just been through, she desperately needed it to shore her up for this evening's discussion with Luisa, Jake, and the girls. Every time she thought ahead about talking this out with them, some unknown force seemed to back her into a corner.

"Thanks for everything, Jerry," she said, reaching out for a final hug, smiling into his eyes. He returned her smile, and looked down at her with a poignant mix of pride and parting.

"Take care now, and come home safe." He coughed a bit, wiped a few more tears, and forced a chuckle. "I'll check in with you to see how the trip went, and Addie, be sure to call me between now and then if you need to, about anything, you promise?" His eyes leaked tears as the last words came out and Addie responded.

"I promise. And when I get back, you're going to bunk at our place for a few days so we can spoil you rotten, okay?"

"Sure, I know I've been a party pooper this winter. Just remember, you will find her, and she will come home safe. I can hardly wait to meet her; I remember holding her at the hospital...and now she's a grown woman!" He looked down, wiping tears and crying more.

He took her hand and they walked outside together to her plane; they both stopped to look out at the sea. Without moving his gaze from their beloved view, he spoke.

"Sometimes I feel his presence here, in the same way that he and I would get those psychic connections back in the old days before he died."

"Yes, I have the same experience. I may not have had him for too many years, but we were so, so close." She got into the plane, and looked out at him one last time for an image she could carry away with her. The plane started with its usual rumble; she knew he was watching her. *Was it for the last time? I bet that thought just went through our heads in the same moment.* To acknowledge their bond and quell his fears, she looked at him again, smiled, and gave him a thumbs-up.

Jerry blew her a kiss and backed away slow. His fist came up to his rotund cheeks and pushed a tear out of sight.

# 32

The short trip from Davenport to her farm's air strip had been peaceful; as if she were carrying Jerry's protective hug with her. Her head felt clear; she had a sense she was ready for anything this trip required. Once the plane was secured, she walked to her car, drove up the hardpan driveway, and paused on the small hill that separated the south pasture from the house.

From the hill, she felt greeted by the acres of orchards, seasonal crops, and the two-acre fishing pond surrounded by willow trees and massive rocks. Childhood memories abounded until she felt she was inside them, pretending to chase Martín as he maneuvered around the pond with her, peeking out at every turn. *So much for a clear head, I can't help but think of him here.* She turned the car off, and decided to gather her energy from the love she felt in this moment.

She could almost hear her young voice calling him to show himself. *Martín, come out, I'm finding you no matter what!* Then his adorable smile, his skinny arm reaching up to push that black hair away from the haunting beauty of his eyes…and maybe uncover the little half-moon shaped scar on his temple. That scar; the only one he hadn't gotten from one of his many surgeries.

There would be no forgetting it. The beach. Low tide. She was helping him over the rocks of a briefly available tide pool, holding his hand so he wouldn't fall, then she slipped and down they went. The cut on his temple was open and bleeding profusely. He screamed as if he were getting heart surgery with no anesthesia. Mama had swooped him away, running with him to Papa while Addie stood crying in the chill of the tide pool, watching Martín's spilled blood lose its shape and color in the water. It wasn't until they had all rushed home with him that she discovered she'd been bleeding from her fall on the rocks, too; a deep gouge where her back had come down hard on some barnacles.

*Martín, I know you are fine, I feel you close by. Give Papa my love, okay?* She gazed at the landscape, drawing strength from everything she saw. *I love this farm, sometimes I feel I was born right out of the ground here, along with the crops. Such a beautiful place!* She surveyed the rich land and its bountiful memories; aware that this day represented a new direction, she gathered the past, weaving it into her strengthening resolve to move forward.

*I love every single thing I see when I'm here; thank God Grandma came to take care of me after Martín died. Mama was drunk all the time, Papa flew to Mexico, had to keep working, until…well, until the crash; then it was just Mama, me and Grandma Luisa, with Mama's parents in the manager's house, keeping their distance. They never liked Papa, probably relieved when he died.* Isabel's ringtone startled her. She shuffled for her phone, knocking over the water bottle she had in the cup holder. Before Izzy gave up, Addie had restored the bottle and answered.

"Perfect timing," Addie chimed to Isabel, "You're on speaker. I'm in the car, just got home from Jerry's. Have to tell the family I'm leaving for Oaxaca in the morning. I'm dreading their reaction."

"How can it be easy? There's just no way. I'd ask you once more if you're sure this is what you want to do, but there's no point."

"I'm at peace with it. Took the plane down to Jerry's; needed to tell him what happened in person. And no, I didn't blab any sensitive info. When I flew out over the water, I felt completely dialed into the mission. And, based on my experience Saturday with that motorcycle practically running me off the cliff just after I came through the tunnel, I say let's go to Mexico before I cash it in here."

"Okay Addie, I'm with you in spirit, and really regret I can't leave this week, but there's too much happening here. Dana's disappointed we had to postpone taking the kids to see the baby elephant seals get born at Año Nuevo; you know how she is. We might get lucky next week, though…hey, maybe we could all go when you get back from Mexico."

"That sounds like fun. Right now, I'm parked on the little hill above the south pasture, just drove from the landing strip. Remember that time you, Star and I slept up here in the tent and roasted hot dogs? I'm sitting here reminiscing about the times Martín and I played around the pond, remembering when Grandma Luisa came here to live." Izzy jumped in, her voice perking up.

"I remember when I met Luisa for the first time, when she and your mom picked us up from that soccer match."

Addie had forgotten it completely. Mama, too drunk to drive, but sober enough to give directions to Grandma, who had to drive the car.

"That was the beginning of so many rescues! Remember when

135

Grandma sold her business and all her property in Mexico, to buy this place from Mama's parents? When she arrived here to help us after Martín died, they treated her like a peon, said Papa ruined their daughter; but when the recession hit, along with health problems, they wanted to go back to France for the free medical care…"

"I remember that! They were so shocked she had the assets to buy the place! And your mama moved into the cottage, leaving Luisa to raise you in the main house. With Luisa's business skills, and your investments in the place, it's all paid off. What a blessing!"

"Ya think? Where would we be without her?"

Izzy laughed, "Luisa's like Mary Poppins, Agatha Christie, Dancing with the Stars and the Psychic Hotline, all rolled into one! Hey, I gotta run and so do you. Love you, I'm missing you already, but I'll be thinking of you cruising to Oaxaca in that chartered jet!" Addie started the car, and crept along the drive toward home, finding it hard to let Izzy go, just kept talking, holding on to her.

"Some flight opportunity, I know. I have to meet Mike and Ana at six a.m. at the airport. They seem to be grounded in this mission too. I figure a guy who was a military munitions expert and a woman who can castrate two Siberian tigers before lunchtime may be more of an asset than we ever anticipated."

"Oh, God, Addie, this is no walk in the park, girl."

"You won't catch me walking in the park, too many weirdos skulking around. Back to the case, though; Ramiro seems like a pretty cool cucumber, but I'd be lyin' if I said I wasn't worried about those Zetas. I keep having to remind myself to focus on the end result.

"That's right;" Izzy's warmth filled Addie, "and my love is onto you like a tracking beam, baby, every mile and minute of this mission; you ever need any, just feel your way toward it, I will be there; and never, never forget, God is everywhere you are, Addison Diaz."

## 33

Jake, with the dogs at his heels, greeted her at the door with a hug, and left flour from his chef's apron spotted on the front of her clothes. Zack came up to her with his tongue hanging out of the side of his mouth, eager to show her he'd been bathed, so she gave him an enthusiastic rub.

"Thank you for bathing this reeking dog! He almost slimed me when I first got home this afternoon, but I had an appointment to go to Jerry's and couldn't do anything about Zack."

"Did it in self-defense, darlin'," Jake said, "he kept at me to come inside, just wouldn't let up. Speaking of coming inside, I hope you're hungry."

Jake's Mississippi accent felt so good as she took it in, along with his grin, his dimples, his generous southern welcome. After she entered, she realized the past two days had felt like weeks, and she felt a physical longing for Jake that was always her response to anything more than a brief separation. She glanced at him, his soft, wavy blond hair had given way to some gray over the years, with not a hint of loss in fullness or sheen. His broad shoulders graced a line to his perfectly rounded derrière that invited a glance and welcomed touch. He walked up to her, hugged her, and was eager to talk.

"I saw you parked out there on the hill, must have been Izzy, huh?"

"Yep, your deductive powers are on track baby," she said with a grin, pulling him closer, wanting more. He shifted gears and went in reverse, pulling back a bit, gave her a quick kiss on her forehead, and changed the subject to food.

"Well, just to show you how far-reaching my powers are, I have shrimp cocktail, grilled snapper, mixed greens with feta, and a cold bottle of chardonnay right around the corner." He bowed and gestured toward the kitchen with his arm. Addie was famished; she reluctantly let go of the connection she'd been seeking, and focused on moving into the kitchen.

"Thanks...I wanted to get down to Davenport right after the meeting, so I haven't eaten since then. Have the girls eaten?"

"They already ate, took their food in Nita's room to watch that movie you gave her for Christmas."

The kitchen TV was on low volume, a commercial for post-Christmas sales was touting half-price electronics, then came the news. Addie ignored the TV and gave Jake his due.

"Jake," she said, "you get five stars from this critic and I'm just going by the aroma."

She sat on one of the stools at the long kitchen counter, and Jake smiled; all blue eyes and white teeth, genuinely pleased with her compliment. They were both news junkies, but he still checked with her at mealtime. He edged to the TV, raising his eyebrows meaning 'leave it on?' to which she nodded, more from habit than interest. She was focused on the harmony between them and leaned in his direction, grinning.

Addie wondered how many nonverbal cues they had worked out over their 18 years of marriage, and recalled how easily they communicated even at the beginning. She never tired of the fact that, both imprinted by the same musical culture, only a month apart in age, they would respond simultaneously to some random situation by singing out a relevant lyric from a popular song they'd memorized years before they ever met.

Her thoughts flashed back to the first week they were living together. *Making up for all the sex we hadn't had while he was finishing up that out-of-town investigative report for the Chronicle.* Falling asleep, she had felt herself float up from her body, into the room, and saw him doing the same. Someone else was there; they felt a strange vibration around them. Startled, she had forced herself awake, awakened him, and before she could explain, he described their event with his typical reporter's accuracy; irrefutable proof that it had really happened.

Freaked by the experience, they had gotten up, turned on every light in the house, and didn't sleep until the sun came up. *Now I realize it was one of my non-physical helpers, offering to take us for a tour of the soul dimension…but back then it freaked both of us completely out. I didn't know then that the vibrations are part of shifting out of the physical, into the non-physical dimension; nothing dangerous about it.*

*And here we are tonight, getting ready to locate courage in our midst, but on a whole new level. Jake knows nothing about the case yet, or the psychic experiences that came with it…but when he does…*

While he was at the stove, she checked her phone for new email, in case any of her other clients hadn't gotten her notice that she'd be unavailable for the rest of the week. She'd been worried about how to talk to Jake about Dean joining the FBI case, but the nightly KPIX crime segment jumpstarted it. There, in a close-up, was Dean, his face filling the screen on the kitchen TV. Addie's countless anxieties shot up from her feet; rattling her insides all the way up, like the seeds in a shaman's dried gourd working to ward off evil spirits.

## 34

The volume on the TV seemed louder as the story began in earnest, with, to Addie's surprise, an actual interview with Dean instead of sound bites. He was introduced as one of the FBI's foremost experts on Mexican cartel crime, the newest FBI weapon for the San Diego bureau, in San Francisco to collaborate on a cartel-related case. Addie thought it was a risky trade-off; an ad for the FBI in exchange for Dean's relative anonymity in California.

The intro to the interview turned out to be a hook for another commercial. Jake plated the food at the stove, and carried it to the counter. A second commercial followed the first. Addie dove in; the snapper, sautéed in butter with a hint of fresh garlic and dill, literally melted in her mouth. She was almost finished with her serving before the interview came back on, then forgot everything around her, focused on Dean's report, and drank her wine.

"In hindsight, we see the North American Free Trade Agreement wasn't just a blessing for the US and our trading partners, it was a boon for the cartels; deregulation made it easier for them to smuggle their poison to California, Arizona, Texas, Florida, then north to every state in the U.S." Addie hoped Dean wouldn't get criticized by his superiors for dissing NAFTA, and noticed Jake's expression sour as Dean's analysis concluded.

"Oh, hell, shut it off, Jake, it's a good thing he wasn't going on like that today at the meeting or Izzy might have taken him aside for a lecture on criticizing the government." She finished her wine; it hit her a bit more than usual.

"He was at your meeting?" Jake blanched, turned off the TV, and grabbed the Chardonnay. He topped off her glass and his, looking up at her. She could tell he was filled, not only with wine, but with questions. Addie jumped in quick, trying to anticipate his concerns and address them before he got the wrong impression.

"Yes, when I saw him it was like seeing a ghost, considering we hadn't spoken in over twenty years. I was so stressed out when I left D.C., didn't want him to know about the rape or the pregnancy. When I told him I was leaving the D.C. job and going home, I didn't leave any room for future discussion. I know he didn't realize what was causing me to leave, but he knew I wanted our parting to be final, and he respected it." Nervous, tired, and still hungry, she drank her second glass of wine.

Jake's mouth hung open, he looked through squinted eyes, his head moving side to side, telegraphing doubt.

"Well…I recall you two had a serious relationship."

Addie saw his anxiety was building; he was worried she still had feelings for Dean, which she did, with no intention of acting on them.

"My intention is to leave what's past in the past. You have no reason to be worried about Dean; I wouldn't pursue a relationship with him because I'm committed to you, and committed to the girls growing up in an intact family."

"That sounds more like logic than love."

Addie didn't want the girls to hear them arguing; she got up from her chair, walked around the counter to Jake, his back against the sink, arms crossed, wine glass still in one hand. She lowered her voice and out it came; she'd held it inside so long, and the wine gave it a life of its own.

"Well, while you're going through this protracted phase of porn, pain pills and booze, maybe it takes logic and a level head; to help me while I wait for you to come back to me—you know, the real me, not one of those sex workers for the porn industry that you think about when you're having sex with me!"

Jake had been spared the brunt of her disappointment up to this point. Now that she'd chosen to hit him with it, he struck back.

"Well, my love, the real you keeps pushing me away, so what do you expect me to do, become a monk?"

"I just want a normal, healthy family, Jake, is that too much to ask?"

She slapped her hand on the counter, furious to be caught in their all-too-familiar circular argument, then moved toward the news that she hoped would focus their attention on Joy's rescue.

"You've been out of town working on that story until today; we haven't even had time to discuss what other bombshells came forward with this case. Dean was the least upsetting surprise."

Jake had gone to the stove for a second helping, had his back to her, but swung his head around when he heard her voice crack and trail off. When he saw her tears, he dropped the spatula on the stove and came to her. Addie was startled by the pinched expression on his face.

*He looks so stressed out right now I don't know how he's going to take this, but what else can I do, I need him backing me up tonight when I tell the girls.*

"Izzy called me into a new case Saturday morning; wanted me to work with the victim's adoptive parents because I was her only FBI-savvy clinician who also understood adoption issues. Their daughter had been kidnapped while they were in Mexico over Christmas."

"That makes sense, sounds straightforward," Jake stayed close, finishing his wine in one gulp.

Addie told him about Ana's Saturday afternoon phone call.

Jake pulled back, stood straight, threw his hands up.

"Holy crap! Your daughter? Why didn't you call me right then?" Her tears in a steady stream, she responded.

"I freaked out! I had a vision I couldn't handle. I saw her as clearly as I'm seeing you now, in an underground bunker with the kidnapper. I ran down the beach and fell, fainted I guess. My phone got soaked. Star and Ben came down for their usual sunset view and found me, took me to their place. I tried to call you later from Star's phone, there was no answer, I just hung up, decided to wait till you got back."

Not too proud to plead for support, she held both hands up toward him. "I have to help, this is my daughter locked up down there!"

Jake gently pulled her close, and hugged her. She could feel the heat of his body along hers, and moist heat from his mouth by her ear as he murmured what she expected to be a comforting salve to her anxious heart. His southern drawl, pulled into rounder tones by the wine, rolled into her ear. Hope crawled from a dark corner of her heart until his petulant whisper found its mark.

"So you tryin' to sugar me up to accept Dean's love child?" Addie pushed Jake away, held her hands up in front of her, palms facing him; her face a grimace, as if he'd slapped her.

"I told you eighteen years ago I knew she wasn't Dean's, I don't want to go over that again! Except for my mother's ancestry, Joy is three quarters Mexican, her birthfather was recruited into a Latino gang in D.C. before he ever got to high school!"

Jake threw his hands up in frustration, walked over to the

refrigerator and grabbed a bottle of vodka from a stash in the freezer, then walked slowly toward her.

"I don't know, I guess I thought you may have gotten the paternity wrong, I remember you didn't do any actual DNA testing, I thought maybe you two figured out it was Dean's kid after all."

"I didn't have sex with Dean during that month's cycle, he was out of town on a case; is that clear enough for you?"

"Uh, okay."

"So that's not the issue. The issue is my daughter needs my help, and I'm going to be working with the team to locate her and bring her back."

Jake was rattled. She watched him, her heart pounding its alarm. He opened the vodka, brought it to the counter and poured himself a glass, his hand trembling as he held the bottle tip over the glass. *What the hell is going on?* Addie wondered, *are these withdrawal shakes, or fears about Dean? Next thing you know he's going to be hiding booze everywhere!* Addie brushed it off, fast. *Too much going on to launch into that argument.* She put her hand over the top of her glass.

"I'll pass, I need to stay focused." she said smiling, hoping to assuage his fears a bit, and maybe her own. Jake stood in front of her; she could see he was breathing harder, his lower jaw moved in a slow grind, his eyes surveyed her from an unfamiliar vantage point. *I'm beginning to think I don't really know this guy…under the charm and the brilliance, what the hell is really going on?"*

## 35

Addie's fall down the rabbit hole of Jake's psyche landed her in the pile of discarded stories he'd told to justify his choices. She saw him look around, as if searching for the ultimate manipulation. He didn't disappoint. His face reflected the existential plight of an abandoned little boy, with a voice to match.

"Addie, since we're on the subject of intuitive thoughts coming out of the blue, I need you to know I don't have a good feeling about you being in Mexico with Dean."

A tear escaped, he avoided her eyes, looked at the vodka bottle, ran his finger around the rim, then, gravel voiced, half-whispered a plea.

"Baby, I'm at a real low point here, and you're heading off with this handsome FBI hero." He seemed stuck, didn't move an inch.

*He's waiting for me to make it all better for him. I wish I could, but the facts will have to do.* In an effort to calm down, she walked to the sink and stared out the window. She had one clear goal for the evening; to communicate what she had learned so her family could see why she had to help Joy. She turned around to see him seated at the counter, his face in his hands. She moved, bracing her hands on the opposite side of the counter, leaning in, keeping her voice as calm as possible.

"We aren't going to get anywhere if we can't focus on the same issue. You're freaking out about our marriage and focusing on keeping me away from Dean. I'm reeling from discovering my daughter in a life-threatening situation. You're asking me to not help her?"

He looked up at her, squinting, tight-lipped, stubborn. Her frustration boiled over.

"Jake! The issue isn't Dean, it's Joy! Your paranoia over an imaginary infidelity can't take precedence over this very real threat to my daughter's life! I chose adoption to keep her away from that D.C. gangster…now my worst fear is playing out and you think she's not worth everything I can do to help her?"

"Addie," his tone was distant and condescending. "Addie, you can't leave me like this, for a second chance with him."

"I'm pressing you to help with something that's really happening, not something imaginary. I've wanted a second chance with Joy for twenty-one years, but it can't happen if she's killed in a turf battle by these gangsters."

She took a risk and laid her hand over his on the counter, calming her voice again.

"I can see you are struggling, Jake, and I'm sorry this is stressing you out. I'm as committed to being faithful to you as I've ever been; the last thing I want is infidelity and divorce. We've had a rough ride since your accident, but we've kept our vows to be faithful, despite our difficulties."

He looked exhausted and detached, a simmering glimmer of rage seemed to be building in the pale blue of his eyes. *He's been playing his poor me card for months on end. I'm done with that game. Time to let him know.*

"Look, we need to stay together as a family and direct our support to Joy's needs right now, and we need to go to counseling when I get back; I'm not riding this codependent merry-go-round into the new year."

Her heart sank as he ignored her, went to the sink, and started rinsing the dinner plates. She tried one more appeal; walked up behind him, her voice steady and calm at the outset, but heard her last words crawl into a howl of desperation by the time she finished.

"My intuition's been telling me since Saturday morning that I must do this." He said nothing.

"For God's sake! I even heard my mother's voice while I was standing in the foyer at my office. She told me I'd regret it for the rest of my life if I didn't go!"

He turned fast and walked up to her, his lips in a sneer, rage squeezing his face tight and mean, his sour, alcohol breath blowing the whispered words at her.

"How convenient for you! You want to fly off to Mexico with Mr. Wonderful, so you construct a psychic message that justifies it. This isn't spirituality, Addie, this is you gambling everything with me and the girls for a fling. If not, you could just stay here and connect with your daughter when they get back, and stay away from that horn dog altogether!"

Addie watched, stunned, as he tore off the chef's apron, threw it on the floor, reached in his pocket for his car keys, and grabbed the vodka bottle with the same hand. His eyes found hers. Glistening points of sweat appeared across his forehead between strands of disheveled hair. Outrage pumped blood into every muscle in his face, raised the tendons in his neck, vibrated through his body with a vengeance.

She felt shot through from head to toe by his desire to crush her, but stood her ground, eyes staying fixed on his. Behind him, the sliding door out to the patio; to her right, the exit into the dining room leading to the front door. He pushed past her, bumped her right shoulder hard with his, so she was forced to turn and watch, stumbling to regain her balance, as he slammed the heavy front door. The exploding sound slapped against her head as he punctuated his escape.

# 36

Addie's entire body was shaking, yet she would finish their after-dinner coffee ritual with or without him. She grabbed her coffee mug and filled it from the fresh pot Jake had made. A round of barking from the dogs let her know Grandma Luisa was at the front door. She yelled for her to come in, hurriedly wiped her tears, and rushed to get the cream and honey into the coffee before their family chat. Luisa found her in the kitchen.

"Want anything to drink?" Addie said, appreciating the strength Luisa brought to her.

"No thanks, mija, I just finished a cup at home, I'm good to go. Speaking of going, what's up with Jake, another assignment already?"

"He's...he's upset." Addie knew Luisa saw her tears, but held back.

"Oh?"

After Addie explained, Luisa gave her a reassuring hug, then whispered a message Addie was more than eager to hear.

"Don't worry about the girls hearing anything, not above the sound of that action thriller coming from Nita's room. As for Mexico, you are going to Mexico to get your daughter, and you would go even if you never had a vision, or if Dean hadn't arrived. You are doing the right thing. Let's get the girls and go over your plans with them. I'll tell them Jake had to leave."

Luisa's petite figure headed to Nita's room. With her stylish short-cropped gray hair, leggings and a colorful knit top, she looked decades younger than her age; Addie hoped she'd have decades more. With her coffee in hand, Addie moved to the living room and sank into the embrace of their big couch. Nita, Lizbeth and Luisa paraded into the living room; Lizbeth busied herself building up the fire with a few more logs while Luisa settled into her favorite chair.

Nita sank onto the giant floor pillow, rebraiding her neon red hair and snuggling her toes further into the fuzzy black slippers she always wore in the house. Lisbeth secured the fireplace screen, slipped off her loafers and curled up in the oversized swivel rocker that matched Luisa's. Addie noticed Nita's comical giraffe knee-high socks, on which the giraffe's neck stretched all the way up to a small head at the top, a gift she'd opened on their trouble-free Christmas morning just three days ago. *How quickly things can change.*

"Let's have it, Mom, what's the twist with this new case that you have to call a family meeting about it? You always say you can't talk about cases, so what's up?" Nita locked on to Addie's eyes and held on for an answer, her look displayed vulnerability, and an equally strong confrontational stare.

"Well, it's a complicated situation, the case started out as a standard referral, but I had to recuse myself from the therapeutic relationship right away, because it turned out we discovered we were, well, relatives, and it wouldn't have been appropriate to continue."

"Relatives? Are you kidding?" Nita was hooked.

"I'll explain in a minute. As the situation developed, the FBI agents, and my former clients and I, all agreed that it made sense for us to resolve this difficulty as a team. So, we'll fly to Oaxaca first thing in the morning, in a chartered jet, and the FBI agents will travel in their own plane."

"Okay, mom, now to the reveal. The situation please," Nita said. Addie complied.

"I know you are nervous about this, but please bear with me, because on a scale of importance from one to ten, this is a ten."

"Did someone die?" Lizbeth lurched forward in her chair, her long black curls flying into her face.

"I should never have said this was a ten," said Addie in a failed attempt at humor. Then she moved forward, knowing she was out on the furthest limb of her decision tree.

"Remember our numerous discussions about the baby girl I placed for adoption before I met your dad?"

"Uh," said Lizbeth, "you're referring to our sister, the one you thought we would have all met by now?"

"Wait!" said Nita, "I know, she finally worked it out to meet us, so WOW, I am ready if that's it, but wait, something's jacked up here, otherwise why the heat? Is she a criminal? Or in trouble?"

"Girls!" Addie blurted, "I'm asking you to listen, you're close but it's not a situation that comes all wrapped up in a bow … it's real life, and in this case, it's way out of our comfort zone."

"Mom," Lizbeth jibed, "that's a bit disingenuous, don't you

think? Considering your FBI work, martial arts addiction, regular firearms training, your hot-blooded horse, your airplane, I don't think you're much of a comfort-zone person."

Lizbeth's description of her hit home.

"Very astute observation, as usual. But when a crime involves a family member, it tests you in ways you never imagined, so I'm guessing it will be painful for you as well."

"So now we get it" Nita said in a pissed-off tone, "this is something that's gonna freak us out, that you are gonna do whether we like it or not, correct? Is she being hurt?"

Addie looked down quickly, calmed herself, and then very slowly raised her head to look directly at the girls. The lights in the living room were on a dimmer, so the fireplace light still set the tone in the room, with some loud pops every few minutes from the fire. *Just tell the truth; your decision has been made.*

"She has spoken to the FBI and her parents several times, it appears she is safe. As for my involvement, I don't think I have an alternative I can live with. It's not something I can watch from the sidelines and just refer out to another professional, because you are right, it involves your sister, and it makes sense to me to use my skills, including my visions—my intuition—which is why I'm not backing out, by the way, because my guidance is urging me forward."

"Okay, did she get involved with a cult or something?" Lizbeth's voice was barely audible.

"No," Addie forged on, feeling tears on the way, "your sister, whose name is Joy…was kidnapped… in Oaxaca, Mexico last week… by three men. One of the men took her to his hideout and phoned Joy's parents about the ransom." *Crap…these tears aren't a confidence builder.* 'So this makes it personal and very, very difficult."

Nita started crying, Luisa went to her and sat next to her on the huge pillow, rubbing her back to comfort her.

"Izzy wanted me on the case initially because she knew I'd understand them better, being an adoptive parent. Hours after I saw the clients on Saturday, the victim's mom called me and reminisced about the hospital, date and time of her daughter's birth because it was Joy's birthday; that's when I realized I was Joy's birthmother."

"You found out Saturday afternoon and you're not telling us

until now? I know, you had to get your ducks lined up first. Could they be the couple we met at church on Sunday?" Lisbeth, legs crossed on the soft chair, sat straight and didn't take her eyes from Addie's face.

"Yes. Ana and Mike. They live in San Francisco; they were in Oaxaca with her for Christmas, but Joy was with some friends in a cab at the time of the kidnapping."

"They pulled her out of a cab for God's sake? Was she hurt? Were her friends hurt? Do they know anything about who did it?" Nita's face twisted with frustration. "Screw this! I don't want to hear any more!" She pushed off the pillow and ran to her room. Addie and Luisa, looked at each other and nodded, and Luisa followed Nita.

"Well," Addie said softly to Lizbeth, "that makes two family members who have voted with their feet. Your dad, and now Nita."

Her hope that the family would rally around this mission was going down in flames.

## 37

"Oh, my God, this is awful," said Lizbeth, "I can't imagine what Joy must be feeling; her heart must be breaking! And, I'm worried about you, Mama."

Addie could hear Nita's outburst from her room, but couldn't make out any details, so tried to console Lizbeth.

"Honey, I know this is rough. If Isabel didn't believe I was needed, she wouldn't let me participate; but that's not what's happening." Lizbeth held her palms up, frowned at Addie, and let her have it.

"Our sister is trapped, is a prisoner of some weird guy in the middle of a gang-infested country, how do you expect to get her for God's sake? And what makes you think you're safe?"

"Okay. I did get hurt once over twenty years ago, true. But I've made it a point to not be on the front lines of any violent confrontations and our plan is to keep it that way. Ana, Mike and I won't be going with the agents to apprehend the criminals and rescue Joy. We will be miles away, safe and comfortable at a lovely inn, ready to greet Joy when she is returned."

"Let's talk in the kitchen," Lizbeth gestured, and headed for the kitchen, "I need ice cream for this, something I can enjoy while I'm listening, because I'm not enjoying this topic at all." Addie followed her, sat at one of the counter stools, then gave her an out.

"You sure you don't want me to stop talking about it?"

"No, Mom, I see you're closing the deal," Lizbeth came to the counter with the ice cream, bowls and a scoop.

"To be blunt, if anything did happen to you I'd feel guilty forever for not hearing you out and supporting your choice—and, once Nita gets over her tantrum, she's going to assume I pumped you for details—she'll want to hear every single thing."

She sat at an adjoining stool and began to pile up the ice cream in their bowls. "It's okay to have double servings in a situation like this, and don't tell me different. Just go ahead and finish. You can have a few bites in advance even."

The audio from the TV in Nita's room found its way to the kitchen. Nita's laughter telegraphed a shift in her mood, relieved

Addie's conscience, and sparked a comment from Lizbeth.

"Sounds like Grandma found an upbeat show to share with Nita, let's hope they forget this ice cream's here, all the more for us!"

"You are so wise, Lizbeth, with your support, and your insights about therapeutic ice cream." The mint chip flavor melted in her mouth. She took another spoonful. *Wonderful!* A deep breath, a generous exhale, and she was ready to continue.

"Okay, for starters, the FBI has made it clear that Ana, Mike and I are going to Mexico as private citizens with no official role in the negotiations with the kidnapper, who, by the way, told the negotiator he kidnapped Joy to bankroll his family's exodus from Mexico."

"So, he's running from something?"

"Unfortunately. For him, I mean, his plan's been compromised, for reasons I can't discuss, so he is very motivated to cooperate with us. He's purely focused on the business end, getting it over with. He has a wife, and a son Joy's age. He's in his 70's, and we believe he has serious health problems. I sense that he's exhausted with worry and wants to get his wife and son into a safer environment with more opportunities, I think he acted out of desperation."

"Mom, you talk about him like any other client, like a regular person, how can you?"

Lizbeth shook her head and looked away from Addie. Addie stood up, went to the cabinet for a bag of Oreos, and gave Lizbeth a reassuring pat on the back as she returned to her seat. Lizbeth grabbed a cookie, pulled it apart and licked the icing. Addie, unconsciously gesturing in the air with her spoon as she talked, tried to give Lizbeth a clear answer, but defaulted into a short lecture.

"Fear and loathing. You've heard Ben talk about how it drags us away from alignment with our common Source. Blocks our empathy and our intuition. It influences our response to the mistakes people make. He is a soul like you, like me, from the same Source. His circumstances and beliefs have shaped his behavior." Lizbeth rolled her eyes, which triggered Addie to press her point.

"Lizbeth, you're old enough to stop judging all criminals in some cookie-cutter fashion. Speaking of cookies, save me a few before you eat them all. So remind yourself, there are powerful psychosocial factors that lead people into organized crime. Boredom, desperation and frustration get them in. Recruiters are master manipulators, seducers, they use free drugs, extortion, violence, force, kidnapping. Once these guys and their girlfriends are in, then it's like trying to get out of a cult; their minds are trapped too, most often they have no skills, no legal ones anyway, and nowhere to go. Joy's kidnapper says it's been fifteen years since he and his wife escaped the cartel, says he's been hiding out since then."

Lizbeth looked at her, still scowling.

"Oh yeah, he's really a good citizen now—no way! I get it though, I know you need to create a psychological profile. You think he is actually someone you can connect with and somehow out of that understanding, you can help the FBI work with him?"

"Yes."

"And use your visions in a way that no one gets hurt and our sister gets to come home with her parents?"

"That's exactly what I mean," Addie said, getting up and taking the bowls to the sink, "except my visions are no guarantee of safety for everyone; I can see things that are happening in the present time a lot easier than I can predict what's going to happen, especially if I'm not in a receptive state, or I'm avoiding something I don't want to see."

She rinsed the bowls and put them in the dishwasher, then began to clean up pans from the stove. Lizbeth put the last few cookies back in the bag, rolled it up, and put it away as Addie finished.

"As for random cartel interference, I'm not saying there's no risk involved, obviously, there are risks; thousands of people are killed every year in Mexican cartel violence. The majority are Mexican citizens, and an increasing number of refugees escaping from the massive gang violence in Central and South America. Lizbeth, the FBI has a plan to minimize risks as much as possible, and we have competent agents whose job it is to keep us out of harm's way."

Lizbeth was looking toward Addie, the tears welled in her eyes, her chin trembled below her pouting lips. She reached for Addie's hand.

"Mama. I need some fresh air. I can't really feel okay about this; not that I think you are wrong, I trust you. It just hurts, all of it. Including whatever the hell is going on with Dad. It's just too much."

Lisbeth stood, walked up to Addie. Addie knew this was as good as it was going to get, and embraced her.

"A walk is always good when you're upset; I'd worry if you weren't upset, you're having a normal reaction, I get it, I love you." They walked together to the front door and stopped. "As for your dad, it's time to get him in treatment; if he doesn't do it while I'm gone, we'll convince him when I get back, and we're not taking no for an answer."

Lizbeth nodded, then slipped on her canvas loafers and headed for the front door with a quiet whistle for the dogs. They rushed to the door, alternating between whining and their happy growl, spun their tails in a frenetic circle, then flung themselves through the door as it opened.

The yard light from the barn and the solar lights along the driveway fence lit the dogs as they raced ahead of Lizbeth. Addie, watching them from the front porch, felt her strength return. Looking out at Lizbeth, the dogs, the farm, reminded her of the vision she had at the end of the Sunday service.

She knew exactly why she was moving forward and not giving up in the face of this crisis—because she had a team that was not only counting on her, they were supporting her—from this dimension and the next.

# 38

An hour later, Addie had showered, checked in on Nita to smooth things out, and climbed into bed early. Despite her worries about Jake, she drifted into sleep faster than she'd thought possible. Hours later she found herself in a dream, somewhere in Mexico. She was outside, searching the ground around an airplane at a furious pace, looking for something.

She felt someone behind her and spun around. It was Jake. Her heart slammed against her chest harder and harder. What was he doing in Mexico? Was this her Jake, or someone else who looked exactly like him? He reeked of sweat and booze, and was frightening her in a way she didn't understand. She backed away from him and backed so hard into the plane it woke her up.

The bedroom was still. Jake's side of the bed was empty, and that scared her. Highway One was hazardous enough sober. The clock's red digits glowed 1:36. She got up, looked out the window and saw his sedan in the driveway. *Oh, thank God, he's okay. Must have fallen asleep watching TV in the living room.* She walked out to invite him to bed. *Would be so nice to make up with him before I leave in the morning!*

Walking quietly down the hall toward the living room, she heard noise from their home office and headed back down the dark hall in the opposite direction. As she approached, she could hear Jake's voice through the door, which was practically closed but not latched. He'd been working on an article for Wired magazine, on internet-based human trafficking. He often wrote at night, so she was hesitant to disturb him. He had some music playing, as usual, but then she heard his voice.

*"Oh yeah, now for the good night icing on the cake!"*

It was silent, except for the music. She heard some motion, then decided he was just talking to himself about something he'd just finished writing. Slowly, she pushed open the door without a sound so as not to startle him. His computer screen was the only source of light coming from the far side of the room.

The familiar contents of the dark room were indiscernible; her eyes automatically went to Jake's outline in the chair in front of his computer desk. There was ample light to see that he was naked.

On the computer screen and emerging from the speakers was a voluble Skype conversation with a young naked woman. *Maybe twenty years old*, Addie thought, *naked except for a tourniquet around her upper arm and a syringe in her hand!* The girl began to inject herself as he watched. Addie felt a bolt of shocked terror explode in her heart, in her gut. She inhaled fast and exhaled loud.

Jake heard Addie's gasp and spun his chair around to look. The loose ends of a firmly tied tourniquet flopped loosely against his left arm, and a few inches below, oddly lit by the computer, blood was slowly leaking out of the vein in the crook of his arm, a not uncommon result of recent injection, Addie knew, and there was the syringe in his hand.

Addie's world exploded inside her. Her marriage, her trust in Jake, the trust the girls had in him, *even Grandma Luisa and Jerry love him like a son.* Their combined trust was the secure center of Addie's universe; now it was obliterated. A gnarled moan filled the room before she realized it had come from her. Jake, groggy already, reached in slow motion, hit the power button on the monitor, and the nodding nude girl smiled out at them no more. He pulled off the tourniquet and laboriously put it with the syringe into a small zippered bag on the desk in front of him. A cruel graveled voice like the frightening Jake from her dream spoke in a curt, slow drawl.

"Shut...the...door...fool! Girls...can... hear...you!"

He needn't have worried, Addie found herself incapable of speech. Her entire nervous system was firing in all directions. Something in her body took over completely, spun her around, and marched her out the door, shutting it quietly behind her. Still the frozen observer, she marched back down the dark hall, moved left through the living room, and out the front door, like a ghost; quiet, so as not to wake the girls, then fast out to the stable where she'd bedded down Amira earlier that evening.

"Amira," she heard herself call. The mare's huge black eyes, beautiful head and effulgent wavy mane quickly appeared above the closed lower half of her stable door. The ceiling light in the barn seemed to be taking its glow from the snow-white mare instead of the other way around. Addie, in stunned passivity, watched her arms encircle Amira's neck, felt the tears pouring into the endless welcome of scented

156

fur, and received the mare's nuzzling again and again, through her hair, across her face, into her neck. How profoundly the mare delighted herself with Addie's scent! The sensual immersion was intensely mutual, and for Addie it sparked a desire to live.

She opened the door, the mare stepped into the barn as Addie grabbed their soft riding pad. Lamb's wool on the bottom for Amira, soft leather on the top for Addie, and light aluminum stirrups. The smell of Amira's body, accented with the stable scent of hay, grain and manure, followed her into the moonlight. Amira snorted and leaned in a gentle hug against Addie. The tears cascaded off Addie's jaw, onto her pajamas. She felt as if the blood in her body had doubled in volume, her heart an anvil, hammered by the painful scene she'd witnessed.

The sea breeze from the distant beach found her tears and made them sting, blew across her short pajama bottoms, whipped her bare legs and feet, and wafted over toes retreating into to the mud. With no memory of cinching on the riding pad, she checked to confirm the cinch was snug, then grabbed two handfuls of Amira's mane; her body launched itself onto the soft pad in a smooth glide. They moved as one; to run, to ride, to cry out.

Amira started with a choppy trot to the back of the property. A drainage ditch ran the entire length of the runway, to keep any runoff from the hills away from the manicured turf of the air strip. Amira slowed, walked past the parked plane, over the ditch's bridge, then picked up her pace. Addie's tears blurred her vision and distorted her view of the hillside. The smudged and twisted shapes of the trees, brush, and moonlit yucca blossoms waved in the wind; like riding into the painful beauty of a Van Gogh painting. She felt her tears whipped straight back onto her cold ears as they plunged ahead into the night.

Amira brought more power to bear as they closed the quarter-mile gap between the strip and the hills, digging for purchase on a familiar trail that went up and over the nearest hill. Addie leaned forward for the ascent along the trail's zig-zag sweep; her muscular frame wrapped around the surging muscles beneath her, feeling Amira forge ahead with power and abandon, grunting and snorting, to the peak of the hill.

The air was cold; their body contact warm. Though the trail continued down the other side, Amira spun around as soon as she

157

reached the top, stomped her feet emphatically, and looked directly toward the distant moon-washed sea. Addie felt her power connect with Amira's. She felt a restored union with every cell in her body.

With the last of her profuse tears, a deafening, raging, agonizing scream rose into the night; the equal of which she'd never heard herself express, and hoped she would never hear again. Before Addie's tortured cry subsided, Amira exuded a loud, deep-bodied screech of her own. Like the lead mare of a wild herd fending off a predator, Amira's guttural scream was terrifying; as if she meant it to be a warning to anyone who would consider hurting Addie again.

## 39

Their ride down the hill felt smooth and effortless, as if they'd become suddenly unburdened after dragging the heavy, freshly-killed body of an evil monster up the hill, discarding it for the vultures to clean up in the morning. Addie grabbed a long jacket from the barn after she had returned Amira to her stall, watched her step into the adjoining corral and hurry through the open gate to the pasture. *I don't blame her for wanting her friends right now.*

As late as it was, and as challenging as tomorrow was going to be, Addie started walking over to Luisa's cottage, her bare feet chilled and numb on the driveway. The scent of the sea entered her flaring nostrils, carried on a gentle breeze that caressed new tears she didn't know she had shed. *Grandma will help me pull it together, and she will take over the girls' care while I'm gone.*

The quiet night gave way to a car engine revving up. *Jake must have taken enough coke to pull out of his nod,* she thought as she saw his car heading out toward the highway. *God, I hope he makes it through this; it's almost as if he knows I'm forced to choose between running after him or flying to help Joy.* Turning away from her parting view of Jake, she walked over to the cottage. *I hope she's up for this.* Addie wiped her muddy feet on the doormat, and rang the bell.

"Addie?" Luisa's voice responded through the closed door. *She sounded alert; she must have been awake,* Addie thought, *my trip to get Joy may be worrying her. Now I'm going to lay this on her? Yes, she needs to know, and I need to get this off my chest before I explode and sabotage everything.*

"Yes, it's me," Addie wiped her feet again as the door opened. Luisa looked at her, puzzled.

"Where's your pants? Is there an emergency?" Addie looked down and realized she looked nude except for the coat that came to the middle of her thighs. Luisa opened the door wider and Addie stepped in.

"There's an emotional emergency," she said, looking up to meet Luisa's eyes; Then she was in her arms, and although she was a head taller than Luisa, Addie felt ten years old again, as she had been when Luisa came to help after Martín died. Luisa had helped her grieve; then in such a short time, they were struck dumb by Papa's death.

Mary had retreated into drunken isolation, while Addie and Luisa coped by walking almost daily on the beach; memorializing Papa and Martín in endless conversations about adventures they must be sharing in the soul realm. Some days, when the pain of separation descended unbidden and stubbornly present, they had stayed home, weeping in each other's arms. *And here I am again, carrying my grief to her, knowing her bond with Jake is strong enough to drag her through hell with me, until we emerge, hopefully healed.*

"Oh, baby, what happened? It's nothing about Joy, is it? Or that kidnapper?"

"No, it's Jake." Addie's tears were coming non-stop, and she felt her breathing go haywire, too much, too little, all out of sync, causing her to gasp, choke, cough, until Luisa spoke.

"Mija, stop for a minute. Do we need to get him to an ER or anything? Did he overdose on those pain pills?" Addie knew she had to get herself calmed down, she started by pacing her words.

"No, he took off. Shouldn't be driving in his condition...girls are asleep, they don't know." Luisa put one hand on Addie's waist and pointed to the living room with the other.

"Come and sit. I couldn't sleep so I was having some tea. Do you want anything?"

"Just a tall glass of water, my mouth's so dry I can hardly swallow."

"Okay, sit. I will be right back." Luisa made a quick trip to the kitchen, joined Addie on the living room couch, and gave her the water. While Addie drank slowly and deliberately, Luisa lit the large candle on the coffee table in front of them. Its clove and cinnamon fragrance gently shifted Addie's focus.

"I see you are calming yourself down. Keep it slow, take your time. I have one of your spare inhalers here if you need it, but it would be better if you could just calm yourself. Let's watch the candle flame for a minute, try not to think."

Addie drank, got her breath regulated. A shudder ran through her body, as if it wanted to expel every thought of Jake. She felt stifled in the jacket, pulled it off, and laid it on the arm of the couch. Clutching her hands together for some gentle reassurance, she stared at the candle flame until her tension subsided. Luisa's face was calm when Addie looked up and began to speak.

"I fell asleep. Woke up around 1:30 and heard him in his office. He was…" her tears came again, Luisa moved closer, and held her hand.

"He was doing drugs, heroin I think…shooting it up…with a naked girl doing it too." Luisa's mouth flew open and she gasped.

"Right there in your office? Oh, my God!"

"No…the girl was Skyping on the internet. He reached over and turned off the monitor, but I'd already seen the girl, looked like she wasn't much older than Lizbeth." Addie saw the shock transform Luisa's rested countenance.

"Grandma…what am I going to do?" Addie pleaded.

"Oh, mija!"

"I feel like a total failure!" Addie jumped up and started pacing the room, shaking her head, crying.

"You think you failed Jake?"

"No, no, I feel Jake and I failed Nita's and Lizbeth's birthparents…they were counting on us to provide the stability and maturity they didn't have back then. At the time we adopted, I believed we were doing great, but it developed into a struggle I never suspected. Her tears fell slowly as she walked, waving her hands in the air.

"Grandma, when you adopt someone's child you're asking for the most difficult level of trust a birthparent can muster; you're being trusted with the success or failure of a human being's life, for God's sake! I believed we were going to be a permanently healthy family for the girls…all the years since we lost Papa and Martín, and through my entire adult life, I've wanted one thing…" her voice trailed off, she stopped and kneeled in front of Luisa, taking her hands, crying more when she saw that Luisa was weeping too.

"I never dreamed about being a champion of anything, or famous—I dreamed one dream—someday I'd have a normal, loving, competent, completely intact family."

Addie's vision of her ideal family seemed to slowly melt inside her, like a photo in a burning room; just the heat, with no flames touching it, melting the images, leaving a misshapen tangle of disappointment and regret.

Luisa freed her hands, placed them on either side of Addie's face, and leaned forward, her eyes filled with tears.

"I honor your ideal, Mija, for I share it as well. Ideals are divine, they live in the creative genius of God, as do we."

Luisa gently combed Addie's hair back from her eyes with her fingertips, and smiled into her eyes.

"That's why those visions feel close enough to touch, even when we miss the mark. Addie, God would not give us ideals without giving us eternal life; more than enough time to learn what needs to be learned, to fulfill our dreams, then dream new dreams. No time clock, endless forgiveness for our mistakes, no judgment outside of our own intolerance, our own impatience."

Addie received Luisa's compelling embrace as she had done in decades past. Succor for their mutual grief had taught them that love between the living would reconnect them with the love of those across the veil; surely, they could get each other through this crisis.

"Gracias…te amo mucho, Abuela," Addie said, regressing to the language they shared extensively during their first decade together.

"I must get some rest; I'm meeting the Doyles at six a.m. for the flight to Oaxaca. Your wise counsel has saved me from taking the wrong path with this experience. You and I will sustain this family, and whatever is needed will be provided. I can feel it. I know it."

"I'll cover the girls for you, Addie, don't worry. I will distract them with baking, barbeque, movies, friends; they will be okay. You and I both know Jake will not be back soon. Oh, Mija, this reminds me of your grandpa Diaz. Such a fine man, ruined by alcohol and drugs; your papa used to get hit by him, just trying to protect me. Oh, Addie, Jake is like a son to me, esto es muy malo, muy malo." Luisa allowed her tears to come. Addie knew how much Luisa loved Jake; he had become the son she lost.

Luisa, who had psychic powers far beyond Addie's, and had taught Addie how to honor her own psychic perception, looked at Addie as if she'd noticed something about her, but Addie had no idea what it was; she responded with her head tilted, brows furrowed.

"Your mother may have passed to heaven, mija, but her presence is with us often, in fact right now. She is the one who spoke to you about going to Mexico."

Luisa stopped and looked up, above Addie's head, as if trying to recall her vision, then spoke.

"Was it in your office foyer that you heard this? When you went to meet your clients?" Addie jerked her head, nodding, shocked, eyes opened big, eyebrows jolted upward, her mouth agape.

"I don't know why I'm surprised, I thought it was her, but now that you have confirmed it, it's going to take some adjustment." She rose, put the jacket back on, and hugged Luisa, her personal font of reassurance and absolution.

## 40

There had been no more sleep for Addie after she returned home from Luisa's cottage; she had finished packing, put her documents in order for Mexican customs, showered, dressed, had a bowl of ice cream and three Oreos for breakfast, and managed to meet the Doyles at San Francisco International on time.

On board the chartered Gulfstream, she had politely bowed out of conversation with Mike and Ana, and plummeted into a series of puzzling dreams, some in Mexico, some in California, some in unidentifiable realms. Following their stint through Mexican customs in Guadalajara, Addie returned to the plane still exhausted.

"You okay, Addie?" Ana stopped at her seat before sitting down with Mike. Addie told a bald-faced lie.

"I got no sleep last night; Nita was worried sick about me and created quite a row. Once it ended I couldn't sleep at all."

"Well then," she reached for a pillow and blanket and handed them to Addie, "you just konk out again and we'll wake you up when we get to Oaxaca. How does that sound?"

"Like a plan I can implement, for sure, Ana. Thanks."

Her grief added weight to her crushing fatigue; in no time she was roaming through another set of chaotic dreams, the last of which featured Ben and Star in ballet attire, doing their best to cheer her up until she fully felt her spirits lift despite the gloom and doom she had brought aboard the flight. More refreshed than she anticipated, she began to stir, waking up in increments, and heard the Doyles' conversation mingled with the power of the jet's twin engines.

She turned her head to the window, sensing the light through her closed eyes, and had to force herself to wake up. Eyes open, she felt her connection to Joy intensify when she saw Oaxaca's Central Valley. The jet seemed to float slowly toward the capitol, resting ahead on the wide, flat plain. The plain's edges curved upward into mountains; Addie sensed Joy was up there, felt their bond growing stronger. The pilot jolted her out of her reverie, announcing their destination, trying to match the aplomb of a museum guide.

"Okay passengers, here's your quick overview of Oaxaca. I admit I just Googled it…never been here before. Here goes. Phonetic spelling is similar to wah ha ka. The state and the capitol bear the same name, but the capitol is technically Oaxaca de Juárez, after Benito Juárez, who was born in a Zapotec village in those mountains you see east of the city. The city's population is approximately 260,000. Benito Juarez was an integral force in the movement against European exploitation of Mexico's resources. He was the only indigenous Mexican to ever be elected President, and the only Mexican president to be elected for five terms." The pilot was on a roll and kept it up. The attendant moved to the rear.

"Indigenous history and art dominate the cultural attractions here. Festivals in July and December are major tourist events. Oaxaca is one of the most biologically diverse states in Mexico, and Oaxaca City enjoys a tropical savanna climate, bordering on a humid subtropical classification, with Pacific Ocean temperatures in the seventies and eighties, Fahrenheit. Elevation on this plateau is like Denver Colorado, over one-mile high, and can result in altitude sickness, usually mild and temporary for most visitors. That's the short version. Time to land, fasten your belts and secure your gear; the name of this airport is longer than its landing strip."

The Aeropuerto Internacional de Oaxaca, located about five miles south of the city, had one landing strip, for which there appeared to be no competition. The pilot cued them, as required.

"Don't know about you guys," Ana quipped, "but I'm ready for food and a margarita as soon as possible, do I have any takers?"

Mike and Addie responded with a simultaneous "Yes!"

Isabel had reserved rooms for them at Posada de Felicidad, a secluded family inn less than a mile away from the city center. Once they deplaned, Addie called Dean's cell to connect before they left the airport; pleased she had bought a new phone after leaving the Doyles on Monday. Leaning against a signpost while Mike and Ana got the cab, she felt reassured once she heard him answer.

"Addie, welcome to Oaxaca."

"We just landed, getting a cab, be there soon."

"Excellent; maybe after you finish some of this great food and have a margarita, you'll have enough energy for real talking...you sound like you're barely holding on, are you okay?" *He read me like an open book.*

"I'm running on fumes. Had a sleepless night. Slept on the flight

165

here, though, but I need more."

"Okay, that calls for lots of rest. And Addie?"

"Yes"

"You don't have to tell me what else is wrong unless you want to. Whatever it is, I know you will be okay. See you soon."

"Okay…thanks. See you soon." *He knows something serious happened.* She tucked her phone in her bag, and lifted her head to look for the Doyles.

A yellow cab rolled up to the curb in front of her. The driver, a tired gray-haired man with a limp, got out and put her bag in the trunk. Ana waved and scooted to the middle of the back seat.

"It's okay, Ana, I'll sit in front, be comfortable." She got in front, put her head back, closed her eyes, and announced, "I'm taking a nap." *Truth is, I have nothing to give, not even small talk.*

The drive north on highway 175 to Oaxaca City and the Posada de Felicidad was brief. Mike paid the cab driver, grabbed Addie's bag and his. Ana rang the bell for entry, picked up her bag, and led their way through the heavy metal gate once it was opened. Addie looked up to see Dean approaching her. He tilted his head sideways, raised his eyebrows, and gave her his 'I'm checking to see how you're feeling' look.

*Tender mercies; he's passing them on right when I need them. A message from Spirit that even though I'm grieved I'm not alone.*

"If you trust me to not drop your tray on the way up, I'd like to invite you to settle in alone and let me bring your meal upstairs. I won't stay, you need some sleep."

"Thanks. Please give my greetings to the team." She turned and headed to her room, tears leaking onto her face, hearing him in the background with Ana and Mike, telling them her nap plan. *I'm not going to tell Dean about Jake yet, he has to stay focused on the case, not on our relationship. I don't want him concerned about my fitness to participate.* She went into her room, sent him a text that she was taking a shower, he could leave the tray on the bed and go take a nap himself.

Before she bathed, she stepped in front of the mirror, and was genuinely surprised her body looked as fit as it had on Saturday when she'd been getting ready for her first appointment with the Doyles. *Because inside I feel broken. Somehow, I expected to see some visual evidence of it.*

She stepped closer and looked at her eyes. There it was, staring back at her. The truth.

*I was living in a fantasy relationship for years! The proof was right there on his computer—over a decade of sexually-explicit photos, different young women in different poses, with him included—I never looked once...until this morning!*

Her vision pulled back, she ran her hand over her bare skin, slow, and felt the contrast. Smooth on the outside, breaking up on the inside; the truth was smashing, slicing and dicing her mistaken beliefs about their marriage, about herself. When her beliefs reflected the truth, who would she be?

## 41

The lunch tray was on her bed when Addie exited the bathroom. She ate because she needed it; she slept because she couldn't stay awake. The combination worked better than she expected. Thinking back on her pre-shower episode, Addie felt as if her internal war had resulted in a truce. Joy returned to her priority position in Addie's heart for now, and with that came relief. *Time to see how Mike and Ana are doing,* she thought as she dressed, left her room, and headed down the terra cotta steps into the angled sunlight.

Addie realized she might as well have been blindfolded when she arrived; she had barely glanced at the inn before running upstairs. Walking from the stairs to the courtyard, she could see the mission style two-story inn was built around a long rectangular garden, with covered decks along each level. A few guests lounged at tables and wooden benches and reclined in hammocks strung between the posts that supported the upper decks.

The wafting scent from the climbing jasmine in the courtyard made Addie's breathing a pure pleasure. She saw Quinn and Silva; two agents Addie had worked with before. They were tech specialists, and masqueraded as newlyweds. Their disguise gave them a perfect excuse for avoiding social activities, and for all the meals they took in their room. Addie could see the Doyles were sitting near the happy couple having coffee in the courtyard with some other patrons. *No one would spot Quinn and Silva for FBI in a million years, an excellent cover.* She knew it was the upcoming confrontation with the Zetas and Ramiro's mini-gang that had them busy up in their room without anyone guessing otherwise.

The two agents were, she knew, assisting Dean with his arrangements regarding weapons, vehicles, medical personnel, supplies, maps, and weather data. Addie also knew they'd be working on the cell phone towers around Oaxaca de Juárez. She remembered Luisa's dream about searching in the hills. It made sense that Ramiro's safe house was up in the hills somewhere, because Joy had blurted out to her parents on Monday that she wasn't being held in Oaxaca City...*it bothered Ramiro enough to take the phone from her...* they had to follow this lead as well as they could.

The sun and the comfortable breeze felt soft on her bare arms. She headed for the patio; its round tables were draped with hand-woven tablecloths, topped with drinks and snacks for about twenty guests. Ana and Mike waved her to their table, replete with sliced fruits, melon, limes, and cold margaritas.

"We took a siesta too, came down about ten minutes ago." Ana said, looking freshly groomed, as if she had showered too.

Addie let the others chat while she sat savoring the tangy sweet melon slices drenched in lime juice. She watched the friendly chiding from two couples seated at the next table who were teasing the 'honeymooners' about spending so much time in their room instead of seeing Monte Alban, the Museo de Arte Popular, and Puerto Escondido. The mirth leveraged her out of the deepest part of her grief, gave her welcome respite, and an opportunity to pay closer attention to the case.

She couldn't resist picking their brains about the port; so she decided to ask the talkative one of the group, a buxom blond tourist, to school her on the sites. She leaned toward their table and interrupted during a lull in the chatter.

"Excuse me…I hadn't planned to take a side trip, but you're making Puerto Escondido sound really inviting," Addie offered, "can you tell me a bit about it? My name's Addie, by the way."

"Call me Lizzie, or Liz, whatever you prefer," she said, adjusting her flowered halter top and sitting up a bit straighter. "Well, Puerto Escondido is terrific. Half an hour by plane, forget driving it unless you want passengers puking in your car. About forty-five thousand population, a small airport, lots of mission architecture, rolling hills, beautiful beaches, swimming, surfers, three-star hotels for sixty bucks a night, and temps in the 70's; the ocean's warm too."

"Okay Liz," her husband interjected, "I don't think she asked for the entire Sunset Magazine article."

"No, no," Addie said to Mr. Liz, "I really appreciate it. Sounds wonderful!"

Agent Quinn leaned toward his ersatz spouse and cooed, "Liz is right, Marta, we should think about getting out and about, especially the beach." He turned to Liz. "You may have started something, feels like an adventure for sure. Maybe in a few days we'll check it out."

Ana and Mike asked questions that required long answers from the inebriated Liz and friends. They snacked in the interim. Addie knew the 'newlywed' agents were sober, but their acquaintances hadn't noticed; it was a laugh-a-minute at their table. Addie relaxed with her drink, knowing more about Puerto Escondido than she'd anticipated.

Dean was nowhere to be seen. She knew better than to say anything. *He must have decided to rest after all, or he's up in his room working.* Addie excused herself after savoring a café de olla. She was too antsy to linger, and decided to text Dean for an update, suspecting there had been a shift in the case.

On her way to the room, halfway up, she stopped to admire a niche built into the exterior stucco wall. It was about three feet high, displaying the beautifully painted clay figures of a nativity scene. Baby Jesus lay small and adored by all the figures around him, even the sheep...*I didn't even see this my first trip up the stairs...*thoughts of Joy came to mind, probably because of the flashback hospital images she had seen during her beach episode, seeing Joy swathed in a blanket in the nursery. *Think of all the people who are focused on Joy's safety today.* Her phone rang as she continued to walk up the stairs. It was Grandma Luisa. Addie felt the fear climb from her gut to her heart and prayed it wasn't a call about Jake dying of an overdose. She noticed her hand shaking as she reached for the phone. *I've known him and loved him for eighteen years; now I feel the man I'm losing is a perfect stranger!*

## 42

She answered Luisa's phone call and let herself into her room, locking the door behind her.

"Addie?"

"Yes," she responded, realizing that hearing Luisa's voice also brought the visual memory of last night's debacle back into her consciousness. She sat in the armchair next to the loveseat and put the phone on the arm of the chair, speaker on. Luisa continued.

"Just checking in to see how you're doing."

"Thank God, I thought maybe…"

"Something happened to Jake?"

"Yes," she sighed, "I feel his survival is up for grabs right now…"

"Are you all right Addie?"

"I'm okay, considering. Had lunch, shower and a nap."

"Gracias a Dios," Luisa exclaimed, "you deserved a break. The girls told me Jake texted them around seven this morning. He said he had to go out of town on a story assignment, but I doubt it."

"It's going to be years dealing with the fallout from this," Addie groaned, "He said the doctor weaned him off the Oxycontin two months after the surgery, but he must have been getting it illegally after that, which is expensive; probably why he switched to heroin. I should have insisted he get help. Now I feel I colluded in his addiction getting out of hand."

"He made the choices every time."

"I know, but the drugs influence your choices. The FDA should never have approved that drug, it's created an epidemic of junkies like no other drug ever has; the US pharmaceutical companies are routing a lot of their drugs into the illicit market, and with their help, Jake is now in real danger."

Luisa sighed, then spoke in a half whisper.

"It all reminds me of what happened to your grandfather, how he went from a healthy life into one that killed him. It is easier to be angry than cry, so I am letting myself be angry at Jake. I pray he heads for a treatment center, before he touches any more street drugs."

The second she heard Luisa say street drugs, Addie felt the

fright roll up from her gut to her brain and couldn't think a positive thought.

"It's the overdose statistics, Grandma! The heroin from Mexico is so dangerous, he's gambling with his life, and, oh, God…must my girls go through what happened to me? Will they lose a father too?"

The thought that her daughters could suffer the loss of their father…and take her into that shock with them…like a reoccurring nightmare of Papa's death, pushed her past any sense of control.

"Grandma, is it hopeless? Some of the cartels are adding prescription strength fentanyl, that synthetic heroin, into the heroin they market, and hundreds of people in the US are overdosing every day! Almost thirteen thousand people died from that poison this year! A twenty-five percent increase, in just one year!"

Addie was up, pacing the room, and looked down at the courtyard. The hammocks were filling up, a few people remained at tables. Before Luisa called, Addie had finally begun to feel more balanced; now she felt like throwing her phone through the window.

"Grandma, I did a search of his computer this morning before I left home. Guess he thought I'd never find his hidden files of personalized photos he couldn't bring himself to part with. Over ten years of files. Many explicit ones with him in the photos. Even if he lives, if he promises to be faithful, how am I ever going to trust him again?" She went over to the bed and flopped down, her anger burning her insides.

"Well, I can answer that question," Addie pushed out the words, "the truth is, I'm never going to trust him again. I might have tried if his affair had been one meaningful relationship, but not this many women over this many years. I don't want Hep C or AIDS for God's sake. I'm pissed at him, but I don't want him to die!" Then it hit her.

"Oh, Grandma, I hope he's not the one that's going to die while I'm on this mission…it never occurred to me before now that his might be the death Mama warned me about."

"Enough for now, Addie, your thoughts are taking you in the wrong direction. You must focus on Joy and put Jake out of your mind for right now. I know, easy for me to say, but try, mija. Get some rest, you will cope better, these people are counting on you to take care of business down there. I will cover things here. The girls do not know what happened. I will not speak of any details. That is for you and Jake to do when the time comes."

"Yes, when the time comes…I trust you completely, you know that. Promise me one more thing if anything were to happen to me, don't let him live on the property unless he is completely clean and sober. I don't want him bringing people onto the property if he's running with a rough crowd. He can't get custody of the girls, Lizbeth's eighteen, Nita's 16. Legally, they are old enough to choose you and the only home they've ever known; no judge would listen to Jake on this. I'm going to put this in writing and mail it to you in the morning. Fortunately, the property is protected by the prenup agreement, with you and I the only owners and the girls listed as beneficiaries."

"I will honor your wishes, Mija. I wasn't going to bring it up. I love you and the girls. I love Joy, as much as my own breath. How I remember her beautiful little face when she was born…oh Dios! Call me, mañana, if you can. I know your heart is broken, I know you are scared. I know you can pour that energy into success. I love you, Addie, I am with you in spirit every moment. So is your mother in heaven as we have discovered; she's not telling us much right now, but she is on the job. Be safe."

"Te amo, Abuela, I will call tomorrow, I promise."

"Vaya con Dios," Luisa replied, then hung up as Addie flopped down on the couch.

She stared at the phone, took her habitual deep breath, then called Jake. When his phone rang, her hope returned, *his phone's not dead, that's a good sign.* Tears poured down her face…then it went to his voicemail. *Maybe he's unconscious somewhere and someone else has his phone…what if he's overdosed?*

"Jake…I'm here in Oaxaca. I'm very worried about you…I'm begging you to get into a treatment center, please. I care about you…please, please get help before it's too late. Call me, let me know you're okay…please." She hung up the phone and tossed it on the coffee table. *Oh, and by the way Jake, all that compassion I just laid out at your feet, was from the part of me that knows what's best. As for the rest of my mind, it's blown, not one good word for you there.*

173

## 43

The bunker door opened, Bella rushed down the stairs and into Joy's arms.

"Buenos Dias." Tonio said with a broad smile, and a glance that told her she hadn't imagined their last conversation.

"I didn't even hear you come down the stairs. What's up?"

"Papa wanted me to bring you up to eat with us. He's anxious this morning. They are packing up all our personal belongings today; my uncle will store them in the bunker when he moves here. We can't take much with us to the coast tomorrow. You ready?"

"Definitely." She had put on the jeans, red tank top, and hooded blue sweatshirt Adela gave her the previous day. They exchanged awkward glances as she moved past him and went up the stairs with Bella.

"I'll race you up the hill," he said, confirming he felt equally awkward about the idea of staying in the bunker.

They hurried up the hill, with Bella running circles around them until the brush got too thick. Their breath labored from the climb; laughing over their competitive ascent, they came through the patio gate and sat down at the table by the back door. Joy grabbed a breakfast burrito, a generous serving of fruit, and paused only to take in the aroma of Adela's spiced coffee. As she held the cup to her lips, she looked up to see Tonio, and found his eyes already fixed on her. His plate and cup were still empty.

"Cutting calories, or feeling too weak to serve yourself?"

"Neither," he said, "I got distracted." She wished she hadn't asked, and pointed at Bella to distract him further.

Bella appeared to be undaunted by the uphill climb, lounging on the warm patio tiles in a patch of direct sun. The macaw was walking around her as if he were seeing her for the first time, prompting her to roll onto her back and stare back at him. With one pounce, the macaw jumped to Bella's chest and launched himself into a celebratory flight around the yard. Bella barked at him, and ran a few circles of her own, with short barks to keep him engaged. Tonio filled his plate, laughing at them, and biting off the end of his burrito.

*Now it's my turn to watch him.* He was wearing a traditional

Zapotec shirt, jeans, and canvas loafers, his hair freshly shampooed and tied in a short ponytail. She watched his strong jaw working on the burrito, then forced herself to look away before he noticed.

Ramiro's booming voice, launched from inside the house, set off an alarm in Joy's brain. Tonio's arm reached out as she bolted toward the gate. She slid through his grasp and almost made it to the gate before he jumped in front of her.

"Joy, please!"

"He's losing it, screaming at Adela like that, let me go!" Tonio didn't move.

"Let me explain. Then maybe I can take you to the bunker, so you can't hear them."

"I don't feel anywhere is safe right now, the Zetas killed Rico, kidnapped Rosa, and..."

"Please, Joy, I'm hurting for Rosa too, she is like a sister to me, like my own blood. I am telling you the truth about Papa, he would never hurt any of us. I would not lie to you about Papa, and I am telling you he is having panic...uh..."

"Panic attack?"

"Yes. He is very scared right now. Mama wants to take me to her sister's in Michoacán, he doesn't want her go because he says there is too much fighting going on between cartels, vigilantes and the government."

"Is there?" Joy's fright abated as the shouting stopped.

"Yes. Let's finish eating quick, then you can help me clean the birdcage. I'll fill you in on Michoacán."

"If it gets loud again I want to go back to the bunker." As he promised, nothing escalated after Ramiro's initial outburst. They finished eating and headed for the bird cage. He grabbed a broom, opened the wire mesh door, began to sweep, and resumed his description of Michoacán's problems.

"It has been very bad in Michoacán at times, especially in the west. The newest cartel, Jalisco New Generation, wants control of the drug transport into California. They are more violent than the Sinaloa cartel, more like Zetas. Many say they are even more sadistic than the Zetas. In May they shot down a government helicopter that was sent to CJNG's territory. One shot from an RPG killed eight soldiers and one federal policeman. Nine families grieving, in part because the US won't legalize drugs their citizens are going to use anyway." He filled the birds' dish with seeds and exited the cage.

Joy gulped, and couldn't talk. She knew of Michoacán's rich indigenous history, rivaling the Aztecs, and had some knowledge of their geography, the colonial architecture, and of course, their amazing art, which she had connected with through a Facebook friend, an artist who lived in the capitol, Morelia.

"I said too much?" he asked. He closed the cage door, and nodded toward the table. "Can we go back? I want some of that flan and another coffee."

As they approached the back door and the table near the grill, Joy could tell the disagreement wasn't fully settled; voices would be raised every few minutes, then quiet down again. She decided to change the subject as they sat down to snack their way through an array of treats.

"Mama is clearing out the food before we leave."

Joy dove into some homemade pastries and coffee. She decided to start off with a casual discussion about their backgrounds rather than focus on Ramiro.

"Tonio, you said you have two fathers…well, guess what, so do I."

Tonio's voice softened and the glistening black of his eyes sought out hers.

"Have you met him?"

"No, I never lived with him or my birthmother. I was adopted when I was born. I have to talk with my birthmother to find out more about him. The adoption agency description was brief. She was a college graduate, in law enforcement. Half Mexican, half French. He was a resident of the Washington D.C. metropolitan area, Latino, around eighteen years old, five ten, a body builder. Sounds like someone she met at the gym and had a fling with, but who knows?" She helped herself to some chocolates Adela had put out with the snacks.

"How do you feel about being adopted?"

"I think I took my cue from my parents, that it was a blessing for them, and a decision my birthmom made to give me a life she wasn't able to. My parents always assured me that she loved me deeply, but what I'm most eager for is to see my Mexican face in hers. When I hear why she did it, I will understand even more." She handed him the last chocolate. "I have a close friend who was adopted, but she feels like she doesn't fit in her family at all. Then I have another friend who was born into his family and has the same problem. I met a birthmother my age who said she was forced by her family to give her baby up when she was in high school. She said she's in a support group with a birthmother who was promised an open adoption with visits, and the adoptive parents ditched her and her family, took the baby, and moved away. The more I learn, the more I see a lot has to be changed in adoption, especially the secrecy part. There may be rare situations that require privacy for the safety of the child, but there could be some separate legal criteria for that." She poured more coffee for both of them.

"This coffee really gets you talking, doesn't it? But really, I think it is good you will be able to meet your birthmother. There has to be a painful truth there, that explains why she felt she had to do it. What pain she must have felt to lose you! Papa Ramiro married my mother and adopted me after my first father was killed; their wedding and my adoption were honored by a Zapotec ceremony. There was no official Mexican court action...the risk outweighed the benefits."

"Such a luscious garden," Joy said, distracted by the view, "in San Francisco, most of the gardens are tiny, you must have an acre inside here...hey, you mentioned the Zapotec ceremony; where did Zapotecs come from? How many remain?"

"A lot. There are more Zapotecs than any other indigenous group in Mexico; in Oaxaca since 700 BC; but during the conquest of the Spanish, their population was reduced by three hundred thousand people." Joy's face registered the shocking news. The depressing subject was countered with lilting music inside the house; they both laughed over the apparent recovery of peace between Ramiro and Adela.

"Sounds like they're chillin' now," Joy said, "go on...the Zapotecs?"

"Well, Despite the conquest, we have utilized our ancient reproductive skills, and have managed to survive through relative isolation. Most don't speak Spanish or English, even now. Our

177

population is about one million in Mexico, and over a hundred fifty thousand in California. If they're undocumented, they are often afraid to seek help."

"I guess they don't know California Social Services doesn't report undocumented residents," Joy said as he pushed away from the table.

"Help me with the garden while we talk, I need to stay busy."

Joy walked with him. He picked up a basket with garden tools, and pointed to a filled watering can sitting next to a wide cistern filled with water. She followed him down the first row as he spoke to her without eye contact, began digging weeds and trimming dead branches. Joy came behind him, alternately raking up the cuttings and weeds, and watering as he moved along.

"Are you going to tell me the rest of your personal story, Tonio?" *I hope he doesn't take offense at me prodding him.*

"I'm not used to anyone asking me this; your curiosity is well meant, I can see that. So, I will honor it." She noted a tenderness, an openness to intimacy she hadn't experienced with him before. *He's decided to trust me; I will need to honor that as well.*

"My parents...it made sense for my mother to marry Papa Ramiro. We needed protection and Papa needed someone to share his grief with, someone who loved my first father as much as he did. And Mama shares Papa's passion for education, so at first, I believe it was a practical decision, then it grew into much more." He looked up at her, gesturing with his weeding tool for emphasis.

"Joy, you ask me all this, but I feel you want to know everything in such a short time."

"Okay, Benito Junior, I admit it, I'm worried about tomorrow. If I'd met you at college, I'd be taking my time, believe me. But..."

He stood, moved very close, until they were inches apart, staring at each other, into an uncertain future.

Bella walked between them with her tennis ball, dripping water from its float in the cistern. She was completely wet, too, and eager to share the refreshing water. Before they caught on to her, she shook over, and over; banishing their blues.

"Come on girl! Dance for Señorita Joy, show her what you can do!" Bella decided to shake again, flinging another large arc of drops. They jumped away, laughed, and mimicked her shake. She barked at Tonio and sat down. He repeated the dance cue, snapping again and again, to no avail.

"She's really good at standing up on her hind feet and hopping around in a little circle dance, but she will only do it for Papa, no matter how often Mama and I try to do it."

"Well," Joy said laughing, "Looks like she enjoys getting you to do your trick of snapping your fingers and imitating your papa. Sounds like a joke a smart dog would enjoy."

"Ahhh, well. Enough of her tricking me! Are you sure you still want me to tell you how we escaped the Zetas?

"Yes, I am sure—really."

His sweatshirt was quickly discarded; the tank top was damp from his work in the garden, but he left it on. Joy prayed his story was riveting; hopefully it would take her mind off his beautiful skin, which had rich brown tones like Adela's. He began to work his way down a row of large planter boxes that abutted the tall back fence, weeding the boxes, trimming the vines.

"Working in this garden has been a chore of mine since we got it started. You don't have to work too, I'm doing it to stay calm. I'm going to miss this place…but I can visit later if I want to, it will stay in the family. My parents always said they would give the place to Mama's brother and his family…when the time came for us to leave."

The planter boxes had trellises to support flowering vines that climbed up the fence and branched out; the effect was an array of tropical beauty. She pitched in to help, ready to listen.

"Well, here goes," he began slowly. Joy sensed his mood shifting downward as he spoke.

"My papa Ramiro and his brother Miguel were conscripted into the Gulf Cartel through threat of death, when they were in their twenties. My papa Diego was kidnapped by the cartel from his parents' car in 1990-something when he was a teenager. When Mama was fourteen, in 1994, her parents paid to be smuggled with her across the

Texas border, but their entire group was stopped near Nuevo Laredo, the headquarters of the Gulf cartel. Her parents were killed, she was taken to the cartel boss as a gift. She refuses to talk about it."

"I can understand that; just the thought of a little girl being used by that disgusting boss makes me want to hit something. Hey, let's take a break and sit over there in that corner."

Tonio nodded. Once they disposed of the cuttings they walked to the small patio in the far corner of the yard. Joy gratefully sank onto the padded chaise, Tonio onto a nearby chair.

"So go on, Tonio, please."

"Okay. Well, compared to the rest of the soldiers, Miguel and Ramiro were getting too old to smuggle drugs and negotiate with the dealers in Texas like they did when they were younger. But they were educated, spoke Inglés, and they knew how to negotiate. So the cartel boss put them in charge of any kidnappings the cartel did for ransom. The cartel's soldiers would do the actual kidnapping, then deliver the victim to Miguel and Papa Ramiro. They had a safe house in Nuevo Laredo, where they kept one or two people at a time, and the turnaround time was rarely more than one or two months. So, the boss knew how to use their skills instead of, shall we say, disposing of them."

"How did your parents get under Ramiro's protection?"

My parents were young and too frightened to try to escape. Papa Ramiro knew they were being abused, so he asked the boss if they could work for him and Miguel at their hideout. The cartel boss didn't want Mama anymore, because she was starving herself and very skinny. So he sent Papa Diego with her to keep the safe house protected, the prisoners secure, clean, healthy and well fed." He got up and retrieved a bowl of fruit from a round table near the chairs, took a mango and passed the bowl to Joy.

"No thanks, I'm eager to hear the rest," she said. He ate half the mango and threw it like a baseball into the compost pile, where it was quickly spotted and attacked by three of the love birds.

"All right, this is where the story gets less painful. Papa Diego was crazy about Mama, and she welcomed his care and protection. They declared themselves married, and Mama began to eat again. She became healthy enough to have a baby, and they had me in '95. My parents and I began to learn English from Miguel and Papa Ramiro."

"Wait a minute, it just occurred to me that Rosa was born in '92. How can Miguel be her father if he didn't move to Oaxaca City until 2000?"

"Because he had work that took him to Oaxaca City. He and Papa Ramiro had a smuggling route for a few years, before they were set up with the kidnapping job. The cartel provided the plane and a pilot, and they handled all the negotiations. Mostly, they bought Columbian cocaine and weapons in Guatemala and flew them north, with a regular stop in Oaxaca City before heading for Nuevo Laredo. Miguel met Rosa's mother in Oaxaca City. He knew she would reject him if she knew he was with the cartel, so he told her he was a business manager for a US corporation with factories in Mexico."

"What a cad," Joy said, "even all those years ago he was a lying manipulator."

"He wanted her bad enough to get married…she was very beautiful, much like Rosa. But after Rosa was born, Rosa's mama found out Miguel's lie and she left him. He made sure she had plenty of money, and pushed hard for Rosa's education in languages, especially after he moved to Oaxaca City in 2000. Probably the only time Miguel had a positive influence on anyone's future!"

Bella started looking for the ball, which had rolled to an unknown destination. Joy grabbed one from under the chaise and threw it to her. She brought it back for Joy to throw again, which she did.

"Okay, history man, tell me the rest." Tonio got up and grabbed the shovel leaning against the fence, went to the compost pile, and began to shovel the processed compost from the base, onto the weeds and cuttings he'd put on top of the pile. Joy stayed close to hear him, and dutifully played ball with Bella while Tonio talked.

"Okay then. Where was I? Oh yes, well, here is where everything changed, mostly the escalation of violence was a response to the Mexican Government cooperating with the US War on Drugs. In the late 1990's, just before we left, the new boss for the Gulf Cartel, Cardenas Guillan, hired over thirty defectors from Mexico's Airborne Special Forces Unit. They were hard core paramilitary troops. They called themselves the Zetas."

"So, they imported their military culture into the Gulf cartel?"

"That, along with the black ops side of military culture. The

181

Zeta leader, Arturo Guzman Decena, was a professional terrorist. He trained both willing and kidnapped recruits at boot camps, taught them specialized torture and interrogation techniques, supplied them with smuggled grenades from the military arsenals of Guatemala; plus, automatic weapons, and RPG's, some possibly from the US black market—plus explosives like dynamite and C-4, the plastic stuff." Shaking his head, he retrieved the watering can, and filled it, pouring water over the compost pile as he talked.

"The Zeta leaders conditioned recruits to terrorize anyone who opposed them. They got everyone high on drugs, then turned them loose to kill and torture people, like villagers who had loyalties to a rival cartel. They often burned them up in their own homes, and once burned down a police station with police barricaded inside."

He walked over to Joy, who was sitting cross-legged on a woven mat in the shade. She had removed the sweatshirt and pulled off the scarf that secured her hair when they got soaked by Bella. Her tank top and jeans were dry enough. The tops of the tall pines were often wrapped in clouds, but the sun was reaching them for now. There was a fluctuating breeze, blowing her hair and his. Joy looked up, willing herself to support his story.

"Joy, by any chance, did you learn in school how the Romans kept hundreds of living and rotting victims on crosses along the roads to a conquered city? Just to terrorize citizens so they would be afraid to fight?"

"Yes, but when I first learned it I thought they were the only conquerors who did that; then I found out ALL the conquerors terrorized people into submission. Testosterone run amuck!" He chuckled at her jab.

"That was the Zeta's goal too. Horrific mutilations were their calling card. Thankfully, we lived apart from the soldiers, who roamed from one raid to the next, or spent all their time with the drug trade, and the boss took Papa's loyalty for granted." He put the tools away and headed for the cistern to get a drink; she followed him.

She watched Tonio as he took the watering can, filled it from the cistern, bent over, and poured water on his head. He used his sweatshirt for a towel, then shook out his hair. His lovebirds had decided to leave the fence for a drink; one came straight for his shoulder; the rest pranced around the edge of the cistern. Tonio brightened at the sight. Joy watched drops of water fall slowly from his wet hair, reflecting the sun as they moved across his skin.

"This is Pico, he is the papa of the babies. He is the one who teaches them how to fly and where to fly, and who to trust. Don't look for the macaw, Joy, he's probably on his perch in Mama's studio." But Joy's mind was elsewhere...

*Predictability, Joy thought, we can't predict our future right now; that's what's making this such a surrealistic experience. Since Tonio moved here, his life has been predictable. My life in San Francisco was planned. Now our lives are up for grabs, literally.* She looked toward the house and wondered why Ramiro and Adela were taking so long to come outside. *Did they get a phone call that we don't know about yet? Are plans changing again?*

## 45

The warm shower had calmed them, and with Tonio and Joy outside, they had the opportunity to share it; Adela always loved the way Ramiro shampooed her hair, then she shampooed his, including his crumb-catching beard. Their decision had been made; they would leave in the morning for the coast, then, hopefully, to the US.

Ramiro had displayed as much confidence in their future as possible, yet Adela, as she followed him into the bedroom, found it difficult to take in his reassurances. She wanted something more comforting than words, and approached him with a smile and a caress.

"Mi amor," he took her hand from his bare chest, kissed it, and looked down into her eyes, then to his flat stomach "you have watched me get old, but it is good you never had to watch me get fat."

"We all get old, it is just not my time yet. If we get to the US, I will be able to see your handsome face again; you will have no need to disguise yourself with this bush!" She pulled gently on his beard and walked slowly backward to the bed. He followed; she could see the pleasure he took looking at her body.

She had changed much in fifteen years; when they were without clothes, as now, she felt beautiful, saw each of her scars as a testament to her strength, as did he, with those he received when the cartel took possession of his life.

He had done an artful job of convincing her she was made pure with each new day. It had taken years, but the traumas of the past had receded as every fresh sunrise promised them another day of freedom. Adela reclined on the colorful quilt; she pulled him close, aware he had things he needed to say.

"Yes, I don't want to die in this beard; it would be good to go where I want without fear of recognition. But, our years here have been a blessing. It has been good to see us heal from the past and learn to love again." Adela rested her head against his chest and surrounded his body with her arms.

"If not for you, 'Miro, the world would never have become mine. I had not read a book, I had never thought I would be speaking English, or Spanish, or become an artist who could sell her work in the US, and surely," she looked up into his eyes, caressing his face with her hand, "I never knew that a man would ever want to give a woman so much pleasure!"

"It is a good thing you learned—now you know what to look for—an equal opportunity lover!" Both of them rolled into laughs and hugs that culminated in a warm, unhurried kiss. He rolled on top of her, their warm skin seemed to merge. He supported the weight of his upper body on his elbows while his fingers combed through her damp hair.

"You are an inspiration, Adela...the healer of my soul." He kissed her face until her smile was filled with teeth, then kissed her nose and lay on his side facing her, tracing a line with his finger up her arm, along her collarbone, and down between her breasts to her navel, which he gently covered with his open hand. A quiet drone of hummingbirds outside the open bedroom window lulled Adela into a sensual calm she welcomed. He continued baring his soul with touching intimacy.

"You could have left here when Tonio's papa died, but you stayed. You could have left me later, after your paintings were selling and you could afford your own place, but you stayed. You could have tolerated me instead of loving me...but you chose love."

"I feel love chose the three of us," she said in a firm tone.

"Adela, my heart needs to speak, so be patient with me. I am remembering, after Diego's funeral ceremony, how you placed little Tonio in my arms and gave me the task to be his father, to teach him what he would need for a good life."

"And you did teach him, more than I ever expected."

"He made it easy for me. The boy is magic; he has a way of pulling you right into the present, with his beguiling curiosity and loving heart; oh, the precious days we shared. I need to say it, Adela, muchas gracias, Adela mia, muchas gracias."

"Five thousand four hundred and seventy-five days," she stated with emphasis. When he looked puzzled, she explained. "I admit it, I used the calculator, but I was in a summing mood this morning, looking back over the fifteen years we have lived here."

Adela moved his hand over her body, watching him respond.

"Let us be together now," she invited him, "tomorrow is very uncertain...we will do our best to survive it without being separated."

185

## 46

"So, I review my turbulent past to satisfy your curiosity. I will tell you about our escape from the cartel, but I need some water first."

Joy sensed Tonio's ambivalence about opening up; perhaps it was too much too soon. She hoped it would proceed smoothly; she had her doubts, but thought it wise to let him take his time. She moved to the cistern, dipped her hands in the water and splashed it on her face; then, considering the birds, Bella, and night visitors to the cistern, she decided to drink the cleaner water from the spigot that drew directly from the spring. It was delicious.

Tonio sat on the edge of the cistern, held his arm out, and, because the papa love bird trusted his arm for a perch, two of his babies followed. Tonio seemed to relax as he caressed the papa bird's head with utmost gentleness, and began to describe the escape.

"The Zetas were out to take over the Gulf cartel, and Papa Ramiro, Miguel and my parents knew they had to escape, and thought it best to sneak out late at night. I was five, so the year was 2000. We headed south from cartel headquarters in Nuevo Laredo, which is just across the border from Laredo, Texas. Our destination was Oaxaca City and the Sierra Juárez Mountains, because my mother had relatives in the Zapotec village that's close to us here. A twenty-hour drive, almost sixteen hundred kilometers. They must have slipped me some allergy meds or something, because I slept most of the trip, except for a few encounters on the way."

"It's so easy to imagine you snuggled in your mom's arms, just sleeping the trip away," Joy said.

"If only it had stayed that way!" The birds startled, and Pico circled the yard with them once, then returned to Tonio. Tonio laughed and did his best to edit his story at this point.

"Highway 85 south from Nuevo Laredo is patrolled by narcos; even now. That night we were spared death only because the narcos were too busy to even see us; they were defending their border crossing into Texas from rivals determined to break through with a big shipment. Mama pulled me down to the floor of the car while Ramiro drove into the desert with the lights off, got around the battle, and rejoined the highway further south. After that, Ramiro says they prayed and drove like maniacs and prayed again, to be spared and allowed to live in peace."

Joy visualized five-year-old Tonio, a refugee from the cartel, escaping death with his loved ones, and compared it to her privileged life in San Francisco. She put her hand on his arm and looked up at him, her heart pounding.

"Tonio, when I think what you went through just to escape! These cartels are like a cancer growing out of control, they seem impossible to stop!" Her fear gained momentum; visions of her kidnapping filled her with rage—like lightening striking dry grass—and the flames exploded. She stood up, looked down at Tonio sitting on the edge of the cistern and yelled.

"Gangsters are just animals! I hate them!" Bella barked at her. Pico, flew off again, his babes in tow. Joy's rant ceased; she knew she'd gone too far. Tonio scowled at her, rose in one move, thrust both hands in the air, and made her work to hear his angry half-whispered response.

"There is no doubt our determination to be free of the cartel finally matched up with God's, because once we committed to our escape, we were blessed beyond measure." He stood up, moved within a few inches of her face and yelled.

"As for the people we left behind, you need to understand something, my lovely Latina! If you had been in their situations, you may have made the same choices. Please don't consider them or us undeserving of compassion! Cartels brainwash these kids!"

"I didn't mean to insult your family, Tonio!" She was pleading, but he wouldn't stop.

"When greedy people control the resources of a country through illegal means, they infiltrate the government and set up everything to take more from the people; lower their wages, take their land, their resources."

Joy began backing up the angrier he got. She knew he was right, so she let him rant. He was breathing fast, passionate in his determination to get through to her.

"Look, the cartels extort the business owners, who then pass the losses on to the poor employees. Poor parents are helpless; they have to leave their children to watch each other so they can work more jobs. Even with a parent at home, the gangsters recruit the kids; the parents don't dare fight for them or the gang will retaliate."

Under pressure but not frightened, Joy backed up to the fence, under the shade of the pines. Bella was too nervous to sit, so she circled around them, and dodged backwards, barking as Tonio's next lecture emerged, then circled around him again, whining.

"So, with their parents intimidated, the kids run loose, easy prey for recruiters. The gangs give them drugs, money, nice clothes and all the food they can eat. They feel they belong to a powerful family that can really take care of them, and their loyalty grows. At some point they cross the line, justify everything they are asked to do, and they are trapped, so there's nothing left but to take pride in living and dying for their cartel. As for the kidnapped, it's simple. Join, or die!" Joy felt the momentum of his anger and turned away from him, only to suffer his reaction.

"Joy! This pattern is taking over South and Central America, Mexico, and now the US. It's a global pattern, destroying democracy. The poor are expendable scapegoats, they work for little or no pay, are imprisoned, forced into crime, children and women sold into sex trafficking, exploited, and exterminated! And yes, they are angry…life itself has been devalued, for their parents, for them, and their victims!"

Joy was crying, unable to argue because she knew he was right, unable to speak because his rage had paralyzed her, but she had to try. Bella was whining by her side; She stopped crying, put her hand on Bella to reassure her, then walked up to Tonio and did her best to be understood. Her voice was loving, respectful, and soft.

"Tonio, have you ever been kidnapped?" He must have been expecting a slap or a fight. She watched his feelings play out across his face; at first it was the tilted head, the wide-open eyes, then confusion…she could almost see his brain firing, desperately searching for her true intentions. Then he got it. He relaxed, shook his head slowly, smiled, and blinked away the tears that pooled in his eyes.

"Only indirectly. I was born a cartel slave. Joy, that's as close as I got to being kidnapped. I am sorry…I wanted you to understand about that cycle of recruitment and victimization. But it brought back your memory of being kidnapped, your rage to fight back, your terror when you knew you were outnumbered." He looked away from her. "And your shame…that you cooperated instead of running or fighting." He walked up close and lowered his voice.

"I was yelling at you to have compassion for gangsters, yet I am guarding you, kidnapped by my papa. And I over-reacted. I know it is hard to see their humanity, once those kids are indoctrinated by the cartels, they can become sadistic robots, it is true. But at one point, they were loved, and a few of them manage to escape and change their ways. I think that's what I wanted to make sure you knew."

Joy felt a flush of relief. She nodded and smiled; she was ready to let it go. *He obviously has passion for the plight of the poor; nothing to be ashamed about there. It's like a re-run of the Spanish conquest, only it's cartels stealing the resources instead of Spain. Tonio sounds like a modern Benito for sure.*

"Let's go snack on some of that food before the birds eat it all." She walked ahead of him toward the picnic table.

"In truth," he said, catching up with her, "Papa has no gang. Miguel saw the news story about your father's project on the internet and read about your family's plans for Christmas in Oaxaca City. Miguel knew Papa had gotten a very bad health report; he convinced him to do this job before he died so he could get us set up in the US." Tonio slowly reached to touch Joy's arm, and when she didn't flinch or move away, he stepped closer and finished.

"Rico, who drove the cab, he was in on it, and the other men you saw, who stopped the cab on Christmas Eve, they are small time hustlers with Miguel down in Oaxaca City."

If Joy believed anything, she believed Tonio was no gangster. Ramiro's mistake had been to let Miguel convince him he had run out of options.

"First, I want to say I'm sorry your Papa is so sick." He nodded.

"And, Tonio, you were right that I reacted to what you were saying. I had a flashback to Christmas Eve while you were shouting, and I felt that rage again. It's anger that makes us stereotype people. My therapist says when we get angry we end up with a distorted perception that lacks compassion; for yourself, or someone else. I see why you got upset."

"You understand. Good. I would like to finish what we started, to tell you what you wanted to know about us, instead of trying to educate you about something you already knew." Joy smiled, shook his hand with mock formality, and cautioned him.

"Talk, and talk quick. You owe me the story and we are out of time, I think, so no long version." He joined in the forgiving ambience she had created and began to finish his tale, grabbing a handful of tortilla chips and a mango. Joy took a mango and poured herself a lemonade.

They headed for the smaller patio near the far corner of the fence. The pine forest began just outside the stucco walls, and for once, Joy felt comforted by the surrounding trees. She sat; he pulled his chair closer to hers, flopped down, and pushed his hair away from his face. His eyes focused on hers as he launched into his tale.

"I mentioned that God blessed us on our trip; to hear Ramiro tell it, God was rewarding their courage to escape what he called the Devil's cartel. Papa Ramiro told me about these years as I got older, so his story and my memories are all mixed up at this point."

"Go on, I just want the story, now I'm more curious than ever," Joy urged.

"Okay," he shifted in his chair, took a few bites of his mango, wiping the juice from his mouth with his hand.

"We were driving on a lonely stretch of road that disappeared into a forested area, we heard a plane, then saw it when it flew over our car; a small plane, sputtering smoke, coming down, right in front of us on the road, trying to land. Their landing was hard to watch, but I could not take my eyes off it. The pilot managed to line up with the road, but the plane bounced again and again, then swerved, and crashed into the bushes and trees." Joy was hooked, and leaned forward to hear every word. He noticed her interest and spoke faster.

"Ramiro drove like a maniac to get there in case it was a family that needed help, but no, it was two men, both dead. Miguel was passed out drunk in our car, so my papa Diego climbed up in the plane, found a fire extinguisher and put out the fire. Then Papa Ramiro went inside. The smoke disappeared in the wind, it was starting to get dark, I got really scared. Mama and I had been told to wait in the car when they ran to the plane, in case things got dangerous."

"Who did it turn out to be?"

"Not what we expected! Papa Diego jumped out of the plane, ran fast to us with two big canvas bags in his hands, and opened one. The bag was filled with cash! Freeze-wrapped packets of hundreds;

packaged just like drugs. Papa Ramiro came out of the plane with more bags, threw them in the car and drove us out of there, fast; felt like the Batmobile! No wonder; altogether, Papa said it was about a million dollars!" He slapped his leg for emphasis, and gave her some backstory.

"A rival cartel was transporting the cash south to Guatemala to pay for a purchase of weapons, chemicals, and drugs. There was a letter to the Guatemalan broker, explaining they had huge markets in the US and wanted to discuss an exclusive trade agreement. The pilot had the shopping list right there in the money bag!"

"So that's how your family got the cash to set up here."

"Our share funded us and helped the villagers for fifteen years."

"That money was a gift from heaven," Joy nodded, "I agree with Ramiro on that. Instead of it going to people who would do harm, it went to take your family out of crime altogether—well, except for Miguel—it was a true blessing."

Tonio stood up and approached Joy. He stopped about an arm's length away, his dark eyes bared his soul to hers.

"Joy…I want to say that I believe you are a gift from heaven."

Joy stood, smiled, and felt so overcome with her sense of connection to Tonio, she looked down at her feet unable to speak. *I have never felt this way about anyone before, as if I've known him forever. How can I be so happy in the middle of all this?* She looked up into his eyes and when she saw his expression, she believed he must have heard every word she had just said to herself.

As if he intended to validate the warm truce between Tonio and Joy, Pico returned with his babies, and guided them to find a perch on their shoulders, heads, arms, whatever they offered. Perhaps he, too, could feel the growing heartfelt ambiance.

## 47

"Adela," Ramiro called from the kitchen, "would you join me at the table for a café de olla?

She was packing some of her paintings in the studio next to their bedroom; praying her work would stay safe.

"Yes, that will be good; one minute."

The smell of the coffee, brewed with orange peel, a cinnamon stick and brown sugar, enticed Adela to the dining room faster than she planned. She saw Ramiro seated at the large table, looking across it, at the window to the patio and garden. She pulled her chair close to his, kissed his bearded cheek, and grasped her coffee cup.

This was their favorite spot. Over the years, they had enjoyed private talks, a huge variety of music, meals, and delectable beverages at this table; often watching Tonio and Bella playing in the garden with a few friends from the village, hunting lizards, dunking in the cistern on a warm day. Now, he sat on the tiles, teasing his birds while they bathed.

"Remember when Tonio got the birds for Christmas? I think my brother was as happy as Tonio, and Bella was overcome with interest." Ramiro nodded and sipped his coffee.

"He was only about seven then," he said.

"And you built the cage so carefully, teaching Tonio how to use the tools, letting him learn, he was so proud!" Adela indulged in the pleasure of the event, the way it had evolved into a true welcoming of new family members. The birds ended up with the big cage against the house, in which to sleep, eat, and, in the case of the lovebirds, breed. A small window gave them intermittent access to the inside of the house from their cage, and often they flew through their cage's exterior doorway into the garden to be with Tonio and Bella. Adela had tried to prepare Tonio for the chance they would depart for the forest if given these freedoms, but they never left.

Adela looked over at Ramiro's peaceful expression, then looked outside again. As she reviewed the years, she believed he was doing the same. Their impending departure had created a presence and power of its own. They sat close, blowing on their coffee to cool it down, enjoying the spicy bouquet as it rose to their faces. As with their recent lovemaking, no detail of these moments was being taken for granted.

Many important decisions had been made at this table, and many delicious meals shared with their friends from the Zapotec village; those they knew they could trust. Adela moved her fingertips around the decorative carved edge of the stained hardwood table. The wood burning tool had been purchased for Tonio when he was about ten. First, she had to master its use herself, thus the hours of work on the table, taken over by Tonio, who had a careful touch and recalled everything she taught him. Tears came unbidden when she recalled teaching him—then fortunately, Ramiro distracted her.

"Adela, my love, look to the garden; Tonio and Joy and Bella, and the birds, hopping onto their shoulders. A few of the baby lovebirds landing on their heads, getting tangled in their hair, requiring rescue...ha!"

Adela looked out through their purple sage vine. For years, it had been growing outside on the trellis that bordered their big window. Its vines were always finding their way across the window, such that seeing in from the outside was almost impossible.

From the inside, they could see out through the open spaces the vine allowed, and fully enjoy their private view from the table. Like the day Tonio tried his first cigarette, sure he couldn't be seen—but they had watched him choke hard—he had thrown it down and stomped on it like a venomous spider, never to touch a cigarette again.

Today's view was one Adela hadn't expected; she followed Ramiro's excited prompt, looked past the vine's fuzzy purple flowers and lime-green leaves, and saw a tall beautiful man, filling out a tank top and jeans like one of those bronze New York models she had seen on television. Tonio had Diego's height. Adela's Zapotec people were typically closer to five feet, so she maintained her curiosity about Tonio's tall European ancestors.

Tonio's flowing black hair, his muscular build, and large delicate hands seemed to move in slow motion as he reached out to carefully untangle the baby lovebird from Joy's hair. For the first time since she arrived, she had loosed her wavy black hair from its tie and left it free, to be lifted here, lifted there, in the lazy waft of the mountain's afternoon breezes. Adela felt she was looking back at her own youth.

"I...I knew when I saw them earlier today...they were mature kids, I could see that, but I was looking at them like adolescents!"

Ramiro laughed, then rubbed his hands over his face as if to clear his vision.

"I know exactly what you mean. In this moment, I see them as they are; a fully-grown man and woman, playing in a tropical garden, with Bella, the birds, the wind, all orchestrated by the love they are in." He reached to wipe her awestruck tears with gentle fingertips, and spoke in a voice more loving than she had ever heard.

"I can tell you now, Adela, what I have waited to tell you. Now that the Holy Spirit has gifted us with a reassuring sign. This is good, very good, because…"

"I already know. You saw the doctor again, then came home and said nothing until now, so I know what he said."

Silence. Adela knew they were both taking in the truth, heartbeat by heartbeat. A minute passed, Adela was mute. Then he spoke.

"Adela, do this for me. Sit by my side here for a while. This may be the last time I will ever see Tonio as I had dreamed he would become; his body powerful and healthy, his mind educated, his heart embracing a truly lovely woman. I suppose it is possible, of course, my soul may be graced with visits after I pass."

"But it will not…be…the same," she whispered, in tears.

"You are right. But some way, I have a feeling it might be even better for you and Tonio. When God's grace helped us escape the cartel, Tonio was five, and you were only twenty. The same age Tonio is now. We never told Tonio—why would we—Diego was strung out on smack and cocaine before we ever left the cartel. We know why he went to Oaxaca City right after we moved here. This home was supposed to be his detox, but he could not do it, so we lost him."

They paused a moment, in the quiet of the room. It was quieter still outside. The wind had picked up, the macaw and lovebirds had gone into their cage; its solid wood sides, bottom and roof created their favorite windbreak.

Jays had invaded and were cleaning up some of the tortilla chips from the picnic table. Adela and Ramiro watched Tonio put on his sweatshirt, and Joy followed suit with hers. What warmth had been present that afternoon was mixing with the wind from the low clouds overhead. Ramiro took his eyes away from the garden, turned in his seat, and took both of Adela's hands.

"So, I was telling you my feelings, while we have privacy, and I do have a deep feeling, you know, an honest feeling, the kind you have learned to trust. I am now seventy-two. You are thirty-five. Much has been accomplished. Tonio is a man, a skilled fighter, fluent in Zapotec, English and Spanish, and a scholar. You have taught me many, many wonderful things since we moved here, things I can take with me when my time arrives." He graced her cheek with his fingertips and shared his prepared speech.

"You have learned Spanish and English, which I know will serve you. Your soul showed you how to paint your unique style, and we found you a way to market your paintings, here, and then in the U.S., and now your associates are putting your designs on sweatshirts and T shirts for stores in California. God be praised for the internet. You will always have enough money to live well, once we get you and Tonio to California." He started coughing, couldn't stop, and had to walk around until it subsided. Adela patted his back when he sat down.

"We don't know if they will really let us go, or if you will go to jail, or we may all go to jail." She began to weep quietly, and put her head on his chest. He held her, and did his best to persuade her.

"My feelings, Adela, I am trusting them. I am too sick to control what happens, but God is not too weak to keep me alive until the time is right for me to go. As for jail, I know enough about the police to know they don't want to put every criminal's family in jail with him because they had some small role." He was still holding one of her hands, and pressed it over his heart. With his other hand, he lifted her chin, so he could look in her eyes.

"This is where I say goodbye, mi amor…"

"What? You just said…"

"No," he whispered, "let me finish." His voice gained a soft volume. "I mean this moment, right now, is the moment I want us to both remember…this is our chance to say goodbye…in love, in peace, in quiet, with no one else around. When my time comes I might die too quick; to save this for later might mean we never get to have it. Can you do this with me, my love?"

Adela shook her head back and forth, slowed, then became still, nodded her head in assent and raised her eyes to his. She took both of his powerful hands in hers, her heart pounding like her papa's Zapotec drum, as if she were drumming Ramiro's departure from his body in this very moment. Tears welled in his eyes as she opened to his farewell message. He spoke slowly. Before he finished, she knew these were his dying words, his final legacy, a structure in which she could remain safe in the world after he passed to the soul realm.

"Adios, Adela. Protect your connection to your soul and to Spirit. Never close that door with drugs, crime, alcohol, a bad man, or a thirst for fame. Just stay with your soul and it will lead you into its plan for you, and out of any kind of pain you will encounter." His hands moved slowly from below her ears, along the edge of her jaw and held there; he stared deep into her eyes. "And most important…live in the company of wise people. Do you promise me?"

"Yes, yes!" Tears gently touched her cheeks and rolled over his hands as she spoke.

"My heart is drumming, to bless you and honor you in this moment." She kissed him on the mouth, "You have been my personal northern star; my guide out of hell, back to my home, near my people, to become who I am. Yes, my love, this is the moment we will remember as our goodbye, with our hearts at peace.

He leaned into her, his arms surrounding her, then turned his head to see Tonio and Joy. She joined his gaze, satisfied and at peace, as if he created it for her.

"After I pass, tell Tonio what we saw through this window. Tell him I have this scene in my heart wherever I am. And know the same goes for you. This moment and all the others we have had." Her eyes overflowed with tears once again, nor could his be contained.

Adela embraced him as if it were truly their last time, and felt his love take its rightful and permanent place in her heart, where it would abide with her forever. She had believed she would never find love equal to his once he passed. His words had changed that feeling. When he declared she would find a worthy relationship, she received a clear vision, a loving gift from Spirit—that Ramiro would be there at the perfect time, guiding the right man directly into her arms.

## 48

While Tonio was talking, Bella had found the giant squirrel of her dreams; perhaps bigger than she felt comfortable with. She started running her paws as she lay on her side in deep sleep, whined, barked, then growled as if fighting for her life; so loud, so angry, she flipped onto her back, flung her head from side to side, flailed her paws in the air in an effort to kick the monster off.

"Bella! Basta!" shouted Tonio, and her eyes flipped open. "Bella, you're okay," he patted his thigh to get her attention. She stood, then shook hard, as if she were trying to shake off the bad dream. She walked to him, and looked around the garden—as if the phantom attacker might be roaming somewhere among the roses and vegetables. Joy gave her a reassuring massage, and moved to the small patio, in the far corner of the yard.

Tonio followed suit. Near the tall fence and the taller trees; they lounged in the padded chairs, enjoying the breeze, watching the birds from the forest swoop down to the cistern for water. The variety of bird calls from the surrounding trees made Joy's precious time outdoors even more magical.

"This reminds me of my early childhood," Joy whispered, hoping the birds wouldn't startle and fly off. "Whenever I would see wildlife for the first time—a bird, a giraffe, whatever—I was sure each new living thing I saw had just been created that instant!"

"I remember some of that, moving from northern Mexico to Oaxaca; the biodiversity here is exceptional, mostly due to the subtropical climate and geography, but as a little kid, wow…it's an endless series of life forms showing up in colors and shapes you never expected. Moving here from the desolate landscape of Nuevo Laredo was like being born again."

Joy wanted to hear the rest of Tonio's story before they were interrupted, so she encouraged him once more.

"Do you feel like telling me the rest?"

Tonio responded with a smile, and a shrug; Joy kicked off her flip-flops, tucked her legs up in the ample seat of the chair, and watched him. Bella curled at his feet.

"And now for the exciting conclusion," he teased.

"I guess the most important point would be that it was a good thing Papa decided to escape when we did, in the winter of 2000, because the insane violence of law enforcement and cartels only got worse after we left. He leaned forward and began picking leaves and twigs from Bella's fur while he talked.

"By 2010, the Zeta's power was undefeatable. They separated from the Gulf Cartel, and increased their numbers with every raid they made. They killed police, federales, thousands of citizens, farm workers and refugees fleeing violence in Central America—anyone who refused to join their ranks or cooperate with their crimes. The US and Mexican governments were pitting different cartels against each other to eliminate them, and it made everything worse."

"It's hard to imagine it could get much worse," Joy said.

"As long as there is prohibition in the US, the cartel's money, power and violence from the illegal drug trade will grow. The Nuevo Laredo faction of the Zetas has had two consecutive leaders since we left, the current one is the sister of the first two, who are in prison for unspeakable crimes. But no matter how many are arrested or killed, there are more to take their place, while homicides and other cartel crimes continue to increase."

"My dad is pretty conservative," Joy said, "but he says it's like the Viet Nam War; the logic supporting US policy was based on a flawed premise, but those in power refused to accept the truth. Millions of people died over those twenty years before the US citizens finally refused to support it. Building prisons seemed like a worthy goal to my dad until now, but he says now it's like building planes to bomb Viet Nam. It's been thirty years since Nixon declared the War on Drugs and the death toll and expense has grown every decade."

Tonio began to pull twigs from Bella's fur, and changed the subject.

"I keep veering from my story of how we settled here in the mountains. When we finally arrived in Oaxaca City, Papa Ramiro told Miguel he couldn't stay with us or ever know where we lived; because of his drinking, he could not be trusted. So, after we left him in Oaxaca City, we came up to the Zapotec village near here, San Pablo Guelatao."

Bella rolled over on her back, and Tonio went to work carefully,

198

easing rather than pulling the small twigs. Joy began to help a bit, but pulled back embarrassed when their hands touched. He changed the focus to Bella, and Joy relaxed.

"She will snap at you if you pull this hair on her stomach," he explained.

The chill in the wind, the diminishing light, told her their seemingly timeless afternoon was mortal after all.

"What do you think is going on with your parents? They've never let us hang out this long before."

"Well, they had an argument, which means they have to make up, no? Maybe they smoked a little...you know" and there was that grin again.

"Okay, I get the idea. Frankly, I don't like to think of my parents or anyone else's parents, you know...just seems weird. Hurry up with your story."

**49**

"Joy, you have been pulling stories out of me for days. I hardly know anything about you. If I did not know better, I would think you were interrogating me for the authorities." Joy tilted her head with a grin.

"That would make you an easy mark for a confession, then, except you haven't told me about any crimes you committed. Look, now I'm feeling guilty. If it's any comfort, my life has had almost no drama at all; at least the part since I was adopted. I grew up in the same house, went straight through school, discovered I loved art with a passion, especially Mexican art, and focused on that. My parents involved me in a lot of Mexican culture as I was growing up. I didn't do much out of the ordinary except to admit I was a psychic and ended up hiding it from my parents. Oh, and I contacted the adoption agency a few weeks ago, and they're going to put me in touch with my birthmother soon. I am extremely excited about meeting her. So that's about it. You go on, I'll tell you more later."

"Well, I do not know how far we will get…where was I? The village, I think. When my mother was young, my Zapotec uncle hunted where we are now, in the deep woods. He's the one who recommended this spot when we arrived at the village. It is perfect. Isolated. There's a year-round spring right here, but not that far from Hwy 175, which is our access uphill to the village, and downhill to Oaxaca City, about 40 minutes' drive. I thought it was a great adventure, living in the wild, learning to hunt. The first year was hard, though."

He paused, she waited. His expression turned into the wide-eyed terror of a little boy who had wandered into the woods on a lark, only to realize he was lost. She saw him look down. He bit his lower lip, then looked to the clouds for the courage to finish.

"Just before my birthday…I was almost six years old. I stayed here with Mama, and my papa Diego went down to Oaxaca City on business. Papa Ramiro got worried when he didn't return, so he made some inquiries and the news was bad. The police had found him. Stabbed to death behind the Cathedral of Our Lady of Assumption."

Joy gasped, feeling guilty for pushing him into this, and shocked, because she never expected anything so horrific. Her mind jumped to her Christmas Eve visit to the cathedral with Rosa and Ángel, mixed with the image of Diego sprawled dead and bleeding.

"You mentioned him when we spoke of our first parents, but these details are heartbreaking. I am so sorry. What a terrible loss, at such a young age."

Tonio's voice trailed off into expressions of pure feeling; Joy could see the rise and fall of his chest as he tried to control his breathing. He swiped his hand fast before the tears hit his cheeks.

"You were so little, how sad it must have been, and how lame I even sound saying this. Death just cold-cocks words, they're useless, Tonio." Joy struggled with the frustration and the desire to alleviate his pain.

He managed to regain his balance; she sat shocked, fighting off tears.

"Papa Ramiro made very discreet arrangements to claim the body for burial, then hired Rico, the cab driver, to deliver him at night out on Highway 175 so no one would know."

"To have to sneak your father's body home for his funeral..."

"Papa said he thought my papa Diego was recognized by someone from their old cartel and they killed him when he wouldn't tell where we were hiding; assassination for desertion is automatic. And I know he would have died before betraying our location, especially since they would have killed him anyway."

"Losing your dad through such a violent act, how did you even begin to understand it?"

Tonio looked at her quickly, his dark eyes wide and pooled with tears.

"Señorita, I have never had such a conversation as this; I am taken by surprise that you want to know such things."

"I want to understand what it means. I have a teacher who says every difficulty is a door to wisdom, that we are souls who incarnate on earth to learn what wise souls know. So, I'm intrigued that you have learned so much, I'm curious to know what you know; not in an emotional vampire sort of way, but because, well...I care."

"Joy, you are a rare kind of person. I will tell you what I can. Every year on the anniversary of his death, I realize I have learned something more about what it means. I'm becoming an expert at analyzing how and why these things happen. If I am blessed with love and with children of my own, it will be because I found a way to make an honest living, in a country that isn't rotting with corruption."

"The US is struggling with its own corruption problems," Joy added, "let's pray they don't get out of control."

Joy thought she saw Ramiro and Adela through the vine-covered window of the dining room. She glanced around the perimeter of the compound, and for the first time felt grateful for the isolation and relative safety of their location.

"Do you mind clearing up a mystery for me? How is it you speak such fluent English? You know a lot for being so isolated up here."

"It's all because Papa was determined to get me out of Mexico and into a good US college. He insisted we get our applications for school submitted and our visas secured. Rosa, Ángel and I were ready to go when Papa decided he needed more cash to pull it off."

"You never told me there was an actual plan in place for college."

"I mentioned our plans, but perhaps I didn't go into any details, so you thought it wasn't imminent." He laughed. "I love that word imminent."

"Okay, wordsmith, maybe I misunderstood," she said with a smile.

"Papa Ramiro and his brother Miguel were the third generation in their family's business to speak fluent English and Spanish. The family was being extorted by the cartel; when their parents resisted, Papa and Miguel were kidnapped to ensure their payments continued. The whole family was under threat to cooperate."

He put his soda to his lips, and drank the entire bottle.

"Guess you were really thirsty! Continue!"

"Papa and Mama home-schooled me here, with supervision from the village school. I graduated, but I think my SAT scores clinched it. I can't be too proud about it though, because learning almost anything comes very easily to me; it's just something I had nothing to do with; a gift. Obviously, I spent way more time studying than most kids, because I've had to stay away from Oaxaca City. Not many distractions here. The village librarian could borrow from any of the libraries she wanted to contact. She could obtain anything I was excited about. For me, discovering books and videos was like my discovery of wildlife, except with all the sciences in books and the internet I can follow the trail of what I want to know about wildlife, geography, astrophysics, biology…"

"Whoa, Tonio! I get it!" She leaned toward him, smiling.

"You know, Tonio, your curiosity is one of your best traits; it's energizing, dynamic." *I heard someone say they considered high intelligence sexy, but it's the first time I've experienced it that way. The way his energy shapes what he learns, then expresses it…with no ego trip. Very nice.*

"What? Oh, yes, I know what you mean…maybe." He appeared a bit flummoxed by her remark, and segued back to his comfort zone.

"Also, after we moved here, we had access to a lot more ways to learn grammatical English and Spanish from television. We have solar power, for TV and lights, and an expensive device that boosts our reception from the cell phone tower; that is when the electricity for the tower in the village is working. They need more batteries to save power.

"Mama begged Ramiro to let me grow up here near her people, so I would know the language and customs, but now she is ready to go. There are a lot of Zapotecs in California, mostly farmworkers, but their lack of Spanish or English skills is causing them big problems…I think Mama wants to do something to help them."

The screen door squeaked open, and Ramiro seemed to pop out of the long, one-story house as the door closed with a loud wooden clap. Joy noticed he had showered and put on fresh clothes. She assumed that he and Adela had finished the heated argument in their bedroom, so his lapse of anxiety made more sense to her. Tonio walked over to him, Joy followed.

"So," Ramiro said with a self-satisfied tone, "you two got plenty to eat, I see, and time to talk. Bueno. Adela and I have a plan of action. Once I explain it to you, I want Joy returned to the bunker for the sake of safety, then you, Tonio, need to come with me to get the gear sorted for our trip. My friend Roberto will use that good road by the quarry off 175 for a landing strip and take us in his plane just before sunrise." He looked at Joy.

"We are going to Puerto Escondido, on the Pacific coast. My

cousin Ruben has a rental house in the hills not too far from the airport." It wasn't until then that Joy realized she'd adjusted to the limbo of her captivity. Now, suddenly, there was a clear plan in place. Ramiro looked at her.

"Señorita, tomorrow you will be returned to your parents in Puerto Escondido. As for the Zetas, and the rescue of Rosa, Ángel and Miguel, the FBI has a plan I cannot discuss at this time."

Joy felt as if his news had reached deep inside her, then yanked her guarded feelings out for everyone to see. The thought—that this was almost over—startled her. Then, as if drawn close, she saw a fuzzy vision of her parents in the forest outside the fence, waving at her.

Tears burst from her eyes, her body contorted with the shocking sweet release of hope. That hope, unexpectedly, also embraced Tonio, Adela and Ramiro with a stronger force than she thought possible. Of course, it could not stop there. *Rosa, Ángel and Miguel, what is happening to them in the meantime?*

## 50

The laughter from the patio at Posada de Felicidad accentuated Addie's dour mood. She was chafing with impatience; felt she was being pulled into a situation she couldn't identify, and the suspense was taunting her, daring her to stretch her vision forward, while her brain moved in the opposite direction, still pondering the conversation with Luisa and the message she had left for Jake. Her phone rang, putting the tug-of-war at an end.

"Hello."

"Addie, it's Ana, can we come up to your room? We need to talk with you."

Addie sat up and checked the time on her phone.

"Sure," she said, "could you bring me some more coffee, soda, anything with caffeine?"

"Will do, see you soon."

She forced herself into the bathroom and washed her face in cold water to perk herself up.

The phone vibrated and rang on the porcelain sink a minute after she'd hung up on Ana. *Must be Ana calling back for something.* She grabbed it up with hands still wet. *Think I'll lighten the mood a bit here...*

"You missed me?"

"Well, yes I have missed you..."

"Dean?" Her heart quickened despite her desire to stay focused on their task.

"You were expecting someone else? I'm calling about the case. New intel on the Zeta's caper." *It was Dean.*

"I thought it was Ana calling me back, she and Mike are coming up."

"Do you have a few minutes?"

"Sure" She grabbed a hand towel, headed back into the main room, flopped down on the bed, and dried her face and hands. *He sounds very awake and busy; makes me wish I'd brought a coffee pot and a pound of Starbuck's.* She put the phone on speaker and tried to relax as he brought her up to speed.

"Well, to summarize, I know we first saw Miguel's drunken screw-up as a potential disaster in the case, but I've been working on it with Isabel, and we think this is an impulsive exposure the narcos hadn't thought through.

"An informant told the local police that the Zetas were in Oaxaca City meeting with some Guatemalans about a new trade route for meth production ingredients, mostly ephedrine. A rival cartel's been intercepting their goods." Dean paused and slowed down; he wanted to be sure Addie had time to digest all of it. Addie cringed and kept her reaction out of her response.

"They went off task when they decided to get involved with Ramiro's job. Doesn't seem like a smart move."

"Maybe not. The Zetas have never regained the cohesion they had prior to the 2014 infighting. However, they are operating cells all over Mexico with various levels of cooperation and competition. Fifty percent of their business is drugs; the remainder comes from extortion, protection rackets, assassinations, kidnappings, weapons trafficking, and more."

"Did the informant know which cell they're from?"

"He thinks they are setting up a new cell in Oaxaca, loyal to the Nuevo Laredo headquarters, so the amount of backup they might get tomorrow at the coast is an unknown quantity at this point. They probably rationalized breaking their cover, figured they would come home heroes if they picked up half a million bucks while they were on the road securing new trade routes."

"Or," Addie interrupted, "They might consider running with the money. In which case, they wouldn't want to call around asking for Zeta soldiers to join them."

"Good point, Addie, so we're looking at confronting just the four of them, or less likely, a dozen. This thing with Miguel's leak just looked like an easy million to them at the outset, to take Ramiro's cash back home to their boss in Nuevo Laredo, or as you say, possibly try to run with it. They demanded half of the million-dollar ransom from Ramiro, but they will likely demand it all once they believe he has it in hand."

"Where are they now?"

"Looks like they're up in the hills north of the Escondido airport. They told Ramiro to meet with them midday tomorrow with the ransom after he makes the exchange for Joy. They have no clue we are cutting a deal with Ramiro. We can't underestimate their ability to recruit some help between now and tomorrow, though. Question is, on short notice, will the guys they recruit have agendas of their own? I mean how convoluted could the situation get by tomorrow?"

Addie's head was swimming with the logistical possibilities. *Feels like tomorrow is going to be as predictable as a roll of poker dice.* She had her misgivings and had to express them.

"This could be a real mess if Ramiro has trouble taking orders from you, even if you get enough agents together to actually pull it off." Dean had definitely had his coffee; he was a fount of information.

"At first, Ramiro was saying he didn't have the men to go after Miguel, Ángel and Rosa, but Isabel and I believe we've convinced him we can have more than enough boots on the ground to tidy up this mess. Ramiro now understands the FBI will have a plan that involves cooperation with Mexican authorities; because the Zetas inserted themselves into a case we're working on, and we can provide the perfect ruse to pull them into our net. Even better if they are from Nuevo Laredo; makes their intel absolutely priceless."

"Dean, explain this to me, I'm behind in my research on this."

"Okay, a third of Mexico's drug trafficking crosses the Rio Grande from Nuevo Laredo into Laredo, Texas, and once it connects with I-35, their drugs are headed for both US coasts and everything in between. In exchange for capturing the Zetas, we expect permission from Mexico to interrogate them."

"And what about Ramiro?"

"I told him the Mexican authorities might let us have him, he might get a reduced sentence in the US since they know he assisted with the sting, plus, if he served time in Mexico, he'd be killed in prison by the first Zeta he encounters, so that would justify extradition to the U.S. Anyway, that's our pitch for now." Addie heard a knock on the door, answered, and waved Ana and Mike inside.

"Dean, Mike and Ana just walked in."

"I'd join you, but I can't right now. Put me on speaker, I want to keep the Doyles in the loop; I've got some good intel, but I also have some not-so-great news I'll do my best to explain."

## 51

Ana and Mike kept quiet and waited on the couch. Addie was aware now that the Zetas killed Rico, so Ramiro would know they were serious...dead serious. *That's how it is with terrorists;* Addie thought, *no killing is just a killing, it's a message.*

"Dean, I'll put you on speaker phone. The room's been searched for bugs by our team."

"Well, you know the saying," Dean joked, "just because you're paranoid doesn't mean they're not out to get you. Go ahead, put me on speaker, I've got info on the cell tower."

Addie switched the phone to speaker, parked it on the coffee table; and sat in the small upholstered chair. Ana put a cup of coffee and a plate of fruit on the table, and Addie was on it quick.

"OK," Dean's speaker voice began, "well, our honeymooning agents have been busy with their cell tower search, which turned up some interesting news. Apparently, there's a grass roots organization, Rhizomatica, who were granted their own cellular spectrum by the Mexican government." Addie gave a reflexive thumbs-up.

"They raise funds and materials, and help isolated rural communities build their own cell towers. They bypass the big providers who don't care about their business anyway, at least at this point. As of last year, they installed nine cell towers in the state of Oaxaca." *Wow,* Addie reacted, *this is power to the poor people!*

"Our agents think Ramiro is living in the mountains, in range of one of these towers. Possibly up in the Sierras, an accessible drive to Oaxaca City on Highway 175. There's a Zapotec village of 1100 people up there who just got their first cell tower two years ago. That may be where Ramiro has been living the life of the invisible man since he escaped the Gulf Cartel, around 2000, right about the time the Zetas were well ensconced as the cartel's personal military terrorist unit."

"What do you know," Ana said, "Ramiro is a criminal with scruples, or just plain scared, or both, that's why he went AWOL from that Gulf cartel."

"Well," said Mike, "I can see why anyone would want to avoid the Zetas. I learned a thing or two about the cartels from that prison project I was on. Zetas have a culture of sadistic torture and gruesome methods of terrorizing the public; chopping people up, burning them, skinning them ..."

"Stop! Enough for God's sake!" Ana yelled. "We get the freakin' idea, Mike, we don't need to hear any more."

"Sorry," Mike offered, unconsciously running his hand through his short-cropped red curls in a self-comforting gesture.

Addie focused on an upbeat remark to Dean in this awkward moment.

"Dean, your info on the Zeta plan is encouraging. We are grateful to have gotten you on board with us for this case. I especially like the optimistic picture you painted of all those arrests you're planning; I'll sleep better."

"I'm glad to be here with you, as well." Dean's phone connection started breaking up, leaving a garbled version of "I'll call right back." Addie decided she needed a moment alone.

"Time for a bathroom break."

Addie got up and went into the bathroom. She wondered about the impact she felt when his deep, soothing bass voice had said 'glad to be with you as well'. Had he meant the singular or the plural you? She took a glass from the sink, filled it, and drank slowly, let it cool her down.

Staring at her reflection in the mirror, she reflected on her feelings as well. *I know one thing for sure; I feel nothing but pain when I think of Jake, and I feel more than just comfort when I think of Dean.* She returned to the room as Mike was offering an opinion on the Zetas.

"Sounds like the Zetas got into their own drug stash; it's possible they're high enough to turn their semi-anonymous presence into a public display of Zeta terrorist tactics."

"Again, stop bringing this up," muttered Ana, "I saw these guys as committed to working out their smuggling plan, which required anonymity. They got involved with Miguel's job on an impulse. If the consequences of the kidnapping get them backed into a corner, yes, I can see how horrific that could become, I admit it." No one spoke.

Addie had heard enough gruesome speculation, and distracted herself with more of the melon the Doyles had brought in, squeezing some fresh lime onto it.

"Excuse me for pigging out, but I always find comfort in food when I'm stressed."

"I'm in your club," Ana said, "but Mike switches from food to whiskey."

"To each their own, darlin'—uh oh, phone's ringin' again."

Dean had called back, the reception was better, so Addie put him back on speaker, then briefly closed her eyes. The deep tones in his voice came right to her, his ever-welcome audible signature.

"I just wanted to close off with one more thing. Emil and I are going to stay with the plan of getting Joy from Ramiro first thing tomorrow morning in Puerto Escondido, Ramiro will be placed under arrest." Addie got the gist.

"What about Adela and Tonio?" Addie garbled, her mouth celebrating the lime-infused melon.

"We'll hold Adela and Tonio for questioning while their role is sorted out. They understand what our plea bargain process is, in theory, that's if they are charged, and Ramiro has helped us facilitate a plan to get his trio from the Zetas." Mike pushed his point before anyone could speak.

"If Joy's being taken to Puerto Escondido by Ramiro, it makes sense for us to be there when you get her from him. That way we could fly back home from there, and not risk any more exposure."

"Agent Chung had a similar view," Dean said, "with the caveat that you and Addie aren't engaged in any of the actions with Ramiro or the Zetas. She used that access road info the Zetas gave Ramiro, and located us something close. Not on the same road of course, two cabins in the hills north of the port, by a small lake. She secured them for tomorrow and Thursday." He paused to cough, then continued.

"The cabins will serve as our base of operations tomorrow. Ideally, if we get everything accomplished early on, we may move out of the hills right away, fly out of the Puerto Escondido airport, then switch to jet transport from the Oaxaca airport to California." Mike and Ana looked at each other like they'd just won the lottery.

"Home tomorrow night?" Ana blurted out, "Now that would be wonderful!" The image of their flight back captured all of them.

"It would be perfect," Dean said, "but, if we have to stay overnight, the agents can restrain the detainees in one cabin and the rest of you can stay in the other one, with enough agents in and outside each cabin to make sure you are fully protected. Isabel told the rental agent we're a church group on holiday and interested in some fresh water fishing." Addie chuckled at the cover story and a got a fleeting vision of Dean giving her a full-immersion lake baptism. She ignored the vision and focused on Dean.

"I got the word that Isabel rented a couple of eight passenger SUVs with four-wheel drive that will be at the airport when we arrive. We have a medical team, too, with a fully equipped med van. Just a little something she worked out with Silva and Quinn's logistical magic. Be thankful we have agents driving the fully-stocked SUVs and the medical van to the coast today; it's a brutal drive through the mountains to the coast."

"We got that loud and clear from Mrs. Liz over lunch when we inquired about the coast," Addie said, grinning and saluting with her coffee cup. "Go ahead, Dean, you're on a roll."

"Well, I am encouraged that things are coming together. Unfortunately, there's some weather Isabel's been watching; that's why she wants us to have a place to hang out away from the port until we are ready to fly out." Ana had been listening and nodding as Dean spoke, then tapped Addie on the arm, and passed on a cue in a half-whisper.

"Speaking of port, Addie, Liz told me to pass this on to you, since you couldn't hang out downstairs much." She reached into her tote bag and produced a bottle and an opener.

"Okay, Dean, go ahead, I'm listening but I'll be forcing myself to give this wine the taste test. Hope it's on the dry side, I'm not a big fan of the sweet stuff." Ana had it open in a flash, and reached into her tote for some plastic wine glasses Liz had provided. Three glasses were poured as Dean finished.

"Regarding criminal charges, once Miguel, Ángel and Rosa are retrieved from the Zetas, they will be offered the same deal. It's clear Miguel planned this with Ramiro. We know from the hotel surveillance that Ángel was involved, but the local police say there's no evidence that Rosa or Rico knew about it. Ángel and Rosa have never been implicated in criminal activity before now, so he may not have told Rosa he was complicit." Mike offered an opinion while Addie and Ana sipped Port.

211

"I'm sure Miguel thought if he disappeared with Ángel and Rosa, the Zetas would give up their threat and go back to Nuevo Laredo." There was a pause, then Dean responded, his energy picking up. Addie could tell he was avoiding the horror of the Zeta's bloodshed on Highway 175, and focusing on the possible positive outcome.

"If that had worked, we could have picked up Joy near Oaxaca City and been on our way. Most local Mexicans would have avoided the exposure and the added driving hours of the southerly coastal route, so maybe Miguel reasoned the Zetas would search for them east of Oaxaca City."

"Guess that Zeta who beat up Miguel had someone keep a closer watch on Miguel and Ángel than they ever assumed. What a screw-up," Mike said.

"Yeah, well, we have a smarter team, so stay as positive as possible. That's it for now. Stay in your rooms tonight, stay close to your phones, and by the way, tomorrow, Quinn and Silva will hold onto your personal phones and provide you each with a clean cell for the trip. Addie, when you get your phone, try to keep it dry if you can."

"Roger that," Addie said, grinning, but deciding to not tease him back, "we'll talk in the morning." But he didn't hang up.

"Just one more thing. I want to say that tomorrow should go according to plan, but we can take absolutely nothing for granted. We don't know exactly how many men the Zetas will have on board; we don't know how the logistics with Ramiro will jive with the Zeta plan. I need everyone ready to leave Oaxaca City by seven a.m."

"The FBI plane will leave sooner, but you three need to be in the air by seven. By the way, this mission is going to be presenting unpredictable logistical variables, complicated by drugged-up, money-hungry cartel soldiers. I don't want to be pushy, but I'm asking everyone on our team to commit to one task tonight."

Ana, Mike and Addie fell all over themselves saying they would do whatever he needed; then Dean's voice came across steady and quiet.

"Pray for a miracle. I have a hunch that Joy and Rosa have opened up a clear channel out of sheer desperation, so log on and listen."

## 52

Addie stood at her doorway and watched Ana and Mike head down the stairs. Mike looked back up at her.

"You sure you don't want to join us for dinner?"

"Well, I want to, but I have to get some sleep; I got about two hours last night at home and a short nap when we got here; that's just not enough. Would you have some dinner sent up to my room?"

Her hunch that they'd be going to the coast had been confirmed, yet the decision to relocate their entire effort to Puerto Escondido weighed on her. Were her adrenal glands finally fed up with the constant pressure and collapsing into a fatigued stasis?

Sure felt that way. *Pace yourself,* she thought, *this is a marathon, not a sprint,* as her first FBI trainer used to remind her. *On the surface, a cliché, but down deep it was potentially lifesaving advice.*

The wine had relaxed her tight muscles a bit, encouraging her to do some yoga until her dinner arrived, announced by an enthusiastic knock on the door. She was greeted with a smile from Liz, who was now quite drunk.

"Surprise! I insisted on delivering your dinner because I wanted a first-hand report on the wine. I don't want to come in, just tell me, wasn't it great?"

"You said it, Liz, thank you so much. Between the tasty port and this dinner, I am going to get a great night's sleep." Liz turned to go downstairs, then looked back at Addie.

"Sleep well, sweetie. To tell you the truth, you looked so sad when you got here I knew you could use it. See you later, bye!"

Addie ate her dinner, thinking about Liz's spot-on observation. She felt grateful for her generosity; another unpredictable tender mercy in her time of need. Her heart felt comforted, enough to ignore the possibility of getting bad news if she were to call Luisa for an update.

Luisa's phone rolled over to voicemail, so she called Lizbeth, who, as usual, answered promptly.

"Hi Mama, I checked the weather for Oaxaca City, looks pretty perfect. How cool is it that December is the best weather of the year in Oaxaca.?"

"It's beautiful; the courtyard here at the inn is filled with colorful blooms of every kind, the food is great, I'm just calling to say goodnight before I konk out."

She paced in her room, tidying up while she finished her call with Lizbeth, and then with Nita. She could see into the inn's courtyard from her window, and the cool evening was proceeding with laughing patrons enjoying drinks and dessert pastries; the innkeeper's extension of the festive Christmas holiday tradition. Colored lights were strung around the columns of the building, and small spotlights illumined the huge oak trees at the center of the courtyard.

The girls updated Addie on their plans for New Years, and seemed to have accepted their father's departure; they believed he'd been called out of town on an emergency to cover a story. Addie was grateful he had called them, whether it was a fabricated excuse or not didn't matter at this point. Nita put the phone on speaker the minute Luisa came in from her trip to the store. Both did their best to be upbeat and optimistic.

It was important to let them know the FBI team was confident about tomorrow's plan; Addie stuck to procedure, revealing no details. The girls and Luisa thought Oaxaca City was the target site for the exchange, and she left it at that. Satisfied that they were unhindered by Jake's departure and not overly anxious about her, she signed off for the night.

It unnerved her to think their team would be one hundred fifty miles away from Oaxaca City, coping with the added complexity of the deal Ramiro made with the authorities. Ramiro had given Dean and Emil the approximate location of the Zetas, and he had convinced the Zetas he was desperate to exchange the ransom for his family members' freedom. The Zeta's had played it by ear up to this point, so it wasn't clear yet how the deal was going to proceed. *I should stop ruminating about this crap and get to work; the fact is that there are a lot of variables that are not under our control at this point.*

As was her habit, she had temporarily turned her bed into a broad desk onto which she could lay out materials; her laptop, phone, charging cords, pens, and notebooks. Even though they were taking a charter plane to Puerto Escondido, she wanted to see a weather update for herself. With a glass of port on the bedside table and her laptop open, she watched the site load. The dramatic weather graphics grabbed her attention.

She'd been following some earlier predictions that a fairly benign tropical storm would be heading up the coast of Mexico, which jived with the weather Isabel discussed with Dean. This latest report, broadcast in English, showed the storm cell picking up increasing force over the Pacific, with the possibility of it being upgraded to a hurricane midday as it approached Acapulco, then losing most of its force when it made landfall further north.

Addie wasn't too concerned; it was moving steadily and was predicted to make landfall far to the north of Puerto Escondido. She watched the video coverage, in which a young, excited meteorologist reviewed the details as he gestured to the computer model depicting the storm's predicted path.

"This storm is part of the very active 2015 El Niño weather pattern we are seeing this winter, created by warmer surface ocean currents across the Pacific. After three years of drought, the El Niño effect is predicted to bring much needed rain at lower elevations, and snow in the high mountains of Mexico and California from December through May." Addie reached for her wine glass, sipped the interesting port, and watched the streaming video.

"At present, Mexico's president, Enrique Peña Nieto has put safety measures in place from Acapulco north to Manzanillo, as he did in October with hurricane Patricia, which quickly became a category five. Thirteen lives were lost in that October storm, prior to which the President sent troops to evacuate at-risk coastal areas. The announcer stopped referring to his maps; the camera zoomed in on him as he addressed the current system.

"Bottom line, this storm's outcome is going to be as impossible to predict at this stage as the others. Do not take this lightly. Take all precautions. Residents in the target areas have been advised to protect their property and be prepared for evacuation. Air and land medevac rescue units are preparing to deploy as needed."

"Landfall may not occur before late afternoon tomorrow, but that could change. You have time to secure windows and anything that could be moved by strong winds. If you are on the Pacific coast of Mexico, stay tuned to the progress reports; if you are south of Acapulco, winds and rain aren't likely to be as severe, but could result in flooding and isolated structural damage even if landfall is further north. That's it for now; we will be providing updates through the night."

*Okay,* Addie thought, *all the more reason to get in and out of Escondido early. If we don't, Acapulco's two hundred miles north of Puerto Escondido. We may get wet, but not blown off the map.* With her confidence boosted, she closed the laptop, moved it to the empty side of the bed along with the other strewn contents of her briefcase, then lowered her head onto her pillow as the wine lubed her slide to sleep.

## 53

The woods around the patio teemed with motion; logic told her it was the wind, but Joy kept looking out through the trees as Ramiro pushed the details of his plan.

"We leave here at 5:30 a.m., meet Roberto at the landing strip; he flies us to the coast. My cousin Reuben will meet us at the airport and drop us off at his rental cabin up in the hills, so we can stay out of sight. Reuben knows nothing of our plans, so say nothing. Señor Dean will pick us up from the cabin as early as he can. If we have any run-ins with the Zetas, Tonio, I trust your military skills over the Zetas any time, considering that I've trained you since you were five years old, and especially because you, unlike them, will have a clear head. We will have our hand guns ready when we get off the plane at the airport, in case the Zetas are stupid enough to jump us there."

With an air of pride, Ramiro turned to Joy and said "this young man is a skilled sharpshooter, and a knife-wielding maniac if need be. We have hunted in these mountains for years. He can survive in the wild with little or no equipment if he has to." Ramiro embraced Tonio, grinning and nodding his head.

"Yes, he is an asset to any team." he released Tonio and pointed to Adela. "His mother, on the other hand, grew up as a farmer in these hills. She considers this compound the only safe part of this wild country. But she knows how to shoot, we made sure of that. Ramiro turned toward the woods and laughed.

"A few years after we moved here she was kneeling down, planting her vegetable garden over there," he pointed to the far end of the thick concrete fence surrounding the compound. "She heard a sound, and looked up to see a full-grown jaguar standing above her on top of the fence. Now, I can personally vouch for the fact that Adela's scream can terrify anyone back to their infancy, and the poor jaguar had no prior experience with such a horrific sound. Adela did not even have to run away; the cat did all the running away that was required!"

Joy realized she was laughing hard, belly and all, a luscious melting sensation. Except for the laugh they had when Bella soaked them, this was her first opportunity in five days to recall what a full-on laugh felt like. She thought about her return trek to the bunker, realizing her fear of snakes and scorpion might be upstaged by the possibility of a jaguar in the woods. Regretting that she'd lost the carefree feel of her surroundings because of the jaguar story, Joy decided to ask for a little help.

"Ramiro, do you have a glass of wine or a few beers I could bring back to the bunker? I'm going to need my sleep just to cope with tomorrow."

"I only have a Valium."

"I'll take it," she said with a faked grimace.

"Bueno," he smiled, "I will go get it." He turned and walked back to the house, posture erect, gait jaunty, still looking very relieved and satisfied that he had, that very day, successfully negotiated a plan with the FBI, the Zetas, and Adela—a veritable trifecta.

The large table by the grill hadn't been cleared. Joy went to it, stacked the plates and disposed of the trash in the nearby bin. The screen door squeaked.

"I will get those, come get your pill." said Adela, coming onto the patio, humming and smiling, her long hair done up Frida Kahlo style. One thick braid was fastened onto the crown of her head like a halo, with a yellow ribbon woven into the braid. Joy saw a beauty in Adela she hadn't noticed before; from her hair, to her multicolored hand-woven top, jeans, and sandals. The faint jasmine scent of her cologne drifted to Joy, who held her palm up to take the offered pill. She was a bit surprised at her own eagerness to take it. She poured the last ounce of lemonade from the pitcher into her glass, and drank it down with the Valium.

"It's going to be dark soon," Adela said as she scanned the sky.

"Tonio, take her back before it gets dark, and get her settled in. There's a flashlight on the side of the top stair of the bunker, you will need it for the trip back to the house." Adela turned to carry the dishes into the house.

"Mama," Tonio said, his voice only loud enough for Adela, "do you care if I hang out with Joy and play some cards for a while?"

"Sure, Tonio, I know you get tired hanging out with us old folks up here. Just behave yourself, and I mean what I say. You lay a hand on this young woman and you will end up in jail…they will forget about their bargain with us! Do you hear me? And get back early to sleep well.

I will help your papa pack your gear. All we have to do is drive down to the landing strip by the quarry tomorrow morning and Roberto will meet us." She stepped closer, articulating their plan as if she needed to hear it again in order to believe it.

"After we leave, Roberto's son will take our car into the city and leave it in Rico's garage. The police have Rico's cab, his family has no other vehicle, so we are giving our car to the family. My brother and his family will be staying here at our house. We leave our truck here for him. Papa is paying him to pack up our art collection, and other things we need, to store in the bunker until we know what we are doing. I made three digital copies of all our photos, in case we get separated tomorrow." Tonio nodded, his eyes downcast. Adela turned to Joy.

"Joy, I am sorry you heard me argue with Ramiro. I fear Zetas, I fear to leave my family and the village, and I feel sad I may never see my beautiful home again. Ramiro reminds me I am expected to answer questions to be part of the FBI plan. And," she grinned, moving close to Joy, "I was able to calm down when he find romance in his heart."

"Okay," Tonio said, looking embarrassed by her statement, "we go; Joy, you can teach me how to play that gin rummy game you think you are good at."

"We'll see who comes out victorious. If it's me, you have to bring me a piece of pastry and a hot cup of coffee in the morning, or I won't talk to you all day tomorrow."

"Let's go," he reacted suddenly, an angry edge to his voice, "I don't want to think about tomorrow!"

Tonio's outburst broke through Joy's denial about Puerto Escondido. She recalled Ramiro bragging about Tonio's fighting and survival skills. This was going to be dangerous. Tonio walked quickly toward the gate at the side of the patio.

Only Joy, who hadn't moved, saw Adela's eyes fill with tears. Only Joy saw Adela returning to spend one final night in her beloved home. Clearly, it had been the shelter and witness to her blossoming soul. Joy's heart ached for her. *She has only one night more, then comes her greatest act of faith since escaping the cartel. Except in this case, she is heading straight toward the Zetas, not away from them.*

## 54

A few yards into the woods and Joy lost her bearings; what remained of the day's light was filtered even more by the foliage. She looked for signs of danger in the jagged shadows that distorted what little light there was, and when she turned to Tonio her voice carried an impatient edge.

"Tonio, please turn on your flashlight, I can barely see where we're going." He pulled out his phone, turned on the app, and directed the light to the next break in the trees.

"Just stay close behind me."

He walked slowly ahead of her, and slowed to help her through the smaller pines and undergrowth.

"I'm feeling all turned around, are you sure we're going in the right direction?" Joy whispered.

"Why are you whispering? No one can hear us. Follow me, I could find the place blindfolded." Joy wondered if she was annoying him, but had to whisper her argument.

"Tonio, what do you mean no one can hear us? A jaguar can hear us, and in this light, she can see six times better than we can. Ramiro told me that when he was warning me to never try to get down the mountain on my own."

"Stop," he said, turning around, trying to whisper. She stopped immediately. He put a hand on her shoulder, leaned down, and whispered an inch from her ear.

"I do not know how much you really know about men," he began, "but if you think we do not get scared, we do, and the more you focus on this jaguar the more I worry, so please, let us just get the hell to the bunker, okay?"

"I'm sorry," she offered, trying to forget how his warm breath had felt on her ear. She pouted a bit, then jerked her head up and whispered. "How about this? I see you have your knife, could you take it out and stay close to me the rest of the way, please?" He nodded in agreement, and with a swift motion, had the knife in his hand.

"Stay close." He stepped ahead of her, she followed. They walked a few meters, consciously trying to be as quiet as possible.

Joy felt a long claw slice her face and cried out. Tonio spun around, knife poised ready to strike, seeing the blood running down Joy's face his head swung back and forth, searching. Joy saw the offending tip of a broken branch pointing at her, and came up close to whisper what really happened.

"I walked into a broken branch! Shit! Oh, it hurts!" Her mom's medical advice immediately came to mind. Joy unrolled one long arm of her sweatshirt, pulled the end of it over her hand until it extended well beyond, folded it back inside out over her palm, and pressed it hard against her cheek.

"I'll be okay, let's get moving. I don't want any cat to get a whiff of my blood. No f-ing way. I shouldn't have taken that valium until I got in bed; it's not exactly a navigational aid."

Tonio slowed down, moved aside, and held back a long branch for her.

"We are about four meters from the bunker," he whispered, "there is a first aid kit there. Let's go."

The outside of the bunker door was so well camouflaged she couldn't make it out when he stopped right in front of it. Dirt and branches had been randomly applied onto a thin layer of mortar over the door years ago, and they always threw on extra foliage and dirt to match the surroundings when they closed it for any length of time. Joy started to let down her guard, and spoke quietly.

"I actually like the fact that this bunker's hard to find, it makes me feel safer when I'm down there by myself, knowing that some random hunter could walk past it and not see it as an invitation to break in." Tonio looked up to speak as he bent down, unlocked the door and began opening it.

"There's buried money and weapons all over Mexico from the narcos stashing it to pick up later, so people do get curious. Once Ramiro found a cache so poorly buried the rains had soaked into the bills and mold devoured them." He stood up slowly, lifting the door.

"Grab that flashlight for the stairs," he said, pointing it out to her with his phone light. Joy grabbed the flashlight, the stairs lit up, and she hurried down while Tonio lowered the door slowly, then locked it from the inside.

"This is the lock you use if you need to keep someone out. We lock it from the outside when we leave so no one but us could get in.

"At least this is the last night I have to imagine the three of you being killed by enemies while I am trapped here with no escape." He started down, and tried to assuage her fears.

"I agree that seems a possibility, but in terms of probability, your chances of dying in here are almost zero percent."

"If you were in my situation you'd realize statistics are no comfort when you're trapped under the ground like this."

When he reached the bottom of the stairs, she stood there, hand pressing the shirtsleeve to her cheek. He grinned and started to tease her, in a voice that implied more conspiracy than privacy.

"I thought we would jump into having some fun when we got here, but no, we have to clean this cut out and get the bandage on." Something told Joy that this medicinal process was going to be more intimate than the standard treatment, even if the final outcome was identical.

"At least we can listen to some music," he said as he found his favorite playlist, turned it on, and propped his phone up on the kitchen countertop.

"I really miss my music; I haven't had my phone since Christmas Eve. It got left in the cab." She walked to the sink, turned on the light over the sink, then turned on the one by the recliner chair and surveyed the illuminated bunker. *My last night in this dungeon.* She looked over at Tonio.

"They returned your phone to your parents, I would think." He went over to the bed, turned on the battery-powered wall light. The twin-sized mattress lay on a platform with a rough-hewn cabinet below. Tonio squatted in front of the cabinet, took out a large zippered bag, sat on the bed, and opened it.

"Everything we need is in here; sterile water, antibiotics, bandages, even some of that paint-on skin, smells like fingernail polish, stings like hell, but, it is waterproof, dirt-proof, and in your case, you will not look ridiculous with a lot of tape and gauze across your face."

"I vote for that; Mom will be pleased with our efforts; she's a zoo vet, very big on being responsible with cuts." She carefully pulled the bloody sweatshirt over her head, letting it fall on the bed.

He took charge immediately, reached to the bedside table and dumped some fruit out of a yellow bowl, then handed it to her.

222

"Hold this under your chin, here, so it will catch the water." He grabbed a blanket and covered her lap. "Just in case," he added, then washed his hands at the sink and rinsed them with alcohol from the kit.

After the cut was irrigated to his satisfaction, he put a thin strip of antibiotic ointment inside, wiped it with sterile gauze, then closed the wound with strips of thin clear butterfly tape, and painted on the liquid sealer.

"Mom would say you have the touch for medical work; careful, tender, and decisive."

"Thank you," he said with a nod. "Papa learned much first aid When he finished, he picked up the bowl of bloody water from the bedside table. He began shaking his head slowly side to side.

"Joy, seeing all this blood makes me think of tomorrow's meeting with the FBI and the Zetas; so much could go wrong...so much blood could flow...from any of us. I'm not saying this to freak you out, but I want to say something in case I am not able to tell you later."

He walked to the sink, put the bowl down and returned to Joy. His phone's playlist was cruising through a series of melodic piano instrumentals; a repeated series of bass notes resonated with the anxiety she observed in his face. She responded to his private revelation with obvious respect, stood up, and walked toward him. She backed up a bit as he came close to her, then nodded her head.

"Go ahead, Tonio, tell me."

Tonio's eyebrows drew closer together, creasing the skin between them into two dark lines, his eyes blinked, his stiffened lips allowed the words to come.

"No matter what, Joy, I want you to know I will do whatever it takes to keep you safe. I pray we make it through this without anyone getting hurt, but this act against your family was wrong, and Papa was wrong to do it." Tears emerged, he ignored them.

"He says he did it for me, so I could have a better life, well, no thank you; how am I supposed to feel good about graduating from a US college if someone else had to be victimized to pay for it?"

"Tonio, you don't need..." He put a finger gently on her lips and continued.

"If there is danger tomorrow, and I know there will be, I want you to know," he paused, she waited—he tried to speak. His dark lashes quivered, his smooth, generous lips trembled, then disappeared as he looked down at the floor, his hair falling forward, hiding his face. Then, like a man awakened by a strange noise, his head shot upward; his eyes bored into hers with an intensity she'd never experienced.

"I will give my life to keep you safe." Her mouth opened slack; her face a dark question mark, eyes widened with fear. Joy turned her head to the side, while her eyes never broke their vigilant gaze on his— —like a horse ready to flee at the slightest muscle twitch from a nearby predator. Stepping back, she faced him directly, almost groaning her words, she scowled at him.

"You really mean it. You're willing to pay the ultimate price to right a wrong you didn't commit or approve of?"

"Yes." Tears covered his eyes. Joy felt a puzzling rage she'd never experienced before.

"Listen Tonio, and listen good! You are really pissing me off! You are not guilty by association! Don't you dare put yourself in harm's way because your Papa defaulted to an old skill set to provide you with a good future. That was his judgment call alone. I can see he's in bad health; he's desperate and afraid to leave you and your mom vulnerable."

He cried, fighting it, sobbing, then shaking it off; anger pulling his face and his hair into a tangle of unfamiliar lines in the half light of the room. When he finally spoke, it broke out through barriers Joy couldn't see; crashing into the room harsh and desperate—like someone shattering a window to escape a fire.

She saw him through the distorted and flooded prism of her tears, he looked as if he were inside a clear cocoon-like liquid; raw, stripped to his essence. Inside the vision she had of him, she felt him transform from a boy to a man, expressing everything, in every way, from each reformed cell of his maturity. His words emerged with jagged edges, as if hastily constructed with the passion and pain of his dilemma.

"I feel like the crime that brought us together is the very thing that will make it impossible for us to stay together! I love you Joy…with my whole soul, I will do anything for you!"

"Then maybe the man who is listening now can understand what the boy could not! Listen to me!" Joy shook, loosing her frustration and passion, no holds barred.

"Tonio! If you don't get what I'm telling you now, then I give up! You have to understand! If what you're telling me is true," she shouted so hard her throat choked with pain, "then promise me this— never take responsibility for someone else's mistakes, even if you unknowingly benefitted. If you really love me," she grabbed his upper arms, gripping them hard, shaking him with all the substantial muscular force in her body, "you will make sure we both stay alive! I promise you I will do the same!"

## 55

Tonio stood his ground, smiling like she'd never seen him smile. The music surrounded them like a soft lasso, pulling them close. The heat and tension held at bay, spilled into the determined gentleness of their kiss. Tonio then took all the force he had restrained from that kiss, and buried his open mouth into the begging curve of her neck, nuzzling deeper, her neck responding with every muscle relaxed, her head at a resting angle to her spine—when he grasped her entire body off the floor and swayed her in slow motion; her hair, loose and long, alternated like a slow pendulum with the sway of her body and the liquid beat of the music.

Joy's arms grabbed onto him as if the air beneath her bare feet extended over an unknown chasm. She clung harder with her whole body as his mouth moved over her ear; his moist warm breath, his words, and a quiet moan entered there. Inside, Joy felt every part of herself churning, expanding through her skin.

Slowly, he lowered her until her feet found the woven rug, and together they sank onto it, stretching out full length to feel the energy moving between them. Joy, cautious of her injury, put her lips on his as gently as possible; routing all her intensity through her hands. Tonio's eyes met hers; Joy felt he dove into her soul and graced it with beautiful gifts she'd be discovering for years.

Their breath came faster, cut in the middle by a distant bark. To Joy it seemed to be barely audible, then it stopped; was Ramiro coming with Bella? Tonio rolled onto his back with a sigh. Joy sat up next to him, took his hand, and pressed her lips slowly into the warmth of his palm. When she looked up, his face was close; he was still holding back his heart's wish, his body's fervent passion, while allowing it to flow unhindered from his eyes to hers.

"The time..." she whispered.

"Isn't right...I agree," he said, holding her in a gentle embrace. The air around them pulsed with the heat from their bodies. Joy, with the uninjured side of her head resting on his chest, felt his heart keeping a fast pace with hers. Her imagination began to follow their hearts' momentum.

A second round of loud barks began. "Your papa?"

"No, he just sent Bella to get me; something he trained her to do when I was little."

Joy looked at Tonio, felt he belonged to her despite any number of future interruptions, then willed herself up to her feet, picked up his phone and put it in his back pocket. Bella whined outside as they moved toward the stairs. Joy kissed him once more as he passed into the stairwell, flashlight in hand. She leaned against the wall at the bottom of the stairs as he headed up, talking to Bella through the closed door. Bella's exaggerated response made them both laugh. Tonio turned and looked down at Joy.

"I just had to see your smile once more." This made her smile grow, until she bowed her head, embarrassed. Before she could look up he was back down the stairs; his arms holding her tight. He leaned down for a long, open, warm kiss; his hair gracing her bare neck, sending chills across her chest. Joy accepted all of it; their passionate bond, the interruption, and the mystery of how tomorrow would unfold and conclude. He pulled away, headed up the stairs, looked back, and spoke to her in soft, loving tones.

"When you get into bed, just curl up and imagine I'm here with you, because I will be imagining the same thing."

"I can hardly wait," she admitted with a smile.

## 56

Miguel was half dreaming, half awake. *Is it the pain pills the hospital gave me?* His mind raced with images, sounds, sensations, but he could not wake up. He wasn't sure where he was—in a car, or stopped somewhere. He tried to retrace his steps, starting with escaping from Oaxaca City in a panic with Ángel, Rosa, and Rico.

He knew the Zetas weren't going to give up on getting a piece of Joy's ransom. Rico had agreed to drive them to Puerto Escondido to hide out. Miguel had told Ramiro he had to make a run for it; all he could think was *get the hell out, get to the coast, into the hills, and disappear.*

He remembered stocking up on a case of tequila, putting it in the trunk of Rico's cab. No one would let him bring a bottle into the car. He hadn't had a drink since his *desastre* at the hotel the night before; everyone had been too pissed at him. He'd been told he'd have to wait until they got to Escondido, which was hours away, and he already had the shakes bad.

In a haze, his regrets appeared. *Nothing went as planned…the Zetas must have been following us to see if we would lead them to Ramiro and the ransom. We thought our diversion worked; got a ride around town, switched to Rico's cab on the edge of town. I thought we were in the clear after an hour on the highway, but oh, how they got us. Rico said he saw that black Navigator approaching—like a missile—they caught up to us in no time.*

Miguel recoiled as he remembered his bad dream turning into a nightmare. Like a pack of wolves, the Zetas had descended on Rico's cab. Their leader held a gun on Rico while three other Zetas grabbed Rosa, Ángel and Miguel at gunpoint, restrained and threw them in the Navigator. *Even from inside their car I could not take my eyes from Rico.* Gordo, the leader, had looked at Rico, Miguel's *buen relativo*, then checked the deserted highway for witnesses, and told Rico in rapid Spanish that the ransom didn't require his return—Rico had been left bleeding to death in the trunk of his cab by the side of the road.

Miguel had seen Rico, his arms and legs hanging limp, blood flowing down his arm onto the road, when the giant Zeta carried him to the trunk of the cab. Miguel knew more than ever before that he had lost his soul to the booze, because from the minute the Zetas opened the trunk, all he could think about as he sat handcuffed, watching the drama through the open window of the Navigator, was *what about my tequila?*

He had even been so bold as to yell at the men, "don't waste that tequila!" They laughed as they pulled out a few bottles for themselves, then stood back as Gordo tossed Rico's bleeding body right on top of the rest and slammed the trunk.

Gordo, massive and mean, his bare head and face tattooed with skillful artistry, had grabbed a towel from the trunk, wiping blood off his clothes and hands as he hurried around the old cab to the Navigator, jumped in the driver's seat, and made Miguel call Ramiro.

Miguel winced, recalling the humiliation he had felt as he explained to Ramiro that the Zeta's wanted half Joy's ransom in exchange for their three live bodies. *Yes, this is all on my head, all my fault.*

Gordo had taken the phone from Miguel and set up his own meeting with Ramiro in Puerto Escondido to make the exchange; Gordo was so high he was rapping out his plan and directions to Ramiro like a narco rapper, and carelessly rapped the name of the access road; so impressed was he by his talent, he never noticed.

The three prisoners were forced to ride with hands restrained behind them, legs restrained, and seatbelts on. They had to stop twice for Miguel to vomit his breakfast, which made Ángel sick both times. Rosa had seemed frozen in place; she knew what typically happened to female captives. They had to put up with Miguel's dry heaves on what seemed an endless winding road. By the time they got to Puerto Escondido, everyone was sick.

Miguel's recollection of all the events since leaving Oaxaca City crawled around in his brain—crabs in a bucket desperate to escape. He finally managed to get his eyes open, and saw the sputtering flame of a candle on a low table nearby. He was still in restraints, covered with a reeking blanket, and lying on a rug. A snoring Zeta was on a couch a few feet from him. If he could have crossed himself he would have in that moment, he was that thankful the Zetas had been coming down off their high enough to pass out for the night.

*If I had the courage, I would do everyone a favor and kill myself...but I am a coward...no matter...with no tequila to stop these shakes, the Devil's hellions will hear me cry...then they will come for me.*

229

The view from 2000 meters aboveground was dim in the haze of pre-dawn, then cleared as they gained altitude and headed toward Puerto Escondido. The pilot was a local, and the plane an unsexy but competent Cessna Grand Caravan, similar to Jerry's but older. Addie realized she had plenty of time to think about their destination. Liz had been right, Addie thought—the innkeepers, restaurant chefs, musicians and artisans of Oaxaca City and Puerto Escondido were worth a long, self-indulgent vacation.

Addie had explored the port on Google Earth; it just made her want to clone herself and send the free-and-easy Addie to eat fresh-caught fish at every restaurant and surf every silver-streaked wave. It appeared to be a relaxing vacation spot, nestled against the sea, and framed by hills ascending into the Sierra Madre Del Sur.

It had all looked great on Google last night, but when she looked out the window of the plane this morning, she knew all bets were off; clouds ahead reminded her their visit to the coast was going to involve a piece of that storm...and what else?

The charter pilot was all business, so there were few humorous quips or tour guide comments coming their way. Ana and Mike were dozing with their seatbelts on. Addie realized she was on autopilot, though the plane was not. *I can't believe how numb I feel*, she thought, *but it's a gift compared to the pain. Problem is, the pain just keeps showing up.*

Her recriminations, powered by a growing sense of betrayal, would not cease. *Jake, you could have asked for help, could have gone to counseling, whatever. Now we're into years of woulda, coulda, shoulda. You just took your hands off the wheel, stepped on the gas, and the life we had planned went into the ditch, with your daughters along for the heartbreaking ride.*

"Addie, you holding up ok?" Addie noticed Mike's tone was soft and kind; he knew she was overwhelmed too, and he didn't even know about her crisis with Jake.

She smiled at him, then saw Ana had roused herself. Her fair skin was pallid, her lips tense and drawn, and the beauty of her blue eyes a pale bleached-out gray. *She looks appropriate for the real-life role of terrified mother, Addie thought. We have all earned our angst.*

Maybe he was dreaming, for no matter how hard he ran, Jake couldn't catch up to his fleeing wife; he heard himself scream.

*Addie! Stop!* The words bounced around inside his head, trapped. *She can't hear me!* Nor could he get any more distance between him and the demons bearing down behind him; first they'd been on foot and he'd thought he had a chance, but now their huge reptilian bodies rode Harleys, their roaring engines splitting his eardrums as they approached. One of them was calling his name.

"JAKE!" A threat had been seeded into that call, from a creature with a sardonic leer.

"Jake, time to rock n' roll, buddy!" Jake looked ahead to Addie, in her plane, taxiing on the runway. Before he could stop her, into the air she went, throwing something from the plane intended for him, he was sure.

"Jake, ready or not, here I come," screamed the ugly tongue-lashing monster leading the pack. Jake's luck held; he made it to the bag she'd thrown for him, threw himself upon it, opened it, found an AKA loaded with ammo. He pissed in his pants as he raised the gun to fire.

"Jake, time to join us in hell, NOW." Somehow, before he got to shoot, the demon got his claws on Jake's arm and shook it.

"Jake," the voice was different; he saw a tall, sinewy black man in his 30's, wearing an artfully designed "CLEAN AND SOBER: NOW IT'S YOUR TURN" T shirt and new jeans. He looked at Jake, shaking his head as if he'd just tasted disgusting, badly spoiled food.

"Welcome Jake, ready for recovery? There's a meeting in the main room in thirty minutes; I'd get cleaned up for it if I was you."

"Huh?" Jake then felt it; he was trembling all over, lying on soaking wet sheets, reeking of urine, his heart still pounding with the life-threatening experience he wasn't sure was over.

"Come on, buddy…uh, Jake…I'm Russel." He offered no handshake. "The shower's right there, see, here's a towel, soap, some clothes, get cleaned up and get your sorry ass to the meeting…there may be hope for you, we'll see."

As the chartered plane carried them toward the darker cloud cover over Puerto Escondido, Addie pulled herself out of ruminations about the past and focused on the future.

"So," Addie turned in her seat, looking at Ana and Mike, "since our pilot's blasting his audio up there, I think we can safely discuss our mission without being overheard…and on that topic, what did I overhear you saying as you stashed your gear when we boarded? You got your hands on weapons while we were in Oaxaca City?"

"Not exactly," Mike said with an elusive air.

"I'll speak for myself," Ana raised her hand abruptly, "I just had to pick up a few tools for the trip whether I need them or not. I borrowed an animal tranquilizer kit from a vet in Oaxaca. I wasn't sure if our trip was going to include opportunities for self-defense or an injured wild animal we could help, but I wanted to have some things handy just in case."

"Wow, that's what I call scoring what you want on short notice," Addie offered.

"Well, I called her the day we decided to fly down here. When I heard the Jaguars were making a comeback in the Sierra Madre Del Sur, and in the Sierra Juarez, I literally cheered. However, if we're going to be tromping through these hills, it's important to remember Jags are the most opportunistic eaters of all the big cats, and they swim for food as easily as chase it up a tree. Aggressive animals, or aggressive people for that matter, can really put a dent in your plans if you don't have tools to discourage them." Addie stared as Ana opened the case.

"A tackle box from a vet?"

"No hooks or sinkers in this one," Ana explained, "this case fits into the backpack I brought; carries tranquilizer darts, and a tranquilizer gun. I used a similar pack when I was in graduate school. We were tracking jaguars for research."

"You tracked jaguars down here?" Addie asked.

"We did; decades ago. They're still endangered, but making a comeback, so it's a rare and wonderful experience to locate them. They love playing in water, hunting around water, they'll dive for fish, crocodiles, snakes. Their jaws are wide, and powerful enough to

paralyze a crocodile by breaking its spine at the neck when it pounces."
Addie's surprise forced an interruption.

"Wow! I knew they swam, but that kind of power even in water, is news to me."

"You would be amazed!" Addie saw Ana's eyes light up for the first time in days, and gave Ana all her attention.

"They'll dive onto prey that are in the water, or they'll swim submerged, sneak up real slow, and attack from there. When I see them thriving in the wild, I swoon with gratitude! So, we may never need these syringes...but my protective instincts make me want to empty this big one into the carotid artery of that kidnapper...just sayin'."

"I think we've all felt some version of that desire," Mike said, "and just so you know, Addie, Ana also got a pistol from the vet, in case an animal had to be stopped with no time to wait for tranquilizers to take effect. For now, I'm keeping it in here."

He reached in his bag, came out with a large Snickers bar in one hand, and a pistol in the other. He put the pistol back, and tore the wrapper off the Snickers bar.

"Just in case the plane crashes, I'm going to eat this now; the deceased don't have to worry about calories. Here, consider this a communion wafer," he broke the bar into three parts. Addie had to laugh, took a small bite of her piece, tasted the chocolate and caramel melting in her mouth, then told them about the weapons Dean had unofficially 'forgotten' in her room.

"Of course, Isabel wouldn't approve, since none of us is here to officially fight anyone, but now we're going to be closer to the action than we anticipated. Last night I was provided with two Gen 4 Glocks. Not my first choice, but; I favor them over Berettas because of the fitted hand grip. And, don't fret, Isabel and I have been to the practice range twice a month for almost twenty years, so have no fear about me shooting your big toe off by accident."

"Excellent," Mike said in a congratulatory tone, "now for a change of subject, what's the word on landing conditions?" Addie wasn't surprised he asked, they had been flying into and above rain clouds for a while.

The graying sky served up a response; sheets of rain provided them about as much visibility as a drive-through car wash. As they gained altitude, the deluge gave way to showers, and the pilot gave them the word.

"Stay seated, stow any gear you have loose and fasten your seatbelts, we have turbulence coming up."

"Landing conditions," Addie repeated Mike's query then answered him. "Dean told me last night he checked out the Escondido airport's weather worthiness. Apparently, in October, the airport upgraded its storm facilities, and new tie-downs for light aircraft were installed. Just in time for Hurricane Patricia."

"Speaking of which," Mike said, "before we got on the tangent about our weaponry, I meant to tell you this charter pilot is on orders to get the plane out of Escondido airport as soon as he drops us off. The charter company doesn't want to risk any damage to the plane. It's only a thirty-minute flight, so when the mission's done and we're ready to leave, weather permitting, we'll have a flight out of Escondido. All we have to do is call them."

As she listened to Mike, the plane began to vibrate, then the whole craft dragged to the right fast. The pilot adjusted course and their forward movement began to pick back up.

Ana readjusted herself in her seat. "Let me see if I've got it straight: Dean and Emil are waiting for us at the airport to take us up the hill?"

"That's right, and since Ramiro is already at his cousin's cabin, Dean and Emil will go get Joy, Ramiro, Adela, and their son Tonio, right after he drops us off at the cabins Isabel rented for us. Ramiro's also bringing his dog; Dean told him not too, but he refused to leave her behind."

"Really?" Ana said, "So is it a pit bull or a poodle? Maybe Ramiro's not as cold-hearted as I'd prefer to believe? Or maybe he enjoys a mean dog, who knows?" Addie laughed and continued.

"Joy will get some comfort from the dog, if it's just a pet, I'm sure, even if Dean doesn't want the dog in the way.

"So," Mike said, "how far are the FBI cabins from the rest of the action? And, if we lose cell service, can Dean can just scout them using the name of the access road?"

"More than likely," Addie said. "Ramiro's cousin rented him a cabin in the same area. So, when Izzy called the property manager in

Puerto Escondido to arrange rental for the FBI cabins, she already had Ramiro's cabin address and the Zeta's access road factored in to her preferences. The property manager said a number of vacationers renting cabins up there had left because people were leery of the storm getting big like Patricia did, so there were plenty of cabins available. He rented her two adjoining cabins in the same general area near a lake."

"And," Mike interrupted, "I hope the Zetas didn't have anyone at the airport to watch for Ramiro and follow him to his cousin's cabin…, oh, crap…too many possibilities; I hope we don't all go nuts before we get our arms around her," Mike started coughing, Addie knew he was trying to choke back the tears, but she saw them come fast and wet. As the plane jostled all of them, Ana reached for Mikes hand; Addie's heart pumped out a feeling of deep radiating warmth when she saw Ana's tears.

Addie couldn't hold back once Ana and Mike started to cry; her tears splashed onto her shirt. The vibrating cabin of the plane felt like a womb, rocking the three of them as their shared longing for Joy filled the space they shared. In a few minutes, they were through it. She spoke quietly.

"Well, first I want to say we obviously needed to let go of those tears, all that backfilled emotion, no point in pretending this isn't difficult. Not to belabor any spiritual aspect of this, but I felt so close to both of you just now, and felt surrounded by a presence so comforting, so strengthening."

"I felt it too," Ana half-whispered. Mike softly expressed his thoughts.

"If we must go through this, and of course we must, I feel grateful we're in this together. Our love for Joy is the presence you speak of, I think, it's just fillin' us and this entire space so much it's become a force of its own."

"So, it's really true what they say about the Irish, isn't it?" Addie said.

"Yes, it's true," Mike answered, "we specialize in poignancy."

235

# 60

Ben was driving south on Skyline Boulevard with Star, heading through the fog toward the Omni Center when Star sighed and broke the silence.

"Good thing we followed your hunch to have breakfast with Isabel; she was startin' to unravel a bit."

"I knew something had changed, knew she wouldn't open up over the phone, so…" His hand reached over to hers and rested. After eighteen years of marriage he'd come to appreciate the triangle of loving support between Star, Isabel and Addie; each of them strong women in their own right; together they shared a creative invincibility he loved.

She laughed and made a joke of the latest shift in the case "So now instead of just Izzy, we're all freakin' out that the whole case got transplanted to the coast."

"Now, Star," he said in a crooning, loving tone, "you aren't going to put your energy into a worst-case scenario, are you babe?" He saw her chin drop to her chest, her eyes closed, a decades-long habit she had perfected; to return to a place of confidence, to confirm an optimum outcome. He drove in the slow lane, giving the speeders room to get by, and waited for her to get squared away.

"I'm good to go now," she announced, "just needed some realignment to put all this new information in the right context."

"Me too. I can see you, Izzy and Addie hopping up and down like eight-year-olds who just won first place in a jump rope tournament!" Star laughed heartily at the scene he described, so Ben knew she had latched on to a winning scenario.

He slowed as they came up on a turnout, pulled off, and parked near some cypress trees.

"Really, Ben, just let those commuters go by." Star turned to check the traffic behind them, and noticed Ben had his forehead resting against the steering wheel.

"Ben?" He leaned back against the headrest, his eyes shut.

"She's coming into Puerto Escondido, weather's rough, wet, windy…" he saw the landing, felt the chaos of wind, rain and people, rushing from planes toward cars. He felt himself jolt when Addie fell. Then a vision of Dean helping her and an announcement about a man's death somewhere near the airport.

Ben decided to keep the difficulties to himself for now, except for the part Star could really use.

"She's got her friend shoring her up, that guy she knew in D.C…he's got her safety covered in ways she doesn't even know yet."

"His name is Dean," she offered quietly. Ben opened his eyes, and looked at Star.

"I really mean it, I think we just received something we needed; a sign that Addie really is all right. He's an interesting guy; I look forward to meeting him."

Star leaned toward him, caressed his face with her fingertips, lightly touching his lips. He loved the graciousness in her touch, felt it move into his body like a warm wind. He gazed at her with a peaceful smile, relieved that Addie was safe.

"I love you, Ben, for your ability to tune into what I need at just the right time."

"Ask and you shall receive," Ben replied. He looked over his shoulder to check the traffic, then pulled back onto Skyline while Star nudged him into a favorite song. She had a healing way to make his day, he mused, and sang with her until he had parked in front of the Omni Center, greeted by the vibrant array of bougainvilleas and hydrangeas celebrating the entrance. They walked hand in hand to the entry, well aware they would have a heightened and beneficial connection with Addie and her team until they returned.

## 61

"The closer we get to the coast, the less I trust the weather reports," Addie said, noting her own anxiety, "but the FBI medical team will be at the airport, so they'll be close if there are injuries. Even if one of the Zetas gets injured, Dean wants to do everything possible to get the Zetas into the interrogation pipeline in one piece." Ana injected some humor, her voice shaky.

"I suppose shooting to kill isn't a first option for anyone today, regardless of our earlier discussion." Mike laughed and added some advice.

"Let's all do some deep breathing, enjoy being warm and dry, at least for a few more minutes."

The plane descended slowly, wind buffeting them in random bursts; Addie, Ana and Mike had put their seatbelts on and secured their gear. Mike looked out his window, his eyebrows shot up, he blurted his news through a huge smile.

"I see the airport, we're closer than I thought!"

It wasn't long before the plane was positioned to land. It dropped like an elevator with a broken cable, and proceeded as if they were bouncing down a stairway of gigantic weather balloons before it leveled off.

Once they made their final descent to the runway, a gust hit them straight on and shook the whole plane in a long stationary vibration. The landing gear presented without a hitch, the pilot focused on their approach, and they met the airstrip. The plane hopped a bit before connecting securely with the tarmac. No potholes, no wet skids, no lightning strikes; they were down, completely safe.

"God, I can't believe we're here!" Ana shouted, laughed, and clapped her hands like a terrified ten-year-old whose nerve-wracking roller coaster ride just pulled to a stop.

"There they are; looks like it's just our folks, and no interference from anyone else." Mike shook his head back and forth as if to shake off his unrealized anxieties. Addie was relieved and started talking off her remaining nerves.

"We lucked out with the airport. No telling how accurate that landfall prediction is, I mean, so far, the weather predictions haven't had much influence on the storm." She had seen Dean and Emil signaling with high-beam lights from the tie-down space next to their plane. It was barely light enough to see.

"Dream on about the storm skipping us," came Ana's voice from behind Addie's head, "I think we're gonna get slammed, but if I've got my arms around Joy and I'm hunkered down somewhere safe, I don't care." Addie turned to Ana and gave her a huge smile, pulled on her jacket, then her backpack, and grabbed the canvas gun bag.

Mike and Ana headed for the door, but Addie felt so much gratitude over their flight, she had to close her eyes and offer a silent prayer. *For all the unseen help we had getting here safely, I want to say thank you. Mama, Grandma Luisa says it was you who locked me into this journey with that message at the office. Now please help get us through this and back home safe!*

As they deplaned, Dean came running toward them, but his eyes were locked on Addie's all the way. Until that moment it hadn't occurred to her that he might have been worrying about her, but he clearly had been. Addie recoiled from the cold wind that reached under her jacket hood and rolled down her back, but the taste of the rain, and the sea's scent in the wind, felt briefly like Pescadero Beach, so she welcomed it.

Dean waved as he approached, a huge smile that she recognized as more relief than joy spread across his dripping face. His jacket, pelted with rain, was mirroring any light that reached him. Lightning broke overhead; the reflected burst made his jacket light up and his smile shine even more.

He yelled with water flying off the end of his nose. "Ready to head up the hill?"

"Yes!" Addie had to shout the rest, "The charter plane is leaving now for Oaxaca, orders from the company, so we'll have to call them whenever we're ready to go."

"Okay!" Dean shouted over the noise of the wind, then turned to Ana and Mike "Come on, let's go, it's gettin' nasty out here!" They ran for the car, eager to be warm and dry again.

Emil was waiting for them in a white Suburban, engine running. Another Suburban, this one red, was filled with undercover agents, as was the third vehicle, a green high-top Nissan cargo van, its rack also sporting vacation gear and fishing poles—no one would recognize it as a fully equipped medical unit. Addie rushed toward the white Sub, grateful they would all have four-wheel drive vehicles in this weather.

A huge gust of wind—like a giant's massive breath—knocked her flat into a widening black puddle. Her head smashed into the tarmac beneath the cold windswept water; pain seared the side of her head far worse than what she would have expected from this kind of a fall.

She lost consciousness, then awakened in a vision, high above the airport, just underneath a black storm cloud. She watched the cloud open slowly right in front of her. Suddenly—coming through it feet first, bent way over backwards with arms and wings hanging limp—a dying angel hurtled past, within inches of her, and seemed to take forever to hit the ground.

# 62

In the rain-soaked hills above Puerto Escondido, Ramiro stood shivering from the damp cold surrounding him, and the fear pumping through his veins. He watched his steamy breath condense on the front window of the cabin as he kept an eye out for Dean's car. He'd refused to let anyone build a fire, didn't want anyone to know the cabin was occupied. Outside, a flash of lightening down the road startled and confused him; he thought it was headlights, then the thunder told him otherwise.

The old furniture and damp wood in the cabin smelled like a neglected basement. A fire would help, but he rejected the thought; not worth the risk. He worried, then obsessed, about Miguel—*probably going into withdrawals by now, which could make him more of a loose cannon. I should have known better than to involve our family in Miguel's job; the asshole had to celebrate by getting drunk, boasting to Lupe about all the money he would have to show her a good time.*

*What were the odds that the Zeta would overhear him and decide to get a piece of the action? Now, instead of having half a million for Adela and Tonio, we lose it to save Miguel, Rosa and Ángel. Forced to buy our way into the US cooperating with this f-ing FBI sting, and an information dump—merde, what a low budget alternative!*

Adela had been quiet; Ramiro could see she was frustrated. She looked at him, then shook her head as if flinging off an annoying fly that buzzed her one time too many.

"Ramiro, please tell us what's going on! I know you're talking to yourself, so stop shutting us out. I will not be just waiting, not knowing what the plan is. Poor Rosa and Ángel, I fear for them. Even Miguel doesn't deserve torture. Please tell me!"

He walked up to her and took her hand, patting it in an effort to bring some comfort. He bent over and kissed the top of her head, and out of the corner of his eye saw Joy watching them with a small private smile. Joy and Adela had been staying warm together on the loveseat with a heavy comforter wrapped snugly around them. Tonio was stretched out on the couch near them, under another blanket. Ramiro stood up straight, feeling what Adela meant him to feel.

*I know about Adela's experience as an adolecente, when she was taken*

241

*prisoner by the cartel; she has good reason to fear for Rosa.* He returned to the window before he spoke; watched their sloped access road give up clods of dirt to the rain; puddles merged and streamed downhill, just like his hope for pulling off this last job and retiring in the US.

"I suppose there will be no harm at this point in telling you the plan; I have been so pissed about Miguel ruining our plans I have been afraid to tell anyone." He paced back to them, and perched on the arm of the loveseat next to Adela; determined to tell Adela, Tonio and Joy as much as he knew. The cabin windows rattled impatiently, as if fatigued from holding back the wind.

"Eso es todo; the FBI cabins, this cabin, and the Zeta's cabin are separated by a few miles of descending elevation. All, like this one, are accessible from unpaved access roads off the main road we took uphill from the port. The Zetas moved into their cabin yesterday after they kidnapped Miguel, Ángel and Rosa.

"They must have planned the kidnapping before they left Oaxaca City, and rented the cabin over the phone so they could use it as their hideout. Or maybe they were set up to go to the coast before they stuck their noses into our plans."

"How do you know they did it in advance?" Tonio's question stirred Bella, and she started pacing again, whining, going to the women for reassurance.

"Because they got high and felt invincible; the boss was singing a narco rap, and rapped the name of their road for the ransom exchange when they called me. Too bad he wasn't high enough to rap out the number of the cabin too; there are dozens of cabins on that road. Of course, he caught himself, then swore to murder everybody if I gave any information to the policía. They are thinking I would never do that…con mi familia." Ramiro had not seen the Zeta's access road sign on the way up; a number of roads had been unmarked. He was worried, but kept it to himself.

"So, I'm still not clear about what to expect. How long will we be in this cabin, and where are my parents?"

"Dean will be coming soon with agents for backup, in case the Zetas are near. Roberto was generous enough to fly us in early this morning to position ourselves for the plan I worked out with the agents. Roberto…now there is a man who knows to keep his mouth shut and

242

his nose out of other people's business. He flew us no questions asked, and I paid him double his usual fare. He's back in Oaxaca by now flying some French tourists to the gulf coast so they can avoid this storm and have sunny beaches."

"What about Señor Dean?" Adela asked.

"He and agent Emil, and the rest of the agents were set to arrive by plane before eight a.m. All of us were going by the weather report, assuming the storm was headed to make landfall north of here. Instead, it sat offshore overnight, now it should be moving north, but the weather report can't really predict when it will move or how far north it will go."

"It feels like it's already hit, there's so much wind and rain," Joy remarked.

"Si, it seems the storm and the Zetas are the wild cards in this game; but the FBI is determined to succeed and wants no casualties; if the Zetas die, there can be no interrogation, si? It is a lucky break we had at least part of the Zeta location and that final agreement before the cell service went out.

"Señor Dean is a man of ideas; he will find a way to lure them into a situation they cannot control. Agent Torres will be pretending to be me at the meeting with the Zetas. Fortunately, we will miss the action." Adela interrupted, her face contorted with anxiety, tears flowing.

"I worry about Rosa with those animals; it is on my heart since we find out. Pobre chica…"

"The price of Miguel's drunkenness!" Ramiro raged, "Everyone else gets hurt right along with him." Ramiro got up and saw Tonio, Adela and Joy all waiting for reassurance; instead he expressed his disappointment in a suddenly quiet voice.

"Why I thought I could do a job with him I will never know, I just got sucked into it," he spoke in an audible whisper; emerging tears sent him walking back to the window; talking mostly to himself, looking through the rain-drenched single-paned glass. *Where is Señor Dean?* He felt Bella rubbing against him, bent to caress her, and finished his thoughts about the Zetas out loud, to help them stay as calm as possible.

"The Zetas aren't expecting a confrontation with the FBI today, that's for sure." Tonio rose from the couch, tossed the blanket aside and stretched. Rain dripped from a seam in the paneling over the couch, so he moved it a few feet forward, then had his say.

"I will bet they even have fantasies about spending that money on themselves, and escaping their cartel altogether, like you did, except you were smart enough to pull it off."

Ramiro sighed, took another look out the window, then responded.

"Si, si… but I doubt they are in any condition to succeed at much of anything; so wasted on their own drug stash, but you never know, as hyped up as they are, if they escape these hills without capture, enough meth and they could drive for days without getting tired, and could get away, no lo sé."

The cabin was cold, Ramiro felt tempted to light the wood stove; the chill went right into his arthritic knees and elbows, his spine, even his wrists. Everyone had kept their jackets on; still, he was literally chilled to the bone.

He walked over to the table, grabbed a soda and a burrito and went back to his post at the window, unable to shut off his rambling brain. Bella moved around the living room of the cabin, her whining almost imperceptible, but a sure signal that she was worried. She moved from Ramiro, to Joy, to Adela, then to Tonio, then to Ramiro again.

"Bella, relax, everything will be okay." Ramiro leaned over and held her face up to his, looking into her eyes, "I know, you feel my fear, it makes you worry." He snuggled his face into the soft fur behind her ears, to comfort them both. Then he heard the zipper on a duffle bag and looked up; Tonio was rummaging through snacks Adela had packed for them.

"Bella's never been away from home before, Papa. I'll find her something to eat." He reached into a bag of venison jerky they had smoked after killing a deer several months ago. Tonio pulled out a long piece and tossed it to Bella, then grabbed some for himself. "Bella, your favorite snack, enjoy!"

The jerky hit the ground at Bella's feet. She jumped when it landed, then sniffed at it as if she'd never seen anything like it before. She pushed it around with her nose, then walked away from it to whine even louder as she looked out the wind-rattled window next to the front door. They all watched her, half imagining that some cranked-up Zeta might burst through the door.

Tonio, mouth full of half-chewed venison, looked at Ramiro and said out loud what they'd all been thinking.

"What if those Zetas saw us coming and they decide to follow us here?" Tonio locked his eyes on Ramiro's and waited. Ramiro shook his head, and walked to the window, bending to ruffle Bella's soft fur again for some mutual reassurance.

"Two of those men are younger than you, Tonio, Señor Dean told me the policía identified them and their black Lincoln Navigator from the dash cam on Rico's cab. Two older Zeta veterans, and two very young recruits."

He saw Adela bury her face in her hands. He knew she was imagining the recruits following orders to restrain Rosa, then recalling her own kidnap and the horrors that followed. He rushed to reassure her, unused to seeing her in such distress.

"Adela, remember a few days ago, they were on a simple cartel chore to cut a deal with those Guatemalans for some ephedrine and chemicals for cooking that crystal meth, hoping to secure a plan to get tons more where that came from?" Adela looked up at him, crying.

"Why should that make me feel better?"

"Listen, they kidnapped Miguel, Ángel and Rosa because they heard Miguel boast about a big job and beat the truth out of him about the ransom the Doyles were bringing. That part was easy. But I believe they have no skills to pull this off, no experience with negotiating ransom, making the exchange, nada, completamente nada."

He looked outside again, feeling cross-eyed, searching the woods for Zetas, watching for Dean's car, *when will this be over, and at what cost?* He turned away from the window, looked back at Tonio.

"Por favor, mijo, keep watch out there while I rest a minute." Tonio obeyed, Ramiro flopped on the couch, patted the seat next to him twice and Bella jumped up, stretching across his lap. Caressing her, he launched another of his inept attempts to reassure everyone.

"I told the Zetas we had more men, more weapons, more experience; they think I was talking about our Oaxaca gang and not FBI of course. I convinced them I wanted Miguel, Rosa and Ángel in a big way, and would do the deal with them no questions asked. If they had ideas about taking the ransom, killing us, and selling Rosa, I think I discouraged that fantasy." He saw Tonio walk to the table for more jerky and a soda.

"Tonio, you keep an eye out for that Zeta Navigator. Shows you what amateurs they were to not destroy the dash cam on Rico's taxi. Señor Dean will be driving a white Suburban with fishing poles tied to the luggage rack. An undercover trick they thought of. No one will be in uniform. If a car drives up, you women get into the next room. Tonio and I will cover it." His intense stare moved to Joy.

"Once you are in the bedroom, listen closely. If you hear gunshots or if I yell Zeta, get out the back door before their car gets close, run uphill with Bella. Adela, you will have your pistol for protection. Stay in sight of the access road and hide in another cabin until we capture them and get them restrained. Tonio will find you." He rummaged in their weapons bag, took out a pistol, took it to the bedroom, and returned, looking at Joy.

Joy returned his stare with an abrupt nod of agreement. *Joy looks exhausted,* Ramiro thought with regret, *what have I brought this child into? I can see the terror in her eyes. I suppose there is no reason to lie to myself; I have changed more than I thought. The evil I held inside is gone; I pray it didn't take my courage with it.*

246

## 63

Adela had finally let down her guard; Ramiro could see she was concerned about the youngsters' welfare. She was up, pacing around the room, looked out the front window, then walked back to Tonio and Joy, her lovely features in a scowl, pointing to them like an impatient school teacher; her authority in this moment was not to be questioned.

"Tonio, your papa knows what he's doing. You and Joy need to do everything he says if you're going to be safe, do you understand?" She sat down next to Joy, and patted the back of Joy's hand, which got no response from Joy.

"Joy, your hand is like ice." Joy's other hand was picking at the threads around the bottom of her borrowed jeans, then moving to her mouth, to renew her discarded childhood habit of chewing her fingernails. Ramiro felt his chest ache, sitting on the adjoining couch, the pain increased as he watched Joy withdraw from everyone, stone-faced and silent.

*A week of captivity has taken its toll on her beauty.* Ramiro recalled how stunning she had looked in the cab on Christmas Eve; now her hair was stringy, her skin ashen, her lips clenched, bitten and chapped. The cut on her cheek was red and a bit swollen. Ramiro shifted his position on the couch and finally spoke directly to her.

"Joy, I can see you are afraid. I would give you a valium, but we have to be very alert for today's job."

He then looked at all three of them, aching to give them some sense of control so they could keep their cool. He rose with a sigh, walked to the window, put his arm around Tonio's shoulders, patting his arm, hugging him close, but unable to resist a peek over his shoulder to check for cars on the mud-soaked road. Lightning flashed, startling both of them. He let go of Tonio, who walked over to Joy, pulled up a footstool, and sat as close to her as possible. *I see the boy loves her; I understand. I pray he didn't go too far, that could get him in jail if she tells the authorities. I can see his hands trembling; the fear he has for her safety overcomes his own. I need to simplify this even more.*

As if answering a sane voice in his head, he replied. *Of course, I know I played a part in setting up this job, I know it's not all on Miguel. But he's the one who blew our cover. I could have gotten away to the US free as a bird with Adela and Tonio instead of the three of us risking this legal mess. I raised Tonio, he became my true son, he made me a father, I would die for him, yet I have put him at risk to save Miguel, Ángel and Rosa.* Tonio reacted as if he'd been listening to Ramiro's thoughts.

"Papa, even if I get some jail time, I read on the internet that you can earn college credit in a California jail." When Ramiro didn't respond, Tonio added "California is better than living in cartel hell, which is what our country has become." Ramiro's face contorted into an unsure and sad expression, muted but recognizable. He wanted to defend his country, to forbid Tonio's broad-brush condemnation.

He felt torn between the Mexico he loved and the Mexico that had corrupted and now terrified him. Just in case it all went bad, he had to clear his conscience. His premonitions were pushing him to get right with God before it was too late. He walked up close to Joy, Tonio and Adela, with Bella at his heels.

"Señorita Joy," Ramiro looked down at the floor, "I apologize for what has happened to you," he looked up, "to your family…your feelings…to your beautiful face…after all these years away from crime I can't explain how I fell back into it," his voice quieted to a sorrowful whisper, tears fell as he spoke, "I have no excuse that is sufficient." Joy looked up at Ramiro, tears painted a clear veneer over her scarred, anguished face.

Lightening flashed, followed almost immediately by a deafening explosion of thunder. Ramiro felt dizzy, ears throbbing as if they'd been struck by two huge fists. Bella barked again and again, running away from the window, around the couch, then back to her duty post at the window despite her fear. A massive gust of wind slammed the cabin, hard, like the concussion from a gas explosion.

All four of them jumped to attention, standing across the room from the front window, their backs against the living room wall. A fat branch at least thirty feet long, its gnarled bark jutting smaller branches that looked like deformed arms, hands and fingers, descended like a giant's spear into the muddy soil. The impact flipped the freshly broken end through the large window, its ancient glass shattering in all directions.

Bella went insane, barking, running to Adela, who held her

close and yelled over the deafening storm.

"Tonio! Pronto! Get the glass off the floor, Bella will run through it, she is scared!" Tonio found a broom in the kitchen, rushed to sweep the glass into the corner, then grabbed the thick blanket he had on the couch, and threw it over the floor with wind whipping his hair in every direction through the gaping, jagged hole. Bella jerked out of Adela's hands, ran over and sniffed the storm's threat, then barked again, and again. Tonio pulled her away from the remaining broken shards sticking up from the window sill, then spoke to her.

"¡Dios Mio! That was bad! Bella is telling us we need to get out of here, aren't you Bella?" He squatted, and she reached up fast, licking his face, climbing on him, while he lifted her like a puppy, and nuzzled his face in her fur, the wind and rain flying onto them unnoticed. Ramiro moved across the room, put his huge hands on each of their heads, rubbing with fatherly affection, then spoke as master, in clear terms.

"We are not going anywhere yet, so you both need to do what I say, then soon we can leave for the other cabin. Bella, why don't you take a nap in your travel crate, you need to relax." As if they needed one more scare, they heard a deep rumbling car engine climbing up the road to the house. Adela called Bella, who jumped down from Tonio's loosed arms and ran to her.

Adela whispered, "Please let it be Señor Dean." Ramiro and Tonio unholstered their guns and signaled Adela and Joy to get in the bedroom. The women ran, and Bella, equally frantic, followed them; as soon as the dog's tail cleared the closing door, they slammed it.

## 64

The Zeta's cabin shook; Miguel felt he was taking a wild ride on an earthquake. He heard the wind tossing branches at the cabin; striking the corrugated metal roof with heavy thuds and odd scraping sounds. He pulled out of his stupor long enough to look around, and saw he was strapped like the legs of a holiday turkey, except in his case it was wrists, restrained behind his back, and his ankles.

He was lying next to a blanket that reeked of vomit, on a wooden plank floor. He could only open one eye; had no recollection why the other eye wouldn't open, but it was enough to see he was in the living room of an old cabin, perpendicular to a windowless wall.

He saw a door in the wall that probably led to a bedroom. The wind was relentless; frightening in its random strength and timing, he couldn't predict its mood or power, thus his fear expanded beyond the building, screaming into the woods, then back with the wind, crashing into the windows and doors so hard they seemed ready to fly out of place. Looking around, he saw Ángel was lying about three feet away from him. *Oh mijo, sweet boy, what have I done?*

Ángel was restrained, hands behind his back, ankles tied, struggling at his restraints and crying. Then came a cry from the next room, and Miguel recognized Rosa's voice, followed by a man's rough voice, grunting louder and louder. Then the sharp sound of a hard slap, a groan from the man, and a terrified scream from Rosa. He heard her attacker laugh, over and over, as if he were enjoying some sadistic cartel version of funniest home videos.

"No, No!" Ángel screamed, his booming bass voice penetrated Miguel's soul, with no apparent impact on the brutal rapist.

"Mijo, por favor, no mas. They will hurt you." Miguel begged Ángel to no avail. Ángel's response was immediate.

"Fuck you! That is your daughter in there! My wife! He is raping my wife! I should be silent?" His spittle, mixed with tears, flew toward Miguel with the force of his rage.

"You put her in there with your stupid fucking alcohol and your whoring ways. I hate your fucking guts!" Then Gordo's booming voice coming from behind Miguel blasted a new threat.

"Callate! Te disparare!" [Shut up! I will shoot you!]

threatened the angry giant. Miguel cringed, *he's probably strung out for three or four days,* thought Miguel. Terrified, he swung his head around to see him. The giant was shirtless; his hoodie next to him over the back of a chair. His tats told his story on his bald head, across his face, down his bulky arms, across his muscular fat chest and grotesque belly.

Miguel knew the man was young by normal standards, probably twenty-five, but, by Zeta standards, what was likely ten years of hard drugs, alcohol, and unremitting violence, had aged and hardened him. The tattoos across his chest seemed to be moving; Miguel squinted his eyes for a closer look.

The Z-shaped snake tattoo over his belly button was moving; the ink started to slowly liquefy, to run and wriggle into a gradually forming den of writhing deadly serpents around his navel, then Miguel saw the cavernous interior of the giant's belly open up—it was their den!

The dark hole was filled to overflowing, expelling the venomous demons onto the floor, their forked tongues reading the air like a map to their victims. Rosa's cries seemed to be coming from every direction, like dozens of screeching crows escaping a wildfire, in search of anyone who might help, or a safe place to hide.

The snakes were on the move, he forgot about Rosa. Miguel's brain, deprived of it's hard alcohol supply since his drunken night at the hotel bar, had marched out his first hallucination like a promo for a TV series; promising many terrors to come.

He feared he was sliding into madness down a muddy slough, destined to drown in the sewage of his misdeeds, wide awake, for eternity. As if in confirmation, Ángel screamed a blood-curdling protest. Miguel had lost track of Rosa's plight and thought Ángel was screaming about the snakes. Still, the giant had warned him to be quiet.

"Please Ángel, do not anger him!

*¡Dios ayudanos! [God help us!]*

Despite his too-little-too-late prayer, Miguel heard a guttural grunt, then saw a short wooden stool flying through the air from the giant's direction. He followed its trajectory until the thick round seat, fashioned from the burl of a tree, found Ángel's skull and knocked him cold. Miguel gasped in shock; Ángel was completely unconscious. The giant had put his body's massive force, plus the force of the drugs, behind that rage.

"Ángel, no, Ángel, mijo!" Miguel pleaded with his son-in-law with not one sign of life in view, no matter how hard he watched to see Ángel's chest lift, did it? *No? What's that on his lip?* Miguel saw blood slowly pumping from the gaping wound high above Ángel's ear, inching its way to his lips and then to the floor.

The long brownish-purple rope of blood seemed to have a life of its own as it started to spread across the planks. The rope of blood twisted and turned, and Miguel saw within it a long centipede, headed his way.

The bloody bug began to consume Miguel's attention; it seemed to get bigger as it moved steadily across the planks separating him from Ángel. Miguel realized he'd gotten so distracted by the bug he'd forgotten about Ángel. *How could I?* Jerking his head back toward Ángel, hoping to see a breath, a twitch, a fluttering eyelash, anything.

He saw instead a hoard of centipedes, faster than the one that was now a few inches from his own face; like ants in a disturbed anthill, some snaked their way into Ángel's hair, one in his ear, another up his nose, spreading out in all directions at top speed, then, a number of them fixed on the trail of blood the first one had dragged with him to explore Miguel. Their undulating legs scurried in unison, like soldiers pushing a battering ram forward in battle, headed toward Miguel.

Miguel could see their heads bobbing, the claws behind their heads preparing to inject their venom. He remembered getting stung by a long, frightening centipede for the first time as a kid; it had wrapped itself around his hand and unloaded all its venom. He'd been unable to believe anything could hurt that bad; it could grab your entire being and dare it to prevail against the searing pain.

A sting across his cheek jerked him back to the present. *No! ¡Madre de Dios!* Miguel squirmed, unable to move, saw the entire swarm of centipedes scurrying over the rough floor planks, just inches from his face. As they rushed inside the collar of his shirt and covered his head, he screamed, and prayed the giant would be as kind to him as he had to Ángel, in his gift of merciful death.

## 65

Except for the vans and the hurried takeoff of the charter plane, the Puerto Escondido airport appeared deserted. Their caravan's departure from the airport was stopped in its tracks while the M.D. and two Medevac agents rushed out of their forest-green 'fishing van,' slogged through the rain, and put Addie on a stretcher.

She regained consciousness and looked around, her head throbbing. The red and white Suburbans and the van looked nothing like law enforcement vehicles; their passengers, dressed in all manner of tourist garb, looked nothing like law enforcers.

On the luggage racks, fishing poles and nets stuck out from under tarps, next to beer coolers, wooden slatted boxes filled with melons, mangos, cantaloupes, and bananas. For a minute, she thought she was with the wrong team; then Dean bent over her.

"Addie," he yelled, "you hit your head, knocked yourself out, Doc here is taking you to the med van for an exam. We'll wait." She nodded. They carried her to the van. The doc was thorough.

"Dr. Diaz, I'm Dr. Jimenez. You have a minor concussion. I want you to rest when you get up to the cabin. You wanna go back and ride with Dean? He knows what symptoms to watch for. You can stay here lyin' down if you want."

"I want to go back."

"Okay, I'd like to see how steady you are on your feet. If you buckle on your way there, the medics are going to carry you right back here for the ride, understood?" He gave the medics a hand signal and they walked her to the white Sub, stripped off her soaked jacket, helped her into the middle seat with Mike and Ana, and handed her two ice packs wrapped in a small towel.

"She's a doctor," Addie pointed to Ana, "she'll watch me," They nodded and rushed back to the van. Ana put a blanket over her. "Hey," Addie begged, "please go slow over the potholes."

Since she couldn't see much of anything through the rain-drenched windows, she put her head back on the seat and held the ice pack to it. Dean's voice came through, soft and supportive.

"Addie, just rest. I'll keep you posted on the route. The rest of you, listen up. We're going from the airport, up the main coastal road, then taking a paved road, Jardín de Helecho, north into the mountains about twenty miles to the access road for the lake, Avenida Lago."

"Okay," Ana said. "Helecho in Español, means fern. Fern Garden."

"Thanks, I knew that..." Addie mumbled; without opening her eyes.

"I think she was translating for me, Addie," Mike said in jest, "I never learned much Spanish in Ireland."

The weight of the vehicle and passengers, plus the 4-wheel drive, helped them maintain traction. Addie was dozing when they turned off the coast highway and headed uphill onto Jardín de Helecho; Ana squeezed her hand gently.

"We're heading up now, but don't doze off, remember?"

"All right," she grumbled, sitting up straighter, eyes still shut.

When they finally reached the turnoff to the access road, Addie was feeling more alert. Ana had prescribed fluids, so Addie was nursing a bottle of water. The signage was exactly as Isabel had described. Avenida Lago.

"Let me make a wild guess," Mike quipped, "Lake Avenue, it's our turn off!" Addie could hear the relief in his voice. Avenida Lago was a serpentine road that wound its way steadily uphill for about four miles through the woods, then surprised them as they moved up and over a ridge capped with granite. Dean announced their arrival, peering out through the drenched windshield as the wipers maintained their 4/4 rhythm. The red Sub and med unit pulled up behind him, waiting for orders.

"Here you have it, my undercover fishing buddies, Lago Verde! The lake's usually a mile across, filling up fast, though. That big lagoon we passed near the coast highway is going to get a lot of runoff from these hills."

He pointed to a cabin built into the slope on the lake side of the ridge; its rear door facing them across the adjacent road that circled the lake. Emil, who was driving the red Sub, and Pedro, driver of the med van, showed up at Dean's window, which he quickly rolled down, yelling his directives over the noise of the storm.

"Listen up; the cabin up top here will be for detainees and agents from the medical team. The second cabin is downhill from it;

254

civilians and four agents will stay in the lower cabin." He turned to Addie. "I'm going to check it out, so everyone sit tight."

Addie, pained but curious, scanned the area from her dry vantage point while Dean explored the site. The granite ridge leveled out for about twenty feet, then stopped a few yards shy of the large downhill slope that held the cabins. The lake was beginning to collect significant runoff from the storm, spilling over into a canyon heading downhill toward the port.

The port was miles away, and from their location on the ridge, she saw nothing but storm clouds blanketing cabins and trees, the hills creating a cone to hold the lake, and the white water of the natural spillway down into the canyon.

Addie was ready to claim the softest horizontal surface she could find in the lower cabin. The sharp pains in her head had turned into a solid ache from the cranial pressure; she didn't miss the more intense pain she had earlier; every surge had brought back the sad image she'd seen in her vision; an announcement of the first death of their mission. She prayed it would be the last, but she knew otherwise.

## 66

Compared to the doldrums of the morning's travel, Dean could feel his energy ramping up, impatient to get Joy into Mike and Ana's arms, then to rock the Zeta's world before more harm was done. He walked with Pedro and Emil to check the driveway leading down the slope to the lake. Drenched by the downpour, they walked back to the other vehicles to talk with the agents and the medical team. They looked anxious, excited, and over-ready to find Joy unharmed; Dean knew why no one mentioned Rosa. He returned to the white Sub and gave his passengers the plan.

"See that big stretch of flat granite to the right? It's the best place for the vehicles. We'll park there and carry our gear to the cabins. The upper cabin's only a short walk from here and there's a long connecting stairway on the other side of it to the lower cabin; so, we won't be slogging through the mud, and won't have any hassles getting the vehicles in and out of here. Let's walk carefully through this, I don't want any more injuries, but be as efficient as you can; we have to get to Ramiro's cabin, back here with Joy, then out again to meet up with the Zetas. We need to get Rosa out of their world as soon as we can."

It took fifteen minutes to unload. Everyone hurried, except Addie. With the storm forcing its way into their mission, all risk factors had been raised; Dean admitted to himself that he'd seen this trip with Addie as an adventure, *like some teenager's fantasy…now the ante has been raised beyond anything we planned, I'm glad she's staying put with the Doyles, safely away from whatever's next.* He exhaled a generous pent-up breath when he saw Addie, the Doyles and two agents, Maria and Pedro, walking on the narrow deck around the cabin, heading for the stairway down to the lower cabin.

Dean noticed Pedro was holding Addie's arm per his orders. Two agents went into the upper cabin to get it set up for the expected detainees. The Medical crew were armed FBI agents, except for the M.D., who was a private contractor. They had their van's engine running, ready to follow Dean and Emil to Ramiro's cabin.

Dean and Emil got settled in the white Sub with their weapons close at hand; Dean signaled the med van, then headed over and back down the ridge to the paved Jardin de Helecho. With a glance over the shrouded hills he turned onto the slick asphalt and headed back downhill toward Ramiro's access road. Dean had passed it on the way up without mentioning it. He had wanted to spare Mike and Ana the agony of having to pass it by and feel the frustration of delaying Joy's rescue, but there was no way he could risk their involvement, no way to know if the Zetas had found them. It was 10:30 a.m., the exchange had been set for noon; but Dean knew terrorists had an affinity for surprise.

He groaned inwardly, *yeah, we're off to pick up Ramiro, Adela, Tonio, Joy—and the dog.* Emil hadn't said anything. It had been quiet most of the way, but when they got to Ardilla Cielo, the access road to Ramiro's cabin, Dean had a question.

"So what the hell does ardilla mean? I know cielo is heaven."

"Squirrel Heaven," Emil laughed. "So did they smoke a bowl of pot before they named these access roads, or what?"

"Who knows? Half these roads don't even have a sign, I noticed that on the way up."

"You know, I did too," Emil said, "it seemed odd then but now I wonder if it was intentional." Dean looked at Emil, his brow furrowed.

"Intentional how?"

"Well," Emil's voice altered enough to tell Dean it was unwelcome news, "remember Ramiro said the Zeta gave up the name of their road over the phone, because the guy was so loaded?"

"Yeah, and?"

"What if…"

"Shit!" Dean hit the steering wheel hard.

"Yeah, if they pulled out a few road signs it would give them the upper hand. They figured Ramiro would have to call them when he got here and couldn't locate their road; it gives them the advantage, setting up an alternate exchange point."

A heavy blast of wind and rain struck the sub; as big as it was, it shuddered, lost traction, and slid sideways a few feet into the shoulder of the road. Dean took the time to shift into 4-wheel drive to maneuver through the mud. He made it back to the pavement, then turned onto Ardilla Cielo. The red Sub and med van followed.

"I bet the Zetas had no clue about the weather that was coming, they figured their cell phones would be fine to set up an alternate plan, let's see, I'm going to try a cell call." Emil gave it a shot, with no results. They were almost a mile down the road.

"We're flyin' solo, mission-wise; looks like all the rest of the big decisions will be made by you, Dean."

"Let's check it out with Ramiro, see what he noticed on the way up. First things first; we get Joy back to her folks, then we see if there's a way to solve the Zeta location. Look through that break in the trees, I think that's the place."

"They said they'd hang something on their front doorknob, but what's that?"

"A plastic garbage bag catching a lot of wind…works for me." Dean pulled up carefully about twenty meters back and waited a few minutes. A tall, muscular man, gray beard and hair flying in the wind, peered out a large broken window; the offending tree branch was lying on the ground in front of it.

"That's gotta be Ramiro. No Zeta ever lives past forty, well, not many. I don't think he'd be alive if the Zetas had been here, but you never know; they may have stashed some men inside." He ordered agents Solorio, Serra, Stone, and Reyes, to enter the cabin from the rear, weapons ready, while he and Emil moved toward the front. The crew in the med van stayed put.

As the agents entered through the rear, Dean and Emil, guns drawn, entered through the front. Ramiro greeted them, arms up.

"Señor Dean, Señor Emil?" Dean nodded.

"I'm agent Culhane," Dean said, "this is agent Torres." He had noticed the obsequious informal style with which Ramiro had addressed them, wanted him to drop it.

"First things first. Where is Joy Doyle?"

Ramiro's hands were now cuffed behind his back by Stone; he nodded to the bedroom door.

"The women are in there, my wife Adela, and Joy, and the dog. I needed to make sure it was you."

Dean spoke quickly, "Any weapons in there?"

"A pistol."

"We will get the women." He turned to agent Stone once Tonio's handcuffs were secured.

"I want the place searched for weapons, and Maria, get ready to search the women, restraints on Mrs. Ortiz."

Dean finished with the agents holding Ramiro and Tonio.

"Stone and Reyes, the Ortiz family will ride back to the base camp in the white Sub with me. Time is short, Emil and I need to discuss the Zeta location with them. Frisk Ramiro and Tonio; be very thorough, then walk them out to the Sub and secure their ankles once they are in. Put them in the rear seat with seat belts on. Leave room for Mrs. Ortiz. Stay with them. Keep the area around the cabin secure while we work in here. Serra, you stay here, secure all the weapons and put them in the rear of the red Sub, then cover the perimeter."

Dean moved to the bedroom door with Emil, each leaning against the wall on either side. Dean knocked on the door with his free hand, and spoke with less authoritative threat than usual.

"FBI, put any weapons you have onto the floor, both of you raise your hands high, and walk out. Joy Doyle, stay behind a few feet and let Adela come first." He heard a quiet 'okay' from one of them and the door opened a few inches at a time. He was getting impatient.

"Just open it all the way, put up your hands and come out." The door opened wide, Adela and Joy were standing, arms up. Stationed in front of them, a low growl coming from her throat, was Bella. Dean motioned to Adela with his free hand, and Adela entered the living room. Bella followed, and once again positioned herself between Adela and Dean. Agent Solorio retrieved Adela's pistol from the floor, removed the ammunition, and put both in Ramiro's duffle bag of surrendered weapons.

"I need a leash for the dog," Dean said.

"Yes sir, a leash is there on the table." Dean backed up to the table, gun still on Adela, saw the leash next to their box of food and sodas, and tossed it to Adela.

"Please have a seat and secure your dog. If she gets startled and attacks anyone, she may get shot. Just tie the leash tight to the table leg, we will bring her out when we are finished here" He covered her while she leashed Bella and tied the leash.

"She has a crate over there." Adela added. Dean nodded.

"Agent Solorio, this is Adela Ortiz, and this is Joy Doyle."

They offered formal, polite smiles to each other. Dean cringed when he got a good look at Joy; he'd seen a few beautiful photos at the Doyles' home, and there wasn't much resemblance.

"Okay, frisk both of them; restrain Adela, then let's get out of here, we're running out of time." Noting Adela's anxiety, Dean attempted to clarify her options.

"Señora Ortiz, regulations require restraints for your family until we reach Oaxaca City where charges against you and your son will be either waved or pressed." Joy looked at Dean.

"Why would she frisk me? I'm the victim."

"Ever hear of Patty Hearst?"

"No."

"Well," Dean warmed up his delivery, "you can read up on her case when you get home. Sometimes kidnap victims switch sides, it's just a precaution. Good to find you safe and ready to go." He walked closer, looking at her face.

"How did you get cut?"

"I walked into a broken branch, no one hurt me," she said. Dean could see she was being protective of her captors, and decided to drop the inquiry.

"Your parents are about five miles from here," he said, encouraging her with a smile. "They are eager to see you. It's going to be okay, Joy, just some bad weather, that's all. You're going to stay in a separate cabin with your mom and dad, protected by agents, until the storm blows over. Then you'll be leaving for California."

The storm swung a massive gust of wind over the cabin; one long shard of glass that hadn't blown out of the front window blew out completely. A metal roofing panel flew off, spinning wildly over the trees. Joy and Adela had been facing that direction and screamed in shock. Bella jumped, barked, and pulled on the leash. A heavy crash on the metal roof startled all of them. Bella whined, looked frightened, and cowered against Adela.

"Sounds like another branch…is it safe on the road?" Joy asked, shivering, her lips turning blue from the cold.

"Well, Joy, I think we have to proceed to the base camp and hope for the best. The trees with the shortest roots will be falling over first if the wind keeps up; we can't afford to get trapped here."

"Solorio, put Adela in the far back seat with Ramiro and their

260

son. Wrist and ankle restraints and seat belt. Joy, I'd like you to ride in the second seat between agents Solorio and Serra, Emil up front with me."

"We have been praying for Rosa and Ángel. I asked Jesus to pray for Miguel, I could not do it." Adela said, trembling with emotion. Agent Solorio put the restraints on Adela's wrists, and she submitted without a word.

"You are fluent in English?" Solorio said.

"My son and I have studied English and Spanish for more than fifteen years, with Ramiro," Adela said. "My native tongue is Zapotec."

"Let's not delay," Dean urged Adela, "I'd like to get Joy to her parents and you into our detainee cabin soon, so we can locate the Zeta cabin and get back before dark. It's hard to see right now, if we wait it will be impossible. We, too, are very concerned for Rosa, Ángel...and Miguel." Adela nodded her head toward the door.

"Our bags are all there by the door, and dog food."

"I'll back the car up to the door. We'll put them in the back after you get settled in."

Everyone filed out to the vehicles with a few mishaps but no injuries. Once everyone was settled in, Dean turned around, looked over his passengers, and gave them a reality check.

"The Zetas may be looking for us, we don't know how desperate or aggressive they may be right now, so keep your eyes and ears open; if you see or hear anything or anyone, shout, and get your head down." As planned, the red Sub and the med van moved ahead of them, ready to scout their exit.

Dean sighed, and checked his passengers again. There was no way he could feel uptight as he looked back and saw Bella stretched out lengthwise across the laps of Serra, Joy, and Solorio. Bella was panting, her tongue hanging out the side of her mouth, and she was looking at Dean with something resembling a grin.

## 67

Luisa Diaz had fallen asleep during her afternoon meditation. The recliner chair in her Pescadero cottage had been unusually comfortable. The music she played to facilitate her relaxation became the background music for a startling dream.

She was in Mexico, unable to recognize her surroundings; everything was shrouded in thick fog. She clutched a cell phone in her hand, and walked at a brisk pace, looking for something she could recognize. The phone rang. It was the ringtone Addie used for Isabel's FBI calls. It kept ringing so she answered it. It was Isabel. But Isabel was calling Addie.

"Addie, it's Izzy, I'm so sorry I can't get you any help right now, I'm surprised you can even get my call in that storm, there's nothing I can do. Addie, I'm going crazy here, knowing you are in so much danger and I can't leave San Francisco. Get out of there, Addie! As fast as you can! That narco, he's going to do something deadly!"

"Izzy, I'm fine." Wind gusted in her face, blowing her hair in front of her eyes. Long, black curls flew in her field of vision. She looked at her hand as she lifted it to push the hair out of her eyes and saw Addie's hair, Addie's hand, Addie's wedding ring. She heard Izzy's voice fade as the wind nearly knocked her flat. The fog congealed around her, cutting off her air. She couldn't see, couldn't breathe, gagged for breath, choked, and fell over a cliff. Her weight pulled her down, the fog cleared, water rose to meet her. She jolted awake, still choking.

Once her breath came and went without struggle, she looked around the living room, and from years of practice, replayed the dream for insights. Her heart raced as if it were running to help Addie before it was too late. *A narco will do something deadly—choking—choking Addie?* Try as she might, Luisa could not sort it out. She rose from the chair, rushed to the kitchen, and pulled her cell phone from her purse.

"Merde!" In her haste, she'd hit the wrong contact, had to hang up and start over. This time she found Izzy's name and hit the phone icon correctly. *Please, please pick up, please don't be busy.*

"Luisa? What's up? You hear from Addie?"

"In a way I guess I did. Izzy, please listen, I need your help. I fell asleep, just woke up from a terrible dream. I was Addie, I was choking, could not get my breath…"

Luisa told her the dream in detail, then demanded Izzy tell her what she knew about Addie's situation. Luisa had been licensed as a P.I. years ago, to work intermittently on cases with Addie; she knew the confidentiality requirements of this case, and reminded Izzy.

"Okay, Luísa, this is what I know; I can't reach Addie, the whole mission relocated to the coast, to Puerto Escondido. I'm stuck in San Francisco on another case. No cell service around Puerto Escondido, and we can't get anyone in or out of there until tomorrow because of the hurricane. For God's sake don't tell the girls I told you this; Addie didn't want them freaking out."

"Izzy, I'm going down there, I have to! I don't know what's happening, if I'm closer I might be able to understand. I promise not to interfere, you know I wouldn't, but I'm calling Jerry. He has many contacts in the jet charter business, he will insist on going down with me to Oaxaca City. It is far enough inland to be out of the storm for now, plus, the storm is supposed to head up the coast toward Acapulco the last I heard."

"Luisa," Izzy implored in the calmest voice she could muster, "I would never dream of trying to talk you or Addie out of any psychic hunches you have; I know you are tuned to the right station and your intel is good, even if it's in code and only you can follow it to the truth. So go, I trust your judgment, Luisa. Keep me informed on your progress, that's all I ask."

"Yes, of course," Luisa said, "I have a friend I invited over for tonight, I'm going to tell Kathy and the girls that Jerry needs me to translate for an urgent charter, they will believe it, it's something we've done a number of times, Kathy will stay overnight with the girls."

"Okay, Luisa. You have contributed to the panic I was already in, but I'd rather know than not know, and I'm sorry I couldn't give you any information that makes sense of your dream. Call me when you get to Oaxaca City. At least I'll be able to have phone contact with you, if not with Addie or Dean. I'm no psychic, but my intuition works pretty well…something tells me you are going to know exactly why you had to get down there!"

263

## 68

The noisy heater fan comforted his rain-soaked legs and kept the windows from fogging, but the wipers couldn't keep up with the deluge. He bent forward, squinting through the fleeting visible spaces on the windshield, using his peripheral vision to stay between the trees on either side of the road. A completely washed-out section of the road, now a rushing creek, waited ahead, but where?

He'd made it through that section on the way in; it would be fuller now, so he proceeded with even more caution. No one had spoken since they left the cabin, so he decided to clarify the plan to ease the tension all around. Emil, in his usual mission-ready mode next to Dean, sat silent and vigilant, so Dean proceeded; talking lowered his anxiety, he hoped it helped them as well.

"Can everyone hear me?" A quiet chorus of responses assured him they could. "Here's the plan. We have a base camp, two cabins, not too far from here, sufficiently separated and well-guarded. Joy will join her parents and four agents in the lower cabin.

"Ramiro, Adela and Tonio, the upper cabin is our temporary holding facility for detainees. I know you three have agreed to cooperate with us fully, but it's protocol to keep you restrained until charges are clarified. Emil and I will go to the Zeta cabin with a second car of agents and the medical van after we drop you off. Ramiro…"

"I understand."

"Ramiro, did you make a map to the Zeta cabin?"

"No, that crazy Zeta was rapping so fast I could barely hear him. I heard the street name, Refugio Forestal. He said to call them to work out the details when we got the money to exchange.

"But the road was Refugio Forestal?" Dean said.

"Here is a big problem, Señor Dean. We looked for the road when my cousin Reuben drove us up early this morning. Reuben noticed right away that someone had removed the road markers. He could not remember exactly where Refugio Forestal Road was located, but he knew it was downhill from Ardilla Cielo. It must be one of the streets with the missing signs, there are perhaps fifteen of those. He had no map or cell service this morning, and was in a hurry to evacuate his family so he could help us no further. He has a property manager who handles his rentals, so he doesn't come up this way enough to know all the roads. I had no phone service up here to let you know. Now you say all the cell service is out. What will we do to reach the Zetas? Wait for the cell tower to connect after the storm moves north?" Dean slowed the Sub to a stop, and turned to talk to Ramiro.

"Emil and I came to the same conclusion about the signs on our way down here to pick you up. I was hoping you had an answer.

He turned and pretended to look out the obscured front windshield, breathing slow to avoid showing how angry he was…not at Ramiro…but the situation, which infuriated him. He spoke without turning around, just watched them in the rear-view mirror.

"Well, they were able to come up with a clever move to confuse us, so I'm not sure what the best plan would be at this point. Looks like it may not be possible until tomorrow. We may be forced to wait on phone service to coordinate with the Zetas. I'm open to suggestions from any of you." He began to inch the sub forward as he watched for the washed-out section of road.

"This is a very bad development," Ramiro exhaled his disappointment with a sad sigh. Adela began to cry, repeating Rosa's name between her sobs. This pained Dean; he kept talking just to feel he was accomplishing something.

"We underestimated them, Ramiro, one of them figured out their location had been disclosed in error, and they rushed out to remove the signs to stall you, to confuse any backup you may have called on. Right now, everything at the port is closed for the storm, we can't get a map." He seethed with frustration, and rambled on.

"We let them get the upper hand in this…I thought they were such amateurs, all wacked on drugs, thought we'd have them locked up this afternoon. He looked in the mirror at Joy, who was crying without moving or making a sound.

"Joy? You okay?"

"Rosa…will she survive a delay?"

He felt her question hit the bulls eye of his frustration and felt his own eyes stinging as he held tears back.

"Our first priority is to get you safely to your parents."

It wasn't the answer she had wanted to hear.

## 69

Dean, in a rush to get Joy settled at the cabin, parked alongside the other cars on the broad granite slab, and opened the car door a few inches. Bella sat up, sniffing the incoming wind, whined, and pulled at the leash in Joy's hand. Dean pulled his poncho on, secured the hood of his poncho over his red cap and conveyed the plan.

"Emil, grab that bag of dog food out of the back of the car; you and I will take Joy to the lower cabin to her parents. We need to work fast on an alternate plan for the Zetas, and I'm praying someone's made coffee. Joy, civilians from the lower cabin may not leave for any reason. We have no idea if the Zetas are scouting us here or are curled around a wood stove in their cabin. The dog can stay down in the lower cabin with you, Joy, you can take care of her."

Dean looked around at the chaotic wind shapeshifting the frantic trees; they looked like hundreds of people waving their arms and bodies in a contorted reaction to an unseen emergency. His respect for the storm's power grew, and rushed him through his orders to the agents in the seat behind him.

"Pedro, get Ramiro's gear out of the back of the car. Then secure Ramiro, Adela and Tonio in the upper cabin, in their own room. Keep their wrist restraints on, remove the ankle restraints and walk them inside. Maria, you monitor Adela to the bathroom, in the bathroom, and back to their room, then get her ankle restraints on. Pedro, same with the men, one at a time." Pedro nodded.

"They have cooperated with us as promised," Dean stressed, "but we can't take anything for granted. Maria, have the M.D. check Ramiro out as soon as he's inside. Ramiro, for everyone's sake, give the doc an honest health history. We don't need any more surprises. Adela, make sure Ramiro's being truthful with the doc. Also, tell the doc that our kidnap victim has a laceration on her face and may require antibiotics. Let's go."

Emil went first, his dripping parka hood obscured his identity until the wind whipped it aside. Dean smiled, noting that Emil was toting the dog food bag under one arm and holding Bella's leash with the other with no free hand to pull the hood up. Emil led the way around the upper cabin's deck, and stepped down the first few stairs to the lower cabin.

He paused for a second to check the remaining stairs, with Dean and Joy right behind. Joy reached out and pulled Emil's hood back over his head, patted it twice, and Emil continued, as if he and Joy had worked out the assist telepathically. Bella started barking as they approached the back door; loud, staccato barks. Emil opened the door and Bella ran in, her leash dragging behind, tail swirling in a circle, leaping into the hallway, still barking. A kerosene lamp hung from an iron hook high on the wall, flooding the space with an odd array of light.

Emil, then Joy and Dean, walked through the door to see Ana and Mike rushing toward Joy down the hallway. As Joy embraced her parents, Addie rushed into the hall, smiling at the Doyles, then approached Dean and Emil, congratulating them. Dean barely noticed Addie greet Emil. His eyes were riveted on the love he saw between Ana, Joy and Mike. He watched them, like three petals of a night-closing flower, folding into each other's familiar embrace; their tears of gratitude shimmering in the light from the lamp.

Dean became nothing but heart, an inclusive unity that drew Addie close, her face warm against his, the alchemy of their tears birthed a promise. As Dean's arms greeted Addie, Bella's head nudged underneath, her body rubbing against their legs. When Dean looked down, Bella looked up and thanked him; how, he wasn't sure, yet with so much gratitude filling the tunnel of the cabin's hallway, how could she not absorb it and be compelled to pass it on?

## 70

Addie entered her bedroom with Dean and Emil, each of them holding a freshly brewed cup of Mike's coffee.

"The heat from the wood stove can't reach us here, but you asked for a private conference, so…" Addie wrapped herself in a blanket and sat on the bed, Emil and Dean kept their jackets on and perched on the two small upholstered chairs near the bed. A piece of cardboard she had duct-taped to the broken bedroom window kept moving from the wind, but remained in place.

"You guys look like you're ready to jump up any second; what's going on? We just survived the reunion of the century, so from here on out the force is definitely with us, right?"

They laughed and tried to relax back into their chairs, but to no avail. She could see the tension in their lips, Emil was chewing on his, and Deans were pursed shut but in constant motion. Dean nodded to Emil, so he presented Addie with their quandary about when and how to carry out the confrontation with the Zetas.

"Oh no!" Addie shook her head repeatedly, then, too loud for privacy, blurted "How can we possibly wait until tomorrow, with Rosa there?" Before she could think another thought, she heard a knock on the door, and jumped to answer it. Joy stood straight, as tall and strong as Addie, who stared as if she were looking into a mirror from her past. Joy jumped to explain the interruption.

"I came to tell you something urgent about Rosa, then I heard what you just said. I think I can help, may I come in?" Addie looked at the men, seeking their reaction. Emil nodded, Dean gestured his assent with his hand. Joy entered, shut the door, and sat on the bed next to Addie, shivering; Addie opened her blanket and wrapped it around both of them. Joy talked so fast they could barely keep up.

"I'm trying to control myself, but it's not easy. I know there was an option to wait until the Zetas call tomorrow, but you can't. I can feel it; she's in big, big trouble. I love Rosa, we have been together for days on end, right up to the…the night they took me." Dean startled, rubbed his face hard with both hands, then rubbed his hands hard against each other.

"What do you propose?" He said. "We just drive up and down

every single unmarked road until we see their Navigator? It's one idea, though how many miles and how much gas…with the storm coming harder, all of us, plus three vehicles, we might lose one completely."

Joy reached up to her neck and pulled the beautifully woven silver necklace over her head, held it out in front of her body; displaying an engraved pendant the size of a US silver dollar. It swung slowly from the woven chain, and their eyes followed.

"I've been working on my psychic skills behind my parents' backs, just didn't want them worrying about where it might lead. So, the teacher I've worked with uses a technique that involves holding an object that someone wore a lot; their glasses, a watch, jewelry, something that's been in their energy field." She slowed her pace.

"It's called psychometry. The unique energy pattern of the person merges with the energy in the object, and you connect with it and with them telepathically. Then you wait for visual clues, smells, feelings, or sounds."

Addie had been nodding her agreement, then spoke.

"I know what you mean, I've done it on crime scenes when we've searched for an abducted victim. Sometimes a family member provides something; a special toy or blanket if it's a child, for example."

"Exactly," Joy held out the necklace, "Rosa gave me this, her dearest aunt had given it to her for graduation. When her aunt died, Rosa put it on, and wore it non-stop for the past two years. She wanted me to have it, gave it to me on Christmas Eve. Addie, I've been wearing it, and picking up her suffering, her cries for help. You must go get her right now! Please, I'm begging you!"

Joy put the necklace in Addie's hand, covered it with her own, and looked into Addie's eyes, imploring her to act.

"Dr. Diaz, the minute you met us in the hallway, I remembered you from your TV show, so I know you can find Rosa!"

Clearly, Mike and Ana hadn't yet told Joy that Addie was her birthmother; so Addie was grateful to be able to stay focused on Rosa's emergency. She closed her eyes, feeling the raised design on the pendant with her fingertips. She felt herself swaying back and forth…then a vision; the wind picked her up and lifted her through the air, above trees, roads, and cabins.

"I see big pieces of broken glass floating up from a cabin

269

chimney, like smoke. As they come closer, the bigger ones have moving pictures; they're like videos embedded into pieces of clear glass, rising in front of me in razor-sharp angled shapes."

Addie had her eyes closed, but she knew they were waiting for something more, so she continued to look at the glass swirling slowly around her.

"One piece is showing me Miguel and Ángel, in restraints." Her vision from the airport confirmed what she was seeing now. Ángel had been killed. "Ángel is not alive, I'm positive. It confirms the vision I got when I fell at the airport. As for Miguel, he is squirming on a wood floor. He's very sick, but alive." She paused.

"Here comes another picture. Two young men, slapping each other, laughing, one is holding up chunks of crystals to admire, crystal meth. Their leader, the big guy, is watching them." She waited. No one spoke. Then, when she saw the last image she choked, choked again, then spoke in a half-whisper.

"The last image, as big as a sliding glass door...oh God...it's a moving picture of Rosa, her non-physical body floating above a bed, and reaching out to me. Blood pouring down from her face. Her physical body's on the bed...a man is on her...like a tattooed pig..."

A painful shudder passed through Addie when she viewed Rosa's desperate plea for help. She looked for clues, moving over the forest below, saw a rain-gorged arroyo hurtling down the mountain, saw the cabin, and the access road in front of it. She felt the wind blow her body hard to the highway.

"I'm going out to the highway, then up to the FBI access road. Okay, I'm going to turn around and go slow down the highway...it's vague...I don't know how far to go. I see unmarked access roads...wait...here's another one with no sign," her voice got louder, "there's a trail of broken glass from the highway, trailing into the woods. Excellent!"

Addie opened her eyes and shouted, "Let's go!"

Dean, Emil and Joy were shocked silent and fixed on her face. She continued to stare at the necklace, then looked straight at Dean.

"I can find it. I know you said I wasn't supposed to leave this cabin until the Zetas were captured and detained; but the main symbol I see over and over is broken glass; I will know that road when I see it."

Dean rubbed his face hard, as if trying to wash away what he had imagined from her description. She watched, aware she had omitted her close-up vision, the terrifying force of the water plunging down the arroyo; it didn't seem relevant to the conversation. Her head bent over the necklace in her hands, she moved only her eyes, looking up at each of them. A quality of inevitability inhabited her voice as she spoke.

"I must go with you. It's the only way." She turned to Joy, and gently wiped her tears with the emerging corner of the fleece blanket. Joy opened her eyes to look at Addie.

"Thank you Joy, you have saved her life." Addie unwrapped herself from the blanket, got up, and stepped in behind Dean and Emil, who were already heading out the door.

## 71

Miguel's delirium was in full swing. Ángel lay on his side, arms restrained behind him, facing Miguel. Miguel knew Ángel was dead; yet when he fixed his glance on Ángel's face, the lips briefly smiled, the nose would twitch, the eyelids would begin to part, then flip open when he least expected it. A stinging pain scorched Miguel's forehead as claws behind the centipede's head injected their venom.

More crawled on him now, but with his hands and feet tied in plastic restraints he could only thrash back and forth, crying out for help. He knew all the snakes from the giant's gut and the centipedes from Ángel's animated corpse were coming for him, every one of them. He screamed, again and again. The Zeta leader slapped his bare belly, his huge bass voice roaring with derisive laughter.

"Ah!" shouted the laughing stool-throwing hulk to his compadres, "el anciano tiene delerium!" [the old man has delirium]. The two youngest Zetas came from the kitchen to laugh at Miguel along with their leader as they watched Miguel, drenched in sweat, screaming in pain.

"Ciempies! centipedes, ciempies!"

They laughed as he cried; Gordo mocked Miguel, screaming in his loud bass voice "Ayudame, ayudame!"

Hearing his compadre's call for help, Manuel, second in command, opened the bedroom door, gun in hand, clothed only in tattoos from the balding crown of his head to his feet, expecting some serious trouble, only to see his Zeta pals in open hysterical laughter—laughter which spiked exponentially at the sight of their short, fat, and naked gun-wielding friend. His mouth gaped in surprise, displaying a few stray teeth, his sweaty hair spoked out in all directions. The four Zetas exploded into a new round of high pitched laughter, bodies contorting into newer, funnier, meth-energized gyrations.

No one noticed Rosa. While the men were captured by the intense comedy of Manuel's demeanor, for which they had been primed by their hours of sadistic entertainment, she was smart enough to run first and worry about clothing later. She climbed out the bedroom window unnoticed, ran behind the cabin, down the flooded road toward the highway.

The blasting wind whipped her long, soaked hair above her head like black streaks of lightening. Mud flew skyward from each frenzied stride she took; her breath wove a scratching groan between the slap of each footfall. Her arms pumped, palms open, as if the rain were a pounding surf trying to pull her under.

Inside the cabin, the Zetas, unaware of Rosa's flight, still hooted at their own jokes, and bragged about a high-income future ahead on the comedy circuit. The two skinny young recruits, sporting fewer tattoos than their seniors, ran shirtless around Miguel and Ángel, teasing Miguel with drug-enhanced creativity. They shouted like little girls running from a centipede stampede, with high pitched squeals, flapping their hands in a swatting motion, running close to Ángel's inert form, giving him a kick in the back, then over to Miguel, to pretend they were seeing the bugs too, yelling everything they could to freak him completely out; succeeding in every way, as Miguel slipped further into his alcohol-deprived, fully insane mind.

A massive bolt of lightning exploded over the cabin like a grenade from an RPG; with a bone-rattling boom that jolted the play out of the revelers. Miguel's eyes opened wide to see Manuel rush to the window by the front door; his tattoos looked like they were extruding ink, running down the length of his naked body into a pool around his bare feet. A second strike hit a tree across the access road. The flash of light illumined Rosa's naked form, skirting down the road like a kite shoved by the wind.

"Gordo! La puta escapó!" [The whore escaped!]

Manuel pulled on the remaining hair that stuck out from the sides of his head, as if to punish himself, then thrust his hands up stiffly, in a pleading gesture.

The giant spun, spit flying with each word of condemnation. "Usted la desató? [You untied her?]

"Si," Manuel said, recoiling in fear.

"La necesitamos para el rescate!" [We need her for the ransom!] Gordo turned to the apprentices, slapped one on the face hard and pointed to their remaining live victim.

"Quédate aquí y no los toques!" [Stay here and don't touch him!].

Gordo turned to Manuel in a panic, then grabbed his gun and

273

his jacket from the table.

"Manuel! Debemos traerla de Vuelta!"

[! We must bring her back!]

Manuel ran naked into the deafening storm, waving his pistol, screaming for Rosa to stop.

## 72

The morning high tide, propelled by the storm surge, had barreled over the sandbar protecting the Manialtepec Lagoon. A few miles south, shop owners and residents of Puerto Escondido rushed to finish boarding up beachside businesses and homes in the whipping rain and wind. Tropical storm Tanya was picking up speed over the warm offshore waters, its way northward stalled, with gusts up to eighty miles per hour.

Coastal birds had abandoned their wind-shredded nests in the lagoon, to seek shelter inland. Tanya was greedily transforming herself into a category one hurricane. The hills fought back; blocking the wind and rain, slowing the power of the storm, but not giving the agents at Lago Verde much of a break in their rush to the Zeta cabin. They had no time to notice their gorged lake was overflowing into its ancient arroyo, slamming thousands of pounds of debris, silt and water downhill, out of sight, to flood the lagoon from its inland side.

They sped around the granite parking area above the FBI cabins, loading the vehicles, eager to leave. Addie's confirmation of Ángel's murder and Rosa's rape had proven they were already late.

She stood next to the white Suburban, her head barely visible under the hood of her jacket. She was shivering from fear; grateful Dean would see it as a reaction to the cold, relentless rain. Dean paced, checked to make sure the weapons, chain saws, machetes and containers of extra gas had been secured on the luggage racks of the vans as he had requested. She could see he wore a holstered Glock, and had put an MP5/10 submachine gun within reach behind his seat.

"Pick your preferred seating, doctor, I'm driving this, Emil's driving the red Sub, full of agents. Pedro's driving the medical van, with the M.D., and armed medics. On the way back we will have passengers, hopefully no deceased besides Ángel. I'm hoping you won't need to use the Glock, but on the off chance…" Addie interrupted him as she tossed the gun bag into the front seat and climbed in.

"I checked them out; noticed the modified sights, which will help if visibility is poor. No modifications on the trigger, if I use it I need to take my time on the trigger press."

Dean got in, and wiping the rain from his face, he frowned in her direction; his tension emanating unabated.

"So, you're good there, and knowing you, you worked with the holsters too. As for our search mission, I'm feeling concerned about gasoline Addie, so rev up your vision process; without it, oh hell, it's stupid for me to worry. Let's stick with what works, Addie. You've done this before, you'll do it again."

"Okay, I've never done it under emergency weather conditions before," she grasped the pendant as if trying to squeeze the information from it, "let me calm myself and focus. Just get us out to the main road, and head for the unmarked roads. The street name the Zetas gave Ramiro was what?"

"Refugio Forestal, Forest Refuge. But hey, if the sign's gone, what good is the name?"

"When something has a name associated with it for a period of time, it's still possible to sense it, even if the physical evidence is no longer there. It's one more connection we are making with that destination; probably hundreds of people have driven up this road over the years looking for that sign, saying the name of the road, seeing it, turning into it, so it adds to the collective psychic information about it. It becomes a denser energy field."

"If you say so, then I'm buying. By the way, I gave the crew a rundown on your investigative skills, how you've located criminals and abduction victims in the past. You know, your street cred."

"Okay, good idea. Keeping them optimistic will help me stay focused. I'm going to center down here."

"I know you can do it."

"Shush."

"Okay."

Dean got the heater, defroster, and wipers going. They fastened their seatbelts. He drove out to the highway, then turned downhill. Addie figured the two crews that followed them had at least some confidence she would find the Zeta cabin.

Eyes closed, Addie held Rosa's necklace, fingers stroking the pendant, sending the strongest emotional directive to Rosa that she could muster. *Rosa! We're coming for you now! Looking for the Zeta's road to the main highway, help me however you can!* Ben Robinson's image came to her mind; she felt he was with her. *Easy for him, he's been doing this remote viewing for decades.*

She heard a tinkling sound, like wind chimes. *Glass wind chimes! The sound is clear, as if it has its own intentionality.* She opened her eyes and looked at the access road signs, just in time to see the first road with no sign. The tinkling sound stopped. Does that mean this is it? Or does it mean it's definitely not it? Nothing else presented, no feeling, empty silence. *That would be a no. If I'm not feeling it, nothing's there.* Without pulling herself out of her semi-trance, she spoke quietly to Dean.

"That's not it, just go slow, I have something to use, the sound of glass; I'm listening for a wind chime. Stay quiet now." Eyes back onto the slight uphill grade to her left, another unmarked road ahead.

She calmed herself, focused on Rosa and repeated the message in her mind. *We are coming closer to Refugio Forestal, I am listening.* She thought she heard panting; looked at Dean; his respiration was slow. *That rules Dean out, but I still hear that panting breath, close by...*she heard fast footsteps, then the panting breath, huh, huh, huh...and...a drum? No...a heart...she felt she was inside it, felt its force, heard its cavernous reverberating boom, then feet slapping against the ground. Breath, heartbeat, footsteps, all moving faster, louder...*are the Zetas on foot, getting ready to ambush us?*

"Look out!!" Dean yelled as they came around a curve. They were heading downhill, with the cliff off to the right side of the Sub, speeding toward the front end of an ancient, rusted truck, coming at them on their side of the road. Dean swerved the Sub into the empty lane as the truck swerved back into his own uphill lane, veering away from Emil in the red Sub. Addie looked around, and saw Emil and Pedro putting more room between the three vehicles.

Eyes forward, another road about forty yards ahead; Addie took long, deep breaths, slowed her heart rate, watched and listened. Relieved, she watched the road coming closer. *Rosa, is this it?* The percussion of breath, heartbeat, footsteps, persisted. She fully expected results from the access road as they came up to it, then crept slowly past. *Nothing! Not a damn sound!*

"Shit! Oh Rosa! Where are you? Help me, help me!" She hit the dashboard, then slapped it over and over.

"Whoa! Addie, please, I know you're frustrated, but you want the right road, correct?"

"Of course, I want the right f-ing road, why would you say that?"

"Because it's there…it's just not here. We want it, we will find it, I know we will. I can almost see it myself. Please get back to calm."

"Easy for you to say, I'm hearing someone's heart beat like a kettle drum, their breath panting, feet slapping the ground for the last five minutes; all this racket in my head, trying to listen for a damn wind chime, give me an f-ing break!"

"Oh No!" Dean groaned, coming around a curve onto a straight section of road. Addie saw it about sixty yards ahead; a pine tree at least a hundred feet long, stretched across the road and over the edge of a steep cliff. The wipers whipped heavy rain with scant space for them to see as they inched ahead, eyes on the tree. Addie checked the side mirror again and saw Emil waving to them; he'd seen it too.

"No wonder that guy in the truck was goin' like a bat outa' hell," Addie yelled, "that tree must have hit the road right behind him! We can go after it with the chain saw," Addie urged. "If everybody helps we could cut out a section in fifteen minutes. Too bad we don't have a wench."

"Guess we don't have much choice," Dean groaned, "first, we need to see if they cut it down to stop us for an ambush." As they approached, about twenty yards from the tree, Addie saw the roots of the toppled tree.

"Good, it just fell. Let's just drive on up to the damn thing, cut it and move on." She leaned down to retrieve her pistol from the backpack. The job would require everyone's help, either with the tree or firearms cover. Reaching for the backpack, the necklace slipped from her hand to the floor; she bent down farther to get it.

As her head leaned down below the windshield's height, she prayed for no sudden stops, then heard what she thought was something smashing the windshield, she pulled her face to her knees and her arms over her head to protect herself from the broken glass. The noise grew, until she caught on and sat bolt upright, saw the windshield was unbroken, while the sound of hundreds of windchimes clanged the most unsettling alarm she'd ever heard.

"Dean, stop, stop, stop!!!"

278

## 73

Dean slowed to a stop and looked at her, eager for a sign. She pointed, her eyebrows and eyes wide with excitement.

Halfway to the log, on the left side of the road, was an access road embedded in the thick forest, so surrounded by trees and undergrowth it was barely visible, like a large cave with a huge tongue of water flowing out of its mouth onto the highway. The chimes rang, incessant, insistent. She yelled over the internal din.

"Go into that entry! That's the one! To hell with the log."

"All right, Addie, all right, let's go!" He stuck his arm out the window and gave Emil a pumping thumbs-up, then turned into the dark arch below the intertwined branches. The minute they drove under the arched canopy of treetops and headed up the flooding road, the clanging noise shifted to a lower volume in her head.

She could almost hear the cheers coming from behind their car, saw arms waving out windows with thumbs-up. Addie was riding on an emotion she'd never felt. *Is this how it is, you keep pushing yourself to grow and there's completely new emotions at every level?* She yelled at Dean.

"Let's go is right, let's get this done!"

"Keep your eyes peeled for shooters," he cautioned, "I gotta watch this creek that's masquerading as a road." He turned on the headlights, then just as fast turned them off.

"Crap; damned if they're on, damned if they're off! This thick patch of forest isn't making it any easier. The clouds are so dark, the sun's dropping behind the mountain, light was low on the main road, now that we're in here I can barely see anything, but if I turn on the lights I'm giving away our position. I'm already keeping the engine as quiet as possible, thank God, the wind's drowning out most of the noise." They crawled forward, the visibility decreased.

Addie reached into the console and grabbed the adjustable flashlight, then jumped out the door, slammed it, and ran in front of the car. Keeping the light pointed down to the ground, she walked forward fast. Her breath pumped, her heart pounded, her boots stomped through the rushing water, forward, aching for results, seeing nothing but the black space in front of her and the gnarled trees scratching at her when she veered off course.

Addie squinted for any sign of light from cabins ahead, saw one dilapidated cabin, half of it collapsed into a heap. She pushed forward, her boots now filled with water, chilling her legs into cold wood.

The road turned sharply to the right, she turned around, carefully signaled Dean and walked backwards slow enough to light the turn. Dean followed, until it was straight again. A massive gust of wind hit her, spun her around and down into low branches that broke her fall. Back on her feet, flashlight still gripped tight, she shoved the flapping hood of the jacket off her head and continued. Dean had stopped and opened his door, but once she recovered and started walking again, he shut the door and drove ahead toward the light she held.

The water that had washed out the first section of road had found another course at the right angle turn they'd made. Her footing was more secure here, encouraging her to forge ahead faster, the light dragging its trail in the mud beneath her. She started making better time. Rosa's necklace seemed to be catching on the zipper inside her jacket, pulling on her neck hard. She reached up and started pulling at the woven chain as she jogged a steady pace, careful to never shine the light anywhere but down.

Her hand reached the round pendant, grasped it and pulled it out. Deafening sounds of gasping breath, uneven footfalls and desperate heartbeats surrounded her as she gripped her silver lifeline to Rosa. Urgency took on new meaning, she was terrified she'd be too late. *Oh God, hang on, hang on Rosa, we're here!* Danger approached, palpable and evil; she let go of the pendant, stopped, bent down, felt for the ankle holster, and grabbed the Glock she had secured during the drive. She ran as fast as she could, digging her boots into the road, ran for Rosa's life, forgot her own, then on impulse, pointed the flashlight straight ahead, until it found Rosa coming up the road, completely naked, screaming, waving hard. Behind her by a good twenty yards, gaining on her, a short stocky naked man, who, when Addie put the light on him, raised his gun.

*Shoot and give up our position to his crew, or not shoot and lose Rosa to that pig's bullet. He's probably on orders to keep her alive for the ransom, so it's me he's gonna try to drop.*

Dean flipped on the headlights, her signal to go ahead and

shoot. Addie dropped the flashlight, stopped, and aimed with both hands on her gun. A close shot from the Zeta hit a tree about three feet from her head.

"Down Rosa!" She screamed, and Rosa dove forward into the mud just before Addie's shot went off. Addie aimed at his knee, hoping to miss his femoral artery. The guy hit the ground screaming, grabbing his right knee with both hands, his weapon disappearing into the mud. She looked ahead on the road to check for more shooters, then back to Dean in the white Sub. Four of the medivac agents rushed forward, guns drawn; two ran to Rosa, and two for the Zeta. Other armed agents stayed behind open car doors, covering them. Rosa started crawling forward, Addie screamed at her.

"Stay down Rosa! Don't move!" Agents rushed to her, one watched for possible attackers while the other threw a blanket around her mud-soaked body, then lifted her as if she weighed ounces instead of pounds, and ran with her to the med van.

Addie heard the wounded Zeta squealing like a massive tortured pig. The horrific sound seemed to have originated in his throat, plunged through his body, and, with the pain, blasted straight out of his exploded knee. The agents had moved him onto a stretcher and were headed for the med van.

She sensed another Zeta's presence but couldn't see him. *The big guy who was spotted on Rico's dash cam...he's here somewhere.* She backed up and braced herself against the massive trunk of a roadside tree. Arms extended, she aimed the gun straight ahead, panning along the brush across the road as the agents rushed past with the stretcher.

Dean and Emil rushed out of the Sub and headed for Addie. Shots exploded from the trees behind her. Emil and Dean hit the mud, signaling her to let her know they weren't hit. More agents ran into the trees trying to get an angle on the shooter. *There's enough cover, just get your ass back in the car!* She squatted fast, shoved the pistol back into the ankle holster, *and stood back up. Now, run like hell!!!*

The giant's hand reached out from behind the tree trunk, viciously encircled her neck, muted her vocal chords, and dragged her backwards, into the forest...like a mountain lion heading for a quiet spot to eat his half-stunned prey.

## 74

"Mom, Dad, no one hurt me! This is a cut I got from a broken branch I walked into last night on my way to the bunker!" The flaming logs in the fireplace by their couch popped enough to startle all three of them.

"Oh, no, just the thought that you were actually under the ground!" Joy looked at Ana and was shocked to see the tension in her face.

"Mom, let's not talk about it right now." Ana recovered, and looked at Joy again.

"Thank God, thank God, we're going to be okay. I hope Addie, Dean and their team don't run into trouble; they may be gone for a few hours."

"Not to change the subject, but what's with the dog?" Mike pointed to Bella.

"It's Tonio's dog, she is the best, no one wanted to leave her behind, she's been with him since he was five. Ramiro got her from a US ex pat in Oaxaca, a retired woman who had brought a breeding pair with her. Dean says she has to stay down here with us. By the way, Dad, that venison jerky you're eating is hers, so you'd better give her some." Mike obeyed, hugged Bella, ruffled her fur, then spoke.

"So Tonio is Ramiro's son?"

Joy wondered how this would go, decided to tell them just enough to assuage their concerns.

"Yes. He is Ramiro's adopted son. He's very kind and well-educated; he's half Zapotec, raised up in the forest near the Zapotec village, in relative isolation. His mom Adela is Zapotec." Joy sensed Ana and Mike had no trust that Tonio was innocent.

"Okay. This is important. You need to know that Ramiro never told Adela and Tonio about the kidnapping until after he did it. He's terminally ill; his heart, I think. He was desperate to get them out of Mexico before it was too late. When they first took me from the cab I was restrained. I was freaked and worried, that's true, but no one said or did anything during the car ride, the other men were dropped off in town, and only Ramiro drove me up to his hideout in the mountains." Joy could see she was making some progress.

"Things got better, and they tried to be as kind as possible; even Ramiro was wracked with guilt, and I think I gained five pounds on Adela's burritos. That's all I'm saying, for now, don't bring it up again until I'm ready. Promise me." She stared them down until they assented. Mike changed the subject as requested.

"Bella's beautiful. She sure loves you, Joy!" He looked at Joy without moving, Bella licked his face, then allowed him to stand up without moving to follow him.

"You hungry?" Joy ached to see him trying so hard. Deep furrows in his forehead rolled into his uncombed red curls.

"I bet you're starving," he insisted, "let me make you some food." He was wearing a plaid long-sleeved jacket over a T-shirt, and khakis spotted with soot from the wood stove. Joy had almost forgotten how adorable he was, and held her hand up to him gently.

"Dad, stop. Mom, I want you to hear this, one last thing; it's really important. I don't want Tonio going to jail, I want him to have a chance. I don't even want Ramiro and Adela to go to jail either. Let the monsters go to jail, there are plenty of those."

Joy was at a loss as to what to do or say next.

"I know, let's make some more coffee." Mike blurted out.

"Do you have any more of the good stuff?" Joy was all over this offer.

"I actually brought a pound. Good thing I bought it ground, right? We've got hot water on the wood stove, let's do this."

Joy could see he was thrilled to have something practical to do for her. Ana stroked her hair and smiled.

"Let me check your cut," Ana said, "this looks a lot better than gauze, and it's waterproof. Whoever helped you with this knew what to do; it's almost as snug as stitches. Did it get washed out properly? Looks inflamed, but not bad." she dug into her medical kit, "here's some antibiotics. Take two now, then one…"

"I know, mom, every four hours. Thanks. Tonio was the one who treated the cut. Cleaned it out with a lot of sterile water and put some antibiotic ointment in before he closed it up." *I'm not telling her we were alone in the bunker when he bandaged it, and, for sure, I'm not saying anything about what happened next!* Joy felt her face flush just thinking about it. Ana noticed.

"You feeling okay? Getting a fever?"

Ana's hand went onto Joy's face with a gentleness that soothed and comforted as it sought an answer to the question.

"Sometimes feeling stressed can cause your face to flush; just relax, Joy. This is almost over. I'm glad you got a chance to clean up and change clothes."

Ana had brought an outfit they'd gotten Joy for her birthday. Joy's freshly-washed hair, turquoise pullover, black jeans and high leather boots appeared to have revived her visage and her spirits. Mike gave her a kiss on top of her head.

"You look so beautiful, Joy...stunning actually.'"

"Okay dad, enough gushing, although I admit I feel somewhat reborn." Ana gave her a hug.

"I just want to hold you and smile at you non-stop. Now I can stop worrying about you being safe. I know you were shocked out of your wits when you saw that Addie Diaz was here helping the FBI with this case. She was assigned to us last Saturday; we had lost our minds and needed them back. The FBI case coordinator, Isabel Chung, wanted her for us because she's an adoptive parent, and a great therapist..."

"And one amazing psychic," Joy said, then Mike jumped in. "Of course, and I know you'll get a chance to really talk with Addie later. They jumped into that meeting so fast when Dean and Emil brought you back here, something about having to come up with a new plan right away, and they disappeared into Addie's room."

"I know, I heard them and went in there for a few minutes."

"You walked into an FBI planning session uninvited?" Joy could tell Ana was shocked. She looked at her, and told the whole story of the necklace, the missing road signs, and Dean's reluctance to go back out without a plan.

"Mom, I knew the Zetas were hurting Rosa, I knew giving that necklace to Addie was exactly what Rosa was trying to tell me to do. Addie got a vision of how to find Rosa the minute she held the necklace, so they left." Joy noticed Ana was ready to open up.

"Joy, you don't have to justify the importance of your psychic gifts to us anymore; We've had quite a tutorial on how legit it is." Ana shifted her position, and faced Joy directly, smiling.

"What is it Mom, I know this look…"

Ana pursed her lips and squinted her eyes in a mysterious expression Joy had learned to love.

"It's really good news. We're all on emotional overload anyway, so what's one more emotional milestone in the mix? Actually, I think it will be more healing than upsetting…"

"So, tell me, if it's something good, of course I want to hear."

"All right, ask and you shall receive. As I said earlier, Isabel picked Addie for us because she didn't have any other therapists who could straddle all the adoption-related fears along with this FBI case…"

"That makes sense, you guys are a little gun shy when it comes to the adoption stuff."

"Well, after our first session Saturday I felt I had to call Addie and tell her you left that message for us on the house voicemail. I was telling Addie you called because it was your birthday; I reminisced about the date and exact time of your birth, your birth weight, how we adopted you, and brought you home from Stanford hospital. Then Isabel called me, I had to get off the call with Addie."

Ana paused, grasped Joy's hands, squeezed, took a deep breath and exhaled slowly.

"Joy, at the Monday morning FBI meeting, Addie announced she had to recuse herself as our therapist; because the information I'd detailed to her about your birth made it clear…" Ana paused, visibly unsettled.

"She is your birthmother. She showed us your original birth certificate on Monday. It matched the one we have. Except for the parents' names of course, so there is absolutely no doubt."

Joy couldn't speak. She looked at Ana, at Mike, as if she'd just been told a UFO had landed in their back yard, and a six-armed alien met them on the deck with gifts. Ana spoke again before Joy could talk.

"Agent Torres had to search your backpack. He showed us the letter from the adoption agency telling you they could connect you with her as you requested, without giving you her name yet." Joy looked more startled.

"I didn't plan to meet her behind your back, I was just checking out the options, so we could discuss it, Mom."

"You don't have to protect our feelings around this, Joy," she glanced at Mike and he nodded in agreement.

"We are more than thrilled to have connected with her. The FBI wanted her to join us here in case we needed help locating you.

She quit her job as our therapist and flew with us to Oaxaca City, then here to Puerto Escondido."

"Oh, my God, Mom, Dad, you're okay with it! With her?"

"Well, it's been five days since we found out; we've had time to adjust," Mike said.

"Addie is thrilled that you, your mom and I love each other like crazy, and…well, that convinced me she's to be trusted…and…she's a lot like you, so what's not to love?"

"Wow…this is amazing." Joy smiled, then cried. "These are happy tears, and tears of relief," she said. Ana moved her hand gently back and forth across Joy's back. Joy wiped her tears, sighed, and smiled at Ana.

"Joy, you have the most satisfied, peaceful smile, the way you used to look at me when you finished your bottle, you'd push it out of your mouth, then look up at me and give me that smile. I would sit there thinking nothing on earth ever made me feel so at peace, so complete."

"I love you, Mom, that's why, I just love you so much. I will never take your love for granted again either. It means everything to me."

"Well, I can tell you I feel the same. That beautiful powerhouse Addie loves you too, and I know you will enjoy her even more than you ever imagined."

"Dad, Mom, this is the first time we've crossed this bridge…things will be different, but not in a bad way. Good different; like other things we've stepped through together."

Joy grinned at them; not just her usual pleased smile. Instead it was her shy, focused grin; the grin that appeared when she took her first steps, when she got on to ride her two-wheeler without the training wheels, when she came out of her room in her first prom formal to answer the door for her date, and a lot of firsts in between. Joy took their hands in hers, leaned back, relaxed her head onto the back the couch, eyes closed. *I can hardly wait for Addie to get back here…safe.*

## 75

When he grabbed her, he pulled her behind the tree, hurriedly frisking her for firearms. Breathless, coughing to the point of choking, he quit just below her knees and stood up, gasping.

"Le rompo el cuello Si gritas! Dónde está la pistola?"

[I will break your neck if you scream! Where is the pistol?]

She mumbled in Spanish, in a choking whisper, that she'd dropped the gun in the mud back at the road. He dragged her away. The giant's grip on her neck required he use his other hand for pushing his way back into the brush, away from the road. They moved swiftly toward her death, slogging through deep mud and brush, around rocks and tree trunks, for about ten minutes. She heard water rushing, getting louder with each exhausted step. The giant's breath came in gasps.

"Mas rapido!" [Go faster!]

He grunted, and pushed her ahead of him, still gripping her throat. They came through the trees, right up to the churning arroyo; a whitewater deathtrap. It sucked trees, boulders and mud into its maw, fueling its violent descent.

"Prepárate para morir! Te hago desaparecer, luego vuelvo por mi dinero!" [Prepare to die! I make you disappear, then go back for my money!]

Addie dropped all her weight so fast he lost his grip on her rain-soaked neck, tripped over her, staggered, righted himself somewhat, then fell backward across her legs. She sat up, tried to come down hard onto his throat with her fist, but wasn't fast enough. He rolled away, then crawled back at her, growling, on his knees, like a Grizzly bear closing in for an easy kill.

She jammed the heel of her boot hard into his face. He fell on his back, the mud exploding upward as he landed. Spotting a large oak tree, she ran; it's girth a ready shield, with half its roots extended into the thunderous white water of the arroyo. As she grabbed her pistol from the ankle holster, her other foot began to sink in the mud near the water's edge. The oak groaned as it moved, offering her a protruding branch. Grasping the branch with her free hand, Addie steadied herself as the tree swayed from the brutal wind above. She felt the trunk vibrate as the water tore through its massive roots; she looked down.

For a second she thought the water had seen her and was coming for her; logic fled, she trembled from head to toe. She saw climbing, desperate waves, grabbing at the tree's black roots as if struggling for a hold, determined to escape the greedy vacuum looting the hillside. A shot in her direction buried itself in the tree near her left hand. Jerking her hand away, she grabbed a stronger branch directly above her head, pulled her boot out of the mud and began an ascent up the tree, her pistol handle in her mouth. She reached the strong cradle of the oak's center, and peered over it to set up her return shot.

He was gone. Her heart thudded; holding onto the branch with her left hand, she freed the other to grab the Glock, got a hold, and spun herself around just as he appeared, grabbed her ankle, and pulled. She shot him as she fell; her weight knocked him off balance and they hit the mud together. He landed on his back. Her face landed in the blood from his chest wound; he coughed, but didn't move. Her arm, with the gun in her hand, was pinned underneath him. She was trapped, inches from the rising arroyo.

His blood pumped, drenching her face. Its warmth entered her skin, forcing her to watch a powerful, eerie vision of a scrawny teenage boy screaming, standing outside a burning house. It was so vivid she felt the heat from the flames. She saw the entire scene; crazed Zetas, flames reflecting across their black tattoos, pointed to the boy's terrified sisters, one a babe in her mama's arms. His papa's hands shook in a prayerful pose, begging for their lives, as the Zeta boss held a gun to the boy's head and placed a pistol in his hands.

*"Matar a tu madre!"* Addie's vision made it clear; the leader had screamed at Gordo, said his mother told the Federales how to find the Zetas. He told Gordo *"Kill her and I will be your father, not like this quivering, weak coward here. Kill her or I will throw you in the fire with the rest of them!"*

Addie, consumed by the vision, felt the giant awaken, grab her neck, garbling words.

"¡Ninguna mujer me mata!" [No...woman...kills...me!]

The pain from his stranglehold felt as if he were ripping the skin from her neck; Addie's gun hand was trapped under the giant's writhing body with her gun still in her grip. She started to lose consciousness as his hand tightened on her throat, so she fired; his upper body jolted up from the ground as if moved by an earthquake.

His scream shook the woods like a monster from the underworld; a deep bass roar with enough ferocity to flush out what few birds had been riding out the storm near them. Addie rolled away fast, she'd lost her grip on the pistol when her shot jolted him up. She located his gun, put the safety on, and tucked it away.

His body lay limp, his head moved slowly back and forth. The black tattoos across his bare skull, down across his eyes, twisted with pain as he wept and moaned. Addie came up close, bent to his face and spoke.

"Escuchar! Un ángel me enseño cómo el líder Zeta atrapó tu alma y te hizo matar a tu madre."

[Listen! An angel showed me how the Zeta leader trapped your soul and made you kill your mother.]

His head stopped moving. His eyes opened wide, startled, staring at her; tears gushed through the mud on his skin. He choked; more blood carried the life from his body, running onto Addie's hands as she held his arms down.

She shouted through his pain, hoping he would hear her; she spoke to the boy she had seen paralyzed in front of the fire, one gun in his hand, one held at his head by the crazed Zeta.

"¡Dios te perdone! Un nino no es rival para el mal, que se retorcio como alambre en su semejanza. Usted era inocente...su familia todavia le espera, yo los veo, aqui mismo! ¿puedes verlos?

[God forgives you! A child is no match for evil, you were twisted like wire into his likeness. You were innocent...your family still awaits you, I see them, right here! Can you see them?]

He moved his head slowly to the side, then looked up in their direction.

"Yes!"

"You are forgiven," she screamed, "go with your family...go now!"

His huge body quivered; she saw a woman...her mother? Her form blinking in and out of sight as she helped him out of his body, guiding him to his family, as the skinny boy he had been the day he lost them, then his discarded body lay still.

The oak tree beside them cried out in a cracking explosion, and, as if enraged over its demise, the trunk fell lengthwise into the churning

289

water, hitting it as hard as possible. Displaced water, like liquid ice, covered the length of her body, loosened the mud beneath her and pulled her backwards. She gripped Gordo's arm. His lifeless body, like a huge anchor, held its ground as the water flowed over them.

She was sliding in the mud, her fingers digging into the cold hand, when she heard Dean's voice approaching and found the strength to move. Grasping Gordo's massive wrist, she slid herself forward, got on her knees next to his body and crossed his hands over his chest.

"Over here, by the water!" Unzipping her blood-soaked jacket, she covered the top half of his body, let her shoulders go limp, and leaned her head all the way back. The pelting rain washed the blood from her hair, from her face, over her body, into the mud.

The more it rained the better she felt. *This is perfect, feels so good, so good.* Her body shook with chills, vibrated as if a low current of electricity were determined to shock every cell, to chase out every vestige of the terror she'd survived. She let the tears come, for Rosa, for Ángel, for the little boy with the gun in his hand, for his family.

Dean ran up to her just as she stood up. Her body felt like cold, wet, vibrating rubber; but inside, her heart was pounding as sure and strong as Amira's. The head pain she'd suffered with since her fall in the airport was completely gone.

"Were you hurt? Addie—you all right?"

"Yes, I'm okay, just had to sit here and get some rain."

"There are at least two Zetas left; could be here or guarding Miguel and Ángel at the cabin, or both. We're exposed, so we need to keep our eyes open until we know where they are." He turned to Pedro.

"Let's go with Addie back to the road right now. We'll send some medics to get photos, get him in a body bag, then into the med van, while we go on to the cabin."

"My pistol's under him somewhere, don't leave it here where some adventurous kid will find it. I have Gordo's here," she pulled it out and gave it to Dean. Pedro kneeled, shoved his powerful arm under Gordo's body, retrieved the gun, wiped it off, and handed it to her with a word of caution and some props for her success.

"Keep it handy on the way to the Sub. If you see one of those Zetas, another accurate shot to the leg would be appreciated; I don't feel like chasing anyone."

Massaging her bruised neck, she shoved her dripping hair away from her face and replied.

"I'll do what I can, Pedro, but no heavy lifting. It's going to take four guys to carry him to the van. I did my part. Even though he forced me to shoot. I don't regret it. He's better off with his family than rotting in an isolation cell in some supermax prison."

## 76

The Zeta cabin wasn't far off; they stopped out of sight, behind a granite boulder larger than the Suburban. Rosa rested in the back seat, medicated and wrapped in a blanket. Emil quietly followed their lead and parked behind them in the red Sub, as did the med van. A few agents did some recon before the rest of them left their vehicles, and confirmed the two young Zetas were inside.

Agents positioned themselves behind large trees around all four sides of the cabin in case the boys decided to come out blasting AK47s. Pedro's voice gave orders over the PA speaker, giving the Zetas one chance to come out, arms up. The intermittent lightning and descending gusts of wind that rocked the Sub made Addie feel under attack already.

She could see the cabin's fireplace chimney from behind the boulder, but not much else. Still, they sat, wondering if the Zetas were going to cooperate or come out shooting. A piece of the cabin's metal roofing, violently yanked off by the wind, spun in an upward draft about thirty feet, then headed down for the white Sub, smashed into the hood and skidded off into a tree.

Dean, Addie and Rosa all yelled when the metal hit the Sub. Addie had been holding an ice pack on her throat; it went flying when her hands jerked up to protect her face. Emil jumped out of the red Sub behind them, and ran over.

"You guys ok?"

"I didn't wet my pants, Emil, but it was close," Dean's hands were shaking as he gestured a bit erratically.

Dean leaned over to Addie, still shaken, but focused.

"Looks like the hood got split open. We'll check underneath before we head back. Hey, Emil, stay here with Rosa when Addie and I go inside the cabin."

Addie turned around to check Rosa, who had yanked herself into a fetal position under the blanket provided by the medics.

"You okay Rosa?" When Rosa pulled off the blanket and nodded, Addie exclaimed "Wow…how did the medics get the mud off you?"

"The women shielded me with blankets while I showered in the rain."

"Are you feeling any help from the medication Doc gave you?" Dean asked Rosa.

"Yes, and thank you both for saving my life." She looked at Addie and smiled, "I see you are wearing the necklace I gave Joy."

"This was how we found you, it was Joy's idea." Addie held up the pendant, "we prayed for signs."

"Oh, I thought the Zetas took all the signs down."

"They did," said Dean, "but Addie is psychic, and when she held your necklace she saw the kind of signs that can't be removed, you know, like visions."

"Señorita Joy has some of that gift; she told me she has to keep it a secret."

"Not anymore," Addie said, "she and her family understand it better now. It's nothing to fear."

"Well," Dean said, "will you look at that; here they come, marching under guard toward their Navigator with hands up. The agents will restrain them in the Navigator and transport them back to the detainee cabin. Rosa, now that the way is clear, I'd like to take Addie inside for a few minutes. I don't want you alone, so Emil's going to join you while we're gone."

They donned fresh parkas, and stepped out. Emil got in the driver's seat. Rosa started to cry, so Addie climbed back into the Sub, kneeled on the seat, leaned over to Rosa, and took her hand.

"You and I both know Ángel is gone, Rosa, even though it hasn't been confirmed with our eyes yet. The agents will bring Ángel's body back to the FBI cabins. We can help with a mortuary tomorrow." Rosa buried her face in her hands, sobbing.

"They killed him, those pigs, just keep those Zeta's away from me!"

"We will, Rosa, try to rest, I'll be right back."

She joined Dean, who was checking under the hood of the Sub.

"Doesn't appear to have damaged anything here, that's a lucky break." He shut the hood and they went to the cabin with the agents.

"Brace yourself, Dean, it's a gruesome mess in there." She shivered from the cold and the shock from Gordo's attack, her teeth chattering so hard she couldn't control it. The minute they walked in

Dean walked over to the pile of medical supplies the agents brought in and grabbed a blanket. While the agents took a look around, he wrapped the blanket around Addie, looking deep into her eyes. She answered in kind. He nodded, then whispered in her ear.

"Our soul-to-soul assessment is complete; let's get to work."

"This is just as I saw it in the vision," Addie said, walking over to Miguel. Miguel and Ángel lay in restraints on the floor, blood pooling under Ángel's silent rotund form. Miguel was breathing irregular, fluid-filled breaths; he reeked of vomit, urine, and feces, and was babbling in a determined, somniloquous tone.

The Zeta's had spent much of their drug-crazed sadism on their only living victim. Old Miguel had been tortured amid advancing delirium tremens, while the generous supply of meth fueled each man's manic obsession with Miguel's withdrawals.

Addie squatted next to Miguel, took his pulse, and as soon as she touched him, got a vision of the scene as it had played out; the men, like cats sharing a wounded mouse, had avoided finishing him off. Gordo wanted him alive for the ransom, yes, but the rest of them just wanted to prolong their entertainment.

Miguel, semi-conscious, groaned and rubbed his face against the damaged floor planks; much of his skin was raw, pierced with splinters, and bleeding. Addie moved as the medics came in; they checked his vital signs, provided first aid to his visible wounds, and checked for broken bones. Dr. Jimenez checked Miguel's abdomen, his cardiac and lung functions, then put away his gear and looked at Dean.

"Agent Reyes found a duffle bag filled with the Zeta's clean clothes; the medics will wash him and get him dressed in something that doesn't reek, then we'll get him loaded up for the drive in the red Sub. I will ride with him to monitor his vitals. I suggest we put Ángel's body bag behind the back seat of the Navigator."

"Really," Dean said, "let those boys ride with their victim."

"As for Miguel, this guy could have internal injuries from being kicked; he apparently suffered a beating prior to this one," he pointed to a soiled bandage next to Miguel. "See the bandage on the floor? That came off his broken nose. He has a host of chronic health problems, the alcohol abuse is front and center right now, cirrhosis of the liver probably, palpation indicates fluid in the abdomen and of course the jaundice is becoming evident."

"Sounds as if he's semi-conscious and still actively hallucinating," Addie offered.

"I'm putting him on IV fluids," Doc said, "laced with a low dose of Diazepam, it may attenuate the detox symptoms until we get him to the hospital in Oaxaca City. Rosa can relax in the back of your Sub, Gordo and Manuel are taking up both bunks in the Med van. Manuel is still yelling about the pain. Of course, Gordo is feeling none."

"What's your plan for Rosa's exam?" Addie said. Doc stowed his instruments, closed his bag, and walked up to Addie.

"I'll cosign the forms after Maria's finished the exam; Rosa will have her own room in the detainee cabin. I'd like Maria to guard her there overnight. We'll submit a report for the court on the injuries she sustained. Rosa's not going to want a man anywhere near her for quite some time, I'm guessing, so it's better if Maria handles the exam; she told me she's certified in the process.

"By the way," Addie cautioned the M.D. and medics, "Miguel watched his son-in-law die and his daughter Rosa's been brutally assaulted and is grieving Ángel's murder. I just got through explaining to her that there was nothing we could do for Ángel, so let's stay sensitive to the emotional injuries." Doc looked puzzled.

"You told Rosa he was dead? How did you know that before you left your car to come in here?"

"I had a vision when I hit my head at the airport; I saw a dead man with an Ángel's wings falling out of a cloud. I knew it was him." Doc looked at Dean as if to corroborate Addie's powers.

"Welcome to the world of Dr. Diaz," Dean said to Doc with a half-smile.

"Which begs the question, Addie, how is your head feeling?"

"Well, strangely enough, Doc, it hurt like hell for hours, right up until Gordo left to be with his deceased family. From that point on, I haven't had any pain. Strange, huh?"

"Don't ask me, you're the psych specialist."

"Well, I'm no psychologist," Dean quipped, "but I'd say you got a blessing for helping Gordo escape."

"I'm grateful the headache's gone, whatever the reason. Let's get going, I want to see Rosa."

When they reached the white Sub, Dean checked on Rosa. She was lying across the back seat, wearing Emil's heavy down jacket, her head on a pillow, the lower half of her body in sweat pants, partly covered with the thick fleece blanket. Addie, in the front seat, listened to Dean's comments, moved to tears by his ability to acknowledge her strength, knowing it would bolster her sense of control.

"Rosa, I admire your guts for escaping and flagging us down on the access road. Your bravery kept us from having to confront all four of them at once. The two young ones lost their courage after Gordo and Manuel took off." Rosa nodded.

Dean went to the boot of the car, put the evidence in, especially the stool he'd found next to Ángel's head. Ángel's hair had stuck to it on impact; Dean had secured the stool for fingerprints of the perpetrator and for Ángel's DNA.

They climbed into the Sub, and Addie put a hand on his arm.

"You noticed those Zeta boys were identical twins, didn't you?" His bravado melted, his eyes misted. The car shuddered from a persistent wind, but it didn't deter him.

"Yes, it reminded me…when my boys got a bunch of those temporary tattoos for their fifth birthday. I found them in the bathroom, applying them with a wet washcloth, and guess what? Just like these Zeta kids, they went to a lot of trouble to put identical tattoos in the same places. So, when those boys walked out shirtless just now, with those matching tattoos, I just wanted to give up. Somewhere, they have families who feel as frightened for them as you, Ana and Mike feared for Joy. And then, I think what they did to Rosa, Ángel and Miguel, and my compassion retreats." He leaned forward and turned on the engine, defroster, and wipers.

"I feel like I'm in a recurring dream every time I start up this car."

"You okay Dean?" Addie leaned over to him.

"I'm just grateful it wasn't worse; now I just want to get all of us home safe. The storm's strong; it could get worse, or move north and let us live. Just pray it goes away without more harm."

Addie put her hand on his back and comforted him, feeling the tension let go as she moved her hand in a slow circle.

## 77

She hoped for no danger on the main road, but between Refugio Forestal and Avenida Lago, the agents had to saw fallen trees apart, and drag them out of the way with the red Sub. The thought of getting out to help move a tree at this point seemed overwhelming, but no one asked. Addie fell asleep, then jolted awake; screams were coming from the med van. When Dean came back to the Sub after the road was clear, he explained.

"Manuel wants pain meds; I told Doc I want him to have a clear head when we get back to the cabins. I want to interrogate him while he's awake and motivated to cooperate with us. We can't get to the hospital until tomorrow, and he's going to need surgery. I want the intel asap; if we wait and he doesn't survive the surgery, we'll lose all those good leads."

"Well, Dean," Addie quipped, "I can see you have returned to the pragmatic view of your job after our poignant hiatus."

Once they arrived at the FBI cabins, the agents were hustling through every protocol they'd been assigned. Debris from the storm was flying over the cabins, forcing Addie and Dean to duck down; when they rose, gusts slapped at the rain-slick stairs, chasing them as they rushed into the lower cabin, their parkas dripping down the hall.

"Come on in!" Mike bellowed, "You missed the action here; the wind took out our big window. But now we have heat, we have food." Mike had obviously been stoking the wood stove since the window incident; the dampness had been baked out of the cabin interior, and the dining table by the boarded lakeside window was filled with food. Joy came up to Addie with a shy smile. Addie had put a spare parka on, with the hood over her hair. She didn't want anyone seeing blood, in case it hadn't all rinsed out.

"Addie? Mom told me about everything after you left, about you being my birthmom." Joy started crying, walked up to Addie, tears falling, arms extended. Addie had still not adjusted; *how could my eight-pound baby have become a woman as tall and strong as I am? Something tells me my shock is the result of having only a newborn baby picture to look at all these years!*

"I'm so relieved you made it back okay," Joy whispered, "the thought of us being separated again scared me more than I want to say." Addie took all the love offered in that strong hug, and gave a lot back.

"Okay," Joy said, "you're freezing; time for a shower, some food, and coffee by the fireplace."

"I think I have just enough energy left for that, but not much more." It wasn't easy to have even a piece of this long-awaited conversation with Joy. Standing this close, yet unable to stop thinking about the amount of blood she'd seen and felt for the last two hours.

Addie excused herself and rushed into the shower. It took a while before the water ran clear and the smell of his blood was gone. She changed into some jeans and a black pullover. The frightening scenes playing in her head continued to be as clear as the more pleasant scene she saw in the living room when she came out. Dean was at the table with Emil and she joined them. Joy walked up with a supersized chocolate bar, took Addie's hand, and placed it there.

"Dark chocolate with a thin layer of the most delicious caramel inside; from Dad to you. May I join you all for a few minutes?"

"I'd say you correctly intuited the price of admission to the table," Addie forced a smile, "so yes, have a seat." *Would she even want to sit with me if she'd seen me kill him?*

"Thank you again for helping my parents accept our reunion." She pulled her chair closer to Addie's and sat.

Addie lowered her voice. Her professional habit took over.

"Joy, your parents jumped through these hoops in a crisis. They may not feel so compassionate once they recover. Adoptive parents can boomerang when it comes to working through these dynamics, and that goes for birth parents and adoptees too. It's about deep-seeded insecurities. When we react with disdain for others, by definition, we don't think they are worthy of our consideration or respect. It's a projection we don't recognize. Or if we're afraid; it's also about our own self-worth." Joy put her hand under Addie's chin, Addie looked up into Joy's eyes.

"Addie, take your psychologist hat off; I can see your heart is breaking." Addie stood up, tears pouring, hugged Joy, and went to her room. Emil and Dean sat like stones, then Dean rose and followed her.

An hour later, Dean emerged from Addie's room, careful to close the door slowly so she wouldn't wake up. He walked into the living room, grateful that Mike had stoked the wood stove for the night. The tech agents were playing cards with Emil at the table. The Doyles were on the couch with Bella in front of the fireplace. Dean set aside his worries about Addie, and did his job.

"Time for everyone to get some sleep; I want us up at six, airborne no later than eight a.m., weather permitting. We have one murdered civilian, Rosa's husband. We have one Zeta with a gunshot wound in the knee, and one Zeta deceased; both of whom Addie took down, including hand-to hand combat with the leader, Gordo, so yes, she's hurting, physically and emotionally. I never intended her to be fighting, but the Zetas surprised us on the road. I don't want anyone discussing our Zeta encounter, unless you are questioned in an official capacity. Our priority tomorrow morning, weather permitting, is to get the injured to the regional hospital in Oaxaca City." He looked at agents Quinn and Silva.

"Sorry Silva, you are guarding the cabin perimeter with Carlos until two a.m. Then switch with Quinn. Joy, you can talk with Rosa tomorrow.

"Is it my imagination or is the storm letting up?" Joy said.

"I think it is, but no telling; an experience like this makes me realize how completely dependent we are on the high-tech weather info, not that it was such accurate info this time around. Okay, enough for now, I'm claiming the couch, so you all need to get to bed."

The Doyles got up from the couch. Bella didn't move. Ana looked toward Addie's room.

"I had no idea she'd been hurt."

"She's an expert in resiliency, she will recover well. In the meantime, we need to be as supportive as possible."

He tossed and turned on the couch for at least an hour. Bella had moved to the fireplace hearth and was sound asleep. Dean, stirred by the vision of Addie dragged off by Gordo, reviewed his regrets; the wrong turn they took running into the woods after Addie, complicated by the low visibility, the sound distortion from the howling wind, and the way he'd found her kneeling by Gordo's body, drenched in blood.

"Dean? You still awake?"

He sat up and stared; Addie had walked right up to the couch and he hadn't even heard her.

"May I join you for a minute? Something woke me up and I can't go back to sleep."

"Sure, I hate to admit it, but the two of us in front of a fireplace, well, it's a fantasy I've had a few times over the years."

"Did your fantasy include the responsibility for two corpses, eight detainees, three Doyles, a doctor, ten agents and a dog?" Dean shook his head sideways, unable to share the humor.

"What's going on? You look so sad."

"Addie, I am so sorry we misjudged the direction Gordo took you. Even with agents following us into the brush, spreading out, we screwed up."

"Hey, it wasn't some urban pursuit; it was acres of thick, dark forest, a storm so loud you couldn't hear your own thoughts. He knew exactly where he was taking me; he was determined to dump me in the arroyo. Please don't blame yourself."

"I'll do my best to let it go if you can reassure me about the load you were carrying when you arrived in Oaxaca City."

"Unfortunately, I have some challenges at home to work on."

"Is it your health?"

"No, thank God, my health is great. I didn't want to talk about it earlier, but now that we're heading home in the morning, what the hell. It's Jake. He didn't want me to come to Oaxaca with you; we had a blowout late Monday night. I accidently interrupted him at one-thirty a.m. in our home office; Skyping and shooting heroin with some naked girl." She paused, Dean waited.

"I didn't even realize he'd gone so far off the deep end until then." She picked up a throw pillow, hugged it to her chest like a security-blanket, took a deep breath, exhaled slowly, and gave him the whole story.

"A year ago, I thought we were just going through some run-of-the-mill marital stagnation; he'd been injured in a car accident and had to have two surgeries. Then I realized he was struggling with an addiction to opioids and alcohol. We grappled with it intermittently, sometimes with success; more often we settled for tolerance without a clear solution."

Dean finally responded in a gentle tone, "It appears he's engaging in very high-risk behaviors."

"Yes, that makes it impossible for me to consider staying married to him. I'm still in the betrayal and shock of it all. Knowing what it's going to do to our daughters."

"Being blindsided hurts bad, yet if you are the one to make the decision to separate, you will be their role model for evolving through all that pain into a life you can respect. Eventually you will make peace with each other, if he's capable of it. The girls will see your friendship survive, even if the marriage doesn't."

"In theory, I agree, but right now I can't see past the shock of it. More importantly, you need to understand I'm not telling you this because I want to make a move on you and complicate your own marriage."

"Too late for that, Addie, as soon as our boys headed off for college, my wife was kind enough to inform me that she and her business partner, who's a lovely woman by the way, someone I really respect, well, they have apparently been in love for years, they just never expressed it to each other until recently." Addie waited for more.

"That's why I took the San Diego job. Easier to heal where the sun shines; plus, the boys wanted to go to school in California and UCLA was the only school that accepted both. You know, the identical twin thing, IVF babies. They wanted to be together through school, since they help each other a lot, and even have a sneaky system of taking tests for each other in a pinch."

"Okay," Addie sighed a protracted sigh, "I really wasn't expecting that at all, because, like you, I've had my fantasies about us over the years, but none of them involved a rebound situation. We're both old enough to know that's not likely to work. Takes time to work things through so they don't come back to bite you."

"So," he said gently, "both of us are going to be doing some serious healing and that takes a while, I agree. I'm willing to wait, well, at least until next week."

"Thanks, I needed that, I admit I was getting way too serious."

Addie and Dean sat in the dark room with the last of the fireplace light burning down. After a few minutes passed, Addie slowly uncrossed her legs, grazing Dean's feet slightly as she moved to stand up on the cold floor, grateful she had put on two pair of socks.

"I'm going to go in and get some sleep; tomorrow might be demanding, or everything might go as perfectly as we would wish; think I should be ready either way."

Dean grabbed his pillow, rolled onto his side, and mumbled "Sane call, Addie. Get some rest. I'm ready to pass out myself."

Addie went over to the chair by the fireplace and grabbed an extra blanket someone had left behind. She walked over to Dean and covered him with the blanket, leaned over him slightly, and gently stroked a loose lock of his hair back off his forehead.

"Goodnight, sleep well," she whispered, and quietly made her way to the bedroom. Passing Ana and Mike's bedroom, she was pleased to know Joy had crawled into bed with her parents. Addie thought the three of them needed something exactly that comforting to make up for a week of painful separation.

## 80

Rosa made it to the bathroom in the detainee cabin just in time. She vomited until she got stuck on dry heaves and couldn't stop. She bent over the toilet, wrists in restraints behind her back, shackles on her ankles, and wished she was dead. Maria was helping her keep her balance.

"Rosa, try to stand straight and breathe real slow. I have some anti-nausea meds I can give you if you can't stop." Rosa tried, and slowly began to gain control of the spasms.

"I'm sorry you have to be restrained, but Isabel will have to give us the word to take the restraints off once the authorities agree they aren't charging you. I recommend you have your medical exam now; I'm a trained sexual assault forensic examiner; just so you know, sometimes this exam can take one or two hours.

"I packed the rape kit for this trip in case we needed it for Joy, but she says they never hurt her. So, the sooner we do it the better the DNA evidence and photographs are likely to be. Plus, you can't really soap yourself down for a thorough bath until after the exam. There's the physical evidence part, and there's your statement, which will take time. We can work on the statement tomorrow, if you'd prefer."

Rosa looked at Maria, then into the mirror on the bathroom wall, stunned by the pathetic woman who stared back at her; black eyes, swollen face, bruises, and bloody lacerations covered her entire body. Maria had temporarily bandaged Rosa's wrists and ankles to cover the rope burns before she put the restraints on. Rosa shivered from the trauma and the cold, then responded to Maria's image in the mirror.

"Do the exam. Whatever happens to me, I want those bastards to pay for this. At least the three who are still alive."

"Okay, do you also want to take the emergency contraceptive pills? I also recommend meds to prevent STD."

"Yes, and yes. I want nothing from them to stay with me. I'm glad that Dr. Diaz killed Ángel's murderer and shot the one who hurt me the most. I wish they were all dead, and I pray to God that none of them had AIDS."

Addie had given Maria an outfit for Rosa, a hooded black sweatshirt and matching sweat pants. There was a small red rose embroidered on the sweatshirt. Maria noticed the rose, and took it to be one more synchronicity among many in this case. When she finished Rosa's exam, she helped her shower and put on the outfit, helped her to the bed, covered her with two heavy blankets, and watched her fall asleep.

With her one patient as comfortable as possible, she relaxed in the upholstered chair by the bed, exhausted. Doc Jimenez had given Rosa a Valium. Just before Maria dozed off, she briefly recalled she had relaxed protocol and moved the wrist restraints to the front during Rosa's exam and shower. She didn't have the heart to wake her up and secure them to the bed.

## 81

Addie planned to go to bed after the fireside discussion with Dean in the living room, but that plan literally morphed before her eyes as she stood at the bathroom sink brushing her teeth. She looked in the mirror; a vision of her attacker coming at her from behind, his sharpened knife blade ready for her throat, leaped into her sight. She jumped aside, eyes on the mirror, looking to see if she had space to break for the doorway.

*I don't have to make a break for it! It's all in my mind!* Tears of relief overtook her. Why in hell was she still carrying that image around with her? It had been almost twenty-two years since the attack, yet right now, her flesh seemed imbedded with the stench of his sweaty efforts, his determination to, as he said, 'make a baby for the cartel' no matter how long it took him to finish. She washed her face with cold water, gave it a swipe with the towel, and went into the bedroom.

As she sat on the edge of the bed in the half-dark room, her head seemed to buzz; an annoying sound that quieted as she saw a vision of the bedroom in the Zeta cabin; Manuel, the Zeta she'd shot earlier on the road, dominated the vision by shouting orders; she saw him insisting that Rosa submit to his every meth inspired whim. Addie recognized his voice, had heard it earlier that day, when he was being carried on a gurney from the parking area to the upper cabin. *Why is this guy's image haunting me? I need to sleep, he's no threat, so what's going on?*

Still sitting, Addie realized she was somehow inside Rosa's mind, reliving the nightmare Rosa had survived at the Zeta's hideout. Addie listened, could understand Rosa's thoughts as Rosa made a plan to kill herself. *'I will tell Maria I have to use the bathroom. She will help me to the bathroom, so I won't trip over my shackles, then she will wait in her recliner chair in the bedroom while I go.'*

Addie saw and heard Rosa's plan like a movie. Rosa would tell Maria it might take her awhile in the bathroom because she was constipated. Maria was exhausted, falling asleep in the chair by Rosa's bed. Rosa would cut herself with a sharp piece of broken porcelain from the toilet tank lid. Addie could see the corner of the lid had broken off and someone had reattached it with a strip of duct tape.

A gasp pulled through Addie's throat in the silent bedroom;

now everything made sense. Her graphic vision in the mirror had put her in touch with the depth and urgency of Rosa's feelings, it had broken through Addie's preoccupation with Dean, and permeated the barrier of her fatigue.

What better way to connect her with Rosa than a flashback to the dilemma searing her soul after the Washington D.C. attack? How she had wanted to die rather than live in a state of mortifying disgust, unable to look in a mirror, unwilling to look at herself, tying her hopelessly tangled hair week after week without brushing it, knowing he had pulled it with such unrelenting searing pain; used it, gripped tightly, in his free hand, the way a new rider clings to a horse's mane or a saddle horn to keep from falling off.

The day she had stood at her bathroom sink and clipped her long hair down to the scalp had been the beginning of her trek back to sanity.

Praying it wasn't too late, she pulled on her wet boots, untied, rushed out of her room, slid past the sound of Dean's snores, down the hall to the back door. She stepped outside, almost oblivious to the wind and rain, and took the first few steps up the stairs. A voice hit her from behind.

"Hey, what are you doing?"

It was Carlos, standing guard on the small deck by the back door. Addie grabbed the soaked railing, turned and hurried back down, getting as close to his face as possible so he could hear her.

"There's a problem with Rosa. I had a vision, she's planning on cutting her wrists in the bathroom, before Maria checks on her."

"Why would she do that? She's safe now." The porchlight made the rain glisten; like fireflies rising past his frowning face. Addie was shocked; Agent Silva walked on the deck. It didn't stop Addie.

"Carlos, I'm gonna make sure Dean requires you to get some real training in working with rape victims when you get home!"

Addie spun herself around, headed back up the stairs, panting, praying she wasn't too late. She reached the large deck situated halfway between the cabins; soaked, shaking, because she'd run outside in wet boots and no jacket; then her breath got tight. *I'm stressing; I have to calm down or I'll be no good for Rosa.*

She saw Pedro standing at the top of the steps, shining his

flashlight on the twenty or so steps she had yet to climb. She took the deepest breath she could and splashed her way up to the back porch of the cabin. Pedro attempted a light-hearted greeting.

"I'm out here in the rain because I've been ordered to do it; what's your excuse?"

"I need to talk to Maria fast, it's about Rosa. She's suicidal, I saw it." Pedro, having seen Addie's visions bring their team straight to the Zeta cabin earlier, did not hesitate. He moved fast, opened the door for her and they both went inside. There was a small fire in the fireplace, the room had a warm glow despite the breeze coming in through the most recently broken window. Pedro grabbed her a towel he'd stashed just inside the door.

"Okay, I'll get her, and a blanket for you. He gestured to the couch by the fireplace. There's some dry wood left, I'll stoke up the fire for you, then I need to get back outside."

"That's fine. The Zetas, Ramiro and his folks in those bedrooms?" She nodded toward the three adjacent rooms on her left. "They're all in restraints, right?"

"Yep, packed like sardines, agents in each room. Good thing this cabin had four bedrooms. Doc moved Miguel in with the injured Zeta, Manuel, in that last room there, so he can monitor them both overnight; Miguel's in pitiful shape. Guess your vision already showed you that Rosa's in that bedroom next to the kitchen, huh?"

Addie was accustomed to rhetorical questions about her psychic gifts and answered him with a grin. He headed for Rosa's room, came out with a blanket, and handed it to Addie along with a dry sweatshirt and some sweatpants. He went over and added logs to the fire, then headed out to the deck. Maria hurried out, crossed the living room to the couch, and sat next to Addie.

"Pedro says you're here about Rosa." Addie was focused on the vision, and started with that.

"Is there a lid on the toilet tank that has a cracked piece of porcelain in it?" Maria squinted hard at Addie.

"Excuse me," Maria digressed, "I guess I fell asleep in the chair; I'll have to get another agent in here who's had some rest."

"Yes, that's going to be important. Quickly though, did you put Rosa's wrist restraints in front when you put her to bed? Are they

307

standard, or softer hospital restraints?"

"First, how did you know about the cracked tank lid and the restraints? Guilty as charged; and second, I'm getting the picture. Oh, Addie, I let my guard down, felt so sorry for her, figured she was too exhausted to try anything."

"I need to talk with her," Addie urged, "it's very important. While I'm in here with her, check with Doc, I'm sure they have padded restraints in the med van. You can secure her with those to the bed frame. Check with Doc about a good sedative. Can you bring her in here with a blanket, and then after I leave, be very aware she can't use the bathroom alone? Even if you took the lid off, there's metal inside the tank she could use.

"Check the cabinets, the bedroom. Leave her wrist restraints in front until I'm finished talking with her, then when you put her in bed, put her on her back; restrain each arm to the sides using the bed frame and medicate her good, because that's the same position the Zetas tied her in. I'll have Pedro figure out who can relieve you, so you can sleep. You worked your ass off all day today, Maria, then did that long emotional examination and cleaned her up afterward; no point in being ashamed about fatigue.

"Ok," Maria nodded, "Thanks, Addie. Of course, you know the reason I chose to get certified to do that exam. Except in my case, there was no exam and there was no conviction for the perpetrator." Addie gave her a hug.

"Maria, you got your power back, that's what matters."

"I'll get Rosa, be right back." Addie turned to watch the fire while she waited, and switched her soaked shirt for the dry hoodie.

Dean was dreaming about his sons, enjoying himself immensely. The living room of the lower cabin wasn't holding much heat; the fire in the fireplace was low, and as Dean shifted his position on the couch, his dream became more vivid. He was sitting on the uphill level of a wide beach that sloped down to the ocean, watching his sons running in the shallow surf, passing a football to each other. Every overthrow was followed by declarations of incompetence and laughter. *Could I love these boys more? I don't see how.*

He felt a hand on his shoulder. He thought it odd that he didn't turn or look, but just received the powerful, comforting energy that descended into his body. He heard a voice. *Be ready and you will live to see them again. Be ready. She will need you. Don't give up.*

The last log he had put on the fire earlier fell off its perch as the log underneath broke into a bed of burning shards. The crashing sound coming from the fireplace arrived inside Dean's dream greatly amplified, forcing him upward, eyes open, ready for ...what? He sat up, looked around, didn't want to bother anyone, but couldn't avoid the anxiety triggered by his dream. He banked the fire and replaced the screen, then decided to rest, and possibly figure out what the voice in his dream was talking about. His gut told him it was about Addie...the part about 'don't give up' gave him chills.

Once Rosa was settled on the couch with a can of soda and her blanket, she seemed more curious than pissed about being awakened; but Addie knew about the kind of rage that chooses an inward course, so she assumed nothing.

"Rosa, I'm sorry to wake you…"

"She thought I was asleep, but I wasn't."

"That fits with why I'm here, being pushy, but for a good cause. First off, please tolerate this off-the-wall question; are you of the belief that prophets, psychics, and mediums are working for the devil?"

"No. I think that's just a way some churches are, all about fear and controlling people with fear. There's other views on TV these days, psychics who really help people, things I've seen on the internet. I heard from Maria that she saw you on TV with psychic investigators, I think it's good. You are helping people, you found me, or I wouldn't be here."

"Okay then, please slow me down if I move too fast, and please call me Addie…I was going to bed a few minutes ago; I had a vision. You had a clear plan to cut yourself and bleed out while you were in the bathroom; a …"

"Yes, the tank lid. A nice sharp piece I noticed earlier today. I was just about to go in when you showed up. Maria, she is exhausted. Addie, she has waited on my every need since I got here. You are sweet to care, and I know you are trained to help people who have been hurt, but unless it's happened to you, you just can't imagine how someone could kill themselves because of it." Rosa looked down at her lap, tears fell on the blanket. She moved her head side to side and wrung her hands.

"I understand more than you think, Rosa."

As she spoke, Addie touched the scar left by the knife that had been held at her throat. Even in the half light of the room, Addie could see Maria had bandaged Rosa's wrists, and saw a fleeting vision of the Zeta Gordo tying her ankles and wrists to the bedposts with some rough hemp rope. Addie turned herself to face Rosa, crossed her legs yoga fashion on the couch, adjusted her blanket, and, in homage, held out both hands, palms up, and bared her soul.

"I was raped, when I was not much older than you. I felt

flashbacks of the pain from the physical abuse, the threats, the terror…felt like I was rotting and dying from the inside…filled with the smell, the sweat, the greed…the evil energy of my attacker.

"My identity vanished; when I'd wake up in the morning there'd be no part I'd recognize. Maybe once in a while I'd get a glimpse of some familiar part of myself, but it would run away when the feelings attacked again. I cut off all my hair because of how he used it."

"Qué lástima!" Rosa wept, reached over and laid her hands on Addie's, "tu cabello, so beautiful, to think you took it all off because of what it had become to you." Rosa paused, then leaned toward Addie so their eyes were in full contact.

"You are strong now, though, I can see that," Rosa said, nodding with conviction. Addie felt relieved, she sensed a shift in Rosa's perception. So she went on.

"My grandma Luisa was abused, humiliated for years until my grandfather died. But she healed. She took all her power back, and she taught me how to do it. What I'm worried about, Rosa, is that if you're released and you go back home with no one to help you, you will kill yourself, and all the love and beauty God put in you will lose its chance to heal you, and through you, to heal others."

"Es verdad," Rosa said. Addie looked for a sign of hope on Rosa's swollen and bruised face. The M.D. had stitched the cut that extended downward from the corner of her lip, accentuating her heartbroken expression. *No hope I can see, please God, give me something that will reach her.* Ángel entered her thoughts, so she trusted the hunch.

"Precious woman, you lost your husband as well; it happened simultaneously, so you are unable to think of one without the other."

"Si, he screamed at the big Zeta, Gordo, because he wouldn't stop Manuel from hurting me. Ángel was tied up, trying to stop it with the power of his voice, he was screaming like a crazy man—until Gordo silenced him." Rosa's tears burst forth; Addie knew she needed to calm her, so they could continue, so she reached for her hands and held them in a gentle embrace.

"Ángel did what he did because of his love for you. Let me say something about healing. It is there for you, but you will have to claim it anew countless times. It takes years, but the more support you have, the fewer years it will take." Rosa nodded in assent.

311

"But," Addie promised, "you need to know you will be stronger than the people who have never climbed such a mountain…that's when your life starts to work in ways you can't even imagine. And all those people who are afraid of their own shadows, afraid to be different, afraid to be shamed out of ignorance, they see your power. If you ever have children, they will see it. They will know they can live through anything and not give up, because they have seen you do it."

"Oh, I do not see how it is possible! Except you are here." Rosa put her face in her hands, and bent into the blanket she had wrapped around herself, her shoulders moving with each sob.

"Before I made my death plan I asked God to give me a sign that there is a God-given life plan for me. I said, 'show the sign to me and if you do I will stay alive and heal, because I will know I'm not alone, and have Spirit's help to get well." Addie sensed Rosa was considering a change of course. *But she's holding something back.*

"I think you got your sign, Rosa, the fact that I had a vision that caused me to intervene seems like a good enough sign, right? I learned lots of techniques for getting your mind back and the evil out. I will help you do it, and so will others. Adela told me the family was planning on you going to California, that the student visas and passports for you, Ángel and Tonio were all set. She said Ramiro was desperate to secure your transition to the states before he died."

Addie paused, leaned toward Rosa and held her hands again. She saw Rosa was caught in recoiling from the experience, the image of Rosa escaping down the road kept showing up. *If she goes off by herself, she will just keep running…*

"Rosa, Dean says there's no evidence you even knew about the plan for the kidnapping. You will probably be released when you get back to Oaxaca City because of that. We have lots of room at our farm; you could stay until you're fully on your feet and ready to get your own place." Rosa seemed to show some curiosity, some hope.

"Adela helped us with the school and the embassy to make sure we had our visas and passports once we got accepted to the university in San Francisco. She and Uncle Ramiro believed San Francisco was the best place for our education, and for her art business."

Addie felt chills run down her arms; she could almost hear Star's voice that Sunday morning at her house, telling Addie there was some

312

bigger plan in motion than her individual crisis; reminding her that everyone involved had a healing opportunity; as if to prove Star's case Rosa spoke up with more spunk this time.

"Miguel tricked Ángel into Joy's kidnapping, I think. He told me we were getting paid as guides for the evening. He and Ramiro got desperate and risked way too much for their retirement plan; esos bastardos! They left the cartel, but the cartel thinking didn't completely leave them. I'm still angry at both of them. Especially Miguel, for his drunken mouth."

"There are many options ahead of you, but healing is your first job, and we can help you with that if you are interested." Addie stopped, tilted her head and looked like she was listening to someone standing next to her. Then she spoke.

"Since you aren't against mediums, I can tell you I do get visions of people who have passed once in a while. Are you okay with me describing something I just experienced?"

Rosa nodded her head and waited with her lips pressed together, her eyes peering upward at Addie, bracing herself as if she were a child who just agreed to have a band aid pulled off fast.

"Ángel doesn't want you to give up. He tells me he's your honorary angel now, and will always be with you. He's got two important messages, he says. One, he wants to explain about the kidnapping." Addie waited a minute, taking in more information, then continued.

"He was in on the kidnapping plan and kept it from you. He never dreamed Miguel would expose you to such harm…the day he agreed to the plan he believed it was planned to be carried out safely…he's very, very sorry for the harm that came to you…he takes responsibility for it." Again, Addie paused, then resumed about thirty seconds later.

"Ángel says, please don't blame Ramiro or Miguel for his death, only the Zetas. He believes that the more people you hold responsible, the longer it's going to take you to heal. In addition, he has one very important request. He says tell you to teach me the recipe he created for the hotel, the lover's bread? Loving bread? I'm not sure. He just keeps holding up a heart-shaped loaf of bread with a red ribbon tied in a bow on top of it, like a box of Valentine candy."

Rosa forgot their plan to stay quiet when she heard Addie's message.

"Amantes Del Pan! Lover's bread! It's a sweet bread he invented, he makes it with honey, ginger, and a few little cinnamon candy hearts in it, here and there. When you find a heart, you must give your lover a kiss or your kissing luck will go bad and you end up with ugly lips and no sweetheart.

Addie, I wasn't going to tell you, but now I must say it. You have proved Ángel is here with me. That's over half the reason I wanted to die, to go find him. Ahora, yo comprendo! He is with me, I don't have to leave this life! He can come with us to California!"

Addie nodded, smiled, and hugged Rosa. She put her feet back on the floor, into the wet boots she hadn't bothered to lace. She stood, slowly. Rosa joined her for a reassuring embrace, silently expressing her gratitude, and said goodnight. Maria came in, said goodnight to Addie, and walked with Rosa to the bedroom.

Addie moved toward the door to the deck, opened it to find the moon shining through a break in the long windblown clouds. *Okay Ángel, you could have kept her out of this entire mess, so you did the right thing here tonight. You owe her big time, so stay with her until she finds a good man, comprende?*

Her mind became quiet; her awareness settled on the sky with no thoughts intruding. Her inner vision took this opportunity to express itself; a vision of Rosa, Joy, Lizbeth and Nita on the beach in California. Addie saw their healing fueled by the power of friendship, the power of the sea, and the power of three ecstatic border collies, Zack, Patch, and Bella, celebrating the sights, sounds, smells and inspired acrobatics of the here and now. *Now that's a vision I can fall asleep to, as soon as possible. Oh, I miss my girls! I'll be so relieved when we come home tomorrow, with the girls and Grandma Luisa waiting to meet all of us.*

## 84

Seeing no one in the room, Dean had glanced at the fireplace but made no connection between its current appearance and the noise that had thrust him from his dream. *Was it a dream? It seemed like something more…something about Addie.* Unable to pull any more clarity from the experience, he paused a moment out of habit. *Okay, whatever this was, or whatever was said, I will know. It will come back to me in an absent-minded moment. I will see it again.*

Satisfied, he rose from the couch to use the bathroom and, yes, to give in and check on Addie. Addie first for some reason. He walked toward the door of her bedroom and saw it was open. A shiver went up his spine, for even before he turned on his flashlight, he knew she wasn't there. Holding the flashlight beam forward, he rushed to the back door and checked outside. Nothing. The chill air grabbed him. As he ran the small beam up the steps to the cabin above, he heard someone walking toward him from the side of the porch he was standing on; the wooden planks creaked with each step.

"Dean, it's Carlos. Remember you stuck me out here? Your idea?" Dean hid his shock; he was relieved to see it was Carlos, but still felt uneasy.

"Any idea where Addie is? I crashed out on the couch and saw her room empty when I got up."

"As a matter of fact, I know exactly where she is." He turned on his torchlight, ran it up the reflective puddled steps past the middle deck, up steps, to the back porch of the upper cabin. Pedro was hunkered back under the eaves of the cabin. A steady sheet of rain was pouring off the roof, and stepping through the runoff came a hooded figure heading down the steps.

Dean could not force himself to wait. He grabbed the saturated railing and, taking two steps at a time, got to the middle deck and halfway across as Addie stepped down a few feet away.

"Addie, you okay? I had a weird dream, couldn't find you in the cabin."

The hooded figure advanced and pushed off the hood; long muscular arms embraced him so hard he thought his ribs would crack.

## 85

The morning light was sparse on the southeastern horizon of the lake as the sun rose. Golden streaks poured through gaps in the remaining clouds. The rain had subsided, however, the remaining surface runoff into the lake was still heavy. It exited down the sole outlet available; the alchemy of the expanding arroyo was turning water into liquid thunder, churning and slamming its way down to sea level. On orders to get the detainees secured in the vehicles for departure to the Escondido airport, Pedro took four agents into the upper cabin to move the two younger Zetas into the Navigator.

Dean had come in to check on the Zetas, Doc, and medical crew. Dean signaled Doc to join him, moving near the door that opened to the road, the ridge and their parking area. Doctor Jimenez had taken his undercover status quite seriously, and regardless of the chill of the morning, wore a brightly colored Hawaiian shirt and white basketball shorts. He joined Dean to report on the detainees, starting with the Zetas.

"Classic methamphetamine withdrawal symptoms, but I'm guessing the younger guys have a different addiction history; they have nausea, shakes, crying jags and almost narcoleptic descents into sleep without warning. Gordo's sidekick Manuel, on the other hand, is in an increasing state of agitated paranoia, resisting being moved to the Suburban for transport. I would say that without some sedation they may be a danger to themselves and everyone around them." Dean looked toward the bedroom the three Zetas were in; agents were giving directives to the Zetas, expressing their frustrations. One agent exited to talk to Dean.

"It's not gonna work unless they're sedated. That Manuel character is convinced we're going to kill him, refuses to let us put him on the stretcher so we can get him in the med van, and he's scaring the crap out of the two young ones."

"Well, considering what he did to Rosa, he's lucky we are capable of restraint. How long 'till you can sedate and load them?"

"I'd say fifteen minutes to half an hour."

"Ok, let me know when they are secured in the vehicles."

"Will do," he agreed with a mock salute. He took his medical bag and went back to the Zeta's room, motioning for more agents to accompany him.

Dean stopped at the door to their room for one last word to the agents transporting them.

"Deliver these three to Emil at the FBI plane at the Escondido airport. Manuel here needs his leg checked at the hospital in Oaxaca City, but only if he's under control, restrained, and has two agents with him at all times. If the plane we flew here is damaged we'll get a charter, or worst-case scenario, drive them to Oaxaca City." The lead agent had a question.

"What about Rosa's husband and Gordo?"

"We'll load Gordo on top of the Navigator, and Ángel on the red Sub; Ángel's wife said there's a funeral establishment down at the port; she wants to make sure he gets there, so she can arrange his cremation. I hope they are located above sea level down there, so they will be available."

"You know the load limit for those racks is only about 200 pounds? Both these guys are way over the limit."

"There are ways to make it work for a short trip; securing to the vehicle and not just the luggage racks keeps it stable enough, may dent a bit...who cares, we have bigger problems."

Dean looked at Manuel and the two teenagers. "Tomas la medecina?" Dean asked.

"Si," Manuel growled, and submitted to his injection.

Dean looked over the scene, smiled, walked out the door and returned to the lower cabin.

## 86

Bella, who had been by Joy's side since dawn, was standing next to her as Joy, holding two coffee cups, called softly to Addie.

"Hello, Addie, it's Joy, I brought coffee for a Happy New Year's Eve toast!"

Addie opened the door, then Bella lost her manners and pushed in front of Joy to greet Addie first. When Addie saw Bella, she looked directly at her, and gave her an affectionate rub.

"Thank you darlin' for shepherding in a miracle," then looked to Joy and her smile grew.

"So insightful of you to bring your own icebreaker, Joy, do come in," and Addie bent forward, gave an old-fashioned bow, arm outstretched into the room to welcome her.

Joy took the gesture as an adorable invitation. Bella took the low bow as Addie's way of saying kiss my face, and so she did, her long tongue gracing Addie's cheek.

"I just wanted to say good morning," Joy gave Addie her coffee.

"Thanks," Addie said, wiping the wet trail of Bella's tongue off her cheek, "and won't we be thrilled when we can just hang out and visit without schedules to keep? I know it's almost time for us to get going." Joy walked up to Addie, gave her a hug, pulled back a bit and looked at her, smiling.

"Addie, thank you for saving Rosa; I know the necklace helped, but your focus in the middle of the Zetas chasing her really took courage. It gives me confidence to keep developing my gift."

"When we get back I'll take you to meet my good friend Ben Robinson, would you like that?"

"Are you kidding me? You know him? I stream their services on my laptop...he and Star are amazing."

"Star's been my best friend since we were two; she's going to love you, in fact, she met your parents at the Sunday service, we wanted to go there and focus all that energy on your successful return."

"Okay then, looks like it worked! Let's get on our way," Joy said, and started to head out the door.

"I'll be right there, I need to grab my phone. As soon as we have reception, I need to call home."

Addie watched Joy walk through the doorway. Bella had figured out they were leaving this morning, with everyone packing up and loading the vehicles; she was excited to get going.

The 'proof of life' Addie's reunion with Joy had provided was its own profound reward. Addie stood alone in the room, aware of something equally profound; she had rediscovered a treasured part of herself, which she realized she separated from on the day they had parted at the hospital. She felt it return; an aspect of herself she had so cherished, so deeply longed for, that she'd confused it with the loss of Joy herself.

Addie picked up the phone from the nightstand next to the bed and shoved it into her pocket. Dean's voice startled her, his face made her smile once she turned around.

"Happy New Year! Looks like the storm has moved on." She looked up and answered with an upbeat tone.

"A great start to the New Year! Finally! Come on in."

"I saw Joy come out, so figured I could get in here quick; just giving you a heads-up, I want to talk with everyone about our plans for heading out of here. I already went to the detainees' cabin and covered details with the agents. We'll drive down to the airport together, then make decisions there depending on the condition the FBI plane is in. I bet Mike's company told the charter jet to get here as soon as weather allowed, so I wouldn't be surprised if it's already here. I'm so eager to get going, it's all I can think about this morning."

"Okay, I assume you came to make sure I was up. I didn't get much sleep, but the midnight talk with Rosa was worth it, without question." He walked up to her, his voice taking a serious tone.

"Yes, what a close call. Without you we would have lost her."

"To hell with being humble; I think you may be right; This thing with my visions; they are so much more frequent than they were. I wonder if this is the new me. That could take some serious getting used to."

"Don't worry about me being put off by it; I think it's just part of evolving. By the way, speaking of natural impulses, I think you bruised a few of my ribs last night on the stairs."

"Hey, I'm sorry I got demonstrative in front of the troops; that session with Rosa rocked my heart to the max; what an adorable soul she is."

"She showed tremendous courage breaking out of that nightmare. Now that she's got you I know she'll find her stride." He took in a deep breath and blew it out with a nervous grin.

"Darlin'—I think this mission is a wrap. I'm relieved we pulled this off, and ready to get back to California as soon as possible."

"Roger that," Addie cheered, "let's go!"

The street traffic on San Francisco's Golden Gate Avenue was light, the Federal Building and US Courthouse, like most criminal justice offices, had round-the-clock activity. The FBI Field Office on the 13th floor smelled like coffee and stale pastry mixed with the janitor's cleaning solution.

Isabel had passed out in her recliner chair for the night, and thought eating breakfast might help. Walking back from the cafeteria, she passed agent Hosepian's office just as he turned on his blender, revved to its most vicious grinding speed, and startled her out of her torpor. *Not the way I intended to snap to this morning, but I'll take it. Good thing agent Hosepian went vegan, or I'd still be staggering back to my desk.*

A pang of guilt hit her, knowing she might miss New Year's Eve with Dana and the kids if the case didn't wrap up today. *Good thing the kids are on vacation from school; she will let them sleep in, then start them off with waffles and a movie, they will care less if I'm there, then guilt trip me for some extra treat tomorrow!*

As she entered her office, the large screen of her desktop computer displayed the weather channel's early morning review. The clock read 7:10 a.m. Just looking at the Mexico map helped her feel connected to her team. Isabel decided to take cover inside the embrace of her soft leather office chair, giving the swivel rocker function a steady workout. Prepared to hear about the hurricane, she clicked on the video update. *Meteorologists live for these storms;* she thought, *but this guy is calmer than he was yesterday, so it must be wrapping up.*

"Communication with Puerto Escondido has been cut off since yesterday; accurate reports will be coming in now that Tanya has lost convection; it appears she did not evolve beyond a category one hurricane. We won't have much to report until the rescue services can relay video and data regarding damage. She stalled over the coast of Puerto Escondido most of yesterday; the high tide surge likely flooded sea level businesses and homes. Tanya moved on shore with damaging winds and rain in the coastal hills and winds up to 82 mph were recorded by the weather service. Services for electric power could take a while, especially in the hills."

"The airport has backup electric power. People will likely

charge their cell phones in their cars; cell phone service may not be restored until later today. The worst is over, but we are watching for damage reports from populated areas of the coastal hills."

Isabel saw a closeup of the map he referenced, zooming into Lago Verde. Her stomach churned, a wave of nausea moved upward; she grabbed her water bottle, sipped cautiously, and focused on the screen and the announcer's voice.

"Lago Verde, a small lake in the Sierra Del Sur mountains north of Puerto Escondido, overflowed. The runoff made its way to sea level, devastating the beautiful Laguna de Manialtepec, and inundating a section of the coast highway 200. The highway is temporarily blocked with trees, boulders and mud. Between the storm surge from the sea and the debris and water from the Lago Verde overflow, the pristine lagoon and its wildlife have sustained severe damage. Residents in and around Puerto Escondido should be seeing the Medevac helicopters, which were deployed once visibility allowed this morning. Stay tuned for videos of structural damage, airport damage, and information on any injuries and casualties. With no major urban areas involved, the number of casualties should be comparatively low."

Isabel's cell phone yanked her out of Puerto Escondido, back to her desk, with Star's caller ID urging her to pick up.

"What's up? Heard from Addie?" Her caffeine high kicked in.

"I was going to ask you the same thing."

"Don't worry, Star, that hurricane wiped out the phone service midmorning yesterday. So, if I know Dean, he followed through on his plan to hunker everyone down in the rental cabins; obviously, the storm made travel impossible. No one, including the weather experts, thought it was gonna dump that hard on the port."

"Isabel, did you get any sleep?"

"I passed out in my chair, but now it's a challenge staying calm without any reassurances from them." Isabel felt tears coming. *Thank God we aren't Skyping, I don't want her to know I'm freaking out wondering if our best friend and my team are alive.*

"Izzy, you're raw, my heart goes out to you. And I know what you mean; overall, I know they are more than qualified to handle this, yet it's unsettling to think of them in the middle of a massive storm with all those logistics to manage. You haven't heard from Jake, have you?"

"No. But you can bet he knows Addie told us what he did, so he'll be avoiding us. For his own sake, I hope he gets his sex addiction and his drug addiction under control. I am so pissed at him! Thank God Addie is connecting with Joy right now, something wonderful in the midst of the devastating news about Jake."

"Okay Izzy, I know you're swamped, I'll let you go. If you get through by phone would you let me know?"

"I will. Don't be too concerned, the agents are skilled, the storm's over, we'll hear from them. It could be hours, though, but I will call you. I'm sure they're doing fine. Oh! Did you know Luisa and Jerry flew down there? They are in Oaxaca City, waiting. Don't know more than that, gotta go. Love you."

As she hung up, Isabel knew her forced optimism had been obvious to Star. Yesterday afternoon, when Escondido was being hit the worst, she had thought about the extra resources she'd ordered for the mission. She prayed they'd be sufficient.

## 89

All four vehicles were fully loaded with gear, sitting on the flat section of the ridge. Dean took the walkway around the upper cabin, crossed its rear deck, and headed down the stairs to the larger deck, halfway to the lower cabin. Agents Stone and Contreras had inspected both cabins per Dean's orders, and were waiting on the deck to fill him in. Dean heard their upbeat banter, chuckled over their smiles and gestures, and knew they, too, were relieved that yesterday's violence, from the storm and the Zetas, was behind them.

"Hey," he said as he walked up, "pretty nice out here, right?"

Stone nodded. "You bet. And these old structures did a great job of toughing it out, too." He gestured toward the upper cabin, which had been built into a cutaway section of the downhill slope, with about ten feet of deck extending straight out, supported with columns.

"Makes me wish we had time for a barbecue out here, I'm lovin' it."

"I know," Dean said, "Feels like we earned it, something so hushed about the place, makes me want to pull up a chair, crack open a beer and cook sausages!"

Contreras laughed and tried to focus on their task.

"Okay, don't want to be a buzz kill, but I know you want our report. We inspected the upper and lower cabins, their adjoining stairs and decks. Some minor damage, about eleven sheets of metal roofing blew off both cabins, but the plywood underneath is solid. I took photos of the damage for the property manager. Can't say much for the walkway from the lower cabin out to the boat dock; the lower half of the walkway plus most of the dock are under water due to the rise in the lake. If the rest of the structures are any indication, it'll all be usable again as soon as the water level returns to normal."

"Excellent," Dean said, the bill on his red cap was pushed up a bit, his uncombed hair hastily hidden in his rush to get going. He looked around, scanning for anything pertinent.

"Okay, enough of this. Everyone in the lower cabin got their gear loaded on the Subs already. I told them I'd come down and get them once the detainees are loaded up. The sun is shining, the clouds are thinning out, looks like we are on our way!"

He walked back up to the detainee cabin with the agents, poked his head inside, and saw that Maria was finishing one more check of Ramiro's vitals, while Tonio sat on the edge of the couch looking very uncomfortable in his restraints. Maria looked happy to be leaving, and greeted Dean with a renewed lilt to her voice.

"Hi, I'll be finished here in about five minutes, everyone's in the vehicles except these two. Could you tell Pedro that Ramiro and Tonio need a trip to the toilet once I'm done with vitals? Then we'll load 'em up."

"Okay, I'll send Pedro to help you," he said as he headed out the door.

On the ridge, Dean checked the Zetas; Manuel was horizontal in the med van. The two younger Zetas were in the back seat of the Navigator. They had been handcuffed behind their backs and shackled to the car seat chassis, then Pedro had put their seat belts on. He passed Maria's message on to Pedro, who left to help with Ramiro and Tonio.

Dean was sure the designers of the Navigator never dreamed a 300-pound terrorist would grace their luggage rack. It wasn't the first time he'd exceeded the load designated in an SUV operator's manual, nor would it be the last; he'd had a hunch they might need extra tie-downs, and was glad he'd followed it. Still, he was relieved to be the director of the task, and not the muscle.

Next, he checked the red Sub. Miguel was secured in the second seat, to be joined by the M.D. Five agents were securing Ángel's body up top, and Carlos gave Dean the run-down.

"We put Rosa and Adela in the rear seat, and they are pissed, just at the sight of Miguel. Everything that can be packed is packed. We got all your crew's stuff onto the white Sub like you said. Backpacks, Ana's vet kit, everything, all secured to the luggage racks with tarps and tie downs."

Dean heard Adela's voice carry far and wide once she began to yell at Miguel. Adela was a very attractive woman, but the vitriol she spewed morphed her face into a frightening mask.

"I hated to think I had to ride in the same car with you but now I'm happy to be here, because I have the way to tell you about my anger. You are only alive today because of the many times Ramiro has rescued you from your drunken decisions. If you're asking God why you lived and not Ángel, keep it up, I would like to know the answer! Who knows what this trip has done to Ramiro's heart, so much worry and pain, to find out you had put everyone in danger and he had to help rescue you again!"

Adela's tirade of shame found its mark; Miguel wept as he'd never wept before, and didn't appear to be capable of stopping. Dean listened with pleasure to hear the women call out the pitiful man, feeling they were finding some of their strength again.

"Yes, Papa," Rosa taunted him, "Running away from truth and into your fantasies is no longer an option. There will be no more alcohol to help you forget. You caused Ángel's death and my torture at the hands of those pigs!"

On that sad note, Dean leaned in the window of the red Sub and filled the women in on his plan.

"Rosa, Adela, I'm glad you're telling him what you think. It's probably the first sober criticism he's heard in fifty years. Sorry you're stuck in this car, but it's just for the trip down to the airport. Pedro's taking Ramiro and Tonio to the bathroom, they'll be here in a minute. Once everyone is secured, Joy and her family, Dr. Diaz, Emil and I will be up here to drive down the hill to the airport with you. All the vehicles will travel in a caravan, so we can coordinate any road blockages together."

"Gracias, Señor, we will try to be patient," Adela said, "I will not strangle Miguel right after you leave to get your crew, I promise."

Doctor Jiménez seated himself next to Miguel, patted the crying man on the leg and gave Dean a parting comment. "I will protect Miguel. After all, I took an oath when I got my license."

"I took no such oath," Adela said, "so don't take a nap on the way or I may give him a permanent pain killer."

Dean had to laugh at her taunt. He moved with a new spring in his step, eager to get to the lower cabin, excited to go give the crew their orders to leave for the airport. The sun broke through, lighting up the forest and the lake, the birds were scouting for food, and for the first time he could see and feel the beauty of their surroundings; a sight long overdue.

## 90

When Addie came out of the bedroom the sulphur smell and the chill of the room greeted her from the damped-out fire in the fireplace, as well as the extinguished one in the wood stove. Regardless of how saturated the cabins and the woods were that morning, someone had followed their fire safety training to the letter. A few portable lanterns lit the corners of the living room that weren't getting light from the windows. Emil, Mike, Ana, Joy, Bella, and one of the medics, Carlos, all looked more than ready to shift directions and get on with their lives. Addie, who had borrowed a scarf to hide the bruises on her neck, felt rejuvenated and ready to roll, and had to mention it to her co-celebrants.

"There's a bit of pre-commencement excitement going on in here, or is it just me?"

"We earned it, graduation from the school of hard knocks; it feels great to launch out of here," Joy said, squatting to pet Bella, who already knew they were getting ready to go, and had been pacing around, looking up at each of them as if to say, 'not yet?' or 'now?'

Dean came in the back door, clomping through the hall at an eager pace, and Bella ran to greet him. As soon as he walked into the gathered group, his on-point energy was palpable.

"So, still no cell phone service. Charge your phones in the car as soon as you can so they'll be usable when the service is available. I don't think there's going to be much in the way of road crews chasing up this hill to see if everyone up here has any problems. I'm sure their resources are stretched thin down at the port. Any other questions, ideas?"

Addie grabbed the last Cliff Bar, couldn't wait, so took a bite and talked with her mouth full, "We're taking the two Suburbans, the Navigator and the Med Van altogether?"

"Everyone's up top, ready to go. Detainees all secured in their vehicles except for Tonio and Ramiro. Pedro and Maria are finishing up with them, but we can go up in a minute."

He checked his watch and continued.

"It's seven thirty; I'd say we have a lot to be grateful for at this point. We got the bad guys, did our best with some unfortunate casualties and injuries, and the woman of the hour has been safely reunited with her family." Addie saw him grin at Joy, who returned it with a big smile. Addie noticed Joy's laceration was looking better, and Mike and Ana looked even more eager to shift gears and get their girl home.

Emil give Addie an unexpected pat on the back. She smiled, he grabbed his parka, repositioned his holster a bit, and gave his kudos to the group.

"You people have been strong and patient. With no phone service to Isabel or your family members it's been worrisome at times. Let's go home."

"I know Izzy better than anyone here," Addie introjected, "and believe me, she's no doubt gone through hell trying to reestablish phone contact since she woke up today; that's if she slept at all. She gambled the weather service was right about the hurricane missing us completely, and that's a bet she lost; she's been envisioning the worst. It's not sitting well with her, I know that much."

"Okay then" Mike added, "Let's get going so we can put agent Chung out of her misery and into a celebratory mood!"

Joy put her jacket on and headed for the hallway to the back door.

"Dean," she said looking over her shoulder, "do you mind if I pop in and talk to Tonio for one second before I get in the car?"

"The Zeta's are restrained in the Navigator, agents are there with them, waiting for Maria and Pedro to bring out Ramiro and Tonio. If you want to scoot up to the cabin you're going to have to hurry. Carlos, would you escort her? We'll be up in a second." Joy grinned her thanks to Dean and headed for the hall. Bella followed her, picking up on her excitement.

"Thanks, Dean, see you up there," Joy stopped at the hall entry and shook her finger at Bella. "I know you heard Tonio's name, but you need to stay here and stay clean for your ride, right Mom?"

"Right!" Ana said, laughing at Bella. "Come on, Bella, time for you to get on your leash and stay with me; no running through the mud for you, too many squirrels around here for you to chase, and jaguars too. Now where did I put that leash?"

She looked up at Joy, who reminded her of a yearling filly at her first official race, and gave her a nudge.

"Hey, hurry up, kid."

Joy eagerly moved into the hall, with Ana, Mike, Emil, Addie, and Dean watching her. Carlos paused a minute to grab his jacket from across the room. Ana spoke quietly so Joy wouldn't hear.

"Her crush on Tonio…is it Stockholm Syndrome or is it love?" Mike looked at Ana.

"She'll be sorting that out with her therapist, more than likely," he whispered, "she'll make sense of it in time."

They all relaxed, and watched Joy feigning a casual pace down the unlit hall toward the back door.

"I'm right behind you," Carlos said as he stopped near the Doyles to put his jacket on, "I have a girl her age," he said, "they're always in a hurry."

Addie heard Joy struggle with the old doorknob, then yell "Open, you stupid door!" then came a hard kick to the moisture-swollen door, until it swung open and crashed into the outside paneling with a hard thud. Joy's first blood-curdling scream echoed back down the hall before Addie knew what had happened. Before anyone had time to respond, Joy's boots hit fast and hard, running back up the hall, screaming in an ear-splitting pitch "MUDSLIDE! HELLLLLP!"

She raced into the living room; they all instinctively held their arms out to her; she targeted Mike, her body slammed into his so hard all he could do was hold on tight as they fell over backwards. The rear of the cabin exploded when the uphill structures freight-trained into it. The force of the cabin's motion rolled Dean away, reaching out for Addie as the joined cabins barreled toward the lake. Ana had thrown herself onto Joy and Mike just as the upper cabin collided with theirs, knocked their cabin off its piers onto tons of sliding saturated hillside, the wood planks screeching as they broke loose and followed the mud to its destination.

The noise of the collision engulfed Addie; she looked for Dean in desperation, screaming where no scream could find space to be heard; drowned out by the eerie groaning of twisted beams and the cracking of wall studs hit by boulders that had lined the driveway. She felt the floor skidding under her feet, lost her balance, flailing her arms, helpless, as her legs, then her body, were entombed by the river of mud from the hallway. The upper and lower cabins merged in a cacophony of violent wreckage; mud flowing below and through the shattered structures, doing its best to choke everything and everybody while its brutal power thrust them into the churning waters of the lake. She held her breath, clenched her jaw shut despite the mud that filled her mouth, and prepared herself to live, or die.

## 91

Gratitude washed over her as she felt the water free her from the tunnel of mud that shot her into the lake—then terror tumbled her blind through water, furniture, mud, and broken wood, until the couch she'd shared with Dean the evening before descended on her legs. Pain exploded in her left ankle; both legs were trapped between the couch and an exposed floor joist half buried in the muddy bottom of the lake. Amid her sightless fright, she remembered the worst surfing experience she'd ever had: thrown over, and over, unable to get to air, then finally able to swim up frantically, only to hit her head on the ocean floor.

Dizzy, trying to discern up from down in the thick muddy water of the lake, she twisted herself sideways; the surging water lifted the couch just enough to get one leg out. She waited for the next lift, then pushed hard on the couch with her free foot, then harder, got her other leg out almost all the way, until she realized the couch had become a tightening vice, twisting her injured ankle, refusing to budge. The cruel pain seared upward, as if her body had caught fire from the inside. *Get me out!* she screamed inside herself. Choking, she stroked the water, desperate to get her head up to the dim hint of light that had come through above her when the couch shifted.

A hand reached down from the light above her head, she reached for it, and saw a young man's face appear in the water, looking at her, reaching for her. They connected, and with a force greater than Addie ever expected, he pulled her so fast she felt she was flying out of the water, then landed tumbling on the shore. She looked around and realized the shore and the lake bore only a tangential similarity to the one she'd left. Her pain was gone. There was no one else to be seen except the young man, who was now sitting next to her, and no sign of any disturbance in or near the placid lake.

"Do I know you?" Addie struggled to remember him. *I believe I was actually very close to this guy at one time, I should remember,* she thought. "You look so familiar, but I just can't place you; did we work on a case together a long time ago?"

"You might say that," he answered, "a case that went kinda cold, but now it's heating up, so to speak. We're currently making huge progress on it, I'm very pleased to see how well it's coming together here." He smiled at Addie with such a beguiling expression, she could sense he was teasing her, inviting her to figure out who he was, and enjoying every second of the process.

Addie searched his face for some familiar feature that would bring it all back; the when, where and why of their prior work together. His nose, his scintillating eyes, his dark eyebrows—and there it was—alongside the outside edge of his left eyebrow; the quarter moon-shaped scar, just barely touching his hairline.

"Martín!" She moved onto her knees in the sand, arms moving to embrace him, hesitating, confused, weeping and laughing, she begged for answers.

"You're not a little boy anymore, you're grown up! Oh, Martín! Has Papa been hanging out with you all these years in the soul realm? I know he must have loved to see his boy turn into such a beautiful young man. Wait…wait…am I dreaming?"

"It's no dream, it's, well, a necessary interlude, to remind you we are weaving our way through the fabric of God's love forever, you and I, and everyone else we love; we can never be separated, and never, never lost. There are more agents working on our case than you can imagine."

His smile radiated such powerful encouragement; Addie felt her being expand and softly rise as he gently took her hands in his.

"Addie, you are going back in a minute; first I've been advised to give you a key piece of information about your powers. Everyone has them, but they get conditioned out of developing them; Papa and Luisa didn't let that happen to you.

"Addie, everyone in the non-physical dimension knows we weren't just created by God, but our awareness is an extension of God streamed into individual form, never separated except by people's beliefs and expectations. Addie, remember this if nothing else—most of your being exists in the non-physical—where all these modes of communication are common, where the connection to divine mind is common. Just realize you are a streamer from this non-physical dimension. Share what you know, especially as your streaming powers expand. Got it?"

The warmth of Martín's love was everywhere, and the sensation she felt from his hands was electrifying, moving up her arms, filling her

332

with vibrant power she'd never experienced before. He rose, floated with her above the sand, looked deep into her soul, stimulating visions that revealed centuries of experiences they had shared together. His eyes were translucent; she knew she was staring into an infinite living being.

A movement in her peripheral vision caught her attention; about fifty feet away, Ben, a bit translucent in the sunlight, was reclining against a rock on the shore, his hands behind his head, elbows out, eyes closed but tilted up to the sun. He knew she'd seen him, opened his eyes briefly, gave her a thumbs-up, and retreated to his relaxing position. Then Martín spoke; Addie searched his face, memorizing it for later, loving everything about him.

"I love you Addie, I always have, I always will. Now—hold on tight—this may be a little uncomfortable," he said, and pulled her upward so fast she got dizzy and blacked out completely.

As her face broke through the oppressive terror of the water, she gasped, inhaled, choked, coughed, and coughed again, then watched carefully, her head half buried in the water, until a dip in the water level gave her what she wanted, one huge breath. *Okay*, she thought as she felt the water swell over her face again, *get ready to yell*, and as soon as the swell passed, she used the available air to breathe and scream.

She heard Dean shout her name, then saw him move toward her, pushing through the chest-high water, passing the couch, which was swaying in the turbulent water, one end sticking out of the water. She stubbornly reached as high as possible and waved her hand, splashing the water to get his attention. Finally, the water swirled away from her face for a brief moment.

"Dean! My foot's stuck! The couch!"

Addie saw him turn, throw himself onto the upended arm of the couch, leveraging it down toward the water with his weight. She felt her foot slip free just as the water-born sound of his scream reached her submerged ears. Her feet searched the lake bottom for earth that was compact enough to push back, her injured ankle recoiled in protest when her feet finally found it. Once she was upright, coughing fluid and sand, her breath returned.

She pushed her way forward with her good foot, her arms and hands furiously pulled, then pushed the water behind her as she swam toward Dean, who was bending over, groaning in pain. He stood straight when he saw her and cried out in sheer agony; his entire face furrowed as his mouth stretched into a grotesque oval, bared teeth and tongue extruding, as if begging every angel in existence to make his pain go away.

Addie looked at his arm, her head jerked up fast, her eyes met his, her teeth clenched tight—felt like a locked pneumatic vice—she was in shock. She couldn't get any sound out of her mouth, it was frozen in fear, but despite the lockdown, she pointed to his arm, anguished to the core.

He looked down and froze. A flap of skin was hanging off his forearm and the sharp broken bone was sticking through it. He'd never admit it to her, but she was sure he had sacrificed a lesser fracture when he jumped onto the couch. The gory compound fracture gaped at her.

Something moved in the distance; uphill, she saw movement as she looked over Dean's shoulder. Medics were coming down from the parking area, racing down an apparently stable slope past a nearby cabin, carrying a stretcher. Until that second, she'd forgotten all the med crew and most of the agents had been safe on the granite ridge with the cars when the hillside on the opposite side of their road had torn the cabins loose.

She waved for their help until she saw them wave back, drop the stretcher on the shore and head into the lake. She was afraid to look at Dean's pain again, but met his gaze and directed all the power of her being into his consciousness.

"I'm…here…for…you!" She felt her energy embrace him as she spoke each word. He reached for her with his uninjured hand and pulled her head close to his, struggling to speak, water dripping like a caress from his hair onto her face. For the moment, her pain retreated.

"Addie…"

He brought his lips to her forehead, then pulled back just enough to look in her eyes. Her hands rose to embrace his face, her eyes searched past the pain that engulfed him. Their lips barely touched. Lingering in assent, Addie released herself from propriety and faced the truth; he'd sacrificed his arm to get her free, she'd be there for him when he needed her, regardless of appearances.

Rain shed light showers on her face; she looked up. A cloud

had coiled around the horizon and risen to block the early morning sun completely. Addie heard Dean's name called by someone coming up behind her, and turned to see it was their comedic Doc; his shoulder length black locks were dripping wet.

The front of his Hawaiian print shirt ballooned in the water, he grinned and placed both open palms on either side of it as if showing off a full-term pregnancy; the split second of humor peeled the stress from Addie's heart as he quickly moved close to triage Addie on his way to Dean. She loved healers who could so blithely move energy to clear a path for healing, and acknowledged him with a comeback.

"Thanks Doc, best you get Dean out of here before you go into labor!"

"You injured?" Addie saw every detail of his bearded face as he tilted it sideways, eyes wide open, about four inches from her face. Desperate for Dean to get care, she didn't stop to check, she just answered.

"My left ankle hurts, other than that I'm okay."

"Dr. Diaz, I'm right behind you." She looked over her shoulder and saw agent Morales looming over her with a solicitous grin.

"I'm working with Ugly Betty here," Carlos said, pointing to Doc. "These civilian contractors are a perfect fit for undercover ops; we've got this, you go ahead." Carlos' attempt at battleground humor didn't make it any easier for her to leave Dean's side; she looked at Dean's face, avoiding another heart-wrenching glance at his arm.

"Okay, Culhane," Addie mustered an air of confidence, "go get doctored somewhere dry. Has anyone seen the Doyles? Or Maria? Maria and Pedro were in the upper cabin with Ramiro and his son. Get some agents on that quick, please! I'm going to find Joy."

"Roger that," Dean said. Addie knew he'd keep her injured ankle a secret until she found Joy. She started to wade into shallower water, following her hunch, grateful her hiking boots were now laced tight enough to support a limp. She wanted all their attention on Dean right now, because all of hers was focused on Joy, and she wasn't going to stop until she found her.

## 92

Before the mudslide, Maria had grabbed her jacket out of the bedroom and joined Pedro to assist getting Ramiro and Tonio, who were in handcuffs and shackles, to the Red Sub. They had been headed toward the rear exit of the upper cabin when it lurched backward, throwing them to the floor. The rear columns supporting the cabin and its cantilevered deck had cracked like a volley of gunshots, and dropped like a sled onto the liquefying slope of the hillside, colliding with the lower cabin, shoving it into the lake.

They had all been thrown toward the impact point, which was now underwater. Pedro and Maria landed in an upsurge of mud that filled the collision point, and scrambled like threatened toads to climb upward and locate their restrained detainees before it was too late. A corner of their cabin was completely open to the lake, and Tonio floated in the sloshing mess, face down. Pedro pointed at Tonio and screamed at Maria.

"You get Tonio, I'm going to find Ramiro!" He turned and started scouring the area, slipping, yelling for Ramiro as he worked his way through the wreckage and shouted a prayer. "Please, God, hold that roof up until we find them and get out of here!"

Maria pushed her boots through broken flooring, mud and water until she felt a whole section of floor move and realized they were still sliding into the lake. She headed for Tonio, got to him, pulled hard, but couldn't move him, he was just too heavy.

"Tonio!" she screamed. Her voice cracked and cut out on her from the sheer force she'd used. The cold water reached her chest. Grabbing her belt, she felt the retracted keychain and pulled the keys upward, finding the one to his handcuffs, she unlocked them, then held her breath, ducked under him with legs in a squat, and pushed as hard as she could under his head and shoulders, pushing his head out of the water.

She stood straight, planted her boots in the muck; her muscles vibrated with the strain of holding his head and shoulders out of the water. She raised her hand, and slapped him as hard as she could across the face—it had been the right move, he choked, puked, choked again, then, at last, got a breath, shook his head, and looked around in shock.

Maria, about four inches shorter than Tonio, squinted at him with her large angled eyes, and pulled a piece of ceiling insulation out of her wet shoulder length hair. He impulsively reached for her stressed face and touched her with his fingertips.

"Gracias, gracias!"

"Stay put, I'm going to unlock your shackles. Don't you dare move or this won't work!" She got her fingers on the key, took a huge breath, and dropped under the water, holding his leg while she felt for the lock, then the keyhole. She prayed it wasn't jammed with sand, then felt the key turn and the lock open. Once his shackles were off, she grabbed them, shot up for air, hooked them next to the cuffs on her belt and shouted at him.

"Find your father! Now! He's in here somewhere!"

Tonio looked around, headed for a dark corner, found only Pedro; they stood and scanned the distorted interior shape of the cabin. Ramiro was nowhere to be seen. They dragged through the most logical spots, knowing he must have been thrown forward toward the collision somewhere. Maria looked again at the gaping hole where the two walls had separated.

"Think!" Maria yelled, "There was mud pouring through here before all this water came in, he probably slid outside with the mud. Get over there quick!"

Tonio rushed through the triangular opening and yelled. "He's in the lake!" She made her way outside, into the lake.

Pedro was right behind her.

"Look Maria, the lower cabin slid sideways as it entered the water, Ramiro must have floated out of our cabin when that one moved." Maria could see the lower cabin smashed against the boat dock in deep water, most of it submerged.

Maria saw Tonio push off and swim through the roiling water, yelling at his father, who was floating lifeless, face down.

"Papa!" he roared, hitting himself on debris as he went, shoving heavy beams aside like they were cardboard instead of pine. Maria saw him reach Ramiro, and with another burst of strength, he flipped the large man over on his back, gripped him enough to keep his head out of water, and towed him like a corpse with the most frantic side stroke Maria had ever seen, past the wreckage, to the intact section of shoreline a safe distance from the mudslide.

She and Pedro moved forward to help but made slow progress. On the shore, she saw Tonio hitting his father on the back. He screamed.

"Breathe Papa, breathe!" His voice started out sounding like a pleading, frightened boy, and finished like an angry forty-year-old drill sergeant.

"Breathe Goddamn you, breathe now!"

Maria moved closer, she saw Ramiro respond, vomiting and coughing up the lake water, then struggling to breathe. In that moment, Ramiro's status as a dangerous perpetrator meant nothing; she was thrilled and reassured to see life triumph over death.

Maria heard agents and medics yelling as they alternately ran and slid down the hill toward Ramiro and Tonio, one of them dragging a stretcher in his wake through the shrubbery, trees, and mud. As she moved forward, her boots stuck in the mud of the lake bottom; she pulled her feet out of the boots and staggered forward without them. Tonio was turning Ramiro on his side, slapping his back to help his father extrude the liquid drowning his lungs, begging him to live, tears falling unabated.

Addie slowed down as she neared another pile of wreckage close to the shore. Dean, flanked by Morales and Doc, waved with his good arm as they watched from the shore not far from her. She didn't want to slow them down. More agents had left the ridge to help them, combing through wreckage from both cabins.

"I'm gonna rest a bit, I'll catch up with you in just a minute!" She felt she had been standing in the water all day; yet the mudslide had happened less than half an hour ago. The water no longer felt that cold, but her ability to move through it seemed to be flagging. As she scanned the scene everything seemed to be happening in slow motion.

The current moving through the deeper water was flowing fast about thirty yards away, crashing down into the arroyo. She could see and hear Ana and Carlos screaming for Mike and Joy while they scoured through wreckage with Pedro. Addie had a flash of insight that filled her with energy and purpose.

*Bella. Joy. Mike. I see it; they're trapped together somewhere that has air.* Addie moved close to a part of the lower cabin that hadn't sunk; one corner had collided with the deep-water end of the old boat dock, nothing was visible above the water but a section of the roof. She saw that Ana, Pedro and Carlos were headed in her direction. She wasn't going to wait for them, but encouraged them with all the strength she had.

"I think they're under that roof, come help me!"

She was almost grateful for the deep water; she thought swimming would hurt her ankle less. By the time she got to the highest part of the cabin roof, which was barely above water, her ankle hurt worse than ever. She heard Bella crying, then a weak bark... *she must have gotten my scent*...Addie rejoiced.

She took a deep breath and swam below the submerged roof line until she found the air pocket. As her head found air, she opened her eyes; everything was black. She blinked, still nothing. The soaked wood smelled familiar somehow, then she thought of her barn at home, could almost hear Amira's greeting, almost see her head bobbing up and down with excitement, reminding her they had a future to share.

"Joy! Mike! I'm here but I can't see you!" Then she screamed for Ana, and Carlos, over and over, while she made her way through the broken boards, sheets of insulation and ceiling joists that had landed on the support columns of the dock.

"Addie! Over here! Dad's hurt, hurry. Bella's hurt too. I'm okay, not bad. Let your eyes adjust to the dark and follow my voice. I can see your head, move to your left about three feet, get over the ceiling beam, that's it, yes, just climb over that beam and come straight ahead."

Addie felt her way over the splintered beam, kept moving ahead to Joy's voice and Bella's painful whine. She got close enough to see a vague silhouette of Mike, Joy and Bella lying on a section of the dock that hadn't broken, with about two feet of air between them and the roof. Recalling the way the structure had looked from the outside, Addie knew her entry was also their only viable exit. A few more thrusts of the rising turgid water and the whole thing was going to slide off and take them with it.

"Joy...is Mike conscious?"

"I am now," he answered for himself. *Groggy but making perfect sense*, Addie thought, *that's good news*. Addie approached with caution, knowing the whole structure could collapse if she put her weight on the wrong support.

"Ok, give me a report, fast."

"Dad hit his head on something, for a while he was knocked out; other than that, he seems to be okay. I'm all right, no major pain from anything, no bleeding. Bella's hurt but I didn't try to check her, didn't want to move until we had help, too worried I'd make everything collapse again."

"You did the right thing, Joy. I'm so relieved you're all alive."

"Me too," mumbled Mike. "Get Joy out of here first."

"Ok, Mike, I'm on it. Carlos, Ana and Pedro are right behind me. Pedro and Carlos can get you, and Ana can check Bella if she feels safe enough to come in here, otherwise, one of the guys can come back for her." A voice came out of the dark, Ana had found her way in.

"Joy! Mike! Both okay?"

"Just...waiting...for room service!" Mike's signature humor had never been so welcome.

"I'm okay Mom, but Bella swam to us after we got up on the dock, she's hurt, mom, she's crying, thank God you're here," the relief and distress was palpable in Joy's voice as she spoke, and rose when she started crying. "I...just wanna go home, Mama...so bad...wanna go home..."

"Okay, Joy," Ana shouted, "we'll get you there."

"Slide off the platform," Addie urged Joy, "easy, very easy, and follow me out." Addie could see Carlos and Pedro had surfaced inside near them, and were ready to take Mike. She heard Bella moan and growl a deep, low growl as Ana slid her onto the water, supporting her with both arms. Ana comforted Bella with such reassuring tones, Addie felt herself calm down more with each word she said.

"Brave Bella," Ana said in a quiet, slow, cooing voice, "you came to find them even though you were hurt, didn't you? Well now it's your turn to be taken care of, don't worry about them, they're okay now, just relax, Bella, Ana's gonna fix you like new; just relax now..." Ana submerged herself and Bella to move out from under the roof.

Within a few minutes, Addie emerged into the morning light with Joy, to find Ana with Bella, and Pedro and Carlos with Mike. Sunlight poured through the thinning clouds, illuminating their position; Addie's eyes flinched from the light. She heard some voices yelling from the ridge and looked up, squinting and straining to make out details.

A whirring sound caught everyone's attention; rising behind the tall trees on the ridge came an oversized rescue helicopter. Car horns began to honk, and Addie noticed two black SUV's coming over the ridge, pulling up next to the FBI team's red and white Subs, the med van, and the Zeta's Navigator. She screamed and waved her hands in the air in absolute jubilation, her one good foot slipped in the lake bed, dunking her under the water enough to get a mouthful. She came back up spitting, wiping her soggy hair away from her face, then screamed out.

"Izzy sent them, Izzy did it, I just know it!" Her chest filled with a sudden burst of constricted aching love as all her pent-up feelings released into the open along with her flooding tears.

"We're gonna be alright, we're gonna be alright!"

## 93

By the time Addie reached the shore, she was leaning on Joy to take the weight off her ankle. Her weight doubled as she moved out of the cold water. It must have been obvious, because Pedro left Carlos with Mike to relieve Joy and shore up Addie's weak side. She tried to smile at him, but couldn't. A hefty breeze slapped against her; rushed across her bare arms and face, and forced a chill through her wet skin to her bones. Pedro held up his hand and looked directly in her eyes.

"Doctor, I cannot let you do more damage to your leg. It may be broken."

Addie didn't argue; she knew he was right, and nodded in agreement; he picked her up with no apparent effort, and carried her up to the spot where Maria was waiting for the chopper with Ramiro and Tonio.

"She needs to stay off her leg. Could be a broken ankle."

Addie felt herself lowered to a semi-level spot on the hillside near the others. Despite the poking of small rocks under her and rivulets of cold water coming from the hillside, she took Pedro's rolled up jacket, followed his suggestion, and went as horizonal as one could go on a slope. *Time to quit trying, quit doing, we have help.* The jacket propped her head enough to follow the progress of the rescue.

Barely above the lapping water of the shore, amidst rocks and shrubs that had never seen the lake this high, Addie could see that Ramiro's body lay twisted into an unnatural shape. He looked more dead than alive, stuck in a position that accommodated the restraints at the expense of all else. Joy came over and stood near Addie. They watched as Tonio cradled Ramiro's head in his lap while Maria moved to unlock his restraints.

Key to handcuffs, wrists free, the old man's arms stuck in place behind his back regardless. Maria worked to get the circulation back in his arms. Addie, more curious about Ramiro than she even anticipated, watched as Maria put Tonio and Pedro to work.

"Pedro, Tonio, move around and rub the circulation back into his arms while I get the shackles off." Addie saw Tonio gently extricate himself from his sitting position. He laid Ramiro's head on the mud as if it were being eased onto the softest pillow.

He took his shirt off, folded it in haste, propped his father's head on it, and made sure he was turned onto his back with both arms free. Pedro began massaging one arm, while Addie was fixed on the combination of speed and caution with which Tonio ministered to his father. She watched as he kneeled at Ramiro's side. Tonio's soaked black hair dripped over his bare chest. He picked up Ramiro's badly chaffed wrist, and with his own hands that also showed marks from handcuffs, carefully massaged Ramiro's forearm.

"Good work, son," Pedro said in his deep, gentle voice.

Addie was fixed on the devotion and care Tonio expressed. The old man's long gray hair had fallen across his face, and the moustache of his bushy, debris-filled beard covered his mouth. She could see his chest rise and fall, but he wasn't responding. Tonio's tears came unhindered as he tried to rouse his father.

"Papa, I love you, please don't leave me, please open your eyes, breathe deeper, you want to see Mama, don't you? She's waiting for you. So is Bella. Wake up, Papa!" Every muscle in Ramiro's body appeared to spasm; he jerked upward, then lay still, coughing hard.

Addie noticed Ramiro's eyes, barely visible under his meandering gray hair, were beginning to flutter and open. She felt herself respond with relief and could barely believe it. *On the flight here, all I could think of was how easy it would be to kill this crook. I was furious he endangered Joy to save his own family. Now I see the loving kindness his son showers on him, I have to think he earned that somehow.*

Addie heard voices behind her.

"Joy," Ana called, "Come help me with Bella; Carlos, can you get my red backpack from the luggage rack on the white Suburban? It has all the vet supplies in it. I see the Medevac crew up there putting up a temporary hospital tent, so take the red pack and I'll meet you there."

Addie wondered how many times Ana had generated this much energy in a veterinary emergency when she was exhausted to the core. *What a woman!* Addie marveled, as Ana dug her worn and wet hiking boots into the hillside and carried Bella up toward the ridge, her mouth set to strong, her blond hair coursed with mud. Joy followed, turned once to look back and wave, just as Tonio glanced up, saw her, and waved. Maria signaled Pedro to help Addie.

The Mexican Medevac helicopter lifted off the ridge and flew

343

to their location, hovering overhead as medics lowered themselves with a stretcher. Pedro excused himself, stood, and walked over to Addie.

"Addie?" Pedro began, gesturing to Addie's blood-soaked pants where the couch had fallen on her leg. "You're hurt, let me help you." Addie looked down and realized for the first time she had a laceration, bleeding and exposed through her torn pants. Addie looked at Pedro, who was soaked and shivering in the cool breeze, and gratefully responded.

"Maybe I can get a lift with Dean, Mike and Ramiro?" Addie asked. Pedro nodded, and spoke to the medics who were already sending up Ramiro to the chopper.

"Esta mujer necesito un paseo. Su pierna se rompe."

"Si," one medic said, and relayed the request by radio to the chopper. The other medic looked more closely at Addie's leg, then at Addie's exhausted face.

"We all speak some English, and Spanish. We will put you on a stretcher after the men go up. Your injuries are a long way from your heart or your brain, but I do not want you in a harness with your ankle hanging; the ankle could bump the hatch when they bring you in." Addie nodded in agreement.

"Okay, a stretcher sounds safer to me too. You know, I'm a little surprised you brought such a large chopper, but it turns out to be the perfect size if these guys need to get to the hospital fast."

"We were deployed because of the storm, then your FBI contacted us through emergency services with your cabin location; we were told to prepare for the worst, with so many FBI agents, detainees and civilians in harm's way. You are going to the hospital too, you need x-rays, a cast, and stitches."

"We'll see, if I can get my leg cleaned up and stitched here, I could stabilize the ankle for now and get it checked tonight at the hospital in California. I'm in a hurry to get home." The chopper was lowering the cable for Dean's stretcher, so the medic began to move, then stopped and looked back at Addie.

"It will not be my decision. But I see you want to go home, and I think I see why," he looked out at the devastation from the mudslide and said, "you are all very lucky, this is not my first scene like this, and often not everyone makes it out alive; you have angels watching over you."

Addie immediately recalled Martín's intervention, his reassurances, and the energy he poured into her, giving her the strength to stay alive until Dean found her.

"Yes, we are very fortunate. I didn't see any angels, but my brother Martín, who died when I was ten...he appeared in the water and saved me from drowning."

The medic nodded, his face took on a reverent expression and loving smile, his awestruck eyes connected with hers.

"Señora, you are not the first person to tell me something like this, I know...es verdad, es verdad."

"Yes," Addie replied, "apparently there's more to rescuing someone than most people understand."

## 94

Addie winced with every unpredictable movement the chopper made, and had her eyes on Ramiro. She stared at his matted gray hair, filled with mud and debris; her fatigue and worry grew. *Maybe he's not going to make it*, she thought. She couldn't see much because the medics were busy with triage, talking with the M.D. on the radio, and setting up help to get the injured to the medical tent once they landed on the ridge.

Dean groaned as the young medic stabilized his arm. All the activity had roused Ramiro even more. He was coughing up fluid; every word Addie heard was weak and guttural.

"Tonio...Donde es...Bella...pobrecita, is she okay?" The older medic was doing what he could to suction Ramiro's excess fluids, while cleaning up his face and hands. He responded to the old man in a quiet voice.

"Señor Ramiro, your son isn't in the chopper, he will meet you up on the ridge as soon as we get to the med tent. Let me get you cleaned up a bit so I can keep an eye on your skin; it is one way I can monitor your blood circulation."

"Oh, gracias." He expelled a rattled watery cough and fell silent. Addie's pity for his condition belied the hateful image she had fixed on him. *Oh, hell, tell him about his dog; he can't hurt you or anyone now, for God's sake.*

"Señor Ramiro?" Addie raised her voice to make sure he heard her.

"Si."

"About your dog. She got injured in the mudslide but should be okay. There's a vet working on her right now up at the hospital tent."

"Gracias," Ramiro's gravelly whisper came with wet coughing; he choked, and the medic made his way to assist him. The chopper turned, hovered, then made a hard landing on the ridge. Addie heard Dean react to the bounce with a deep groan that made her cry more. *Get a grip, stop crying; you don't need everyone fawning over you when Dean is in serious trouble.* She grabbed a corner of the soft blanket they'd covered her with and wiped her tears and their streaks of mud before anyone noticed.

As she tried to regain her composure, the thumping engine went silent, the door to the chopper opened fast, and two medics from the hospital tent came through the door. The first one who entered gave loud orders military style, and made no effort to conceal the sense of urgency the doctor had communicated to him.

"Everyone listen up; the doc wants you to move to the med tent for triage and transport planning. Each of you must have a medic in charge of your exit from this chopper. No one goes in or out of the med tent without assistance. One lane of the road from here to the airport is now open for vehicular travel for able bodied individuals.

"This chopper will fly one group of injured down the hill to the Puerto Escondido airport once the doctor is finished here. Those persons who the doctor wants checked at Alta Regional Hospital in Oaxaca City will all have air transport downhill to the airport right away. Detainees and agents will fly in the FBI plane, and there is a charter flight waiting to take non-detainees to Oaxaca. It is a miracle you people survived that mudslide. Do not forget to give credit where credit is due."

Addie was so numb she had struggled to hear his orders, but the last one penetrated through to her soul; Martín's appearance in the middle of her losing struggle with the lake would be extremely high on her list of miracles. Every other blessing she had witnessed over the past week began to waft through her imagination, and as she pretended to look interested in whatever else the strident medic was telling them, she was indeed busy, giving credit where credit was due.

## 95

Ana stepped out of the hospital tent by the granite slab, her view unencumbered with the upper cabin gone. Bella, sedated, with a cast on her leg, was resting in her travel crate in the white Suburban; leaving Ana to cherish the calm that had settled on their crisis. As the medical crew packed up for the trip, she saw Emil.

Earlier, he had hooked up a hose to a spigot on the large water tank, created a semi-private shower curtain stall, and collected dry clothes and towels from the crew to share with the mudslide victims. Ana had showered, and wore what she suspected had been Emil's black sweats with a San Francisco Giants logo. Her blond hair, pulled back into a ponytail, was secured with a strip of gauze from the med tent.

"Emil, do I have time for a ten-minute mental health hike? I'm getting a real pull to just go over there and see what I can see, maybe say my goodbyes before we head out."

"You earned it, Ana, if you're not back when we're ready I'll whistle for you." She walked away from the tent, and followed the shelf of boulders along the ridge; drawn to the intact hillside beyond the muddy slope where the cabins had been. She walked until she heard no voices, then stopped, took a deep breath, exhaled the morning's experience, and looked around the visible perimeter of the lake.

Color began to appear before her; the clouds thinned and lost their power to paint trees, water, earth and people in dull monochromatic hues of gray. The sun had reappeared; reminding her it was always there, always pouring its life into the space between them, blessing her infinitesimal point of life. Ana felt invisible, as if she had been absorbed by everything around her; as if she lived in the sparkling water that slapped the shore, in the dark earth that turned to mud at water's touch, in the green breath of pines reaching for the gift of penetrating light, in the great black hawk's swoop to the pine's tallest branch.

She walked about halfway down to the lake, sat on a shelf of rock between two boulders, and waited. The hawk perched at the top of a tall sparse pine, looking at the shoreline for stunned fish, frogs, a snake, any sign of life the generous storm may have provided.

Ana noticed she too was looking across the shore for signs of life. A large dead tree, half in, half out of the water, caught her attention; a small animal wiggled in the crook of its divided trunk. Would the hawk go for it? Then, her peripheral vision picked up something moving downhill a few meters away; a large shape making its way through the trees, emitting a deep, rolling, growl in rhythmic bursts.

Her eyes returned to the log; the small, tan, black-spotted form moved up; the welcome call from her mother pulled her closer. Tears of unbounded awe blurred Ana's vision as the massive jaguar made a slow grunting descent past Ana, down toward the cub. Another cub, proudly sporting her mother's colors, appeared next to Ana and looked up, receiving a smile in return. A black streak, powered by mischievous forces, pounced onto the first and rolled her over the toe of Ana's hiking boot.

The mother's broad head had been busily inspecting the runt as they made their way back up the slope. Startled by her cubs' squeals, she turned and looked at Ana, who sat awestruck on the rock shelf between the boulders, the two cubs playing on the slope in front of her.

Ana saw the mother's belly, well rounded from a recent meal. The cat's wide jaws opened, a louder deep-chested growl caught the cubs' ears, and they obeyed, with a few swipes at each other on the way, they met her as she and the runt moved up from the shore. Ana's heart pronounced a slow drumming beat that radiated through her body.

The hawk screeched, diving off his perch, in a straight descent toward the hillside. The deep thumping roll from the jaguar's throat announced she was ready to disappear with her reunited family into the forest. She paused, straight and proud, her cubs bounding around her, the intricate black and tan designs of her fur burst in the returning sun. Her ears pointed toward Ana, and twitched a few times. As Ana stared transfixed, the mother's penetrating eyes telegraphed a healing farewell.

## 96

The quick chopper flight downhill to the one strip Puerto Escondido Airport overwhelmed Addie's senses. Mudslides, damaged buildings, cars drowned in flooded areas, some upended downhill from the road, satellite dishes still attached to blown-off sections of roofing. The powerful rhythmic vibration from the chopper claimed Addie's entire body as they flew over the highway leading downhill to the port.

The chopper crew checked for mudslides, cars and trees blocking the road, so they could radio the crew who were driving down and tell them what to expect. There were obstacles here and there; they would have to proceed with caution but fortunately nothing appeared that they couldn't clear or drive over. Dean pointed out a few families en route.

"Let's hope all they got was wet."

As Addie strained to see, her heart ached. People who looked too small for the problems they were facing could be seen along the route, some of them drenched in mud, walking out of the foothills with their children toward downtown Puerto Escondido in search of assistance. Addie's hopes for the stranded families rose when she saw rescue vehicles, moving to make order out of total chaos.

Dean pointed to the intact cell phone tower as the chopper descended.

"With clear skies and an intact tower, we should be able to call out. Let's wait until we have everyone settled, though, don't want to lose our focus."

She saw the charter plane that brought them the day before, parked near the FBI plane, which sat undamaged and ready for boarding. As the chopper landed, Addie's heart gradually slowed into a peaceful, but still noticeable cradle-rocking pace. She thought of her reunion with Joy. *Not to miss her, what a gift...*

Addie was talking with Mike while Miguel, Ramiro and Dean were moved out of the chopper. When her turn came, Addie stood up, grabbed her crutches, and with Mike behind her and a medic in front, she got down.

"Thanks, Mike. How's your head feeling?" The medic wanted to hear his answer as well.

"It hurts. I feel a little spaced out, not too bad. Doc said he didn't recommend flying for brain-injured cases, but he knew this was a brief half hour and low altitude, so even if my noggin had some problems, the flight wouldn't make it any worse." Addie nodded, then teased.

"You seem to be making sense—that's a plus."

"I'll do better when Ana and Joy get here; at least we didn't have to wait for the charter, the pilot must have figured if the weather here was clear, he'd just come on ahead."

They made their way to the charter plane, a gentle breeze caressed her face. This was the first friendly weather they had seen since they had left Oaxaca. Once on board the plane she reassured him.

"Don't worry, Mike, they'll be here soon. Plus, I'm sure Ana has Bella with her, keeping her under observation, so she'll need to come with us. Say, do you think I could borrow your phone and try for a quick call to my family? I lost the FBI phone in the lake this morning."

"Are you kidding me?" Mike's mock disdain made her laugh so hard she even felt it in her injured leg.

Mike didn't let up, "you've wrecked two cell phones in one week! Why should I risk losing mine? Oh, all right, I'll throw caution to the winds, here, take it," he gave it to her, lost control, and laughed.

"No more pain pills for you, smart ass," Addie joked.

"Well, we wouldn't even have my phone if Dean hadn't insisted we get all our gear packed into the Suburban last night; guess you missed that suggestion. By the way, while I'm under the influence, humor my macabre curiosity and let me know what's happening with the deceased; seeing them strapped to the top of the cars was a surrealistic experience, for sure."

"Well," Addie began, eager to get to her phone calls, "Dean told me they are going to Funerales Ayala in Puerto Escondido. One of the agents located it; the police wanted it open today to handle casualties. Good thing, because the examination of any homicide victim is best when embalmed within twenty-four hours and available for examination by the coroner, to secure evidence for the court. Ironic they're going to be delivered together, considering one's the killer and one's the victim."

## 97

Thanks to Mike, Addie was settled on the plane waiting for the Suburbans to deliver her fellow passengers. She was used to briefly reporting to Isabel on an out-of-town case before she phoned home, so even though she wasn't officially on the payroll, she knew Izzy was waiting to hear her voice. When Izzy answered the call, Addie's heart radiated a poignant, visceral celebration; welling deep throughout her chest, pushing through her throat, triggering tears.

"Mike?

"Izzy, it's Addie! I'm using Mike's phone; the one Dean gave me is at the bottom of the lake somewhere."

"Oh my God, you're okay! Emil just updated me on the detainees and the mudslide. Oh, Addie, I'm so sorry." Isabel was crying, Addie knew, so she wanted to reassure her.

"No one died in the mudslide which was a freakin' miracle if you saw the wreckage. A few injuries. Everyone has an excellent prognosis, except for Ramiro and Miguel. Miguel's son-in-law and the Zeta leader didn't survive, but I'm sure Emil told you."

"And you? Come on, tell Mama all about it."

"I swallowed a few too many gallons of nasty lake water, we should get hazardous waste pay, considering a few septic tanks slid into the lake with the cabins. I cut my leg, and maybe broke an ankle. We're about to fly out to the hospital in Oaxaca City, I need to call Grandma Luisa and the kids before we lift off."

"No problem, Addie, thanks for letting me hear your voice; now I can start to relax. I'll call Star, so you can focus on calling home. Be sure to call me when you get home and have a chance to talk. I love you, Addie, and I thank you for everything you did."

"Izzy, the details of this mission will blow you away, but for now I gotta go. See you soon!"

The pilot had apparently come in while she was talking to Izzy with her back turned to everyone. He was seated up front. Still no sign of the Suburbans. Hurriedly, she called Lizbeth. After three rings, Lizbeth picked up.

"Caller ID says Mike Doyle?"

"Yes, Lizbeth? It's Mama, I'm using Mike's phone; mine got

wrecked. We have Joy! She's safe and sound! No time to explain stuff right now, but I don't want you upset because I didn't tell you. Bottom line, we had to move to a location on the coast, got caught in a storm. There was a mudslide, but no life-threatening injuries on our team. I hurt my ankle, but I'm okay, we're all okay, and after one stop in Oaxaca City for some medical care we're flying home; probably tomorrow morning. I can't wait to see you! How's Grandma and Nita? Have you heard from your Dad?"

"Whoa, Mama, you sound a bit rushed, what's going on?"

"I'm sitting in a plane at the Puerto Escondido airport, the cell tower here doesn't reach far, so I can't call you back until later if the plane takes off."

"Ok, I'll talk fast then you call us all back tonight. Grandma left us a note last night that she had to help uncle Jerry with a charter flight; her friend Kathy came to hang out with us until you get home. Wow, that woman can cook!

"Nita just went to the store, as for Dad, hold your horses...he checked himself into a rehab program the day after you left. He says we'll all be coming to a few sessions in a week or so, which is fine with us. Aren't you glad Mama? I have no idea what triggered him to do it, but thank God, it was only a matter of time before he really wrecked himself."

Addie started to cry and couldn't bring herself to stop.

"Oh, Lizbeth," she struggled for words, "I am happy, even if I'm crying, it's a huge relief. Oh, baby, I love you so much, I miss you so bad, I can hardly wait to hold you in my arms...all of you...so dear to me...so precious."

Her tears poured unhindered, her gratitude kept pushing them out; the fears she had held about Jake overdosing left her along with the tears.

"Hey!" Addie heard Mike yell and point out the window to the arriving caravan. Emil pulled the Suburban as close as possible, and Mike hustled out to talk to him. Lizbeth's voice brought her back.

"Mama, what's all the yelling?"

"Joy and her mom had to come to the airport by car, they just drove up to the plane; Mike was getting worried."

"Well, put me out of my misery, please! Is my sister okay? No injuries?"

Addie could tell Lizbeth was crying. Through the window of the plane, Addie could see Joy approaching her dad with open arms. Ana was directing an agent to carry Bella in her travel crate into the plane.

"Yes baby, everyone is fine. Your sister Joy is laughing and boarding the plane now with her parents. We're all coming home safe and sound. You'll see them tomorrow or if not then, very, very soon."

"Oh, Mama, I can hardly wait…Nita's going to flip when I tell her. Don't forget to call us tonight. I love you so, so, much Mama. Never, never forget that. We all love you way more than you even know."

"Okay, that is a LOT of love, baby, I love you too, so much. I will call you tonight, okay?"

"Bye, mom, and I'm running out to tell Amira you are okay, and she'll see you tomorrow. She's been in the pasture with Leah and Missy since you left; she's too busy to miss you the way I do. Before I hang up I want to know if you're in a lot of pain from your leg injury."

"I'm okay, Lizbeth; after twenty-one years of waiting, I found Joy…it's the best pain killer I've ever had."

"That's so wonderful; I can only imagine how amazing you must feel about actually being with her. I can hardly wait to see her! Send us a picture from Mike's phone when you can. Anyway, I'm hanging up, I love you, bye…"

Addie heard the dial tone and leaned back in her seat exhausted, tears streaming, grateful she'd survived, proud of Lizbeth for being so comforting, and relieved beyond belief that Jake had sought help.

# 98

Within three hours, steeped in the smell of antiseptic, bleary-eyed from fluorescent lighting and pastel walls, tired of being x-rayed, poked, prodded, injected, blood tested and bandaged, their injured crew members—civilians, agents and detainees alike—had been evaluated and treated. The ER director made it clear they weren't the only casualties of the hurricane being brought in, and said the protocol required every one of them be showered and washed down with antiseptic soap due to their exposure to so much mud and contaminated lake water. When and how that occurred would depend on the extent of their injuries.

Manuel, whose knee bore testament to Addie's courage and skill under fire, was rushed to surgery, flanked by four armed FBI agents in a segregated security section of the hospital. Ramiro and Miguel, in adjoining rooms, also had agents guarding them, but neither of the brothers were well enough to walk. No one considered them a serious flight risk, but they were considered at risk for assassination…gossip about their kidnapping fiasco had very likely reached their enemies.

Addie had her laceration stitched, her leg x-rayed, and a temporary cast applied. When she came out, Emil and Dean were waiting. Dean was in a wheelchair with his arm in a temporary cast.

"Hola señor Torres, señor Culhane, que pasa?" Addie was high on codeine and pain free at last.

"Te estabas buscando," Emil pointed at her cast, "good looking cast, what did the x-rays show?"

"A simple fracture, should be fine as is, but we'll see what the ortho specialist at Kaiser says about it. Any news about the others?" Emil filled her in.

"Our friend Dean here is still a bit woozy from his procedure, so don't let him tell you different. Ramiro and Miguel are in serious condition, they've been admitted for treatment. Frankly, their prognosis isn't good. Mike, Ana, and Joy are testing the cafeteria food, Tonio and Adela are in Ramiro's room.

"What about Rosa?"

"Rosa had her exam, then went to sit with her father. He's in a room near Ramiro. The agents watching Miguel have also been alerted

355

to watch Rosa. She says she's no longer suicidal; swears she'd come and talk to you right away if she was having problems. She called her mother, who's been separated from Miguel for decades, but is coming here to see Rosa and check on Miguel. Rosa said we should mention nothing about her problems to her mom, she will tell her what she wants her to know."

"Rosa also said something that may surprise you; her mother told her she'd better thank her father now in case he dies, and she misses her chance. She asked why, and her mom reminded her about the million in cash they found in the downed plane during their escape from the cartel."

"She told Rosa that Miguel never spent his portion of the million they found in that airplane. He invested it in US Treasury bonds, to be distributed to Rosa and Tonio equally at the time of his death, to be used for their education, and to atone for getting Ramiro involved with the cartel."

"He must have done that decades ago," Dean said, "before he screwed up Rosa's life with this nightmare. It's completely out of character for a guy like him, but I love being surprised like this! What a blessing for the kids! Just think of having college paid for. Rosa must have gotten a huge boost from that; now she can focus on school and not have to work on top of it, at least for the earlier years while she's recovering." Addie had one more question.

"Speaking of family, Dean, I returned Mike's phone, may I use yours to text my family? And, when we get to the inn tonight, don't let me forget to get my personal cell phone back from our techie agents. In the meantime, your phone? I'm not up for conversation, but I need to check in." He handed it to her with a smile; she figured that at least for now he'd lay off teasing her about losing phones.

"I'm going to find some coffee," Emil announced, "I'll check in with you two later."

Addie nodded to Emil as he departed for the cafeteria. She wrote her brief text report, then sent it to Izzy, Star, Ben, the girls, Grandma Luisa, and Jerry. Her thoughts returned to Dean.

"So, you escaped extensive surgery?"

"They did their best, got it x-rayed, clean, set, and stitched, with some hardware I'll see on the next x-ray. I don't recall any of it. Then

they woke me up and said see an ortho specialist as soon as I'm home."
He looked down at his injured arm, paused, then looked up with a
tentative expression, his eyebrows furrowed.

"Addie, I may need more advanced surgery on the arm, and
frankly I'm not feeling so hot. The FBI plane's going to drop me off in
San Diego tomorrow. When Isabel does the debriefing with everyone,
I won't be able to be there. I'll have to Skype it." He heaved a deep
breath, then managed a smile and changed the subject.

"No one's flying out of here today, good thing I kept our rooms
reserved at the Inn."

"I guess that calls for dinner and a margarita at the Inn tonight,"
she said with a grin.

"Sounds like an excellent idea." Dean sat closer to Addie, with
a change of demeanor that told her he was going to get personal.

"Addie, I know there's a lot going on, and we may or may not
be able to arrange any privacy tonight at the inn with everyone there. I
just want to say this once, and, frankly, it's nothing we need to discuss
any time soon, but I want to just put it out there for you to mull over,
even if it turns out to be something you can't decide on for sure, one
way or the other."

## 99

"Okay," Addie felt butterflies in her stomach despite her pain meds, "I'm already nervous about hearing this, so I'm going to go with your suggestion. Whatever it is you want to say, I'm going to agree to think about it, period, and there will be no discussion any time soon."

"Right," he reached with his uninjured arm, and pushed his hair back, then squirmed in his chair; Addie could see he was nervous.

"Well," he began, "I am ready to accept that you will work things out one way or the other with Jake, and this could take some time. That being said, I want to let you know that ever since my divorce, I have been considering retirement from the FBI, and taking my skills into the private sector. I'll have more flexibility as a private consultant, and there's certainly more than enough investigative work out there." He cleared his throat, shifted around in his wheelchair, and threw his best pitch out to Addie.

"I think we work together well. We did before, our personal relationship notwithstanding, so I'd like you to just file this info, and stay open for working some cases together in the future."

"Okay, I have no problem considering this idea. I agree the timing isn't right, but maybe down the road, we can discuss it further."

"And," Dean said, "I talked to Isabel about this current case; she said she's coordinated with the Mexican authorities. They agree with her there's not enough evidence on Rosa, Adela or Tonio to charge them. They all have visas. Ramiro insisted on it months ago, so they are free to come to California." Addie was thrilled.

"Dean, I'm up for taking Rosa, Adela and Tonio tomorrow with us, especially so Rosa can get into treatment right away, and be living in a supportive environment. Adela and Tonio may want to stay with us until Ramiro's plea bargain is sorted out. Adela is going to be thrilled to hear about the college money Miguel gave Tonio. Maybe it will make it easier for her to forgive him. She already has good income from her paintings, she can set up a studio wherever it suits her, but I hope she stays close by; I think Tonio may need Adela close to him more than he knows."

"Okay, I can see you already thought this through. I'm sure Joy will be thrilled to hear that, but how do Mike and Ana feel about Tonio and Joy?"

"You remember being that age, the odds are against it lasting very long, but while it's happening I'm not worried about any major paranoia on their part. I think they are thrilled they made it through this with Joy and their ransom money intact...and just think, now they never need to worry again about me showing up and wrecking their relationship with Joy, we trust each other. I don't have to wonder if Joy's okay, she doesn't have to wonder about me, I don't have to worry about her liking me or not, she doesn't have to sweat what I will think about her—same goes for Mike and Ana—so it's an anxiety purge for everyone."

Once again, Dean shifted uncomfortably in his chair. Addie regretted getting carried away over the Doyles, she sensed something difficult was coming up.

"Since we got to the hospital I've had Pedro, Carlos, Maria and Leticia hanging out in Ramiro's and Miguel's rooms undercover as visiting relatives. More to protect them in case some random person with a grudge manages to ID them.

"And get this, a hospital volunteer and an orderly gave Ramiro a shave and a haircut, then monitored the brothers in some kind of sit-down shower, and got them tucked in their beds. I stopped to see them on my way here, and you would not believe the transformation in Ramiro's appearance! All that shaggy hair trimmed up, beard gone, he's quite the handsome fellow."

"Now, that I'm ready to see! A clean-shaven Ramiro!" Addie stood up and stretched. Emil sauntered back into the waiting room with three coffees, safely capped for wheelchair use.

"Thanks for the coffee, Emil." Dean leaned forward and spoke quietly.

"Only one problem right now, Addie, the doc said Ramiro is in critical condition. The tests show he's had several heart attacks since he was here a year ago. He has congestive heart failure so bad they are struggling to control the fluid in his lungs. The heart just won't pump enough for his lungs to disperse fluids, and his episode in the lake was the final insult to his system...they don't expect him to make it." Dean's phone rang; it was still in Addie's hand, startling her enough that she just shoved it in Dean's unbandaged hand.

"Hello, Dean Culhane…yes…yes she is here…yes. Oh, I can help with that, yes…very good. She's here in the ER waiting room with me." Addie had held her hand out to take the phone, and was surprised he ended the call, and stared at her as if her head was on backwards.

"What's going on? Who was that?"

"It was your grandmother Luisa. She's here at the hospital, down in Ramiro's room; Adela asked her to pray for him. She wants your help. Are you up to it? If so, get back in that wheelchair."

Addie got into the chair, holding her crutches. Emil signaled an orderly to push Dean's chair. He pushed Addie through the double ER doors into the hallway leading to Ramiro's room. The orderly kept up with them, and Addie pressed for info on Luisa.

"What's Grandma Luisa doing in Oaxaca? Lizbeth said she'd gone with Uncle Jerry on a tour or something, to translate."

"I think there was a white lie involved," Emil said, "Luisa said she had a vision yesterday that convinced her she had to be here this morning, so Jerry pulled some strings for her and booked a flight. Luisa got here while you were in with the doctor. We were in the waiting room when Adela came to check on you, and I introduced Adela to Luisa. The priest had just finished last rites for Ramiro, Adela was crying and asked Luisa if she would pray for him, so off they went. I could see Luisa had her arm around Adela, comforting her."

"Luisa probably called my phone just now because you texted her from my number," Dean said.

"Well, push faster, for God's sake!" Addie said. "Now I want to know what's happening. She said it was urgent? I hope she's okay."

The orderly and Emil picked up speed, jockeying around people in the hallway, doing their best to avoid reprimands from the staff. When they came to Ramiro's room, Luisa was waiting outside. She bent to hug Addie, and said hello to Dean.

"So, what's up?" Addie needed answers, and Luisa complied.

"Addie, I had to come to Oaxaca, I had a vision about an emergency here. I couldn't reach you by phone. So I asked Kathy to stay with the girls and Jerry found seats for both of us on a jet to Oaxaca."

"Grandma, there's no emergency, we're banged up as you can see, but we're okay…I'm happy to see you, for sure, but there's nothing to worry about."

"In my vision I was you, and I was choking to death, unable to breathe. I had to get here."

"Grandma, there's too much to explain right now, but your vision already played out around eight this morning, a mudslide swept our cabin into a lake…I almost drowned…Martín was there, he saved me!"

Luisa stared at Addie, the features on her face seemed to be misshapen, pulled into simultaneous expressions of surprise and distress.

"That's how your leg got broken? Oh, Addie, thank God you are alright. I can hardly wait to hear about Martín!"

"Grandma, the Doyles and Joy are here in the hospital somewhere…"

"I know, Addie, but mija, we have to see them later, right now there's something I need to tell you, but there's not much time."

"What is it? Please, you are scaring me."

Luisa seemed to float over to Addie in one motion. Addie sensed and almost recoiled from the force of her grandmother's mysterious, adamant intentions. She could see Luisa's confidence was shaken.

"Listen, Addie, I called Isabel when I had my vision; she encouraged me to go, gave me the name of the posada and the hospital. When we got to the airport Jerry needed to rest, so he went to the posada, and I came straight here. You were with the doctor, Emil introduced me to Ramiro's wife Adela. She was distraught. I couldn't refuse her when she asked me to come pray for her husband."

"I'm not upset with you praying for him, Grandma. God knows he needs it." She felt the pain meds loosening the reins on her emotions; the pain up her leg was serious. *Don't know why the damn doctor pushed and twisted it so much before deciding to x-ray it. I am not going to start crying…too afraid I wouldn't be able to stop.*

"Yes," Luisa agreed, "he's made decisions that had dire consequences, I know. When Adela brought me to his room…"

Luisa pulled her shaking hands up to her face for a few seconds, then down again, exposing her tears.

"Addie, this is so hard for me to do right now, because you look so stressed, so exhausted, I don't want to put more on you, but this isn't something I can control."

"I don't care," Addie pressed her, "What's one more thing after all we've been through—if I need to do something, then you need to tell me!

## 100

Luisa nodded, then gently reached out and took the crutches from Addie's hands, and gave them to Dean. She took hold of the wheelchair handles; her hands shaking even more than before. Someone in Miguel's room across the hall knocked over something heavy; Luisa's diminutive frame jerked as if she'd heard a gunshot. She turned her head to Dean and strained to speak. Every word seemed to suffer through an arduous passage before it was spoken.

"Dean...please wait...Addie is going to need you...please?"

"Yes...of course...but what..."

Addie was equally puzzled. *Is this some attempt at a miracle healing, or what?"*

"Please." Luisa's final word, a barely audible guttural whisper, sounded as if it were being spoken by another entity and channeled through her.

Dean nodded, signaled the orderly to roll his wheelchair to the wall of the hallway opposite the door, as if he needed the support to keep him in place. Emil squirmed like a man who had walked into a stranger's hotel room and witnessed something he wished he hadn't.

"Emil," Dean said, "why don't you check in on Manuel's whereabouts, he should be out of his knee surgery; good chance they were going to amputate. Make sure with your own eyes that he's still under heavy guard in the security area. If he lived through the surgery, let me know. I have another round of questions for him once he's conscious. I don't want to take any chances, don't want him to die of an infection before I know what he knows." Emil nodded and left. It was obvious to Addie that Emil knew some weird situation had arisen with Ramiro, and he preferred to not be involved.

"You seem optimistic about Manuel's value as an informant," Addie said. Luisa clearly wanted Addie in Ramiro's room and wasn't appreciating the delay.

"You need to go in, Addie, suffice it to say he's been with the Zetas for decades, he knows they'd consider his handicap a liability, he'll sing for me." Dean nodded to Luisa, whose perturbed expression softened. She pushed Addie's wheelchair close to the door. She spoke, barely loud enough to be heard.

"Addie, I will open the door…you wheel the chair in on your own…he's still alive, but running out of time."

Addie put her hands on the wheels and pushed while Luisa held the door open. Adela and Tonio watched her come in. Both bore an air of worried expectation, holding onto each other for support on the far side of Ramiro's bed. The nurse looked over to Luisa and Addie as they came through the door.

"Nurse, this is Dr. Diaz, she has come to see him," Luisa whispered.

The nurse walked forward as they entered, her cap and stark white uniform reminded Addie of her childhood; going with Mama and Papa to visit with little Martín after each of his heart surgeries. She'd been frightened by the old style colorless decor of the hospital, and intimidated by the staff swarming in a blur of white uniforms. *It's 2015, this nurse is from the old days!*

The nurse's hands, clasped at her waist, held a rosary. Again, this was an anomaly, as were her lips—a straight line, thin enough to have been drawn in one swipe with a red marker, defying interpretation.

Addie guessed that perhaps Adela, Tonio, the nurse, and Luisa needed her to help them orchestrate a union with forces of healing and forgiveness. Whatever they wanted, the priest hadn't been sufficient. Her hands, reluctant but obedient, pushed the wheels of the chair forward to the head of Ramiro's bed. He was lying on his side, his back to her, facing Adela and Tonio. His clean-shaven skin and a short haircut exposed the cartel tattoos and what looked like deep, circular burn scars on his neck and ears, previously hidden under his shaggy long hair and beard. She saw more of the same scars on his back, where his hospital gown had separated. *Injuries from his cartel days,* she thought.

*God knows he needed cleaning up, I pity the orderlies that took on that task, it must have taken an hour. It took me almost that long just to get the mud out of my hair, not to mention the second skin of silt we all wore in here. What is it I'm always preaching to the kids—do your best to have compassion for criminals? If the girls only knew how I feel right now.* Her stomach twisted, as if someone had grabbed it from the inside. A vision played out in her mind's eye; Ramiro taking Joy down into the bunker to lock her up. *The terror she was feeling! If I'd been there I would have shot him as he walked her down. Right between the shoulder blades and through his heart!*

364

The heavy hospital door jolted Addie when it shut. She grasped the arms of her wheelchair, looked, and saw Luisa standing just inside the door. Addie's heart struck her chest in protest; a threatening anxiety that insisted on answers, lest it force the issue with some drastic move she would regret. No one said a word.

She looked around at them again, and got nothing but a visceral array of fear—as if she were a priest they called in for an exorcism, and its success depended entirely on her ability to summon God's power.

*Okay, I'm pretty good at it; having compassion for hard-to-love people, looking for the context that spawns every behavior; but this is way more complex, I can sense it, I'm in over my head! I don't know how to care enough right now! Too much stress…too much pain medication…don't think I can…*

"Here, Dr. Diaz, I will adjust the bed." The nurse acted as if she knew what was expected; something that involved Addie ministering to Ramiro. The nurse moved to the bed, stepped on a lever, and lowered the bed; Ramiro began to stir.

Addie felt she was coming out of a trance; seemed like an hour but it had lasted only seconds. Luisa walked up to her, stood next to her wheelchair, and reached over to Ramiro's shoulder. He began to cough, slowly, then the mix of fluid in his lungs was audible. Addie recalled watching him choke on the lake shore. The horror of the mudslide returned. She pulled back from the hospital bed and looked at Luisa, as if she needed her permission to pull back.

"Addie, it's time." Again, Luisa left her puzzled. *Time for what? Somehow, she knew Luisa had decided she had to figure it out for herself. All she could imagine was that Adela and Luisa had tried to help Ramiro and got a wild idea Addie could summon powers they could not, was that it?*

365

## 101

Still under the surrealistic influence of his surgical anesthesia, Dean sat immobilized, his wheelchair still against the hallway wall, trying to imagine the mystery unfolding in Ramiro's room. The doctor and orderly who had rushed past him into Miguel's room reappeared in the hallway pushing Miguel's bed, which was being rolled out of the room, down the hall, and into the elevator. The agents who were posted to his room followed quickly, and took the stairs. Rosa and her mother scurried to the elevator. Dean saw Rosa, the bruises still prominent on her face and arms, pushing the half-closed elevator doors back open, urging her mother to enter ahead of her.

Whatever concerns Dean had about Rosa's resiliency were put to rest when he saw her strength and determination, and for that he was grateful—considering how eagerly he had set up the Zeta Sting, and how deeply he regretted his team's late arrival—and the horrific damage done to Ángel, Rosa and Miguel in the interim.

*Guilt by hindsight*, he thought, *let it go*. His medication had almost worn off, so he stashed his wheelchair in a nearby alcove, and walked the hall impatient, but thankful for his clear head.

## 102

The nurse stepped forward and gestured for Addie and Luisa to give her some room. She left the bed at its lowered height, but raised the head, and moved Ramiro onto his back, sitting up against the raised portion of the bed. She straightened her white cap, moved across the room to her supply cart, got a new oxygen cannula, then stopped to watch Addie.

Addie had avoided looking at Ramiro; she got up from the wheelchair, grasped the bed rail and stood with her eyes closed, praying for Ramiro, assuming that's what they wanted. *I've got nothing left. I don't know what they want from me, but they all expect something.* Addie heard Ramiro's coughing clearing up. She visualized him strong and healthy, but couldn't hold an image. She knew why, she wasn't just tired. She hated him. She was too exhausted to fight the truth. *Hey, I'm no saint like Ben, sometimes I just don't care.*

Her rage pulled her, she resisted, it pulled harder, and threw her into a flashback. Ramiro's suave voice coming to her during Isabel's Saturday morning phone call, Ramiro traumatizing Joy, Mike and Ana, dragging them into a nightmare on Christmas Eve.

Then the gut-wrenching memory of her horrific panic attack, when Ana called to reminisce about Joy's birthday message, and Addie discovered Ana's kidnapped daughter was the same child Addie had grown inside her body—the child she believed she had placed out of harm's way with a good family.

*It might as well have been Ramiro who threw me on the seaweed in Pescadero, made me relive the heartbreak of Joy's birth and adoption…then the added insanity when I saw the vision of Joy—buried in fear—literally locked underground! And the impact on Jake and the girls, terrified they could lose me through this case…then Jake risking his life even further because he couldn't get me to avoid Dean and abandon my role in Joy's rescue!*

Addie felt her stomach squeeze its contents upward. She swallowed, fighting the acid back down as her memories flooded in. She saw clearly, how Ramiro's and Miguel's botched plan had put everyone through hell, including the hell of Ángel's death, Rosa's horrific abuse, *and the Zeta battle, barely won. Then the suffocating hell that trapped me under the water, hearing Dean's scream when his arm was broken and torn.*

She opened her eyes, and looked at Ramiro, the hate churning like a flashfire through her body. She heard the blood pumping loud in her ears, felt her hands become hardened fists, but he spoke first.

"Addie?" His voice was stiff with effort. He strained to hold back another coughing fit.

She stood speechless, her hate spinning. She saw Papa's handsome, fully recognizable face looking right into hers; his head on Ramiro's body. Her brain imploded like an overstressed fault line, the aftershock slammed into every cell of her body. Some of Ramiro's history had been described to her—if Ramiro was really Papa—and she could see he clearly was, then it meant only one thing. He had faked his death and joined the cartel.

Immediately, she looked at Luisa, saw the grief and hope in her eyes, and only then, knew exactly why she had called her into Ramiro's room.

"Addie—forgive him," Luisa urged, "he is your father!"

"NO!" She screamed in Luisa's face; Luisa recoiled, raised her hands to cover her ears.

The nurse dropped the new oxygen cannula and her rosary at the same time.

"Dios!" Swiftly, she bent to save them from more contamination. When she rose, she squared her shoulders and her jaw, and dared Addie with a stare.

"Take the upper road, Doctor Diaz," she said, proud of her ability to give Addie a directive in English. Addie recognized the misspoken idiom, and silently cursed the nurse's interference.

Behind her, Papa's coughing began to build into a repeated effort to find room for air amidst his flooded lungs. He managed two words before Addie lost it.

"Please Addie..." Addie spun around and unloaded on him, yelling loud enough to be heard into the hallway despite the heavy wooden door. Her freshly washed hair, wild with dark curls, enunciated every head-bobbing phrase that flew from her mouth to his ears.

"I believed you loved me—all these years at least I had that to hold onto. You liar! How could you leave me to grow up without a father! You were keeping your pledge to a filthy drug cartel instead of me!" She wept inside her rage, fueling it beyond containment. Adela and Tonio wept in silence, averted their gaze to the window.

"Please try, Addie," Luisa begged through her tears.

"No! To all of you!" She looked at the nurse, Luisa, then past the blur of Tonio and Adela, and back to her papa.

"You're putting it on me to tie this up in a pretty little bow, Papa—you locked Joy all alone under the ground, offering to sell her back to her parents like a shipment of cocaine! I put her up for adoption to keep her away from a dangerous gangster, only to have you traumatize her! You put your wife and son at risk too! Make nice with you? Hell no, I'm out of here! Open the damn door!"

Luisa appeared to have shrunk in the face of Addie's tirade. Crying, she opened the door and held it open. Addie, back in her wheelchair, looked at the floor directly in front of her, and wheeled herself out the door, her chest heaving, jerking in and out, her tears practically spitting out of her eyes, her mouth poised as if ready to bite the first hand that reached out to her.

## 103

Dean had no clue what was going on with Miguel's emergency, and the silence in Ramiro's room gave him nothing to go on—until he heard Addie's fury coming at him through the door as if it were made of paper. *What? How in God's name can Ramiro be her father?* With a few calculations, and the story of her father's death that Addie had told him years before, plus the history they had on Ramiro, he pieced some of it together. Regardless of his confusion, it had to be true because Addie and Luisa had recognized him.

The door opened, and Addie came right to him in her wheelchair, blind to the fact that she almost rammed into a nurse exiting Miguel's room with a supply cart.

"Addie, hold on, hold on." Dean walked up to her, grateful again for his newly acquired balance. Addie almost jumped into his arms, somehow missing a collision with his injured arm, her fingers digging into his back so deep it stung. An orderly stopped her chair's backward course, pushed it next to Dean's in the alcove, and hurried after the nurse.

"Dean," she looked up to him, her curls and fresh-scrubbed skin reflecting the garish fluorescent ceiling lights. She begged him, like a child running from a playground bully, pleading for understanding.

"My Papa is a bad man! I had it all wrong, He never loved me!"

"I heard what happened in there. I guess Luisa misjudged how it was going to hit you, Addie, she was hoping it would work."

Wracking sobs radiated into Dean's chest as she buried her face against him, begging him to do something, do anything.

Adela opened the door and walked toward them, opened her purse and took out a legal sized envelope with 'Dr. Addison Diaz, 2020 Pescadero Creek Road, Pescadero, CA 94060 written on the front, and handed it to her. Addie took the envelope, ambivalent about whether or not she would read it. Then Adela pressed her case in person.

"He wrote to you last week when the doctor told him he wouldn't live much longer. We confirmed you still lived in Pescadero, and he asked me to mail it after he died. We had no idea you were working on the Doyles' case. You might feel better if you read it now, but at least hear this much. He risked everything to get the money for

Martín's medical care; the bills were way beyond their ability to pay."
Addie looked up at Dean. He knew Adela had Addie's attention, and
nodded, encouraging her to listen to the rest. Adela's pained expression
grow more optimistic as she continued.

"Miguel apparently had a debt to repay the Gulf cartel, so he
suggested your papa fly some drugs for them into the US, to make
enough for the medical bills. So, he flew for the cartel for five years,
until Martín died. He tried to quit the cartel then, but they drugged and
tortured him for weeks, told him his Mexican family and his California
family would be murdered if he ever left; then they dumped his plane
in the Pacific to fake his death." Dean watched Addie's expression
begin to soften as Adela spoke.

"Miguel had been flying some smuggling routes with your papa.
The cartel captain kept Miguel prisoner as well, for more leverage. They
resigned themselves to their fate. By the time I met them they were
doing high profile kidnappings. One of the new Zetas killed Ramiro's
old Gulf cartel boss, and your papa's family information died with him.
Their hold on him was gone. He and Miguel were able to rescue us and
escape to Oaxaca." Adela stood in front of Addie, her soft voice
became a half whisper as she confided in Addie.

"Doctor Diaz, we did everything we could to never tell Tonio
what that cartel did to us. It broke us…scarred us in so many ways. We
were a traumatized family when we came to Oaxaca in 2000; it was the
Zapotecs' protection and care that brought us back to life, and it took
many, many years. Tonio was our reason to keep trying." Addie's
expression was frozen; Dean had no clue where this was headed, and
feared Addie was going to bolt down the hall, broken ankle or not.

Addie's breath was coming through with less effort; her eyes
fixed on Adela. Dean wondered if she had uncovered a half-forgotten
landmark to her previously cherished childhood. Could she read the
truth in Adela's eyes? Would her body pause its flight? He could see
Addie wasn't ready to disarm, but knew her training had conditioned
her to respect new facts. The tears on Adela's face seemed to move in
slow motion.

"Doctor, let your heart open again, for your own sake. When
your papa heard the news about his impending death, it triggered a
terror in him that I had not seen in decades, he could not escape it;

371

nightmares and memories haunted him. He became obsessed with the belief that we would not be safe in Mexico without him. Miguel saw it too, and used it to recruit your papa; the night he went to Oaxaca City to kidnap Joy, he was driven by that delusion, blind to the consequences. I am not making an excuse for him; I am saying that he did none of his crimes for personal gain, but out of desperation to protect his family." Adela took Addie's hand, and dared to comfort her, cupping her other hand gently on Addie's face, wiping a tear with the soft stroke of her thumb.

"Dr. Diaz, he gave you ten years of love and encouragement before he disappeared; his fear for your safety, his shame and grief kept him from you, but nothing stopped his longing for you. Please come back inside and say goodbye." Adela lightly touched Addie's arm, nodded to Dean, and returned to the room.

Dean and Addie stared at each other, both of them wise enough to know that words were unnecessary. Dean reached over to the wall where he had parked Addie's crutches, and handed them to her.

## 104

Ramiro woke up when he heard the door close. His congested lungs labored to make space for even the smallest breath. Strangely, it didn't frighten him anymore. He'd been dreaming about his beloved Mary, who had just brought Martín to see him. *I can't get used to Martín being a young man, I've always thought of him as a little boy since he passed away. Until yesterday at the lake, when he came to us on the shore. Tonio was screaming at me to breathe, and I could not do it; Martín came and told me it wasn't time for me to die yet, and he gave me some kind of energy shock that woke me up, now that I remember...*

"Señor Ramiro, put your oxygen back on!" He opened his eyes, couldn't get them open beyond a slit, but saw the nurse's white uniform, then her hands in his face, and felt her replace the small oxygen tubes in his nose. Everything was too much effort. He heard Adela, then his mother's voice, and Tonio's.

Ramiro couldn't get his eyes open. *What's Mama doing here again? He felt so confused; did she die? Did I die? Dios! Are we all dead? I must be dead. What's going on?"*

He forced his eyes to open, just a bit. The nurse raised the head of his bed, he started coughing, then heard his mother's voice next to him.

"Javier...Javier, wake up... now...it's Mama! Remember your name? The one I gave you? My, you are still very handsome." The nurse nudged Luisa closer to him, gesturing with her hand, making kissing gestures with her lips.

"Are we dead?" he asked, as their faces and everything in the room swam around him in a blur. Luisa bent over and kissed him repeatedly, all over his face, her tears pouring onto his skin while the nurse stood back, smiled, and wiped a tear she'd been unable to contain.

"Javier, mijo, I'm still alive. I've been living with Addie in California all these years."

"I dreamed about Addie, Mama...my...worst fears came true...she hated me."

"Mama?" He opened his eyes more; the nurse gave Luisa a damp cloth for his face. She wiped his eyes and forehead with loving deliberation. He swooned with the pleasure of it amid so much discomfort.

"I used to do this with a cool cloth when you were little and had a fever." His mama's voice was as soft and soothing as the cloth on his skin.

He rubbed his eyes. As he became more conscious, he looked around the room. Adela, Tonio and Joy were in a half circle at the foot of his bed. His beloved Mary and Martín, appearing translucent and beautiful, were standing in the few feet of space between the head of his bed and the window to the garden. *I didn't even know my Mary had died. I never thought I would consider that a good thing, but since I'm dying, and I know I am, it is a very good thing.*

He opened his eyes in their direction and smiled. "Mary? Martín?" They smiled back, both nodding.

"Papa?" He wasn't aware he'd turned his head in her direction, but discovered his eyes were fixed on hers. *Of course she still has my eyes, why am I shocked? My little girl, so tall, so beautiful! Just like in my dream, but she hates me.*

Her eyes fixed on him. Luisa stepped back, her face glistened with tears, her lips spread in a celebratory smile. Addie reached the bed rail, handed Luisa the crutches and took his hand.

"Forgive me, Papa." Her tears fell onto his hand…which she held tight; as if she were trying to keep him from slipping away. Adela explained everything to me. It is a tragedy with many faces…too complex for me to judge… I see that now."

*So, I was not dreaming. But you came back.* Finally, he could speak.

"You know I never stopped loving you mija, even when I had stopped loving myself."

"Grandma Luisa says God's love is unconditional. Forgive yourself, Papa, you are free to just let go, the price you paid was high enough. Sometimes we try to fix something and it doesn't work out."

His dry lips broadened to hear such news, to discover he believed it. He reached with his free hand in Martín's direction. Martín leaned down, smiling.

"Papa, I'm the one who gave you that hard punch in the back, during the kidnapping, I was giving you a sign, so you would know later that even if I couldn't stop it, I was with you and Joy through all of it." Ramiro saw Joy standing with Tonio and Adela at the foot of his bed, tried to clear his airway by coughing before he spoke.

"Joy," he said, weakly lifting his hand toward her, "no comprendo… how this all came to be…I thank God I got to know you…I regret I can never pay you all back…for the pain you suffered because of my choices." Joy blew him a kiss, then moved her upraised palm over her heart, releasing her tears. Tonio, his face initially solemn, put his arm around Joy's back, and gifted his papa with a beautiful smile.

A loud bass voice boomed from the doorway.

"What about me? Talk about paying people back? Javier, my buddy, you still owe me five more payments on that Cessna you crashed in 1980, plus compound interest for taking so damn long!"

Jerry walked in, laughing so hard, his broad eighty-pound belly bounced as if it were celebrating independently. Adela, Tonio and Joy made room for him; his girth took up all the space at the foot of the bed. Javier looked up and tears gushed as he coughed a sodden cough over and over, finally giving up the task and talking through the bubbling congestion to deliver an important message.

"My friend…Jerry…you look old as hell," he coughed more, "I don't know…how you are still standing…last time I saw you…" Jerry roared in response, his chins dancing.

"Was thirty-five years ago, bro, thirty-five years with nothin' but those ugly snapshots of you to look at in my office every stinkin' day since. Compared to them photos, looks like you kinda went over the hill too!" Javier was laughing inside, but couldn't find the strength to express it, so he smiled; it would have to do.

"Oh! I forgot!" Jerry leaned in more but didn't lower his volume. "You also owe me for Addie's flying lessons; you're lucky she was a fast learner, she got her pilot's license at seventeen, my friend, or you'd owe me more."

He bent his tall, rotund body forward over the bed, his huge overstuffed hands gripping Javier's legs, his soul-searching eyes direct and clear, his voice declaring his intention to tease his friend eternally. Jerry grinned a sardonic grin and continued.

"On second thought, forget the clause in your will that clears your debts with me, bro; the doc told me last week I've got a one-way ticket scheduled for the great beyond very soon. Just make sure you save me a seat in whatever you decide to fly when you get there, we have a lot of fun to catch up on."

Javier felt infused with love from everyone. *How do I deserve so much love after all this time? Is it because I never stopped loving them, not for one day?* He coughed, started to talk, choked enough to get the nurse to his side, coughed again, then calmed himself and looked at Jerry.

"Jerry...muchas gracias," he turned to Luisa, "and to you Mama...for loving me... staying with ...Addie."

Luisa's lips were clamped, her face soaked with tears, her chest rose and fell swiftly; he felt her love as if no time had passed.

"I'll be waiting for you Mama, when your time comes...Miguel, too...he..."

Luisa motioned for Adela and Tonio to join her; then leaned over and kissed her son goodbye.

"Vaya con Dios, mijo, yes, Miguel will be with you soon enough, and, as always, he will look to you for guidance." she stepped aside, and Adela and Tonio, weeping, kissed him. Ramiro saw someone appear and disappear behind Tonio. *I'm not afraid of these phantoms now that I am becoming one,* he mused. As if in response, Diego showed himself again, smiling. *I think he's congratulating me on the good job I did raising Tonio!*

Adela, Tonio, and the translucent Diego moved back. Before he could see where they moved to, he became very light-headed. His body felt like a human-sized helium balloon, floating gently up and down a few inches over the bed. Martín reached over and gently caressed his face until he turned his head. His son's form was more visible than before. Behind him, Mary beckoned him with her hand.

"Come fly with us, my love." He heard her summons, and felt surrounded and filled with a strong vibrating sensation. He could feel Mary and Martín lift him into their arms, their essence refueling his, inviting him into a synchrony reminiscent of the joys they had shared. He smiled, nodded once, and in the slowest of imperceptible increments, he felt himself moving with them through a soft welcoming light, filled with penetrating, comforting energy.

Secure in their embrace, he released the weight of every recrimination, every regret. He discarded his conflicted feelings and guilty memories—the way he'd tossed the first English language book he mastered, and the second, and the rest after that. *It's what I learned that matters, that's all that matters. There's an eternity to recover what's important;*

*for me...for everyone.*

He radiated his happiness to Addie, Luisa, and Joy, who had tilted their heads to watch him join Mary, Martín, and Diego.

He could see that everyone else, especially Tonio and Adela, had their eyes fixed on his inert body in the hospital bed; except the nurse, who, unobtrusively, looked at her watch, checked his nonexistent pulse, recorded the time on his chart, crossed herself, and kissed the cross on the rosary she had tucked under the lapels of her uniform.

Mary and Martín embraced their loved one. He paused to look at his body on the bed, finally at peace, free from pain, and said farewell. They calmly turned and walked through the hospital room wall, with Diego alongside.

"He's gone." Luisa said to the weeping onlookers. "The force of our love was so true, so powerful, it gathered us here, from our longing to see each other again."

Addie grabbed a tissue from the pocket of her vest and heard something hit the floor—her inhaler. A sense of peace enveloped her, settled inside her. A profoundly deep breath formed in her lungs. She let it ease out, held her crutches in one hand, bent down slowly, and picked up the medicine; it looked as if it belonged to someone else. Before she hobbled from the room, she tossed it in the waste basket.

Letting go...letting go.

## 105

Thanks to Jerry's behind-the-scenes planning, Inocencio, the innkeeper of Posada de Felicidad, set up a long table in the courtyard and provided an unforgettable New Year's Eve banquet for Dean and his FBI crew, and Addie and her San Francisco-bound contingent. Everyone sampled Inocencio's raw mezcal, blew off more steam than they planned, then promptly passed out in their rooms.

Mike had chartered a larger plane for their morning flight to San Francisco, a heavy Gulfstream IV charter jet with beige leather recliners, couches, game tables, two pilots, and a flight attendant. Jerry and Addie were the last two to board. The attendant helped Addie hobble to a seat close to the front, then checked on Jerry, in the seat across from hers. He struggled to get comfortable, asked for water for his pain pill, then passed the water over to Addie and looked at the attendant, a short-statured young man with 'TONY' inscribed on his nametag.

"By the way, Tony, my Cessna Caravan is parked at SFO; all of us will be taking it down to Pescadero. My friend here will need a wheelchair; she's a klutz with those crutches and I can't bear to watch it." He glanced at Addie, and despite his pain, conjured a smile. "You're going to fly my Cessna when we get to SFO, right?"

"Uh...okay...if you want to force me." Addie laughed at Jerry; "You know I'm a sucker for that plane!"

"Well, do me a favor and take a pain pill yourself so you can get some rest before we get there." Addie saluted Jerry, dug the pill bottle from her bag and dutifully took one while he watched.

"Good girl...hey, check out our group...everyone safe and sound. Well, except for your pop, and Rosa's husband, and that Zeta kid...well, we know they are all safe and sound, but in an adjacent dimension." They both laughed at his joke.

Addie looked back, and felt a deep wave of relief and gratitude. The gripping stress that had occupied her body for days dissolved into comfort at the sight before her.

Joy, determined to get Mike comfortable with Tonio, had seated them together, insisting they keep each other entertained because she needed to sit with Ana, within chatting distance of "the two amigas,"

Luisa and Adela—so dubbed by Tonio. Addie looked over at Rosa who was near enough for chatting, but for now was wrapped in a red fleece blanket, her head on a pillow, in a semi-doze from her medication, listening to Tonio's downloaded tunes on his phone, headphones in, cruising.

Joy approached Rosa, carrying a box of chocolates and a greeting card. She lightly kissed the top of Rosa's head, Rosa opened her eyes, grinned, then Joy, who was proudly sporting a new handmade Oaxacan dress, pushed her curls away from her face, straightened up, and focused on her plan.

"Rosa, I want to give these to you before you get into your nap. I'm going to read to you what I wrote on the card, okay?" Rosa nodded and smiled as Joy read the note.

"Dearest Rosa," Joy looked up, eyes pooling with tears, then dropped chin to chest and forged on. "I felt a special kinship to you when we met, which only grew during our museum-hopping days together. When I found out Ramiro...uh...Javier, was Addie's father, I realized that you and Addie are first cousins! So the kinship we felt when we met each other was deeper than we thought. Our souls are rejoicing, I'm sure of it!"

Joy placed the chocolates and card in Rosa's lap and gave her another quick kiss. An announcement from the pilot broke through everyone's conversation.

"Five minutes, everyone needs to get seated. Seatbelts on." Joy waved at Rosa and headed for her seat.

Addie saw Tonio opening a package, then realized it was a travel chess set with an easy-release Velcro board. Tonio leaned toward Mike.

"Interested in a game, Mike? I found this at the hospital gift shop." Mike nodded, licking his lips looking eager for a game. Ana was grinning an enigmatic grin, which Addie understood immediately.

Addie could also tell by the pleased look on Tonio's face that he was going to transform Mike and Ana's stereotypic assumptions of him. The plane began to move, Jerry stirred from a brief doze; Addie had to let him in on the humor unfolding over the chess set.

"Jerry, see Tonio and Mike? I already gave you the backstory on Tonio and Joy, so now watch this event. Most likely Tonio will checkmate him before he knows what hit him, then do it again, and

379

again. And because Tonio is so charming, Mike will be able to appreciate the irony, and if he starts betting with Tonio, it'll be like Miracle Gro for Tonio's college fund. I'd say this flight to California will have the equivalent power of Tonio coming to dinner at their house at least four or five times." Jerry chuckled, his belly moving like a wave at low tide.

"Tonio's a genius," Jerry said in a loud whisper, "moving in on more than one front, and so smoothly too; think I'm gonna like that kid!"

Adela, who had impressed Addie with her decision to accompany Tonio to California, chatted with Luisa; Addie overheard something about Miguel's ex-wife, Rosa's mother; a 'young' forty-five-year-old who had been separated from him for twenty years but never divorced him. Addie eavesdropped as she explained.

"She decided," Adela said, "to take responsibility for Miguel's palliative care, and for Javier's cremation." Addie's attention homed in on Adela's report.

"Your son wanted his ashes scattered in California," Adela told Luisa, "when she sends us the ashes do you want to have a ceremony with lots of picnic delights, down on the beach? It would be beautiful, we can all take turns throwing his ashes into the sea." Adela and Luisa looked at each other and started crying.

"Adela," Luisa said, wiping tears, crying more as she spoke, "I look forward to you and Tonio telling Addie and me stories about Javier's life that we missed; so many years of wondering, now I can fill in the blanks. We have a lot of catching up to do!"

"Well, you will be happy that I brought a digital copy of all the photos we took the last fifteen years, so we can go through them together a bit at a time." Addie knew the bittersweet images that Adela's offer elicited would touch Luisa deeply. Luisa grabbed a packet of tissues from her bag and dried her face, thanking Adela repeatedly.

Addie got distracted by Bella, who fussed nearby, inside her large canine container. Adela leaned close to Bella's wet nose and spoke to her. Addie sensed Adela was counting on Bella to cheer her up.

"En diez minutos," cooed Adela, "when we are up in the air, Bella, you can come out and sit with me. I have a little pill here for you that Dr. Ana gave me. You'll take a nap and you will not get sick in your belly. You will be out of there soon enough. Lie down." She gave her the bacon-flavored pill through the grate of the container, and Bella obediently lowered herself, resting her chin across her paw.

Luisa was now smiling a brave smile right along with everyone else. Addie loved to watch her healing way with people; she knew Luisa was an accomplished octogenarian who had learned to ride the waves of grief like a pro, with the warm beach in her line of sight all the way. Rosa and Adela would not be able to resist her. Luisa nudged Adela; Addie had seen her do this emotional recovery dance with Nita and Lizbeth numerous times.

"Adela, do you mind if we share some new recipes once we get to the farm?" Adela smiled a sad smile and nodded, raising her eyebrows with a bit of authentic curiosity.

"Well, there is much to do if your spirits need lifting. We have a large patio with padded chairs and a grill the size of a picnic table. We can cook and eat together often. Adela seemed to brighten, and leaned closer with a question.

"I had a patio like that in Oaxaca, I will love it! How far from you will we live?"

"The house, where you three can settle for the transition, is on our property, maybe a hundred meters from my cottage and Addie's home. It used to belong to our farm's manager. It has three bedrooms, and a fifty-inch TV screen, so we can watch movies from Mexico when we feel homesick. And last, but not least, I belong to a dance club in San Francisco that is devoted to Argentinian Tango...oh, a captivating and very stimulating dance, that tango! You will see, the women are supportive, and the men are real gentlemen. Not much inappropriate flirting.".

"So that leaves room for a bit, just not too much?" Adela had been lured out of her grief long enough to anticipate a tango, and Addie silently applauded Luisa for her gift. The picture Luisa had painted for Adela was beguiling; honest laughter echoed through the plane. The pall everyone had carried in with them dissolved with ensuing giggling from the new friends. Addie felt her heart take in the hope released from Luisa's alchemy. *I love you, Grandma, for showing again and again, that a life can be rebuilt at any point along the way...*

## 106

The jet, moving through clear skies, leveled off at cruising altitude. Rosa was in her healing modality; blanket, pillow, music, eyes closed. Jerry and Addie sat across the aisle from each other, also close to the front of the cabin. Luisa and Adela behind them, then Mike and Tonio, who were holding off on their game until the plane was airborne, already engaged in a lively conversation. Addie noticed, as did everyone else. Ana and Joy kept glancing at Mike and Tonio, and were laughing like two conspirators. Addie marveled at the upbeat mood, considering what they had all been through.

Then Jerry reached into his carry-on bag, removed a large manila envelope, and placed it on Addie's lap.

"Happy New Year, Addie, the Cessna Caravan's all yours; lock, stock...and no barrel rolls or dives allowed."

"What?!" Addie felt her entire body lit up by all that was associated with this gift.

"The doctor told me last week I need to retire immediately and turn over the business to someone who will really appreciate it. I'm hedging my bets; it's all yours, all of it. You know my hangar manager and flight trainer have been with me for twenty years; the mechanics are stellar, what's not to want? So, my sweet one, you can take your time finding just the right person who will love it as much as I have. Keep the Cessna, sell the business, and use the proceeds to put Nita and Lizbeth through college. Don't say any other word than yes."

Addie felt the loving, bittersweet tears, but concentrated on her answer being very clear.

"Yes, Jerry, that's a definite, unequivocal yes."

"So be it." Jerry said with his signature sigh of approval, topped by a truly beautiful smile.

From the back of the plane, Bella, who had been released from her crate, limped forward to greet Jerry and Addie. Addie enjoyed running her fingers through the downy fur on Bella's neck, and surmised that Ana had passed a sharpie around; Bella's cast had signatures, happy faces and miniature flowers drawn all over it. Addie chuckled as Jerry patted his leg and invited Bella closer, then scratched behind her ears as she looked in his eyes.

"She's another sign that we were on a trajectory to reunite with Papa," Addie said, "What were the odds that, in a country filled with chihuahuas, Papa would end up with a Border Collie? Adela told me some ex-pat resident of Oaxaca City had a Border Collie litter and insisted on rural homes for them. Tonio's birth father had just died—it was a match made in heaven, I'm sure." Jerry piggybacked on her comment with more enthusiasm than she anticipated.

"Ya know, Addie, I used to think that ol' sayin' was just something people said but didn't really believe for sure. Now I think our worlds do connect, way more than we know."

Bella suddenly jerked her head away and moved to the one empty seat closest to the front, barking loud, running in a circle, then barking more.

Alerted, and smiling even as their tears welled, everyone but Rosa, who was sound asleep, looked up at Bella. She was so excited her tail kept wagging even after she sat down. She looked up at the empty seat, lifted the paw of her broken leg to its soft armrest, looked up again, as if to say, 'see my cast?' She then stood back on all fours for a second, leaped onto her hind legs, and, using those two capable hind paws and every muscle in her body, hopped in a tight circle.

Her brown eyes flashed with excitement, her front paws and nose raised high in the air, her luxurious white fur in motion, the black patches on her face and neck reappeared with every turn. She hopped around and around, miraculously maintaining her balance in the blessed absence of any turbulence, celebrating her airborne dance.

When she finished, she returned to all fours, sniffed the air, put her nose to the floor, gimped through her habitual 'nesting' circles, and snuggled down in front of the seat to take a nap.

Addie, Joy, Tonio and Adela knew who had invited Bella to dance. Tonio told Mike, Ana, and Luisa about his father being the only one who could get her to do the trick. Luisa nursed a satisfied smile. Jerry looked over at Addie, wiping the mist from his downcast eyes.

"He's sitting in that seat, Addie? For real?"

Addie, chin up, looked straight at the seat under which Bella lay curled. Papa, his form looking like a hologram, seemed to click in and out of visibility. He was leaning back, his seat swiveled to face down the aisle of the plane at his loved ones. His smile, big, robust, energetic, seemed to radiate his joy upon everyone.

"Yes, Jerry, for real, I really wish you could see him; he is so happy."

"I love that man, and to think that soon I'm going to be feeling healthy and happy again in his company. It just takes all the fear out of dying. I've been really scared, that's why I avoided everyone the last few months. But now I believe I've got what you call a healing destination, Addie, am I right?"

"Yes, Uncle Jerry, you are completely right."

"Amazing man, your pop. Think he'll stay with us through the party?"

"What party?"

"Oh, well, Lizbeth and Nita want to meet Joy, feed everyone, then one of them will give the Doyles a ride to their car after dinner. Then, and only then, can they put their heads down and sleep in peace in their own home."

"That may be a hard sell; I can only imagine how much Mike and Ana want to get home after all this."

"Not so hard a sell, Addie, I already talked with them about it and they are definitely ready to reward Nita and Lizbeth for suffering through your prolonged absence."

"Oh well, then!" Addie perked up, felt her heart beat with enthusiasm, imagining the evening's conclusion with the Doyles on board. "Sounds like we may have a celebration we won't ever forget, if I know my girls!"

## 107

Home! Their transition from the jet to the Cessna Grand Caravan had been smooth, and the flight to Pescadero one of joyous anticipation. They had all napped on the flight from Oaxaca, and were ready to party. Addie's descent from the Cessna's cruising altitude was breathtaking; no fog, and a stunning immersion through another golden ochre sunset. As they flew over the high tide foam of the breakers on Pescadero beach, Addie compared the colors to last Saturday's sunset; the night Ben and Star found her at the same beach.

Both experiences, two sides of one priceless coin; providing more healing than Addie had ever known possible. Jerry, in his tour guide modality, spotted two migrating gray whales with calves; Addie flew close enough for everyone to enjoy them before she banked the plane inland to the farm; her heart lighter than it had ever been. The sun disappeared behind the horizon as they landed, and the Cessna coasted to a stop; as if the turf on Addie's grass strip had lifted every blade to welcome them home.

Jerry phoned Lizbeth, who had appointed herself event planner, and requested shuttle services for their group. One truck for luggage and two SUV's got to the strip in less than five minutes. The dogs knew the homecoming routine, and had hopped into the truck bed. Both sisters and their boyfriends greeted all nine passengers as they exited the Cessna. Bella, who had been crated for landing, was the last to be carried down. Ana opened the crate, and, without a visible cue, Bella exited the crate, and proceeded to dance on her hind legs to insure a memorable first impression. Patch and Zack watched with rapt curiosity; their heads stuck in a befuddled sideways tilt as she introduced herself.

Everyone had exited the Cessna with palpable excitement; squeals abounded. Addie kept her balance on the crutches as Nita and Lizbeth welcomed her with an embrace and a promise to spoil her rotten for the next week. They released Addie, then hugged everyone once, and gave a second hug to Joy and Tonio before they drove everyone to the hilltop overlooking the pond, to share the surprise.

As they all looked down on the pond, it was obvious that Izzy, her wife Dana, and their three teenagers, plus Star and Ben Robinson, were more than ready to light up the night. In the recently plowed field next to the pond, fireworks lit up the black sky, releasing a flashing bird's-eye view of the pasture, the barn, the patio draped with Christmas lights, and the three houses. Christmas music blared on the outdoor speakers in the patio.

Rosa, sitting next to Joy and Tonio in the SUV, threw her arms up and exclaimed "Joy, it is not mariachi music, but it feels like the zócolo did as we watched the parade on Christmas Eve. I think it's a sign! A heaven-sent remake!"

Joy was dazzled by the display, and raised her voice over the noise.

"I'll accept a remake of that night anytime! This is just beautiful!" She squeezed Tonio's hand, and Tonio smiled as if he'd won the lottery.

They watched the fireworks from the hilltop, a brief display to spare the dogs' nerves, then drove to the parking area between the barn and the main house. As they made their way through the front door into the living room, all three Doyles cried delighted tears when they saw the huge tree, decorated freshly for Christmas, with gifts galore underneath, a fire in the fireplace, and in plain sight, the big dining room table with a candle-lit, poinsettia-graced buffet of holiday food.

Lizbeth, enjoying her role to the hilt, let them in on their surprise.

"Joy, Mike, Ana, on behalf of everyone here I want to welcome you to our home and our hearts. Christmas in Mexico was stressful this year, to say the least, so here's an improved version to reframe Christmas 2015 as a divine triumph of the spirit!" Ana and Mike smiled and lifted their empty champagne glasses high in an anticipatory toast.

Ben popped the cork on the first of several champagne bottles. "And here's a toast to 2016, Happy New Year!"

Mike and Ana were the first to fill their glasses and swoon over the mind-boggling variety of holiday food. Jerry ogled Nita's famous sweet potato pie, and chose it for his first course, buried in whipped cream. Nita headed down the hallway with his suitcase, laughing at Jerry, then re-entered the living room, saw Jerry sporting a whipped cream mustache, and told him what he already knew.

"Uncle Jerry, your luggage is in the guestroom, we'll fly you home tomorrow; so just relax and let us spoil you. And before you ask, yes, I baked you an extra pie to have with your coffee in the morning!"

Bella, Zack and Patch were so thrilled to hang out, they bypassed butt-sniffing and started rolling with each other all over the carpet, breaking apart now and again to rush down the hallway, through the kitchen and dining room, then back in front of the fireplace, panting with their tongues limp, salivating from exertion and the smell of the roast turkey. Zack and Patch hardly noticed that Bella passed on the races and focused on modified roughhousing on the carpet, all the while every bit as excited as they were. Finally, she rested in front of the fireplace, a satisfied gimp.

Star and Izzy fussed over Addie as she hopped to the restroom on her crutches.

"I don't need help," Addie asserted.

"We're not doing this to help, babe," Star said.

"We just want to get some firsthand highlights of the trip," Izzy said in her most cajoling tone.

"Well," Addie said, "after countless years of sharing bathrooms, I guess privacy isn't an issue...okay." The three friends seemed to skip down the hall to the bathroom; Addie's crutches were no hindrance.

Luisa took Tonio, Adela and Rosa out the kitchen door to the patio and pointed toward the former manager's house, lit with Christmas lights and a sign in huge red painted letters, WELCOME ROSA, ADELA, TONIO AND BELLA!

"Well," Luisa said, "we found our Joy in Mexico, and brought her here. This is where you will heal and find your own joy." Luisa said to them.

Tonio, who had been with Luisa, Addie, and Adela at the hospital, and shared their grief over his papa's passing, still had not spent time talking directly with Luisa. In this moment, he walked the few feet that separated him from Luisa, and bent down a bit to look directly in her eyes. She looked up at him with a warm smile.

"Señora Diaz…"

"Call me Luisa, please."

"Luisa," he said with shy deference, "it is an honor for me to meet you, and to have an opportunity to get to know you. Papa spoke of you often. He would say 'Mama would love that flower,' or 'Mama

387

read this story to me when I was a boy like you."

"Did he ever tell you his grandma, my mama, used to take him camping so they could watch the meteor showers together?"

"Yes! The first time he took me to do the same. He treasured her, and you."

"Tonio," Luisa responded tearfully, "you are so sensitive to share these gifts with me. I adored your Papa, and I intend to keep my promise to him, to make sure you have what you need. We will have quiet times to visit once you get settled."

"Thank you. Oh—I forgot to say that, at the hospital, Papa told me you loved dancing more than anyone, and that if I wanted to be a fine dancer, I should ask for your help."

"That I will do," Luisa smiled, "Javier used to do ballroom dancing with me when he was a boy, we had such great fun!" She took Rosa's hand, "You will find that this dancing lifts your spirits for days afterward. Rosa, you can have days of remembering it, and then days of looking forward to the next time, such a gift."

"I believe you, Luisa, I see you are in high spirits a lot, and I will get there too. Adela, we need to go shopping for dancing shoes and dresses!"

"It is settled then," grinned Adela, "Of course we will pick out Tonio's outfit with him if he's going to do the Tango with us, si?"

"May I bring Joy? I know she would love it." Tonio looked to see Joy coming his way. As Joy approached, Luisa took her hand and looked at Tonio, who nodded to her for encouragement.

"Joy," Luisa began, "Tonio wants to go with Rosa, Adela and I to our Argentinian tango class, he is hoping you might want to join us? It's in San Francisco, La Pista Tango! We go every two weeks. Think it over. Just so you know, the studio is moving to a larger space next year, with a 1500 square foot floating wood floor!" Luisa took Joy by the hand, and led her away from the group a few feet.

"Joy, I want you to know I held you the day you were born. You looked into my soul with your beautiful eyes, and I knew then, without a doubt, that we would be together again."

Joy, a head taller than Luisa, wrapped her arms around her and squeezed her hard, then spoke.

"You've always loved me, I can feel that, and my heart is open wide to love you right back!" Tonio put his arm around Joy's waist as she and Luisa let go of their hug, and they all looked at the sign on their new house. The word WELCOME seemed to broadcast a greatly amplified meaning for all of them.

## 108

Soon, the youngsters piled up their plates and headed for the patio tables, taking the dogs with them. They seemed to inhale their food, and once the plates were empty, Lizbeth put two fingers to her lips and a loud, shrill whistle went across the property. Zack and Patch knew the drill, and raced out to the south pasture to round up the approaching horses. Ana, curious about the noise, came out with Bella on her leash, reminding her that her chance to race with them would have to wait a few months.

In a few minutes, Amira, Missy, Leah and the collies bolted into the corral that abutted the barn. Amira brought her 900 pounds to an artful, abrupt stop a few inches from the driveway fence, snorted steam from her nose in the floodlight from the barn, edged the other horses to the side, and stomped her feet. She looked for Addie, flipping her head up, her long mane flying free, and called for Addie in a frenzy of excitement.

"Look Joy!" Nita shouted, "They're rarin' to go! Want to race the horses down the driveway?" Joy gave her a thumbs-up, prompting Nita to give her new big sister an impulsive hug and proclaim, "You do? Let's go!"

Addie had heard Amira's call, and having figured out the rhythm of using crutches, hurried out the front door and over to the corral to join them. The commotion attracted everyone else out the front door. The night filled with hoots, laughter, and bets thrown down for the first nighttime two-furlong race of the year. The driveway's solar lights marked the track in two straight lines out to the wrought-iron gate near Highway One. Someone with a sense of humor played "Joy to the World" from the patio speakers into the night sky.

Addie felt the phone vibrate in her pocket, took a look, and saw Dean's number on Mike's phone, which she'd forgotten to return to him.

"Yes Dean, I still have Mike's phone...you figured as much?"

"Hey, it didn't take much figuring at all. Happy New Year, Addie, how's the homecoming?"

"Spectacular! Fireworks, music, a Christmas tree, huge buffet of food, and guess what...Jerry gave me the Cessna!"

"I'm happy for you Addie, I can't even find the words. You helped everyone come through this with flying colors. Everyone on the team really pulled their weight too. I thought when we got to Mexico you'd be sitting on the sidelines per protocol, but you have become a spirit who neutralizes containment."

"I sure can't contain my happiness right now."

"Me either, but that's because I'm celebrating with you; my boys are on a double date—go figure—but altogether, what an amazing week. Anyway, let's touch bases soon; in the meantime, enjoy yourself to the hilt, you deserve it."

"I will. You have a glass of champagne, unless you're already halfway through a bottle, and take care of your arm, get some rest. I have a hunch this will be a busy year, once our bones recover from the trip."

"I agree, and if you're not doing anything tomorrow morning, why don't you give me a call and we can chat over coffee."

"Sounds like a plan. Until tomorrow, then."

Joy walked up behind Addie as she put the phone in her pocket. She put both of her arms around Addie's waist from behind, and hugged her tight, tucked her head next to Addie's, and crooned in her ear.

"Thanks for everything you did for Rosa, and for my family and Tonio's." Joy moved around in front of Addie, put her hands on the upper part of Addie's arms, and stood close to her face, her tears shining in the light from the barn.

"I wouldn't be here if you hadn't decided to carry me full term; I know it wasn't an easy decision. Dad, Bella and I wouldn't have gotten out of that mudslide trap alive if you hadn't had that vision just before it collapsed. This gives me a very strong feeling that you and I have something important to accomplish together. Got any hunches about what that might be? Or maybe we should wait…you can tell me when Mom, Dad and I see you at the Robinsons' Sunday service. Should we meet you at the nine or eleven o'clock session? Do you have room in that fancy new car to bring Tonio, Adela and Rosa too?"

"Yes I do, if they want to come, that would be great!"

Addie had already decided to keep this morning's powerful vision of their next adventure to herself for a while; maybe write it

391

down, mail it to herself and keep it sealed in a safe place. Until the day arrived when she and Joy would open it together, for a glimpse of the journey that lay before them. For now, she would let it incubate.

"Any hunches I have about our future adventures will have to wait, Joy. Right now, you have a race to run, but remember, the race is just for fun. Amira always decides who's going to win, so just enjoy the ride." They looked up at Nita and Lizbeth coming out of the barn with the three mares saddled, snorting, prancing for a run. Addie greeted Amira, kissed her soft nose, told her to behave herself, and handed the reins to Joy with a wide smile.

Amira pushed a chest full of air through her vocal chords and lips; the mare's loud, heart-sent guttural sigh and percussive lip-flapping greeted Joy as she took the reins from Addie, stuck her left boot into the stirrup and sprung into the saddle. She balanced her weight on both stirrups, leaned forward for a sniff of Amira's aromatic neck, stroked her, and turned to smile at Addie.

"Guilty pleasures, Addie, she smells wonderful!"

"Joy, we didn't even discuss it when we talked in Mexico, but wow! I'm not surprised you're a horse lover. Have fun, girl!" Amira was revving up; scooted hard to the side of the driveway to flaunt her dominance, backing into Lizbeth's mare, who objected with a squeal.

Addie watched Joy's instincts and skill take over, and in that moment, Amira's new respect for Joy allowed them to connect. Amira turned her head around to look at Joy, then tipped both her ears to Addie and see-sawed her head up and down in Addie's direction, as if to say, 'Of course I'll make sure we win, those mares haven't beaten me yet!'

"Get on your marks!" Addie yelled, her heart leaping.

"Get set!" Three horses lined up, three girls, ready...

"GO!"

# APPENDIX

# I

## About the Author

Maryl Millard (pronounced mare-ul mul-ard) grew up in California's San Joaquin Valley. She holds Bachelors, Masters, and Ph.D. degrees in Clinical Psychology. Her early decades of professional experience involved work with a wide variety of populations, including full-time work in locked mental facilities, group therapy and counseling with addicts and alcoholics, counseling and in-prison participation with young male felons attending the Squires Program at San Quentin Prison, training foster care social workers, counseling foster children and foster parents, and adults whose children were removed due to abuse or neglect.

Maryl's focus on adoption and infertility research, counseling and education arose during her Master's program in Clinical Psychology, and remains a priority. In 1984 she settled in the San Francisco Bay Area and continued her career as a psychotherapist, educator, researcher and national adoption and infertility consultant. Maryl is the birthmother of two daughters (now 54 and 42) who were adopted at birth and raised by their adoptive parents in closed adoptions, but have contact with her as adults. Her two youngest daughters (now 24 and 30) were adopted by Maryl and her husband as babies through open adoptions.

For the past six years, Maryl and her husband Larry have been raising three grandchildren under legal guardianship, now ages 9, 11, and 12, in a 60-year-old farmhouse on 12 acres in the Sierra foothills. Their mother Lara, who participates generously in the children's lives, has a separate home on the property. For the past six years she has been in recovery from a traumatic five-year marriage to an addict whose birthparents were addicts. They lost him to the foster care system at age of two, and later died of drug-related causes. He was adopted at age 2 ½, by a family with two adopted daughters. He has struggled with attachment disorder since childhood, and drug/alcohol/legal problems as an adult. Drug addiction and drug proliferation impact every city, every school, every family, sooner or later.

Correspondence may be sent to BloodDilemma@gmail.com.

# II

## Perceptions of Mexico, Canada, and the United States

I chose to locate half this story in Mexico because of what I love about Mexico, *not* because I have a desire to discourage friendship, trade or tourism between our countries. However, the US and Mexico share considerable pain because of our interrelated and problematic drug policies. US gangs and Mexican cartels have responded with aggressive recruitment and competitive wars against each other and against law enforcement.

Thousands of parents have lost children to drugs and drug crime; thousands of children have lost beloved parents, siblings, friends and family in the same way. We need to create more effective solutions, *especially since the United States citizens who use illegal drugs are the primary customers fueling the violence and growth of Mexico's cartels, and US gangs.*

George Grayson's report, published by the US Army Strategic Studies Institute, states that of the one hundred ninety-four independent nations who have diplomatic relations with the U.S., "...none is more important to America than Mexico, in terms of trade, investment, tourism, natural resources, immigration, energy, and security." I would add that Mexico's wellbeing is extremely important to the United States—because our shared 1,993 mile border (700 miles already fenced) is a fated relationship.

Mexico has suffered horrific difficulties because of the drug trade we share, and US citizens are sidelined into prison culture by the thousands every year, many with serious drug addiction problems. The Drug-Addiction Epidemic Creates Crisis in Foster Care by Teresa Wiltz (2016) Pew Charitable Trusts/Research and Analysis, states "The tragedy of drug addiction is extended to the children of addicts, who are overwhelming the foster care resources of every state."

The foster care system had many financial and logistical challenges prior to the current level of drug-related foster care placements. The legislation that was to address these needs, the Family First Prevention Services Act, HR5456 has not received enough support in Congress to pass. Congress has also failed to support more comprehensive drug addiction treatment for the parents of children in foster care.

Canada has its unique drug use patterns and economy, costing approximately 23 billion dollars a year, and Mexican cocaine is in increasing demand. Latin American traffickers are taking advantage of the Canada-U.S. easy-access border. *It is the longest border in the world* (5,525 miles) and is regularly scouted and crossed by Latin American drug smugglers. Traffickers are using 100-foot-long submarines—each one built to smuggle two tons of drugs northward, some for direct coastal delivery in the U.S., some for Canadian users, while most submarine deliveries are destined for Canada, are there to be distributed back into the US from Canada. Hundreds of these submarines have been constructed, and production is continuing at a steady pace. One jungle production camp was verified to have produced over 70 in one year. (Joint Interagency Task Force, USA, Rear Admiral Charles Michael, June 19, 2012).

In September 2016, the US Coast Guard intercepted and boarded a self-propelled semisubmersible, carrying more than 5,600 pounds of cocaine, with an estimated street value of 73 million dollars. This interdiction brought the total amount of cocaine seized in fiscal year 2016 (10/1/15 to 9/30/16) to over 416,600 pounds—an amount valued at more than $5.6 billion. (Business Insider.com).

We have friends, family, political relationships, trade, and a huge criminal drug industry crossing our north and south borders. Despite cartel and gang crime, there are still many places in Mexico and the US that provide some of the most hospitable and safe destinations in the world. Will we be able to say that in ten years? Only if we act to improve our policies and the laws that enforce them. A viral phenomenon is spreading; inaction is not an intelligent choice.

Education regarding the components of the drug crisis is the first step toward a workable solution. Section III has an overview of publications relevant to crime and drug policies for readers who are interested in understanding and influencing the history and the scope of these problems.

# III

## Publications Relevant to Crime and Drug Policies

*Most of these books are available for audio download and are well-narrated.*

**Thieves of State: Why Corruption Threatens Global Security by Sarah Chayes.** One of the most esteemed journalists and writers of the decade, Harvard graduate Sarah Chayes describes the democracy-killing behaviors of corrupt organizations, criminals, politicians and mismanaged government policies at a global level. Our current period of history is exponentially more chaotic due to the globalization of the internet and the related vulnerabilities of critical infrastructure (transportation, water and power companies, military security, computer and media networks, etc.). Cyber war, terrorism, nuclear proliferation, and increasing major weather disasters and fires from climate change are on the rise. Chemical and biological weapons continue to have a place in the arsenals of dictators and terrorists who prey on innocent citizens.

**Tim Weiner won the Pulitzer Prize for his work on the Pentagon and CIA—Legacy of Ashes (2007) and a ground-breaking factual history of the FBI—Enemies: A History of the FBI (2012).** *This is newly released information Weiner compiled from previously secret government files, released through the Freedom of Information Act.* His caveat: "No republic in history has lasted longer than 300 years, and this nation may not long endure as a great power unless it finds the eyes to see things as they are in the world."

These institutions have been through earlier eras of gross mismanagement, and at their core are struggling to evolve in the growing complexity of our current geo-political situation. At present, the FBI is generally well respected, and, as Trump's firing of FBI director James Comey attests, the institution strives, under pressure, to stay independent from the interference of changing presidential administrations. and committed to a focus on the rule of law.

**The Social Order of the Underworld: How Prison Gangs Govern the American Penal System, by David Skarbek (2014).** The United States, China, Russia, and Brazil have the largest prison systems in the world. Prisons in California and Texas house 70% of our nation's prisoners. This scholarly economic model of prison culture can be extrapolated to other systems outside the US.

Government policies that marginalize and incarcerate poor people instead of educating and employing them, steer them into an underground black-market economy. Of course, the disenfranchised must organize and survive: both in and out of prison. Skarbeck, a brilliant scholar, shows how millions of prisoners govern their gangs' activities.

**British Journalist and Mexico City resident Ioan Grillo has provided an impressive and comprehensive history: El Narco: Inside Mexico's Criminal Insurgency (2012) and Gangster Warlords: Drug Dollars, Killing Fields, and the New Politics of Latin America (2016).** Gangster Warlords describes the Latin American trend away from nation-focused political wars to boundary-defying organized crime wars. Brazil, for example, has the fourth largest prison population in the world, and, as in the U.S., and Mexico, incarcerated gang leaders participate in the management of gang activities far beyond prison walls.

**Don Winslow, authored two highly crafted historical novels Power of the Dog, (2005) and The Cartel,** (2015). Both novels personalize the well-researched interwoven, intricate relationships between Mexico's organized criminals, US and Mexican authorities, and Mexican journalists. Winslow's ability to show historical facts through the eyes of one DEA (Drug Enforcement Agency) agent, personalizes the plight of many agents and Mexican citizens—those who sacrificed their lives to expose the drug cartels' rampant terrorism—corrupting Mexican business, military, legal, political, and judiciary institutions. Winslow's historical chronology across both books spans forty years, from 1970 to 2015.

A report published in 2015 by the Didactic Press, The **Los Zetas Drug Cartel, Sadism as an Instrument of Cartel Warfare in Mexico and Central America**, was written by George W. Grayson, and originally published by US Army Strategic Studies Institute and US Army War College Press. He is also the author of **Bad Neighbor Policy, Washington's Futile War on Drugs** (2003). A 2015 Congressional Research Service Report states "80,000 people have

401

been killed in Mexico due to organized crime related incidents since 2006." CNN Library (2017).

**The Fire Next Door: Mexico's Drug Violence and its Danger to the United States (2012).** Ted Galen Carpenter's thesis: *The US strategy of drug prohibition, like the US prohibition policy on alcohol, does not work, and exponentially increases cartel violence in Mexico and excessive imprisonment in the US for non-violent drug offenses.*

The solution: decriminalize the use of drugs, as did Portugal, and overall drug use will not expand. If the production and use of drugs were decriminalized, *most of the 20 to 39 billion dollars a year that US citizens pay to black market drug suppliers would be eliminated.* Cartels would lose their billion-dollar incomes, and would not be able to maintain their current level of acquisition of weapons, political influence, and soldiers.

Drug-addiction treatment would be the intelligent alternative to prison, because upon discharge, clean and sober addicts will return to society sooner, healthier, with services to assist with education and employment. In this decriminalized scenario, addicts can avoid recruitment into gangs, and avoid the trauma and cult-like conditioning of the gang lifestyle inside prison and after release.

**Javier Sicilia, well-known Mexican novelist, essayist, peace activist, poet, college professor and journalist:**

> **"The flawed premise of prohibition is the mistaken belief that criminalizing drug use, drug production, and drug sales, will lower sales, production, use, and related violence. The facts are that the war on drugs has increased and continues to increase the destruction of individuals, families and the rule of law." Javier Sicilia.**

"The legal prohibition of drugs, as always, has bankrolled the industry of organized crime, as it did in the days of alcohol prohibition in the United States. Now, the escalation of organized crime into a wealthy, heavily armed military power, has pitted it against the military power of Latin America and the United States in the failed war on drugs."

In closing, democracy and the rule of law are the only solutions that allow equitable protection of US citizens and global alliances built on trust and strength. Knowledge and unity is power. It's not too late to pull our government back from the brink if we can organize effectively and remove those in in the US Congress and state government who promote destructive drug policies—such as more police violence and expensive, overflowing prisons—when we know current policies are not working, but are escalating the wealth and power of organized crime on a global level.

# IV

## Author's History of Adoption and Infertility Research and Clinical Practice

> Adoption, like marriage, is an opportunity, not a commodity. It does not come with a guarantee. Life itself is an opportunity—to heal and create our own happiness—without making it conditional on the love or approval of any one person.

Dr. Maryl Millard was one of numerous pioneer "open" adoption reformers in the United States who, from the late 1970's onward, provided research, education and psychotherapy focused on the emotional crises of birth mothers, birth fathers, adoptees, and infertile adoptive parents. Her master's thesis (The Hidden Side of Adoption, 1981) focused on the psychological impact of secrecy in "closed" adoptions.

Secrecy creates closeted grief and developmental issues for birthparents and adoptees, and provides no legal recourse to locate and invite a lost relative into a relationship. Secrecy harms adoptive parents, who live with the stressful and unrealistic fear that their adopted child's birthparents will locate them and alienate them from their children. Only a small number of adoptive parents take steps to open their closed adoptions for the benefit of all concerned.

As a birth mother/first mother, Maryl helped many adoption triad members search for lost family throughout the 80's and 90's, and counseled them through reunions. She completed her own search for her daughters, but did not have an opportunity to meet them face-to-face at that time. Her experiences with adoption search/reunion made her determined to find out why adoptive parents were so fragile, insecure, and distrustful of birth parents.

The adoptees in her research were aware of this fragility, often describing their parents as pathologically 'phobic' regarding birthparents. Adoptees often felt obligated to protect their parents, often searching in secret or not searching at all. Maryl knew these parents were protecting deep wounds to their self-esteem due to their infertility and subsequent adoption experiences. This led to the focus she chose for her doctoral dissertation.

## Infertility Stress Syndrome: PTSD in Adoptive Parents

During the 1990's, Dr. Maryl Millard served on the board of directors of the San Francisco Chapter of Resolve: The National Infertility Organization, and regularly presented workshops at San Francisco Resolve's two annual Symposia, focusing on Infertility (medical and psychological challenges) and Adoption (logistical and psychological challenges).

The focus of Maryl's workshops: (a) Making the transition from infertility treatment to adoption, and (b) Post traumatic stress disorder in infertility and adoption, (c) Open vs. Closed Adoption, (d) Common Fears in Adoption, (e) Relationships with birth parents, (f) Raising adopted children in open adoptions.

Maryl's Ph.D. dissertation was a statistical analysis of Post-Traumatic Stress Disorder in infertile pre-and post-adoptive parents who were traumatized by the experience of infertility, and often traumatized further by the stress of the adoption process.

The research confirmed significant stress from miscarriages, long-term hormone treatments, invasive surgical treatments, in-vitro fertilization procedures, and marital conflict.

Couples experienced stressful alienation from the understanding and the social support of family, friends, coworkers, and employers, as well as massive financial debt for under-insured medical procedures, and lost time at work. The couples in this study were heterosexuals, and had statistically significant gender differences in stress-related behavior (which added more stress to their relationship).

Last but not least, as walking wounded, the couples in this study experienced significant stress navigating the adoption system, which is fraught with adoption agency "professionals" who facilitate adoptions "in house" without providing qualified, fully separate adoption counseling for all parties. This group of agency adoption practitioners suffers at one end of the spectrum from a lack of transparency, and at the more independent or private adoption end, the industry has a significant number of greed-driven private adoption attorneys and facilitators (who also lack transparency and undervalue counseling for their clients during and after the process).

Before open adoption was established as a healthier alternative to secret adoptions, the highly-stressed population of infertile couples (and some single adopters) feared contact with birthparents, and they initially opposed open adoption. Many still choose closed adoptions, and some choose international adoptions in an attempt to permanently avoid contact with birth parents.

A combination of PTSD diagnosis and treatment, plus supportive counseling and mediation for adoptive and birth parents during the adoption process, creates a context that mitigates fear and shame. Clinical social workers and members of the adoption triad have stated their preference for open adoptions nationwide.

By the 1980's, open adoption became the professionally preferred model of adoption by the professional community of clinical social workers and psychotherapists in the United States. For a copy of the Infertility Stress Syndrome research, and an overview of how these couples successfully adopted through open adoption, see **Infertility Stress Syndrome, A Study of Pre-and Post-Adoptive Parents**, by Maryl Millard, Ph.D. Copies are available on Amazon and Kindle.

In many legal jurisdictions, open adoption is the only way that adoptive parents can obtain a copy of their child's original birth certificate and birth parents' contact information. Likewise, for birth parents, open adoption provides a way for them to consider many prospective adoptive parents, and personally choose who will adopt their child. Open adoption also provides birthparents with the accurate identification, background and contact information on the adoptive parents.

Open adoption contracts pertain to informal agreements regarding contact between the birth parents, the adoptive parents, and the child, both before and after the legally binding adoption is filed with the court. Regardless of how they are crafted, they are not a formal, legally binding part of adoption law; they are 'good faith' contracts, the success of which depends on the dynamics that evolve between the parties after the adoption. As with any relationship between relatives bound by blood or legal agreement, there are vicissitudes of compatibility throughout the family members' developmental stages.

There is no factual support for the fear-based myth that birthparents will interfere with the adoptive family, or in any way harm or alienate the child from the adoptive parents. Isolated cases may result in adversarial relationships, but are not numerous enough to create any significant predictive probability of failure. Most importantly, open adoption provides a starting point for an extended family relationship, which will likely fluctuate, depending on each person's values, geographic location, and psycho-social dynamics. In adoptions that involve parents whose children were removed due to abuse or neglect, how open the adoption is depends on responsible safety assessments, especially when birthparents are incarcerated, or drug-addicted. In many cases, foster children who are adopted often have relatives who can offer support and family of origin information while the child matures within the adoptive family.

Dr. Millard continues to support open adoption as a preferred model of adoption. People who cite this model as "failed" because the ongoing contact initially desired may not work out in every adoption, would also be advised to look at the model we have for marriage, which has a fifty-percent divorce rate, yet still serves as a meaningful, viable family relationship with legal and social obligations for support. Open adoption offers reassuring "proof of life" to birthparents, and opportunity for contact, but it is no guarantee that birthparents will not experience significant grief. Adoption abuses, such as coercion and intimidation, have wrongly removed children from birthparents throughout history.

*Adoptees are the only citizens in the US who are denied* (in 43 US states) *the civil right to obtain their original birth certificates,* and they deserve to have this right. At the present time, open adoption is the only way to provide this document prior to the adoption being legalized and the original record sealed by the court.

Open adoption may provide full information at the time of the adoption, but in most states adoptees cannot obtain their court-sealed original birth certificates from the state in which they were born, if the document provided earlier were lost or destroyed. **A federal law, recognizing this civil right for all US adoptees, is the only way this right can be guaranteed** (See ALARM on Facebook—Advocating Legislation for the Adoption Reform Movement—for information on this civil action).

Blood (genetic) relationships are important, and so are adoptive relationships. They are so important, that people hold very strong opinions and beliefs about every aspect of genetic and adoptive relationships. Nothing is more counter-productive than generalizing or being harshly judgmental about any of these relationships without being privy to all the facts involved in every relationship. Until that day arrives, being anti-adoption or anti-open adoption is an act of desperate oversimplification in the face of a highly complex issue.

## V

## Publications Relevant to Adoption and Infertility

### Infertility Stress Syndrome, a Study of Infertile Pre-and Post-Adoptive Parents by Maryl W. Millard, Ph.D. 134 pages.

A statistically supported study of infertility/adoption-related PTSD. Comes with questionnaires created by the author from her clinical experience. A cornerstone measure of the study, the Impact of Events Scale (Mardi J. Horowitz, M.D.) is one of the most valid and reliable measures used in PTSD research. This was the first study to validate statistically significant gender differences in PTSD scores. Any of the questionnaires in this study may be utilized in assessment of PTSD for the same population, (pre-and-post-adoptive parents in open adoptions). Available on Amazon and Kindle.

### Adopting After Infertility by Patricia Irwin Johnston

Infertility always has an impact on the quality of the adoption experience, before, during and after the adoption. We need counselors, therapists and educators who understand the ongoing legacy of infertility-adoption stress. When adoptive parents are helped through the maze of their insecurities into healing, they can avoid damaging the relationship with their adoptive children; they can embrace the value of their children's origins. In this way, their adopted children do not need to compartmentalize their relationship with their birth parents when such a relationship is available.

### The Family of Adoption: Revised Edition
by Joyce Maguire Paveo, Ed.D., LCSW, LMFT

"I am most interested in the best interest of the baby and child, not for just one moment in time, but for all moments of that child's lifetime. Adoption is not an event. It is not a snapshot in time. It is a moving picture that goes on through this life, and into the ones that follow." Dr. Joyce Maguire Paveo.

- **The Spirit of Open Adoption by James L. Gritter.**
- **Life Givers: Framing the Birthparent Experience in Open Adoption by James L. Gritter**

James Gritter is one of the most intelligent and compassionate writers on the subject of adoption. His understanding of the birthparent experience and his support for the birthparents' dignity is timeless. Life Givers is a book filled with respect for every birthparent; and honest discussion of how the adoption industry has treated birthparents in the past, with recommendations for better practices. In the future. Birthparents who read it may have their first opportunity to be in the presence of someone who fully understands and respects them.

- **Lost and Found by Betty Jean Lifton**
- **Journey of the Adopted Self by Betty Jean Lifton**

The 1980's and 1990's were filled with an outpouring of powerful feelings and desires that adoptees from secret/closed adoptions found a way to express—including intense experiences of grief, frustration, rage—and personal power.

Lifton's books helped adoptees understand that they didn't agree to this robbery of their origins, nor did they agree to the "gag order" that expected them to remain passive in the face of inhumane adoption practices that in some cases were (as many still are) more similar to slave trading than compassionate family options.

**The Girls Who Went Away: The Hidden History of Women Who Surrendered Children for Adoption in the Years Before Roe v. Wade by Ann Fessler**

Focused on the Baby Boomer era, yet relevant to birthparents, adoptees, and adoptive parents who participated in closed adoptions no matter what era.

**The Baby Scoop Era: Unwed Mothers, Infant Adoption, and Forced Surrender by Karen Wilson Buterbaugh**

Another insider look at adoption industry malpractice.

*My apologies for not including many, many other wonderful authors; check out the author's names I listed in the acknowledgements and explore their publications.*

# VI

# MOVIES

## Domestic Adoption

The Other Mother (NBC movie 1995) (from the book of the same name written by Carol Schaefer in 1991). Available on You Tube. A true story, of Carol's 1965 teenage experience with an unplanned pregnancy, a Catholic "unwed mothers" home, the subsequent adoption of her son through a closed adoption—culminating in a search and reunion in 1985. Realistic and well done. Reminds me of my own path to sanity following my search and reunion experiences.

## International Adoption

Lion (2016 Biographical film, based on the non-fiction memoir A Long Way Home, by Saroo Brierly). A touching story about a five- year-old Indian boy who falls asleep on a train that travels far from his rural village, becomes lost in a big city, speaking a regional dialect that cannot be identified, and is placed for adoption with an Australian couple. At age 25, he decides to search for his mother's village with no memory of the village's location or name. An Academy Award and Golden Globe award winning film.


*To the reader: please let me know if you know of other movies about adoption, especially a filmography someone has already published, and I will include it in the revised edition.*

# VII

## Thoughts On Our Current National Crisis

As a 72 years-young witness to the 50's, 60's, 70's, 80's ,90's, and beyond. I have witnessed the Republicans in Congress abandon morality for fielty to their rich donors, and have witnessed too many people behave like the citizens in the Emperors' New Clothes, none of whom could admit that their leader had fallen for a scam and believed his tailor's magic talents dressed him in the best of the best...when in fact he was traipsing around in the nude. No one but a clear-thinking child had the courage to say exactly what he saw!

This is how the Republican Congress has behaved under Trump, with a decreasing percentage of US citizens who support them. The Republicans are repaying their wealthy donors with a tax bill that will put over 90% of the country's assets in the hands of the 1%. And, they ignore the facts outlined in **The Dangerous Case of Donald Trump**. This book, written by 27 of our country's esteemed mental health professionals, provides their learned analysis of his mental illness and the danger it poses to our country.

The American Dream is dependent on a system that supports the rule of law in a democracy designed to provide upward mobility and inclusion of *all* our citizens in the health, education, and self-actualization that comes from a united citizenry. Only patently ignorant or selfish people deny the value added to our communities through public support for higher education. Millions of people are ready, willing, and able to contribute greatly to our country's fiscal health and growth, if we can contribute to their education and training.

No one can say they love this country if they refuse to support civil rights and education for all its citizens. Without unity, we devolve out of a true democracy, into a predator-prey paradigm. Many short-sighted people who say they want the US to be powerful, are forgetting that our *only* viable competitive edge for leadership in the global economy, fostering global health and welfare, is our *unity* within the country and within the community of free nations around the globe.

If you are sounding the alarm with your representatives in

government, if you are working to elect the legislators and policy makers who support the programs that educate, heal, protect, and unite our diverse citizenry, then, at this sensitive point in history, you are contributing to the survival of a *United America*.

Made in the USA
Columbia, SC
06 January 2018